The Bestselling Novels of TOM CLANCY

THE BEAR AND THE DRAGON

A clash of world powers. President Jack Ryan's trial by fire.

"HEART-STOPPING ACTION . . . CLANCY STILL REIGNS."

—*The Washington Post*

RAINBOW SIX

John Clark is used to doing the CIA's dirty work. Now he's taking on the world. . . .

"ACTION-PACKED."

—*The New York Times Book Review*

EXECUTIVE ORDERS

The most devastating terrorist act in history leaves Jack Ryan as President of the United States. . . .

"UNDOUBTEDLY CLANCY'S BEST YET."

—*The Atlanta Journal-Constitution*

DEBT OF HONOR

It begins with the murder of an American woman in the back streets of Tokyo. It ends in war. . . .

"A SHOCKE YOU'LL WONDER W ."

nt Weekly

THE HUNT FOR RED OCTOBER

The smash bestseller that launched Clancy's career—the incredible search for a Soviet defector and the nuclear submarine he commands . . .

"BREATHLESSLY EXCITING."

—*The Washington Post*

RED STORM RISING

The ultimate scenario for World War III—the final battle for global control . . .

"THE ULTIMATE WAR GAME . . . BRILLIANT."

—*Newsweek*

PATRIOT GAMES

CIA analyst Jack Ryan stops an assassination—and incurs the wrath of Irish terrorists. . . .

"A HIGH PITCH OF EXCITEMENT."

—*The Wall Street Journal*

THE CARDINAL OF THE KREMLIN

The superpowers race for the ultimate Star Wars missile defense system. . . .

"*CARDINAL* EXCITES, ILLUMINATES . . . A REAL PAGE-TURNER."

—*Los Angeles Daily News*

CLEAR AND PRESENT DANGER

The killing of three U.S. officials in Colombia ignites the American government's explosive, and top secret, response. . . .

"A CRACKLING GOOD YARN."

—*The Washington Post*

THE SUM OF ALL FEARS

The disappearance of an Israeli nuclear weapon threatens the balance of power in the Middle East—and around the world. . . .

"CLANCY AT HIS BEST . . . NOT TO BE MISSED."

—*The Dallas Morning News*

WITHOUT REMORSE

The Clancy epic fans have been waiting for. His code name is Mr. Clark. And his work for the CIA is brilliant, cold-blooded, and efficient . . . but who is he really?

"HIGHLY ENTERTAINING."

—*The Wall Street Journal*

continued . . .

And don't miss Tom Clancy's fascinating nonfiction works . . .

SPECIAL FORCES

A Guided Tour of U.S. Army Special Forces

"CLANCY IS A NATURAL."

—*USA Today*

CARRIER

A Guided Tour of an Aircraft Carrier

"CLANCY IS A MASTER OF HARDWARE."

—*The Washington Post*

AIRBORNE

A Guided Tour of an Airborne Task Force

"NOBODY DOES IT BETTER."

—*The Dallas Morning News*

SUBMARINE

A Guided Tour Inside a Nuclear Warship

"TAKES READERS DEEPER THAN THEY'VE EVER GONE INSIDE A NUCLEAR SUBMARINE."

—*Kirkus Reviews*

ARMORED CAV

A Guided Tour of an Armored Cavalry Regiment

"TOM CLANCY IS THE BEST THERE IS."

—*San Francisco Chronicle*

FIGHTER WING

A Guided Tour of an Air Force Combat Wing

"CLANCY'S WRITING IS SO STRONG THAT READERS FEEL THEY ARE THERE."

—*Boston Sunday Herald*

MARINE

A Guided Tour of a Marine Expeditionary Unit

"NO ONE CAN EQUAL HIS TALENT."

—*Houston Chronicle*

AT BOOKSTORES EVERYWHERE!

Novels by Tom Clancy

THE HUNT FOR RED OCTOBER
RED STORM RISING
PATRIOT GAMES
THE CARDINAL OF THE KREMLIN
CLEAR AND PRESENT DANGER
THE SUM OF ALL FEARS
WITHOUT REMORSE
DEBT OF HONOR
EXECUTIVE ORDERS
RAINBOW SIX
THE BEAR AND THE DRAGON

SSN: STRATEGIES OF SUBMARINE WARFARE

Created by Tom Clancy and Steve Pieczenik

TOM CLANCY'S OP-CENTER
TOM CLANCY'S OP-CENTER: MIRROR IMAGE
TOM CLANCY'S OP-CENTER: GAMES OF STATE
TOM CLANCY'S OP-CENTER: ACTS OF WAR
TOM CLANCY'S OP-CENTER: BALANCE OF POWER
TOM CLANCY'S OP-CENTER: STATE OF SIEGE
TOM CLANCY'S OP-CENTER: DIVIDE AND CONQUER
TOM CLANCY'S OP-CENTER: LINE OF CONTROL

TOM CLANCY'S NET FORCE
TOM CLANCY'S NET FORCE: HIDDEN AGENDAS
TOM CLANCY'S NET FORCE: NIGHT MOVES
TOM CLANCY'S NET FORCE: BREAKING POINT
TOM CLANCY'S NET FORCE: POINT OF IMPACT
TOM CLANCY'S NET FORCE: CYBERNATION

Created by Tom Clancy and Martin Greenberg

TOM CLANCY'S POWER PLAYS: POLITIKA
TOM CLANCY'S POWER PLAYS: RUTHLESS.COM
TOM CLANCY'S POWER PLAYS: SHADOW WATCH
TOM CLANCY'S POWER PLAYS: BIO-STRIKE

Nonfiction written with John Gresham

SUBMARINE: A GUIDED TOUR INSIDE A NUCLEAR WARSHIP
ARMORED CAV: A GUIDED TOUR OF AN ARMORED CAVALRY REGIMENT
FIGHTER WING: A GUIDED TOUR OF AN AIR FORCE COMBAT WING
MARINE: A GUIDED TOUR OF A MARINE EXPEDITIONARY UNIT
AIRBORNE: A GUIDED TOUR OF AN AIRBORNE TASK FORCE
CARRIER: A GUIDED TOUR OF AN AIRCRAFT CARRIER
SPECIAL FORCES: A GUIDED TOUR OF U.S. ARMY SPECIAL FORCES

INTO THE STORM: A STUDY IN COMMAND *(written with General Fred Franks)*
EVERY MAN A TIGER *(written with General Charles Horner)*

Tom Clancy's

NET FORCE®

CYBERNATION

Created by
Tom Clancy and Steve Pieczenik
written by Steve Perry

BERKLEY BOOKS, NEW YORK

TOM CLANCY'S NET FORCE®: CYBERNATION

A Berkley Book / published by arrangement with
Netco Partners

PRINTING HISTORY
Berkley edition / November 2001

For information address: The Berkley Publishing Group,
a division of Penguin Putnam Inc.,
375 Hudson Street, New York, New York 10014.

For more information on Steve Pieczenik,
please visit www.stevepieczenik.com.

Visit our website at
www.penguinputnam.com

ISBN: 0-425-18267-3

BERKLEY®
Berkley Books are published by The Berkley Publishing Group,
a division of Penguin Putnam Inc., 375 Hudson Street,
New York, New York 10014.
BERKLEY and the "B" design
are trademarks belonging to Penguin Putnam Inc.

PRINTED IN THE UNITED STATES OF AMERICA

10 9 8 7 6 5 4 3 2 1

"The issue before us is one of no ordinary character. We are not engaged in a conflict for conquest, or for aggrandizement, or for the settlement of a point of international law. The question for you to decide is, Will you be slaves or will you be independent?"

—President Jefferson Davis
Confederate States of America
Jackson, Mississippi
December 26, 1862

PART ONE

The Lines Are Down

PROLOGUE

Friday, December 23, 2012—7:03 A.M.
Scranton, Pennsylvania

Cameron Barnes jabbed one finger at the phone's keyboard, hitting the "O" button over and over.

"Dammit, what the hell's wrong! C'mon, C'mon—!"

From the kitchen, Victoria said, "What?"

"I'm not talking to you, I'm talking to the stupid phone!"

Victoria stuck her head through the doorway. "Excuse me?"

"The phone, the *phone* is out of order. No dial tone, nothing."

"Use your digital."

"I already tried that. Same thing."

"Maybe your battery is—"

"No, the battery is *not* dead, I checked it!"

"Well, don't take my head off! It's not my fault!"

"I'm sorry. But, look, I *have* to make this call—if the customer doesn't hear from us by seven-thirty, we're screwed. I'm gonna lose my commission!"

"Use my cell."

He started to ask, but she beat him to it. "In my purse."

Cam found her purse, pulled the little folding phone out, opened it. He tried voxax first, telling it the name to call, but that didn't work. Neither did the buttons.

He was going to lose his commission. Eight hundred bucks. Shit!

Austin, Texas

Rocko Jackson stared at his computer screen and cursed. "Son of a *bitch!* Don't you do this to me now!"

In the cubicle next to his, Tim Bonifazio stood and peeped over the short divider.

" 'S'up, white boy?"

"The damned system must be locked up again. I can't get it to access the net."

"Hold on a second, lemme check. It's probably just your station, you know how the mainframe hates you."

Tim disappeared from sight. After a second, Rocko heard, "Uh-oh!"

"Aha, so the mainframe hates you, too, don't it?"

"No, man, it hates everybody. My *laptop* and wireless modem ain't working, neither."

"So what are you saying, the net is down?" He laughed.

"That's what it looks like from here."

"I don't even want to hear that."

Silicon Valley, California

Rachel Todd arrived at the conference room at the same time as Dal Ellner and Narin Brown.

Rachel said, "What is going on, guys?"

Both Dal and Narin shook their heads. "Got me," Narin said. "All I know is nobody can get on the web. Not with hardwired, laptops, digital phones, nothing. Even old man Johns's virgil isn't working. It's like the net just . . . died, or something."

"Can't be," Dal said.

"Maybe not, but I know of at least fifteen major ISPs—from local to New York to London to Hong Kong—that are flat out inaccessible."

"This is bad," Rachel said.

"Bad? It's catastrophic! Every hour we're off-line costs us half a million bucks! In a couple of days, we'll be in the toilet!"

"Us and everybody for as far as the eye can see," Narin said.

"That doesn't make me feel any better."

Cheyenne Mountain, Wyoming

"Lieutenant, you want to tell me what the hell is going on?"

"Unknown, General Harmon, sir. All network operations are snafued."

"You mean we are deaf and blind here?"

"No, sir, we have landlines that still work, we can call in launch codes manually if we have to."

"And how do we open the silo doors?"

"Hand cranks, sir."

"Not acceptable, Lieutenant. I want the situation rectified."

"Sir, according to landline reports, the problem is nationwide—we can't fix it from here."

"God dammit!"

"Yes, sir."

Dry Wells, North Dakota

Chief of Police Steve Cotten stared through his window at the icy morning outside. The new power grid had just up and shut down. With the temperature at minus fourteen and the windchill factor pushing minus *fifty*, the lights, electric heat, and all phone and net service simply stopped.

The citizens of North Dakota knew how to deal with cold, and usually had enough wood stockpiled for such emergencies. The chief himself had six split cords under a tarp next to his garage, but there were people old enough so that splitting and then hauling in firewood would be a hard chore. Four men had already had fatal heart attacks; two others injured themselves badly enough to require hospitalization. Chief Cotten knew there would be another group unable to heat their homes who were likely to die from hypothermia.

The chief sighed. It was turning out to be an all around, in the toilet, crappy morning here, oh, yeah.

***On the Gambling Ship* Bon Chance**
Somewhere in the Caribbean

Alone in his cabin, Jackson Keller slipped the headset up, pulled the earplugs loose, shucked his haptic gloves, and grinned at the holoproj's test pattern. "Way to go, team," he said. "Let's see how they like *that*!"

They weren't gonna like it at all. Jay Gridley especially wasn't gonna like it.

He laughed. Ah, this was going to be so much fun!

1

Net Force HQ
Quantico, Virginia

Alex Michaels, Commander of Net Force, swore softly at the empty computer screen on his desk. He picked up his phone and said, "Jay Gridley."

The voxax circuit made the connection, but internal coms were pictureless. The voice on the other end said, "What? I'm kind of busy here!"

"Jay. What the hell is going on?"

"Oops. I didn't check the ID sig, sorry, boss. We got problems."

"Really? You think so?"

"I guess you wouldn't be calling if you didn't already know that."

"What's up?"

"I don't know. Our main server is off-line, and all wireless external phone lines are bollixed. My virgil's emergency circuit says there are outages like this everywhere, all over the country."

"Great."

"I'm trying to run it down, boss."

"Don't let me keep you. Call me back when you get something."

Michaels put down the phone. Well, wasn't this just peachy? A few minutes ago, he'd been patting himself on the back, telling himself how great things were going. Business had been slow, Net Force had been on top of computer crime like never before, even the director had called to congratulate him on how good a job they'd been doing. He should have known better than to feel good about this. It was as if while God was having his morning coffee, Michaels had strolled by, full of hubris and proud of himself, and bumped God's elbow, sloshing hot coffee into His divine lap.

Oops.

Here, son, let me show you what goeth before a fall . . .

He should have *known.*

He was paying for it now. Because he knew that whatever the problem was with the net and phones, it was going to be Net Force's responsibility. No question about it.

"Sir?" His secretary.

"Yes?"

"The director is on the intercom. Line one."

Michaels nodded. Of course she was. He sighed and reached for the phone.

Helsinki, Finland

Jasmine Chance walked down the hall toward the office Roberto had cleared of furniture and made into a workout space. Music drifted out of Roberto's makeshift gym, drums and the singsong twang of *berimbau*, an instrument that looked vaguely like an archery bow strung with a metal wire, and with a gourd attached to one end. Roberto had explained the workings of this device in much greater detail than Chance had ever wanted to know. The instrument was played by hitting the wire with a little stick while rattling a gourd filled with pebbles in the same hand, and the musician could alternate between two notes by touching the wire with a coin or not. Santos liked to have his players use a Krugerrand, gold giving the best tone, so he said. The simple rhythms produced were part and parcel of the acrobatic African/South American martial art of *Capoeira* that Roberto Santos—a black, Brazilian master of the dance who bore the title of *Capoeirista Mestre*—practiced for hours every day.

Chance stepped into the doorway just as Roberto leaped into the air and turned a back somersault, landed neatly on the balls of his feet, then dropped into a spraddle-legged posture, sweeping one foot along the floor in a broad half-circle. Only the palm sides of the hands and soles of the feet were ever supposed to touch the ground, he had told her, that was part of *O Jôgo*, The Game. *Capoeira* was a fighting system developed by slaves, and while one school of history had it that it had been disguised as a dance so as to fool the white masters, Roberto had been quick to point out that such thinking was simplistic.

Most of what she knew of *Capoeira* she had learned from Roberto in bed, between bouts of an art at which *she* was an adept. Roberto was barely thirty years old. He was a decade younger than she was. He was handsome, had great stamina, and his body seemed chiseled from hard cocobolo wood. There was no fat on him at all. He had been a diamond in the rough when they had met. She had polished him and taught him how to be a skilled lover over the year of their association. He was coming along nicely.

Now, wearing only a pair of thin, calf-length red-and-white striped cotton pants, Roberto glowed with passion and sweat as he practiced his exercises. Though he preferred to be musically accompanied by three or four of his fellow game players—you had to learn to play the instruments as part of the dance—the music now was recorded. When he saw her arrive, he finished his sequence, then padded across the bare floor to the sound box and shut it off.

When he spoke, he had an accent, the soft liquid flow of Portuguese translating to his English, a rounding of hard consonants and lengthening of vowels.

"Ah, Missy. How goes the battle?"

She smiled, flashing perfect teeth—all marvels of expensive orthodontia, a thousand dollars a cap. "Keller says the first sortie went perfectly."

Roberto picked a towel up from the floor and wiped the sweat from his face and shaved head. "Jackson, he's a fine boy, can make them computers dance like nobody else."

Chance smiled. That was true. Jackson Keller was a wizard with hardware and software, as good with those technical things as Roberto here was at bashing heads. CyberNation did not hire second-class talent for its key positions. There was much to be gained—or lost—in this game, and cutting corners on personnel would be shortsighted and stupid. When you were trying to create a virtual nation from nothing, to give it weight and substance, you had to do some very intricate things if you were going to pull it off. Having good help alone wasn't sufficient. You needed the best. All of Chance's people were just that—the best. And she wasn't so bad herself, though her talents were somewhat harder to quantify. The higher-ups in CyberNation called her The Dragon Lady when they thought she couldn't hear, and she took that as a compliment.

To Roberto, she said, "Yes, but this is the easy part. Scrambling software gets their attention, but they'll fix that, and all it will cost will be some tired programmers and a few hours' downtime. The next stage will be more difficult. If it gets to that."

And of course, it *would* get to that soon enough—the nations of the world weren't going to just roll over and give away anything, certainly not the kind of power CyberNation wanted for itself.

"You worry too much, Missy." He grinned. "That part won't be no harder than Jackson's *jôgo*, only different."

"Good to see you haven't lost your confidence, Roberto."

"Ah, me, I ain't lost nothin'."

She closed the door and locked it. "Talk is cheap."

He hooked his thumbs into the waistline of his pants and skinned them down, peeled them off, one foot, then the other, and tossed them to one side.

She laughed, and reached for her shirt buttons. "We'll have to hurry," she said. "We have to leave for the ship in an hour."

"Only an hour?"

"We have to pack."

"Let me show you how to pack," he said.

She laughed again. Life was good.

Washington, D.C.

Somebody screamed bloody murder, jerking Toni from her half-doze into full alertness. She came off the couch and onto her feet and into a defensive stance, expecting to be attacked, before her brain got back on track.

It's only the baby. Just Little Alex.

Toni relaxed. Aloud, she said, "Yeah, little Alex, the demon child from the lowest pit of Hell." But she was already on her way into the bedroom, and at the baby's crib before he could get through the second outraged scream.

"Hey, hey, hey, baby boy, what's the matter? Mama's here, it's okay."

He stood balanced precariously on his little fat feet, holding onto the rail.

She picked the baby up, put him over her left shoulder, and patted him gently on the back.

He gave out one more half-hearted yell, just to let her know he wasn't happy it had taken her all of thirty seconds to get from the living room to pick him up, then trailed off into a quiet burble before shutting up completely.

"Oh, you're happy now, are you? Brat. Monster." She leaned him away and cradled him, smiling with a fierce possessive joy at him. She hadn't slept for more than four hours at a stretch for what seemed like forever, but he was such an angel when he smiled his new-toothed grin at her, as he was doing now. He was a beautiful child. Yeah, yeah, she knew that every mother thought that about her babies, but objectively speaking, he really was. Objectively speaking. Anybody with eyes could see that.

She smiled at that thought and at Alex Junior—a name his father had fought against but lost. Yes, she had agreed, a junior had a lot to live up to, and no, it wasn't necessarily the best thing to tag a baby with that. The choice they'd agreed upon was "Scott," giving him his paternal grandfather's middle name. But when the nurse had come in with the little flatscreen to log in the newborn baby's stats, Alex hadn't been there.

"What's the baby's name?" the nurse had asked, ready to log it into the system.

And Toni had smiled and given it to her. Alex hadn't really been that upset. Secretly, she was sure he was actually very pleased.

Little Alex made sucking noises, but it was not time for his feeding yet. He had gotten off the breast and was taking milk and some solid food full-time now. And she no longer leaked milk when he cried, thank God. That had gotten a little embarrassing while sitting in a restaurant or even just out pushing the stroller.

She walked into the living room, cooing at little Alex, looking for his binky. They had half a dozen kinds of different pacifiers, but somehow, the baby could tell the difference among them, and would spit out all but his favorite. This had caused some not-so-funny moments while they turned the house upside down looking for it against the background of unhappy baby squawls. Unfortunately, the favorite binky had come as a baby shower gift from somebody, and neither Toni nor Alex had been able to find a match for it anywhere. There was no brand name on it, and nobody remembered who had given it to them. A web search came up empty, and friends with babies were no help, either. Normally, they had the thing strapped to a clip attached to the baby's shirt so they wouldn't lose it, but somehow, they managed to lose it anyhow.

Jay Gridley had come up with a tiny responder that could be hooked to the clip strap. All you had to do was say "Binky!" in a loud voice, and the electronic device, about the size of a penny, would say "Here I am!" over and over until you could find it and squeeze it off. Jay had put the thing inside a little sleeve of waterproof silicone, just in case little Alex managed to somehow get that part into his mouth.

Life since the baby was just full of these kinds of problems, and they only sounded little to people who didn't have children of their own.

And being a full-time mama was a far cry from being a Net Force operative second in command to her now-husband, or working for the mainline FBI as a special liaison to Net Force.

Just then, the baby distinctly said, "Da da."

Toni stared at him, astounded. "What? What did you say?"

Little Alex smiled and said it again, repeating it a third time for good measure: "Da da da."

She had to call Alex! He had to hear this, this child was a prodigy, a genius!

She hurried to the phone, picked it up, and punched in Alex's number.

But naturally, the phone wasn't working.

Okay, fine, she'd tell him when he got home. Meanwhile, she could bundle the baby up, put him in the stroller, and go for a nice long walk. It was chilly out, but at least the sun was shining, no rain in the forecast. Some fresh air would do them both good.

"Want to go for a walk, sweet babboo?"

He understood her, and she was sure he nodded, a little bit. Of course. He was a prodigy, after all, wasn't he? The smartest, prettiest, best baby in the world. Without a doubt—none at all.

2

Madrid, Spain
Summer 1868

The summer's day was scorching in Madrid, time for siesta.

Jay Gridley sat in the shade of a wide awning at a sidewalk café, sipping warm red table wine, waving flies away from the dirty checkered tablecloth, and watching a sleeping dog under a nearby table twitch as it dreamed its mysterious canine dreams.

Isabella II, eldest daughter of Ferdinand VII, still sat upon the Bourbon throne on this hot day, but her rule, balanced precariously as it had always been on a high wire, was finally about to come to an end. Isabella had sporadic popular support, she changed her cabinet as often as she changed her underwear, and the lumpy stew of monarchists, moderates, progressives, and radical unionists in late 19th-century Spain was about to come once again to a roiling boil. Her military politicians, the generals Ramón María Narváez and Leopoldo O'Donnell, were both dead by now. Led by Serrano y Domínguez, the Duque de La Torre, who had run things before Isabella's ascension, and Juan Prim y Prats, the prime minister, Isabella was about to be booted out of the country in the Revolution of 1868. She would flee to Paris, where she would stay until her son, Alfonso XII, eventually ascended the Spanish throne some six years later, but even then her influence upon him was to be minimal. She would, however, outlive the leaders of the revolt against her by long margins. Prim would be assassinated a mere two years after the revolution, and while Serrano lived until 1885, Isabella lasted until 1904.

Living long enough to spit on your enemy's grave was a certain kind of revenge.

Jay sipped his not-too-bad wine and grinned. Well, what was the point of creating a VR scenario if you couldn't make it sing and dance and do tricks like you wanted it to do? Being a history buff could be a lot of fun, if you let it.

In the Real World, Jay sat in his office at Net Force HQ, part of the almost four-hundred-acre FBI compound at Quantico, plugged into full wirelessware haptics, including top-of-the-line optics, otics, reekers, droolers, and the brand-new version of spray-on WeatherMesh, which could be set and controlled by your computer to plus-or-minus one degree Fahrenheit, and none of the Madrid afternoon was the least bit real. But it looked, sounded, tasted, smelled, and *felt* real—close enough for government work, anyway.

Sure, you could still input everything into a computer with a keyboard or voxax, or read words scrolling up a holoprojic screen if you wanted to, but with VR software as good as it was, why would anybody *do* that if they didn't have to? When you could get the same information you needed and be entertained at the same time, why wouldn't you, unless you were short on imagination?

A short, balding man wearing a clean but out-of-date summer suit strolled toward Jay, mopping his florid face with a handkerchief he pulled from one jacket sleeve.

"Señor Gridley?" His name came out as "Greed-lee."

"Sí."

"Por favor, Señor, I have a message for you."

Jay nodded. He indicated the chair across from him. "Have some wine, Señor . . . ?"

"Montoya. Jaime Montoya. Muchas gracias."

The little man sat. A waiter appeared with a glass, plunked it down, and sauntered away. Montoya poured himself a glass of the wine, took a long sip, then sighed.

"Ah, good. Hot today."

"Mucho," Jay said.

The man removed a folded parchment from his jacket. The yellowish document was sealed with a dollop of orange wax, imprinted with the signet of a local marquis. Jay expressed his thanks as he took the parchment, thumbed the seal open, and unfolded the document.

Sure, he could have downloaded this file to his system and scanned it. And sure, if he needed hard copy, that would be courtesy of the office printer, on so-so grade ink-jet paper and not parchment, but what the hell—if you couldn't have fun, why bother?

It was what he had come to find, but a quick read told him it wouldn't do him much good. The hackers who had attacked the net servers were too good to leave an obvious trail he could follow. The marquis could not point him in the right direction, *lo siento.*

Oh, well, how big a surprise was that? The shock would have been if somebody good enough to rascal their way into major computer nodes *had* left obvious clues to backtrack.

"Personal call override" came a warm and sultry voice. "Saji on line one."

Jay cancelled the VR scenario with a finger-weave in the sensor grid and told his phone to put the call through. It came across in visual, so he could see her sitting in the kitchen at home. She was, as always, beautiful.

"Hey, babe," he said.

"Hi, Jay. Have you once more made the world safe for democracy?"

"If you count Republicans, safe enough. What's up?"

Saji—Sojan Rinpoche, his fiancée and the world's most beautiful and bright woman—said, "My mother needs my help picking out the bridesmaids' dresses."

"And I can help you do this how?"

"Not at all, wiseguy. I was just calling to let you know I was going to look at bridal magazines with her."

"In Phoenix?"

"No. She's visiting my aunt Shelly in Baltimore. I'm going to take the train up for the day."

"You're gonna ride the *train* to Baltimore? Are you crazy? The local is full of perverts and weirdos! Why don't you just do it in VR on the net?"

"Because it isn't the same for my mother, she wants to sit next to me on the couch, and I'm trying to connect with her on this. You want her to like you, don't you?"

"Well, sure. But—what's this got to do with liking me?"

"You want me to tell her you said I couldn't go see her?"

"I didn't say that. And it wouldn't do me any good if I did say it, would it?"

"No. Besides, I used to take the train to see my aunt every time I came to Washington, three or four times a year. Nobody ever bothered me."

"I don't like it."

"You don't *have* to like it. I'm just telling you as a courtesy, idiot-mine. I don't recall either of us planning on putting anything about 'obey' into our vows."

"Yeah, well, I don't mean to come off as some kind of authoritarian jerk here or anything, sweetie—"

"Oh, I don't think of you as *authoritarian* at all, Jay." She batted her eyes at him theatrically and gave him a big, fake smile.

"You're a Buddhist, you can't convince your mother that VR and RW are essentially the same?"

"They aren't, and you know it. We've had this discussion before."

He grinned. Yes, they had. Several times, and a couple of those were after mad and passionate lovemaking.

"I'll be back before it gets late, and I'll have my com. I'll call you when I leave for home."

He nodded at her. "Okay. It's just that I worry."

"I know. It's sweet. Don't do it anymore. I'm a big girl; I can take care of myself."

"Not so big."

She laughed. "I love you. See you later."

Jay nodded, and said, "Love you, too."

She disconnected and his screen went blank.

Given that she had hitchhiked across most of Southeast Asia when she was seventeen—once fending off a gang of bandits who wanted to steal her backpack—and ended up in a temple in Tibet where she stayed for three months, Saji could indeed take care of herself. Riding a train to Baltimore and back shouldn't present much of a problem. Although he felt that since they were getting married, that should become his job, taking care of her.

He wondered if most guys felt that way about their bride-to-be.

Well. He could watch her anyway. When you were Smokin' Jay Gridley, the fastest computer cowboy at Net Force, tapping into the surveillance cams on the trains that ran the corridor between D.C. and Baltimore was nothing. He could do that one-handed, with a head cold and a hangover. Saji didn't ever need to know, and if something happened, Jay could have the transit cops there in an instant.

***On the* Bon Chance**

Jackson Keller went to the main computer complex. There were only eight programmers and netweavers here, aside from himself, but they were certainly among the top twenty or thirty such people worldwide. Bernardo Verichi from Italy, Derek Stanton and William Hoppe from the U.S., Ian Thomas from Australia, Ben Mbutu from South Africa, Michael Reilly, the Irishman, Jean Stern the Israeli, Rich Rynar, the Swede. There were a few better, but the ones without *vision* didn't interest him. Keller's people had to be good, but as important as that was, they also had to be *believers*.

Skill without direction, without purpose, was wasted.

It was too bad he couldn't approach Jay Gridley. Jay was the best he'd ever known, as good in school as Keller himself had been, maybe even better. They'd been friends then, trailblazers on the web, adventurers in cyberspace. But Jay had gone over to the dark side, become a Net Force op. One of the enemy. A man whose vision now stopped at the end of his nose. He fought to preserve the status quo, he lived in a tower of decay.

What a waste of a great talent.

Well. He had made his choice, Jay. Now he'd have to suffer the consequences. The train was leaving the station—no, the rocket ship was lifting for the stars, that was better—and Jay hadn't booked passage. He would be left behind. Sad.

CyberNation was going to become reality, *that* Keller never doubted. How long it might take, exactly how and when it would come to pass, well, those were not things he could predict with certainty, but the end was a foregone conclusion. This was the information age, the time when knowledge and accessibility to it were the two most important things in the world. That genie wasn't going back into the bottle, not ever. The world was going to undergo a change like nothing it had ever seen in all its history.

Jackson Keller was the best of the best, and he was leading the way to change.

One of the netweavers, Rynar, had just pulled his sensory gear off and was stretching when he saw Keller come in.

"Jackson," he said. "How are we?"

Keller smiled. It was a running joke—Cyber-Nationalists often spoke in collective terms.

"Why don't you tell me?" Keller said. "What is the status on Attack Beta?"

"Going quicker than we'd hoped," Rynar said. "ZopeMax programming is one hundred and nine percent of goal. DHTML and GoggleEye Object Links are six by six."

"How is Willie's Ourobourus?"

"Well, the python is choking on its tail a bit, but he says he'll have it fixed in a day or two."

Keller nodded. "Excellent. Anything new I should know?"

"Well, Net Force is after us. Perhaps we should be quaking in our shoes?"

They both chuckled.

"Do they have anything?"

"No. They don't have a clue. Don't know who they are chasing, where to look, how we did it. I think you give your old friend Gridley too much credit, Jackson."

"Maybe. But he's pulled down some other big players who didn't give him enough credit. Better safe than sorry."

"I hear you. We'll keep shifting the cover."

Keller nodded again. He headed for his own workstation. There was much to be done yet. Best he get to it.

Net Force Shooting Range
Quantico, Virginia

John Howard had already put half a box of ammo through his revolver waiting for Julio. It was the first time he'd been to the range in at least a month, and he felt a little rusty. He was used to stopping by once or twice a week, and since he'd been gone, making the drive from town seemed like a real chore sometimes. Just for fun, he'd been shooting 9mm. His Phillips & Rodgers K-frame revolver was unique among wheelguns, in that it would load and shoot dozens of different calibers, ranging from .380 auto to .357 Magnum, this made possible by a clever spring device built into the cylinder's rod housing. You had to adjust the sights if you wanted to do precision work when you changed calibers—the flat-shooting nines went to a different point of aim than .38 Special wadcutters or .357 hollowpoints did—but at combat distance, it didn't matter all that much. A couple of centimeters one way or the other, it didn't make any tactical difference.

He'd reset his command ring before starting—he was inactive, but still technically on call—so he was good for another thirty days before they changed the codes. So far, the smart-gun technology the FBI mandated for all its small arms had not failed any of Net Force's operatives, though there were supposedly a couple of incidents at the FBI Academy range with Glocks where there were failures to fire. Howard didn't know if that was due to the computer-operated smart tech, or the Tupperware Glocks, but he hoped it was the latter. What you did not want was for your weapon to turn into a paperweight when the bad guys started shooting at you.

And, while he worried about that, so far at least eight or nine regular FBI agents had lost their handguns in fights and the smart guns had saved them from being shot by their own weapons. If you weren't wearing the control device, either a ring or a watch, the guns using them simply would not go bang. Made keeping a piece at home in a drawer at night safer, too. While Howard's son was trained to shoot, and well past that age where he might accidentally blast himself or some playmate, a lot of federal employees who carried guns as part of their daily wear had small children at home.

Well. It wasn't really his problem at the moment, was it? He was on "extended leave," which was probably a prelude to full retirement. Somebody else's worry, now.

Here finally came Julio. Howard nodded at him. "Lieutenant."

"General. Sorry I'm late. Your godson."

"How is little Hoo?"

"Oh, *he* is fine. It's Joanna and I who are tearing our hair out. How come you didn't tell me what would happen when he got seriously mobile? One second you're standing there trying to take a leak and he's in the doorway, the next, he's in the kitchen pulling stuff out of the cabinets. It's like he can teleport—zip, and he's gone!"

"You have to kidproof the place, Julio. Get those little latches that install inside doors and drawers, plug all the electrical outlets, put everything you value high enough so he can't reach it."

"Right. We thought we had done that. Yesterday, he climbed up onto a chair, leaned over, and punched the power control on the DVD player half a dozen times before I could grab him. He's turned into this little tornado that destroys everything in his path. We clean the house top to bottom, spic-and-span, and five minutes later, there are toys, books, food, clothes, you name it, piled a foot deep everywhere. I've been picking peanut butter out of my running shoe soles for a week."

Howard chuckled.

"It's a conspiracy, isn't it? Those of you who have had children deliberately kept the knowledge from those of us who didn't, right?"

Howard laughed louder. "Of course. If people knew how much trouble they'd be, they'd never have kids, and the race would die off. Soon as you figure this out, you get a call from the Parent Police, and you have to take the secrecy oath."

"Once I would have thought that was funny. Now, I halfway believe it."

"You going to shoot, or are you going to bitch?"

"Well, sir, bitching is more fun, and probably I'm better at it, since I'm getting more practice doing that than shooting. The little brat is a full-time job. I get to sleep maybe two hours uninterrupted a night."

"Life is hard."

"Like you would know? How is retirement, General? You been gone a while now, you sure you still remember how to shoot? The bullet comes out of that end, right there."

"Tell you what, Julio, I could leave this handgun on a shelf for ten years and still be able to outshoot *you.* I'll spot you the first attacker, just so I don't take advantage of a tired and bleary old man such as yourself."

"Keep your charity. I'll shoot your ass off half-asleep and with one eye closed."

"Not with that beat-up old Beretta of yours, you won't. I'll even let you use your cheating laser grips."

"I don't need those to beat an armchair, nap-taking commander such as you, General Howard, sir."

Both men laughed.

Gunny came on the intercom. "I hate to interrupt your waste of good ammunition, General Howard, sir, but you have a com."

"Tell them to call back later."

"It's Commander Michaels, sir."

Howard looked at Julio, and his old friend smiled—butter wouldn't melt in his mouth.

"You knew he was going to call me, didn't you?"

"I'm sure I have no idea what the general is talking about."

"He's going to ask me to come back, isn't he?"

"What—I'm a mind reader now?"

Howard shook his head. He went to take the call.

3

In the Air over the Central Atlantic Ocean

Roberto Santos prowled up and down the aisles of the private jet, a stretch 737 rigged with all the comforts needed to keep a bunch of corporate fat cats happy. No gym, but at least a couple of flat spots wide enough to lie down and stretch out. That was good, 'cause sitting for a long time on a plane trip could cause blood clots in your legs. Santos had an aunt who died that way. She was taking a trip from Rio to London, and she'd been jammed into one of those little seats between two other people for like eighteen or twenty hours. Only time she had gotten up was to go pee, and then only a couple times, 'cause she didn't want to cause the guy sitting on the aisle any problems. For being so nice, Aunt Maria had gotten a blood clot that had cramped her leg so bad she'd started screaming. They were a thousand kilometers away from anywhere, and by the time they landed, the clot had broken loose and gone to her heart or lungs or something, and she'd been dead ten minutes before they got her off the plane.

Roberto might die young, but by God, it was not going to be from sitting in one place too long.

He dropped to the floor next to a pedestal table and did fifty quick push-ups, flipped over onto his back, and did fifty twisting crunches, alternating from side to side, to work the obliques. That was what kept a man's stomach pulled flat, the lateral muscles, not the abs in front.

He snapped up to his feet with a gymnastic move, a kip-up, then headed up the aisle again.

Jasmine was asleep in one of the recliners up front, the chair leaned back to make a bed, her seat belt fastened across her lap. Damn, but she looked good for a woman her age. Good lay, too, she knew some tricks. Maybe he should wake her up, join the mile-high club. Well. Renew their membership, anyway.

And maybe not. She was mean as a snake if anyone woke her suddenly. Besides, they had done it on the plane before. And on trains, buses, taxicabs, and once, in a horse carriage going around Central Park in New York. Never done it on a boat, though. When they got to the gambling ship down in the Caribbean, that would be the first chance to do it there.

He grinned at the thought. Nothing was better for a man than pussy.

Besides pussy, Santos had but one passion, and that was The Game. *Jôgo de Capoeira*. It wasn't just for fighting, though it gave you that. There was so much more—the music, the rituals, the manners, the company of fighting men. Yes, one learned the way to position oneself, the *posicionamento*, so that one could *ataque* or offer proper *defesa.* And all the flashy, acrobatic moves that impressed the unwary were necessary, but at the higher levels it was the subtle dance that played. The slight lean this way that told your opponent he could not touch you if he attacked. The shift that way that opened up an attacker like a blank book upon which you could write whatever you wished. It was art.

When first he had begun The Game, Santos had wanted

only to know the fastest way to knock an opponent from his feet, the methods to throw a powerful fist or elbow or knee that would send a man sprawling. And he had learned those. But real mastery lay in the small details, the constant circle in and out that hypnotized opponents, whether one or five of them, caused confusion and missteps that an expert could use to his advantage. The real experts were fifty, sixty years old, and you could not touch them no matter how fast or strong you were, because they knew what you were going to do before you could do it. He was getting closer to that, but he was not there yet. He would be, eventually.

And the money he was making as Field Operations Head of CyberNation's security force was very good—enough that after a couple more years, he could retire, go back to Rio, and study and teach The Game full-time. Work out all day, screw all night, sleep on the weekends. What more could a man ask for?

Net Force HQ
Quantico, Virginia

In their third meeting since the electronic attack on the net and web, Alex Michaels and his team had figured out the easy part of the Five-W-and-One-H question: They knew what, when, and how. What they didn't know was: who, why, and where they were.

Now in the conference room with Jay Gridley, Lieutenant Julio Fernandez, and Major Joseph Leffel, the acting head of the military arm, Michaels raised his eyebrows at the others. General John Howard would be arriving later in the day. It had taken some talk to get him to agree to come back, and he had to go home and tell his wife face-to-face before he would agree to it. But Michaels had had a bad feeling about this, and he wanted Howard—who had proved himself more than a few times—back on the team, at least until this was cleared up. He had a hunch it might come to guns, and when and if that happened, he wanted his best man leading the troops.

"Gentlemen?"

"Nothing new, boss," Jay said. "My guys are back-walking every trail, but so far the pirates covered their asses pretty good. The regular feebs' Carnivore and NSA's snoopware have come up zip. The hackers had to be coordinating stuff on-line, there's way too much going on, so we're looking for ways they hid it. We've got random sampling of JPEGS, GIFS, TIFFS, PICTS, and all the common sound files attached to e-mail running through the stegaware plexes, but so far, nothing."

Fernandez said, "Somebody want to translate that for the computer illiterate among us? Meaning me."

Michaels grinned. "Jay is talking about steganography. Hiding things in plain sight."

Jay, already tapping away at the keyboard of his flat-screen, said, "Check it out."

A holoproj shimmered into view over the flatscreen. It was a picture of the Mona Lisa. "What do you see?"

"A famous painting of somebody who probably didn't want to smile too big 'cause she had bad teeth?" Fernandez said.

"But that's all," Jay said. "However, we touch a button, *presto!* and look again."

The image melted, and left several words floating in the air: "Up yours, feds!"

Fernandez looked at Jay.

"We got this off a steganography website run by a ten-year-old kid.

"The word means 'covered writing.' It goes back to the Greeks," Jay said, "though the Chinese and the Egyptians and Native Americans all did variations of it. Since the Greeks gave us the word, here's how an early release worked: Say Sprio wanted to send a secret message to Zorba, so what he did was, he had a slave's head shaved, tattooed the message on the scalp, then waited for the slave's hair to grow back. Then he sent the slave to his bud, who shaved his head again. Slave didn't even know what it said. Even if he could read, he wouldn't be able to see it."

"Clever. But kind of a slow process," Fernandez said. "How long it take for the hair to grow back enough to cover it? Five, six weeks?"

"Those were the good old days. Um. Anyway, you can do much the same with electronic pictures. They are made up of pixels, millions of them in some cases, and some aren't as important as others. Without getting too technical, you can take a standard RGB—that's red, green, blue—image and, with a little manipulation, hide all kinds of information bits in it without affecting what a human eye can see. If you run it through the right program, the hidden stuff shows up.

"So, you send an e-mail addressed to your mother with a picture of your beautiful two-year-old boy, and right there in the middle of his face can be the specs for how to build a nuclear bomb."

"Great," Fernandez said.

"Welcome to the future, Lieutenant.

"See, if somebody sends a big bunch of encrypted material and we happen to spot it, we might get suspicious. Everybody is watching the net these days, and a lot of e-mail gets scanned by one agency or another. Even if we can't break the code, it might alert us enough to track down who sent it and received it, maybe pay them a little visit to see what they look like. But a picture of a little kid sent to his grandma? Who'd suspect that?"

"Some paranoid Net Force op who couldn't find anything else?" Fernandez said.

"Right. And if you really want to make our jobs hard, not only do you hide the sucker in the middle of somewhere nobody is gonna look, you also encrypt it, which is double protection. Use a one-time-only code, and by the time anybody might be able to break it, whatever you were talking about is ancient history."

"All of which is fascinating but not helping us find the bad guys," Michaels said. "All right, let's break this up. We'll meet again in the morning, call if you get anything useful before then."

Jay nodded.

Jay watched the others leave, until only he and Fernandez were left in the conference room. He said, "So, you up to speed on all this, Julio?"

"Might as well have been speaking Swahili far as I'm concerned."

Jay laughed. "Maybe I can translate. How much do you know about the net and the web?"

Fernandez shrugged. "There's a difference between the net and the web? I dunno if you remember or not, but it took me six months to figure out where the on/off button was on my issue computer. I got a few things from Joanna since then, but I'm basically an analog kind of guy. I figure if God had wanted us to count higher than twenty, He'd have given us more fingers and toes."

"Okay, let me lay it out for you in base ten, Jay Gridley's quick and dirty history of computer communications."

"Fire away."

"Right. The original Internet was designed so it couldn't be taken out. It was decentralized, nodes and servers all over the place, so if one went down, information flow could be rerouted. Think of it like a sixteen-lane superhighway. Block one lane, you just jump into another and keep going in the same direction. Only with the net, there are a whole bunch of superhighways going in all directions. Blow up a whole freeway, you just take an off-ramp to another one. Might have to get to San Francisco by way of Seattle and then Miami, talking a big loop, but you don't have to pull over and stop 'cause there ain't no more roads."

"Okay, I can follow that much."

"So, what this meant was, if the Soviet Union, who

was our worst enemy in the bad old days, dropped a nuke on a city, it didn't much matter in the grand cosmic scheme of things."

"Except to the people vaporized in the aforementioned city," Fernandez said.

"We're talking bigger picture here, Julio. What I meant was, it wouldn't significantly disrupt the net elsewhere. Like those giant fungus-thingees that are spread out over a thousand acres, but are still only one plant—cut a chunk out here or there, it doesn't matter. The beat goes on."

"I got you, babe."

"Funny. Thing is, as the world wide web came into being and expanded, with everybody and his kid sister logging on, a lot more information started going back and forth, a whole lot more than the original guys ever figured on. This was set up pre-WWW, remember. Anyhow, along the way, things wound up getting more clumped together than the net founders intended. Everything started getting run by computers. In the beginning, when most everything in the phone company—and there was only one big phone company back then—was mechanical, you couldn't really hack into much because there wasn't anything much to hack *into.*

"Now, the phone companies are like everybody else, slaves to the computer, and what one programmer can make, another one can screw up. Shut down any substantial amount of phone service to a big city, and that city is whacko. Sure, some of the big companies have landlines to other cities that don't run through MCI, AT&T, Sprint, and so on, but the little guys who use dial-up or T1 or DSLs and such—and there are an awful lot of little guys—they're screwed, because no matter how good their ISP's securityware might be, bottom line is, you can't spike paper without a paper spike."

"No shirt, no shoes, no service?"

"Exactly. Even if the phones work, there are ways to bollix things. The web itself these days, there are a dozen main DNS servers, or name servers—these are the ones that map from domain names, like www-dot-whoever-dot-com, or dot-org, or dot-biz, or dot-whatever. Then the raw Internet Protocol addresses, those are the IP numbers, one-eight-four-dot-two-dot-three-dot-blah-blah-blah. They all have backups, of course, but there are ways to get into them electronically and rascal 'em. So that can mess things up real good by itself."

"Sounds just swell, Jay."

"Hey, we aren't even talking *social* engineering yet. Bribing a guy who's got the password is a real easy way to save yourself a lot of trouble.

"The big multinational corps all have their own servers, of course, and even if you manage to throw a monkey wrench into the big DNS guys, the pool of corp info and connections won't be affected right away—this gets kinda technical here, but let's just say it's kind of like shutting off a big power grid. Some houses will go dark, but a lot of folks have personal generators at home they can crank up, and they'll work fine until they run out of gas."

"I'm still with you."

"But if you know what you are doing, you can maybe time things so that the big blackout hits long enough to make folks kick on their little generators, then it seems to ease a little. About the time the little generators are running out of gas, another big blackout hits. It's tricky, but not impossible."

"Okay. Blackout."

"All right. But to complicate things further, there are some new, big, centralized broadband backbone switchers that serve a lot of traffic. And while a bunch of the traffic is encrypted or stegawared, especially in the military and banking areas, there are servers that have those encryption sequences or picture decoders who serve a whole lot of folks. Rascal those, and you get another kind of shutdown. Think of it like somebody not only shut off the power, they stopped the natural gas flow, or maybe flattened the tires of the heating oil trucks so they can't deliver, and turned off the water while they were at it."

"This all sounds complicated," Fernandez said.

"Boy, howdy, is it complicated. There are so many triple fail-safes built into the system that making a major dent in the web, much less the entire net, is almost impossible without a multipronged attack perfectly timed. I wouldn't want to try it without a herd of expert hackers and programmers, and even then, it'd be iffy at best. Before this happened, I'd have said it couldn't be done."

"Except that somebody did it."

"No way around that, somebody did—unless it's the biggest coincidence of all time, and I don't believe that for a second. I'd sure like to know who ran the teams. He's good. Real good."

Better than I am, Jay thought, but he kept that to himself.

"Sounds like it would be easier just to go to the servers and cut the wires."

"If you knew where they were. These places are kept out of public view, and even if you knew where to find 'em, you'd still have to get past rabid armed guards who'd just as soon shoot you as look at you."

"Now we're talking my language."

"There are a couple of major switchers that carry a substantial portion of net traffic now, more than they should, some fiber-optic, some wireless, and if you blew 'em up, it would be like stopping up all the toilets at a championship football game at once—civilization wouldn't exactly grind to a halt, but you'd be knee-deep in feces in a hurry. We're talking billions of dollars in downtime, so you can't just waltz in and snip a few light cables with your handy-dandy wire cutters; it would be more like breaking into Fort Knox."

"But it's possible."

"Sure. And you could do it other ways, too, and never have to get in the building. FCGs, MHGs, or HPMs."

"Excuse me?"

"Electromagnetic pulse bombs."

"Ah, yeah, EMP I've heard of. Nukes."

"Oh, that's last century's news, Lieutenant. EMPs come in a rainbow of flavors these days, non-nuclear, no messy radiation to deal with. Got your Flux Compression Generators, MagnetoHydrodynamic Generators, and the dreaded Virtual Cathode Oscillators, aka Vircators. These babies are packed into conventional bombs, use easy-to-find high-speed explosives and off-the-shelf electronics, and can be shoved out the back door of your basic twin-engine FedEx delivery plane for an air burst high enough so the ka-blooey doesn't even scorch the building's paint. But even hardened electronic components will shimmy if a big one of those suckers goes off directly overhead, and all the nonhardened stuff gets turned into chicken soup."

"My God, you computer geeks are a dangerous lot."

"Nah, computer geeks don't *do* things like that, Julio. We sit in our offices and push buttons and talk about it. You ain't gonna see a bunch of guys with pocket-protectors storming a backbone server, shooting it out with guards, and throwing hand grenades, dropping bombs, that's . . . not *cool*. Not to mention most geeks I know outside the intelligence community would collapse under the weight of a flak vest, and probably pull half the muscles in their body trying to toss a baseball, much less a grenade."

"Yes, of course."

"Jeez, don't be so quick to say that when you're looking right at me, dude."

"I've heard about your field exploits, Jay."

"And this is why I get paid the big bucks to sit in my office and do what I do. Let guys like you do my heavy lifting, thank you very much."

"You're welcome. I'd rather be throwing grenades than pushing buttons any day."

"Yeah. So anyway, how they did it was as computer geeks and not commandos. They electronically attacked the phone companies, the big servers, the backbone routers, the comsats, they bought some passwords and strolled right on in, and probably stuff I haven't even thought about, the whole enchilada, they did it in very precise stages, and they were good enough to cause the snafu they caused. Numbers aren't in, but if they managed no more than a fifteen-percent disruption, even twelve-percent, they burned up billions and billions of dollars, reals, pesos, or whatever in downtime.

"The real question is, *why* did they do it? What did they hope to gain?"

Fernandez shrugged. "That's for you and the other Net Force computer ops to figure out. Me, I just go and shoot who they tell me to shoot."

"Must be nice."

"Yes. It is, actually. Much easier."

The two smiled at each other. Everybody had to be somewhere, Jay figured, and if he ever wound up in a dark alley in RT, he'd want Julio Fernandez watching his back. And his front, too . . .

4

Alex Michaels leaned back in his chair and stared at his monitor's splash screen.

"Okay, what else is on our agenda today?"

The computer's voxax circuit came to life and told him. Among the other items on his list was a meeting with the director to discuss his testimony before the Senate Committee on Electronic Communication. Apparently the political pressure from CyberNation was on the rise again, and some of their promises were being examined. A totally secure net/web connection was one of those promises, and the committee wanted to know if that was possible.

CyberNation. Michaels wasn't sure how he felt about them. More a political movement than a web site, CyberNation was trying to get the world powers to recognize them as an actual country, a nation without cities, a nation without borders, a nation that existed only in the virtual world of the net. But a nation with real power nonetheless.

And that was the scary part. It seemed that a lot people didn't know whether to laugh at them or join them. Could such a thing really work? Could a country exist without roads, without buildings, without farms and rivers and lakes? Could a country exist without really *existing*? If it could, what did that say about the nature of countries . . . or of citizenship . . . or of life itself?

To an extent, Michaels could appreciate their vision. These days in particular, in the age of the Internet, an era of ever-increasing globalization and the constant movement of people, information, and ideas, the dream of a truly borderless country held a certain kind of appeal. Not that it would fly, of course. Not yet. Not today.

The chances of any major country granting CyberNation's patrons the status of nationals and exempting them from taxes was about as good as flying to the moon by jumping off a tall building and flapping your arms. It made no logical sense that if you lived in, say, Dubuque, Iowa, you could use the roads and infrastructure of the city, state, and country, but be exempt from paying anything for the privileges. Of course, you'd have to give up social security and welfare, but if you could afford to join CyberNation and pay their fees, you were better off than most anyhow. And their claim that megacorps and even nation-states were going to pay that freight for the rights to reach billions with their advertising was such a vaporous castle in the air that even psychotics wouldn't try to live there.

CyberNation said it would offer all information to all its "residents," for free. Music, vids, books, medical formulas, whatever. It was a chaos engine looking for a place to have a train wreck, and anybody who believed it would work was a few sandwiches short of a picnic.

Still, they had money, and they were willing to spend it. And enough money could, if used correctly, translate into power. Otherwise, would a senate committee be calling the head of Net Force to the hill for a little chat? Not likely.

Michaels hated this part of his job. The glad-handing he had to do, the whole political game. It was necessary, he knew that, and the director could deal with a lot of it and more power to her, but now and then it fell to him. Politicians did things for reasons not connected to logic or science, but because they were trying to please voters back home; being re-elected was always in the rearview mirror for professional politicos, and some of them wouldn't go to the bathroom without taking a poll to find out if it was okay to unzip.

He sighed. It was always something. He wished he could just take the day off, go home, and be with his wife and baby son. Sitting in a rocking chair with a sleeping baby on your lap was a lot closer to paradise than listening to the director caution him on anger management against the likely possibility some fat cat senator from Bug Dick, Arkansas, asked you a question that would insult the intelligence of a retarded moron . . .

***Aboard the Gambling Ship* Bon Chance**
Somewhere in the Caribbean Sea

A long-legged, blue-eyed blonde in her early twenties, hair down to the middle of her back, and wearing just enough to be legal for network television smiled, showing perfect teeth. She inhaled, and breasts too perfect to be real nearly broke free of their translucent gauze microbikini top.

"*I'm* in CyberNation. Why don't you join me?"

She moistened her ruby lips with her tongue, then drew one finger down her cleavage, down her belly, and to the hem of her bikini panties.

A phone number and e-mail address appeared in the air next to her as she inhaled again.

• • •

Jasmine Chance touched a button on the remote, and the hologram froze. She looked at Roberto. "What do you think?"

"I wouldn't kick her out of bed."

Chance laughed. "You wouldn't kick a crippled blind *pig* out of bed if it was dark enough so you didn't have to look at it. I meant as an ad. We're running it on the TV nets, movie house commercials, and the big servers and comware."

He shrugged.

She said, "Yes, it goes straight for the groin, nothing subtle. If we could get away with it, we'd have her say, 'Join CyberNation, you can date me, *and* I do housecalls.' "

"Yeah? You have her number?"

"No, but I've got *your* number. She isn't even *real*, Roberto, she's a computer construct."

"Too bad."

"It's end-justifying-the-means," she said. "They join, they'll get more than their money's worth, in the long run. But we need bodies. If we have enough members, we can start to get things done."

"I thought the exercise with the computers was getting things done."

"Yes, but our fork has four prongs. We do ads, we do politics, we rascal computers, and if push comes to shove, we hit hardware with hardware. We have to come at this from every angle we can think of."

He shrugged again. "You the boss."

"No, I represent the bosses. I'm just the hand."

"What does that make me?"

"A finger."

"Ah. Which one?"

She showed him.

He laughed. "Want me to show you what I can reach with that finger?"

"Go for it."

Washington, D.C.

When he finally got home, Michaels was tired, but looking forward to seeing Toni and the baby.

She met him at the door. Before he could ask, she said, "He's asleep. I just got him down. Wake him up, and you die."

He chuckled.

"Let me go turn the baby monitor on and I'll be right back."

When she left, he opened his briefcase and removed the gift-wrapped present he'd hidden there. He had spent some time looking for it. It wasn't their wedding anniversary, but the anniversary of the day they had first kissed, sitting in that old Mazda MX-5 he had bought to restore, somewhere in Virginia. It had taken a while to find what he wanted, and it had cost five times what it had sold for new, only a decade back. He'd stashed it at the office for a couple of months after he'd gotten it. He hadn't wanted to wait, he'd wanted to give it to Toni the first day it arrived, but he'd held off. She was gonna be surprised, he was sure of it.

When she came back from Little Alex's room, he had set the blue foil-wrapped box casually on the end table.

"Chinese food'll be here in about ten minutes. Hot and spicy chicken, purse shrimp, chow mein, dried, sauteed string beans."

"Sounds good. How's the boy been today?"

"An angel."

"But of course."

"Better enjoy it while we can. We—what's this?"

"That. Oh, you mean that package there? Got me."

"What did you do, Alex?"

"Me? I didn't do anything. I never saw that before."

She grinned and picked up the package. Shook it.

"What's it for?"

"You've forgotten what today's date is?"

"January 15th, isn't it?"

"Toni."

She grinned wider. "And they say women are romantic. No, I haven't forgotten. It's the day you bought the Miata."

"And . . . ?"

"Isn't that all?"

"You're scum."

She laughed. "Our first date, first kiss, and the first time you were able to admit what I had known for a long time before that. You didn't need to buy me anything."

"No, I didn't *need* to, I *wanted* to. Go on, open it."

She did, ripping the paper off with abandon.

"Wow. Where did you *find* this?"

"You like it?"

"You're an idiot. Of course I like it."

"It's a first generation," he said. "A collector's item."

She turned the old VHS videotape box in her hands, and he smiled at her happiness.

The tape was an introduction to *Pukulan Pentjak Silat Serak*, techniques from djuru one, as taught by Maha Guru Stevan Plinck. There was a web address and a picture.

According to what Michaels had learned, the vid had been shot in a borrowed kung fu school in Longview, Washington, ten or eleven years ago, the first one of a series, about the time Americans started realizing there *were* such things as Indonesian martial arts. Toni had another tape by Plinck, an intro to *Bukti Negara* shot a couple of years earlier, also in the old VHS format. The *serak* tapes were harder to find, since they were self-marketed by Plinck in the backs of martial arts magazines, and from a single web page on the net. Most of the commercial producers had gone to DVD or super SQD formats years ago, and the old magnetic tapes were harder and harder to come by. The instructional video consisted of Plinck, who looked to be in his early forties, lecturing on laws and principles of *serak*, then demonstrating them on various students, along with the students punching, kicking and bouncing each other off the floor and walls. The players all wore T-shirts, sweatpants, and sarongs, most of them men, a couple of women. One of the women was even smaller than Toni.

From his web research, Michaels had found that Plinck, a former Special Forces soldier, was one of the senior students of Paul de Thouars, a Dutch-Indonesian who, with his brothers Maurice, Willem, and Victor, had been among the first to bring the nasty and violent Javanese martial arts to the west. Probably the brothers all knew Toni's teacher, the old lady Toni just called "Guru."

Toni could slaughter most men with what she knew, size notwithstanding.

She hugged him. "Thank you, sweetie. This is terrific."

He smiled. Since Toni had been teaching him—he was up to *djuru* eight of eighteen—he had gotten more than a little interested in the art's history in the U.S. One of the brothers—the youngest one, Victor—had apparently written some books on *serak,* and Michaels had a web search going to find those for Toni's birthday.

"Okay, sit right there, I'll be right back."

"Going to slip into something more comfortable?"

"No, goat-boy. I'm going to get your present. You really thought I forgot, didn't you?"

"No, of course not."

"Liar."

He smiled, and she was back in less than a minute. "I had this hidden at the bottom of the spare Huggies pack. I knew you'd never find it there."

"Hey, come on! I change diapers all the time!"

"Here." She handed him a rectangular wooden box, hinged on one side, about the size and shape of a small hardback book.

He undid the brass latch and opened it.

"Whoa!"

Inside, nestled into recesses carved out for them, were two small knives. They were *kerambits*, all steel, no handle scales, a quarter-inch thick, each with a short, sickle-shaped blade on one end, and a finger ring on the other. The edges were smoothed and scalloped with fancy filework. Toni had a pair—he'd used them once, against a drugged-to-the-gills psycho who'd wanted to kill him—and these looked almost identical, a little fancier with the filework. He took them out and without thinking, automatically slipped his index fingers through the rings, holding them in a reverse grip with the points curved forward and extending from the little finger edges of his hands. He regularly practiced his forms with her knives, so they felt comfortable.

"I couldn't find the knife maker who did Guru's," she said, excited for him. "But there's this guy down in Baton Rouge, name of Shiva Ki, who specializes in custom-made stuff for martial artists, an old warrior himself. I sent him a picture and a tracing of mine, and he made these. They are nickel Damascus, almost like traditional *kerises*, too. I figured you should have your own."

He put the knives back into their case, and hugged her. "Thank you. They are beautiful."

"So maybe now I'll go slip into something more comfortable," she said.

"Yeah, hurry, before the monster child from hell wakes up."

Toni left, and Michaels leaned back on the couch and looked at the little *kerambits*. He wondered what normal couples gave each other for anniversaries. Surely not a tape of how to stomp attackers into hamburger, or a pair of custom knives designed to fillet muggers? He laughed. What you got when you fell in love with a serious martial artist who converted you.

"What are you laughing at in there?"

"Nothing. Hurry up, I miss you."

Already his day was a thousand percent better.

5

***On the* Bon Chance**

Chance strolled through the casino, listening to the background sounds: the rumble of conversation from people playing cards, the musical tones of slot machines, the big, old-style roulette wheel with its clattering marble. Yeah, you could gamble on the web, do virtual games that looked and felt almost perfect, but there was always going to be a market for the high-end experience. Anybody could plug in and go on the web for VR; that didn't get you bragging rights:

"So, how was your weekend?"

"Pretty good. Went to the Caribbean, played a little blackjack."

"Yeah? What program?"

"Nah, man, no program—real world."

Except for the staff, none of the gamblers here had a clue as to what this ship's main purpose was. Oh, sure, there was money to be made, and it did that, a handsome profit every month that got plowed back into the cause.

What went on below the casino and cabins, in the electronic heart of the vessel, that was the important thing.

This was one of the three main mobile loci for CyberNation. From here and from the other mobile and hardset locations, a virtual country was going to arise, and that was ironic, since it was going to be helped along in no small part by people who'd rather do things in RW than VR.

"The web is the future! Information should be free! Access is all!"

Yeah, right.

The CyberNationals—her term for the human engines that drove the concept—really wanted this to happen. They believed the slogans. They ate, slept, and breathed the idea. And they had plenty of support, especially among kids who had grown up with computers as much a part of their lives as cars and television. Kids who figured that whatever they wanted, be it music, or vids, or books—those who could actually *read*—games, whatever, should be theirs for free. That some artist might spend a month or a year of his life creating something didn't mean anything to them. Why should they *pay* for it? Take it, put it on the web, make it free to anybody who wanted to crank in and download it, that was how it should be, and screw anybody who didn't like it.

To these people, the concept of intellectual property, those who even understood it, was passé, a product of the Dark Ages, and those times were past. Extinct, like the dinosaurs, and good riddance.

The way it should be? Well, from each according to his ability, to each according to his need. They didn't have a clue where that idea originally came from. They had no sense of history.

Lenin must be laughing in his grave.

Chance was a player, but she didn't share the fanatical ideology the movers and shakers of CyberNation and their most rabid supporters embraced. It was a job. Well-paying, exciting, interesting, but a job, nonetheless. She could toe the party line, mouth the slogans, but she wanted to accomplish CyberNation's goals for her own reasons. She was a winner. She didn't like to lose.

Roberto, dressed in a tuxedo, drifted over to intercept her. He looked good in the dress clothes—he looked good in any clothes, and out of them, too—though it had taken her some time to teach him the casual attitude he needed to make a tux work. *Pretend you're wearing a workshirt and blue jeans,* she'd told him. *Clothes don't make the man, the man makes the clothes.*

"Missy," he said. "How goes it?"

"Fine. Meet me in the greenroom in ten minutes. I have a small chore for you."

He grinned, probably thinking it was carnal.

Four decks down, past a heavy, locked steel door operated by a fingerprint reader, and manned by a pair of armed guards, was the greenroom. The term came from the entertainment industry: It was the traditional name of the place where actors, prepared to go on camera, waited until they were called.

Roberto was there when Chance arrived.

"What do you have for me?" he asked.

She smiled. "Keep your shirt on, bucko. Don't be so eager."

"That's not what you usually tell me."

She allowed herself a tiny smile. "We have on board tonight Mr. Ethan Dowling, of Silicon Valley. He's doing fairly well at the tables, up about five or six thousand dollars at the moment. He is also VP of Programming for Blue Whale Systems. We need to know everything he knows about the security codes for his company."

"No problem."

"Well, that's not strictly true. First, we can't do it here. You'll have to follow him and grab him elsewhere. His chopper will ferry him to the airport in Miami, where he has a corporate jet waiting to take him to San Francisco. We want him to be on the Mainland, and preferably back on the West Coast, when this goes down."

"Still no problem."

She handed him a holograph of Dowling. He looked at it, nodded.

"He has a pair of armed security guards with him. They are ex-FBI, expert shots, big, strong, and well-trained in *mano a mano* combat, too." She gave him two more pictures, and he glanced at them.

"Only two of them?" He flashed his white teeth in a big grin.

"God, you're an arrogant bastard, aren't you?"

He shrugged, still grinning. "Why they call it 'Blue Whale?' "

"Because that particular creature has the largest backbone of any animal on Earth. His company is a backbone server, and if not the largest, quickly getting there."

"Ah."

"It needs to look like an accident. If anybody suspects his brain has been picked, they'll start changing codes."

"No problem."

"This is important, Roberto."

His smile vanished, and for just a second she saw a feral gleam in his eyes. "This is what I do, Missy. You don't need to tell me about it."

She felt a chill course through her. Looking at Roberto now was like being inside a cage with a partially tamed jaguar. It could kill her with one swipe of a paw, and only its conditioning kept it from doing so. "Of course," she said, with an offhand ease she did not feel. "That's why I'm asking you to do it."

Asking. Not *telling*. Roberto was picky about such things.

"Then you must consider it done," he said.

She nodded. "Of course."

Net Force HQ
Quantico, Virginia

Mid-morning in his office and fairly quiet, Michaels got a call.

"*Aloha*, bruddah," the voice said.

The call was vox only, but even if the ID hadn't been working, Michaels would have known who it was. The caller was Duane Presser, one of the FBI close-combat trainers, a big, broad-faced Hawaiian who'd been with the Bureau for fifteen or so years.

"*Aloha,*" Michaels said. "What can I do for you, Duane?"

"Make me skinny and handsome and rich."

"You don't want me, you want a magician. And he'd have to be the best one who ever lived."

"You a funny man, bruddah."

"Convince my wife."

"Now who needs a magician?"

Presser used his island-boy talk to lull people into thinking he was maybe a little slow; anybody who thought that would, however, be making a mistake. Michaels knew the man had graduated first in his law school class, and was sharp as a room full of razors.

"Why I'm callin', we got a new class of recruits to the point they think they each can whip a platoon of Marines. I thought maybe they tried to see how their stuff works against a fat old haole Net Force Commander and his scrawny little wife, it might make 'em think twice."

"You want Toni to do a demo. Why include me?"

"Just bein' polite, bruddah. 'Sides, she needs somebody to throw around. I'm too old to be hittin' the mat dat way."

Michaels laughed. "You and me both."

"Think she'll do it?"

"Probably. I'll ask her. When?"

"Whenever she wants. Dey mine for a while yet. I don't want to turn 'em loose stupid."

"I'll check with her and call you back."

"Thanks, bruddah. *Mahalo.*"

Toni would probably jump at the chance. She enjoyed being a mother, and Little Alex was the light of both their lives, but she had mentioned more than once that she needed to get out once in a while. With her mother visiting from the Bronx—staying in a hotel, fortunately, because she snored like a chain saw—they had a baby-sitter they could trust, so they might as well make hay while the sun shone.

He told his phone to call home, visual on.

"Hi, Alex. What's up?" Toni lit the comcam; she was breathing hard, in a sweatshirt. Probably just finished working out.

He explained about the call from Presser. As he figured, she was eager to play.

"When?"

"You tell me, I'll tell him. He'll set it up. Probably in the big gym, the new one."

"What does he have in mind?"

"He didn't say exactly, but probably a short demo, then some hands-on stuff. Apparently some of the recruits are starting to think they are invincible."

"We can fix that," she said. "How about we set it up for day after tomorrow, about ten A.M.?"

"I'll pass it on to Duane. How's the boy?"

"Down for a nap at the moment. He had a big yellow poo, I changed him, and he conked out, so I did *djurus.*"

Michaels smiled.

"What are you smiling at?"

"You. You're so cute." What he was thinking was, *Here I am, a grown man, talking about baby poop with my wife. Isn't life strange?*

He heard a thin squawk in the background. Toni said, "Oops. Gotta go. He's waking up. You gonna be late?"

"Nope."

"I'll order in Thai tonight, that okay?"

"Great."

The baby's I'm-awake-cry grew louder as Toni broke the connection. Michaels smiled. Whatever was going on with work, life wasn't so bad. The first time he'd become a father, he'd spent way too much time away from home. That had cost him his marriage, but it wasn't all bad. Susie would always be his little girl, and he'd never have gotten together with Toni if he and Megan hadn't split. His ex had remarried, she had a new baby boy, Leonard, and her husband was a decent guy.

Sometimes, things worked out for the best, though it didn't seem like they would at the time. He couldn't complain.

6

Mardi Gras—Fat Tuesday 1970
New Orleans, Louisiana

The evening was warm, the smells of too many sweaty people and too many spilled beers heavy in the damp air as Jay wandered into a bar named Curly's on Canal Street, just outside the mobbed French Quarter. The floats were still rolling, various krewes throwing beads and coins and candy to the crowds packed shoulder-to-shoulder next to the streets, and the volume was turned way up.

Not that the bar was quiet or empty, far from it—but at least the patrons weren't throwing hurricane glasses from Pat O'Brian's at each other, and they all had their clothes on. A fair number of them were sailors, dressed in their whites, and while the atmosphere was festive, it wasn't quite as manic as the bars on Bourbon Street in the Quarter had been.

Even though it was 1970, there weren't a lot of long-haired hippie types in here. The sixties came late to the South, and a sailor's bar was probably not the best place to find the counterculture in any event.

Tomorrow was Ash Wednesday, the beginning of Lent, and the party would be over as good Catholics gave all this up—until next year, anyway.

Jay found an empty stool at the bar and slid onto it. The bartender, a woman of maybe thirty, with dishwater blonde hair and a harried look, spotted him.

"What can I get you, mister?"

"Beer."

She nodded, reached into the cooler, came up with a cold can of Jax, opened it, and slid it to Jay.

In his research for the scenario, Jay had learned that Jax was a local brew, and there was a rumor (which was untrue) that the water they used in making it was drawn straight out of the Mississippi River, passed through a strainer no finer than needed to keep the crawfish out, and mixed with the other ingredients just like that. Given that there was a major petrochemical complex eighty miles upriver that used and discharged a lot of the water, and this was just before the days of OSHA and the EPA looking over everybody's shoulder, the river would have been pretty vile for a whole lot of reasons. According to the locals, it was like the old saw about only mad dogs and Englishmen going out into the noonday sun, only in this case, only mad dogs would drink the water in New Orleans. They said that fishing was easy at night up over the levee, because the fish all glowed in the dark . . .

The can was icy, and the beer cold enough so it didn't have that bad a flavor. Besides, even if it was poison, it wasn't going to kill Jay in VR.

Next to Jay, a sailor, a petty officer, held a leather cup with a pair of dice in it. "Wanna roll for drinks?" he said.

Jay shrugged. "Sure."

The navy man shook the cup a couple times, upended it on the scarred wooden bar, and lifted it. He had a four and a two.

Jay took the cup, put the dice in it, rattled them around, and poured them onto the bar. Six and a two.

"You win," the sailor said. He held up two fingers so

the bartender could see them, then pointed at himself and Jay. The woman came over, put two more beers on the bar. The sailor put a couple dollar bills on the bar, the woman took them, then hustled off.

"David Garret," the sailor said, offering his hand.

Jay shook his hand. Davy in the Navy. "Jay Gridley," he said.

"You . . . Korean? Japanese?"

Jay grinned. "Part Thai," he said. "Born here, though."

Garrett shrugged. "No offense. I just got back from duty in Southeast Asia, off the coast of Vietnam." He pronounced the last part of the name so it rhymed with "ma'am" and not "mom."

"Picked a good time for shore leave."

"Hell, yeah. I been balling chicks left, right, and center. One big party. Had to stop and top off my tanks before I get back into it." He waved vaguely at the door.

Jay took another swig of his beer and said, "So, you being a Navy man, you probably know about all that business with the minefields."

"Minefields" in this case was VR scenario-speak for the problems with the net and web.

Garret finished his beer, put the can down, picked up the fresh one. "No more than anybody else," he said, offering another shrug.

"What do you hear about it?"

"Usual stuff. Somebody seeded a whole bunch of the suckers where our ships would run into 'em. Nobody knows who, but I got a buddy in Navy Intelligence says it might have been CyberNation did it."

Jay was surprised to hear this. "CyberNation?"

"What I heard."

Jay thought about that. Why would CyberNation want to disrupt the web? With it down, that could only hurt their business.

Maybe not, said Jay's little internal skeptic.

No? Why?

Remember the detail shop guy?

Jay looked at the dirty mirror behind the bar, got a glimpse of himself looking thoughtful. *Ah.*

Net Force HQ
Quantico, Virginia

In the commander's office, Jay sprawled on the couch, looking at the boss.

"And what exactly does this reference mean?" Michaels said. "Detail shop?"

"Well, if the CyberNation folks *did* do it, they are smarter than I would have guessed."

"I'm listening."

"Last time I went home to visit my folks, there was a local scandal. A guy had gone into business detailing cars—waxing, buffing, cleaning up dead paint, like that—and business had taken a downward turn. So late one night, the guy took a run through a fairly well-off neighborhood nearby and spray painted squiggles on fifty or sixty cars parked outside of their garages."

The boss nodded. "Okay."

"You see where this is going. Guy got an immediate influx of new business the next day—he used a kind of paint he knew he could get off without too much trouble—and he had to hire a couple of kids to help him, he had so many new customers. He didn't get them all—some owners did their own cars, and there were other detail shops—but he got twenty-odd cars, at a hundred and fifty a pop. After paying his new helpers their minimum wage, and allowing for buffing pads and polishing compounds and all, he cleared almost three thousand dollars. Not a bad return for an investment of fifteen minutes and a can of spray paint.

"Business tapered off again, so the guy waited a couple weeks and then did another midnight graffiti run. This time, he made almost five grand.

"Now, if he'd quit then, he'd been ahead of the game. But it was easy money.

"So, every couple of weeks for the next few months, the detail man would sneak through a nice neighborhood and make work for himself. The local police figured the painter was probably a teenager bent on nothing more than half-witted vandalism, and the detail guy might have kept his scam going for years, but he tripped himself up. Not wanting another shop to get too many of his customers, he tended to hit the same neighborhoods, those close to his own place of business. One of the car owners whose car had been decorated three times got pissed off enough to set up a videocam watching his driveway. The detail man had been smart enough to pull a ski mask over his head when he ran into somebody's driveway, so nobody could see his face. And he had driven a different car each time, belonging to customers who'd left them overnight. Thing was, the cam picked up the license plate on the getaway vehicle. The cops were able to trace it to the owner, who supplied them with the information that the car had been at the detail shop on the night in question. They found the empty spray paint can in the guy's trash bin, leaned on him, and he gave it up. End of crime spree."

"All right, I can see where you're going, but I don't see how it applies. Didn't CyberNation's customers have the same problems everybody else had when the net and web went wonky?"

"Funny you should ask. I checked it out. During the outage we had, everybody who had logged on through the affected phone companies and backbone servers had the same problems. But none of CyberNation's customers using their hardwired-direct server connections lost their links. Now maybe that doesn't mean anything by itself, but it would be a big selling point! Hey, when all the other servers were scrambling around to figure out which way was up, we here at CyberNation had our act together!"

"That's a reach, Jay. Didn't lots of folks who weren't CyberNation customers sail along just fine?"

"Yep, that's true. But at least it's a possibility. Any time a big server has problems, they lose customers. Fifty years ago, nobody had a computer at home, nobody was doing biz on the web. Now, a lot of folks make their living from it. Before telephones, people wrote letters or did things face-to-face—now, every company has a phone, and most of them with any brains have a web presence. You have to have one to compete. Shut any of that down, and they look for a fast fix. Switching servers is easy. If you can claim yours is reliable, you'll get some of the movers."

Michaels nodded. "All right. What do you have in mind?"

"I'm thinking that unless I turn up something that shows it definitely *couldn't* be them, maybe I ought to keep looking at things in that direction. It's not like we have a lot else to go on. Well, until next time."

"You think there will be a next time?"

"I'd bet money on it, boss. A disruption on that scale took a lot of time and money and talent. It wasn't something a couple of high school hackers dreamed up just for the hell of it over chocolate shakes at the malt shop. We'll see these guys again. They have something in mind, and that first time could have been a test run. Next go 'round, it could be worse."

"Find them before that happens, Jay."

"I'm working on it, believe me."

San Francisco, California

The thing with professional bodyguards was that they were so predictable.

Santos watched the pair escorting his target to a limo, and smiled. This computer guy was a low-priority item.

With only two guards he was not seriously protected—somebody who was in real danger of being snatched or killed would have six or eight armed bodies working him, at a minimum, and if they were any good, you would only see the ones they wanted you to see, the others would either be out of sight or somebody you wouldn't consider a guard or a threat: a woman pushing a baby carriage, an old man leaning on a cane, somebody who appeared to be something he or she was not.

Mr. Ethan Dowling, of Silicon Valley, had only the two show guards, and these would be enough to keep honest people from bothering him. They might be tough and well-trained, but they were limited because they were right out there in plain sight. If all he wanted to do was kill Mr. Dowling, that would be easy: set up a hiding spot four or five hundred meters away, line up with a rifle, wait for the right moment, then spike him, end of mission.

Santos had undergone the sniper training program from the rebel paramilitary organization Blue Star, which was almost exactly the same as the one used by the U.S. Navy SEALs. With a good bolt-action rifle, he could get off three aimed shots in less than two seconds. These days, you didn't even have to worry about methods of estimating range. A good sniper scope would have a built-in range finder. Line it up, look at the readout, adjust your sights for elevation and windage, *blam*! the man was dead before the sound of the bullet reached his ears. By the time the guards pulled their heads out of their asses, you could spike both of them, too, if you felt like it.

But this was an information-gathering mission, not a simple assassination. He had to put the bodyguards out of commission, capture the target, get what he needed, then kill them all so their deaths would appear to have been an accident, which—despite what he had told Missy—was not so easy.

Still, as he watched the limo pull away from the curb, with both guards in it—one driving, the other in the front seat—he was confident he could do the job. It would require a little preparation, but he had the resources of CyberNation at his disposal, including large amounts of electronic cash, and he would have all that he needed in a few hours. Throw enough money at some problems, they got buried. Just like Mr. Dowling and his two bodyguards were going to get buried—after he had what he needed.

***On the* Bon Chance**

Keller lay naked on his back on the bed, exhausted.

Next to him, Jasmine Chance, as naked as he was, rolled over onto her belly and smiled at him.

Keller said, "If Santos knew you were with me, what would he do?"

She shrugged. "Probably nothing. He doesn't own me."

"He strikes me as a man who might be prone to jealousy."

"Are you worried?"

"Damned right. He could kill me with one hand."

"I bet he could do it without using his hands at all," she said.

"Great. I really need to hear this."

"Are you unhappy with the sex, Jackson?"

"No. No, the sex is terrific. Very, uh, relaxing."

"That's good. I don't want you tense. How is the next attack shaping up?"

"Almost done. A few more tweaks, some more security, we're ready to launch."

"Excellent."

"That is, if Santos doesn't come back from his mission and decide to beat my head in for sleeping with you."

"I won't tell him if you won't."

"We aren't the only two people on the boat."

"Leave Roberto to me. I have ways of calming him down."

"That I believe."

"Come, I'll show you something new."

"I can't. The beast is in a coma, sorry."

"Want to bet your next month's pay against a dollar on that? Have you ever heard of the Viennese Oyster?"

"Can't say as I have."

"Watch."

She rolled over onto her back and did something with her legs he wouldn't have thought she was nearly flexible enough to do. Both feet behind her head. Damn.

A good thing he didn't take the bet.

7

Washington, D.C.

Another day had passed without any major assaults on his domain, and Michaels was careful not to allow himself to feel too good about that. He didn't want to incur the wrath of a bored angel. He had finished his workout, and was looking forward to a beer and a quiet evening, maybe turn on the TV to watch some mindless sitcom, no heavy lifting.

He had just gotten dry from his shower and was reaching for his bathrobe when Toni told him to hold it—then told him why.

"Excuse me? You want me to try on a *dress*?"

"Not a dress, Alex—"

"Okay, fine, a skirt."

"A *sarong*. Some places they call it a wrap. Half the men in the tropical Third World wear them every day of life."

"Not this man. That's why God made short pants."

"Think of it as a kilt."

"A kilt, a sarong, a sixty-three Chevy Impala, it doesn't matter *what* you call it, it's a skirt!"

Toni laughed.

"I won't wear it."

"Oh, yes, you will. *You* volunteered us for this demo, remember? And when we do formal demonstrations of *Pukulan Pentjak Silat Serak*, we wear formal clothes. You saw that Plinck videotape. You bought it for me."

"They were wearing sweatpants underneath," he said.

"Fine, you can wear sweatpants under yours if it makes you happy."

"It will make me less unhappy."

"Come on, Alex! You can't have any doubts about your masculinity. The baby looks just like you."

"No, he doesn't. He looks like you." He tried to keep a straight face, but finally gave it up and laughed.

"That's what I thought," she said.

"Admit it, I had you going for a minute there," he said.

"Did not."

"Did too."

He followed her into the bedroom. She opened her closet and came out holding two hangers. "Okay, which do you want, the celestial or the bamboo?" She held up two squares of brightly colored cloth. "Genuine handmade Indonesian batik from Bali, the finest one hundred percent rayon."

"You don't think I'm gonna wear a *girl's* sarong?"

"Give it up, Alex. They're unisex and one size fits all." She pulled the garments off the hangers and unfolded them in a cascade of patterned azure. One, with what looked like stars drawn by somebody tanked up on psychedelic drugs, was dark, mostly indigo; the other was also blue, but lighter, with bamboo plants done in blues and whites.

"Maybe the bamboo. Jeez, it's as big as a tablecloth!"

"Come here, I'll show you how to put it on."

"Hey, I can wrap a towel around my waist, thank you."

"And it would fall off the first time I threw you."

"You'd do it on purpose."

"Damned straight."

He smiled. She handed him the bamboo-patterned cloth, which *was* as big as a tablecloth, had to be seven or eight feet long by maybe four feet wide.

"Watch me."

She demonstrated the way to put it on. "Okay, you wrap it around, like so, then fold it on your left side, and back upon itself, this way. Traditionally, it'll stay in place with just folding it, but since we are going to be more active, we'll use a safety pin for the demo, one here, then fold it back to the right, another pin there, then fan-fold it back and forth narrowing it each time, like this, then roll it down in folds to make a waistline, and shorten it at the bottom, see? It should hang to your knees."

"You wish."

"Not as much as you do," she said.

He watched, tried to duplicate her moves. When he was done it looked pretty good—until he let go and it fell down in a pool around his bare ankles.

"Great. Won't that look good in front of the FBI students. The Hawaiian will laugh himself silly. Two pins, you said?"

"Yes. In your case, I think diaper pins would be best."

"Ha, ha. You are so funny."

"Yes, I am, aren't I? Try again. Keep tension on it with your elbow, here, then here, until you get the waist rolled down to lock it into place."

He did what she said, and this time when he let go, the sarong stayed in position.

"Well?"

"Have to admit, it's comfortable."

"No worse than wearing a towel wrapped around you when you get out of the shower."

"Except I wouldn't wear a towel in front of a bunch of people in public."

"You do it at the gym, don't you?"

"That's different. It's just the guys."

"Ah, now we get to it. You're worried that some strange woman might see your wee-wee?"

"No."

"Well, you should be. I don't want you showing that to other women. Small as it is."

He laughed. "I just don't want to feel like some kind of weird pervert is all. Men don't wear skirts in this country."

"As opposed to a nonweird pervert?"

"You know what I mean."

"So the half-billion men who wear these are perverted?"

"I didn't say that. Speaking of which."

"Of which?"

"Perverts. I had an interesting visit with Jay today."

"Nice segue there. I'm sure Jay will love the transition. What about?"

"You aren't gonna believe it. But given the direction of the conversational road you're dragging me down . . ."

"Me? I'm not the low-self-esteem-I-can't-wear-a-sarong-because-people-will-think-I'm-funny-looking guy here."

He shook his head.

"Okay, so what about Jay?"

"You're kidding," Toni said.

Alex shook his head. "Not according to Jay."

"And how would Jay know?"

"That was my first question, too." He grinned. "He said a good computer op has to do enough research to know the field."

"And how does his fiancée feel about this *research*?"

"I didn't ask."

They had moved into the kitchen, Alex still in the sarong. It was very thin cloth, and he looked sexy in it. She glanced at the carrot she was about to slice. She held it up, then used the Japanese chef's knife to lop the ends off.

"Is that an editorial comment?"

"Make of it what you will."

He laughed.

She went back to dicing the carrot for their salad. With her mother watching the baby at her hotel, they had the place to themselves. Well, for a couple more hours, at least.

Alex said, "It doesn't really surprise me, when I stop and think about it. There has always been a certain amount of porn on the net, even back in the very early days. Newsgroups dedicated to various perversions, web pages where you could download pictures or movies, even some chat-room interactive stuff. And with scenarios in VR getting better and better, it was only a matter of time."

"But fully interactive internet sex? That seems so-so—"

"Weird?"

"That'll do for a start, yeah. You wouldn't think it would be possible."

"Well, according to Jay, it's been possible since before the turn of the century. In the early days, you could buy things like full-sized silicone dolls, with functional, uh, *apertures*, complete with vibrators. Plug 'er in, and go to town. But that was just high-tech masturbation. Now, you can connect yourself to various, ah, *machines*, dial up a friend, log into a joint VR sex feelie, and what you see is what you feel. Jay says the machines started out as things like phone pagers, but got a lot more sophisticated pretty quick. Some of them can mimic a penis or a vagina, either with expandable silicone rods, or as many as sixteen sequentially motor-driven, heated silicone undulant pads."

"Do I want to hear this?"

"I dunno, do you?"

Toni thought about it for a second. "Sure. Never let it be said that after I got married and had a child I automatically turned into an old stick-in-the-mud."

"The folks who are really into this call the sex devices McCleans."

Toni finished the carrot, reached for another, and raised one eyebrow.

"It's from an old limerick, according to Jay."

"You don't need to keep saying, 'according to Jay.' I'll take your word for it."

"Um. According to—I mean, you know about haptic mice and input pens and such. The McCleans came out of research for blind computer users. The top-of-the-line units have oral/genital/anal plugs or cavities, depending on the users', ah, physical configurations and desires. The headsets come with Aromajet's DigiScents modules that can mimic certain body smells. They call these 'reekers.' There is a tongue wafer from Taste-the-Real-Thing-dot-com that is electronically controlled to offer various tastes, and naturally, they call these 'droolers.' "

"Reekers and droolers," she said. "Sounds like some kind of medical condition."

"Or a law firm," he said.

"Um. Anyway, the best units include form-fitting memorymesh that can apply pressure in various ways, heat or cooling along any of the mesh ladders, along with vibrations."

Toni disposed of the second carrot, then went to work on a sweet purple onion. She said, "So you plug into a high-tech vibrator, or one into you, depending on your gender, slip into some mesh thingee that is really comfortable, dial up the taste and smell of warm whatever, and join your unseen loved one on a beach in VR somewhere?"

"That's what I am given to understand, yes."

"And how is it compared to the real thing?"

"Well, according to Jay—and I am in no way otherwise knowledgeable about this, believe me—it's not as good as the real thing, but it's better than being alone. And in some cases, there are sensations available you can't get with a real partner. The Electric Tongue can actually deliver enough low-amperage-but-high-voltage to make your hair stand up. Then there is the lifelike vibrating anus . . ."

"Yuck! This sounds totally disgusting!"

"Well, sure," he said, "because *you* have *me*. You are forever spoiled for other men and machines."

That cracked her up, as he knew it would.

"Say, fellow, is that a banana in your sarong, or are you just happy to see me?"

"It's a banana."

She laughed, and somehow his sarong fell down again.

8

Nicasio, California

The night was cool, but not too cold, and the winding and hilly road fairly quiet. The target and his bodyguards were on their way back from visiting some movie people who had a place in Lucas Valley. Santos didn't know a lot about movies, he did not spend much time in theaters, but this place, a ranch hidden from the road, was apparently pretty famous.

Santos had picked several places along the route where he could make his move, some better than others, but all should be workable if he did what he needed to do.

The limo passed his position, and he waited until it was a half-mile ahead of him before he started the big motorcycle's engine and pulled out behind the car. There was no worry that he would lose them, for he knew where they were going.

They weren't going to get there, though.

Thirty minutes later, the limo approached his primary location choice. But there was a car pulled off on the shoulder on the dark stretch of road, a big American sedan, just sitting there. He didn't see anybody silhouetted in the vehicle, but that did not matter.

It was a complication, and he let the limo drive past.

Five minutes past that, the secondary site loomed, but this time, the traffic was heavier than he'd expected.

The third choice was another six or seven minutes away. If there was a problem there, then he would scrub the mission for tonight and try again tomorrow.

As the road narrowed and curved, however, Santos saw that they were alone. He checked his speedometer. The bodyguard, who liked to drive fast, was going ten miles an hour faster than the posted limit.

Perfect.

A flip of a pair of temporary switches on the handlebar lit the flashing lights and cranked up the siren.

Ahead of him the limo slowed, and pulled off in exactly the place where he hoped it would. It was dark enough so any passersby wouldn't see anything except the bike's flashing lights—that's what they'd be looking at as they went past. And he wouldn't need more than a couple minutes to do this.

The limo stopped, and Santos pulled the motorcycle up behind the car. He killed the siren, left the lights going, dismounted from the bike, and walked to the limo. The driver powered the window down.

"What's the problem, Officer?" the driver asked.

In his best U.S. accent, Santos said, "You were going a little fast there, sir. Could I see your license and registration, please?"

"Aw, come on, you're not gonna give me a ticket, are you? Out here in the middle of nowhere, no traffic?" The bodyguard opened his wallet and flashed a badge and ID card. "I'm Russell Rader, King Executive Protection Services. I'm a former LEO–FBI, retired, working a bodyguard assignment for Blue Whale. This is Mr. Ethan Dowling, the vice president." He nodded at the passenger in back, who smiled. "Cut me a little slack, okay?"

Santos pretended to think about it for a couple of seconds. He closed the fake ticket book he held. "Retired FBI, huh? Well, I suppose I could let the speeding slide. But did you know your license plate was about to fall off?"

"What?"

"Screw must have fallen out, it's barely hanging on. Have a look."

Santos moved back, and the driver alighted. Both men walked around to the back of the car. "Looks all right to me," Rader said.

Here was the tricky part. Santos squatted behind the car, put his right index finger on the plate holder. "No, sir, see, right here?"

As he expected, the bodyguard squatted next to him to get a closer look.

As soon as the car's occupants couldn't see them, Santos used his elbow.

Normally, a squatting man wouldn't have particularly good balance or leverage for such a strike. But Capoeira was an art based on movement in odd positions. Santos's balance was superb.

He slammed the bodyguard flush on the right temple. The man fell as if somebody had chopped off his lower half.

Good night, Mr. Rader.

Santos stood. He walked around to the passenger side of the limo, leaned down.

The second bodyguard lowered his window.

"Your friend is trying to fix the license plate, but his knife isn't going to do the job. Do you have a screwdriver in the car?"

As the bodyguard opened his mouth to speak, Santos drove his fist into the man's throat with as much power as he could. He heard the voicebox break. The man clutched at his neck, and Santos fired a second strike, this one with the heel of his hand to the man's forehead. A punch that hard likely would have broken his knuckles, but the heel of the hand was padded—you hit hard with soft, soft with hard, if you wanted to avoid damaging yourself.

The man's head snapped back. Before he could move, Santos jerked the door open and grabbed the stunned guard's neck with one hand and pinched his carotids shut. Ten seconds was more than enough. The man's eyes rolled in his sockets, showing white. He was unconscious.

Santos released his grip. He didn't want to kill him.

In the back, Mr. Dowling started sputtering: "What the—! Hey—!"

Santos could have pulled his pistol out and used it like a magic wand to silence the man, but he didn't need it. He smiled, a broad, teeth-flashing grin. "This is a kidnapping, Ethan. You be quiet, or I'll have to kill you."

The man was terrified. He shut up.

Now, all Santos had to do was immobilize the bodyguards. He hauled the second one out of the car and dragged him to the back. He expertly tied both unconscious men, using the soft cloth ties he had tucked away in his pocket. He didn't want any ligature marks on them. He placed a loop around each neck and to the wrists, so they wouldn't struggle when they woke up. He opened the trunk and hoisted the tied pair inside, then carefully shut the lid. He walked back to the bike, glanced at Dowling as he did to see if he'd make a break for it—try to get into the front seat, get the car started, or maybe just open the door and run.

Dowling sat, not moving, and Santos smiled. He hadn't thought the man had it in him. He was a good judge of such things.

He killed the motorcycle's flashing lights, unclipped them and the siren and controls from the bike, then pushed the two-wheeler into a clump of bushes nearby, so it wasn't visible from the road. Now it was just an ordinary motorcycle. By the time somebody found it, this would be all over. And there wouldn't be any way to connect it to Dowling and his bodyguards anyway—the rest of the night's business was going to happen thirty miles away on a different highway. The motorcycle wasn't stolen; it had been bought under a fake name, and there was no reason to link it to the limo. It would be another of life's little unsolved mysteries.

Santos walked to the car, opened the driver's door, and sat behind the wheel. "Just sit there quietly," he said. "We'll go for a ride, then we'll have a chat. Behave yourself, and all it costs you is a little inconvenience."

A lie, that. Dowling and his two guards would be dead within an hour, all things going as planned. But no point in upsetting the man, was there?

Net Force HQ
Quantico, Virginia

It was the nightmare that had finally pushed Michaels into it. He'd awakened in a sweat, heart pounding, from a dream in which the psychotic doper Bershaw had come to his house and captured Toni. In this one, the would-be killer had Little Alex and was holding him by one ankle, getting ready to smash the baby against the kitchen counter.

Michaels hadn't been able to go back to sleep after that horrific image.

John Howard had told him whenever he was ready to give him a call. As soon as it got late enough, he did just that.

Now, they were in Michaels's office.

"I've been meaning to do this for a long time," Michaels said. "Thanks, John."

"No problem. Makes perfect sense to me," Howard said. "In your place, I'd have done it a long time ago."

"I mean, even with all of Toni's expertise, and the knives and tasers and stuff we have laying around, somebody has twice shown up at my house with murderous intent."

"I remember the last incident quite well," Howard said. "It's about time you got some more serious hardware."

"Yeah. I want to be a little better prepared if it ever happens again."

"I expect this will do the trick," Howard said. "Let me show you what we have."

Michaels nodded and looked at the gun case, which seemed to be some kind of brownish-gray canvas or oilcloth, darkened here and there with splotches of lube.

He untied a string at the fat end of the cloth case and slid the weapon out.

"This belonged to my uncle," he said. "It's what they call a 'coach gun,' being the kind of weapon a lot of the stagecoach drivers used when they rode shotgun guard duty back in the Old West. This one is a European American Armory Bounty Hunter II, actually made in Russia for export. My uncle used to use it in cowboy action shooting."

"Cowboy action shooting?"

"A competitive sport. Men and women get dressed up in pre1900 costumes like those that might have been worn in the Old West, give themselves names like 'Doc' or 'Deadeye' or 'The Kid,' and while in persona, shoot for scores using period weapons—single-action six-shooters, rifles, usually the lever-action kind, and shotguns."

"Really?"

"Yep. A grown-up version of cowboys 'n' Indians. Got Native Americans who wear period stuff and compete, too. Everybody wears hearing protectors and safety glasses and all, but otherwise the look is usually pretty authentic."

"Huh."

"My uncle used to love it. There were a fair number of black cowboys on the frontier. After slavery was abolished, and before Jim Crow got going, nobody much cared what color you were, long as you could ride, punch cattle okay, and could shoot snakes or rustlers if they showed up. At least that's the story I heard growing up."

"Interesting."

"It's not a particularly expensive gun, basic walnut stocks and case-hardened color. The Russians don't build 'em pretty, but they are very solid and mechanically well-made. Uses 12-gauge shells, the short ones, two-and-three-quarter inchers only. Just as well—the high-powered three-inchers would have a fierce recoil with a barrel this short."

He pivoted a lever in the middle to one side, and opened the breech. "Got twenty-inch-long double barrels, extractors that pull the shells out, but not ejectors, so it doesn't throw them on the floor. External hammers, they call them 'rabbit ears,' see? This one is a modern copy of the old ones, so the hammers don't actually hit a firing pin, but cock internal strikers. That way, you can use a hammer block as well as a trigger-block safety, here, this button. It's about as simple as you can get. You open it up, put a pair of shells in, close it, then cock the hammers. Got two triggers, one for each barrel. Slide the safety off, aim it like you would a rifle, or if somebody is in your face, poke them with it like a stick and pull the trigger."

"What if I miss? Is this going to go through the wall and kill my neighbor in his bed?"

"Not if you use birdshot. You don't need buckshot or slugs for close range stuff. Combat distance, a load of bird- or rabbit-shot works just fine, and the little bbs don't go far after hitting couple of layers of sheet rock and siding. Even though you could get a permit for a handgun, this packs a lot more punch, it's safer, and it's legal to own here in the District, even for civilians."

Michaels took the gun, worked the action open and closed, then tried the hammers out. It had a nice, solid feel to it.

"You should drop by the range and put a few rounds through it. It'll kick some, but you can hip-shoot easy enough if you don't want a sore shoulder. Just like pointing your finger."

Michaels nodded.

"And here's the gun safe."

He held up an oblong box big enough to hold the shotgun, with an image of a hand on it.

"This is titanium, lightweight, but strong enough to resist somebody trying to pry it open with a screwdriver. It'll hold a couple of long arms. You bolt it to a couple of wall studs in a closet in the bedroom, put your gun and ammo inside it. It's got a fingerprint reader in the handprint here that will accept sixty-four different ones, so you can program it to read yours and Toni's and anybody else you trust. Uses a lithium-ion battery to run the reader, battery is good for five or six years, and when it starts to run low, it flashes a diode, right here, so you know to replace it. It can also be wired into your house alarm system if you want."

"Seems, well, *safe* enough."

"If you really want, you can get Gunny at the range to install the electronic safeties we use in our issue guns, get a transmitting ring, and cover it that way, too. That way, if an unauthorized person should manage to get it out of the safe, it won't shoot for them—but I wouldn't worry about that.

"So if somebody starts kicking in your front door in the middle of the night, you can get this out and ready to go in a few seconds. Anybody who sees you standing there with a piece like this is apt to think twice about proceeding in your direction. A lot of guys who would charge a pistol will pull up when they see the muzzle of a shotgun yawning at them."

"I can understand that. Looks like a cannon."

"Downside is, you only get two shots. A pump would give you five rounds minimum, more with an extended tube.

"You ought to consider taking the FBI/DEA house-clearing class for shotguns. As head of Net Force, they'd be happy to have you, and it would be worth a Sunday afternoon to learn it."

"You think I need something like that?"

"Yes, sir. For instance, if you see somebody prowling your house with a gun who doesn't belong there, what would you do?"

"Tell them to drop it?"

"Not according to home defense experts. You should just go ahead and shoot them."

"Excuse me?"

"Law enforcement officers are required to try to catch bad guys alive, homeowners aren't. If somebody is in your house with a weapon, they are ipso facto to be considered a deadly threat. In your case, this has happened a couple of times already. You ordering an armed housebreaker to put his weapon down will just as likely get you shot as not. You hear a *clunk*! in the night, what you are supposed to do is lock yourself and your family in a secure room, get your gun, com the police, and stay put until the cops arrive. You aren't supposed to stalk down the hall like Doc Holliday with your shotgun looking for the bad guys. If you do, however, and you see one, and he's armed, you shoot first and ask questions later."

"Jesus."

"Not likely He is gonna be breaking into your house. Take the course, sir. There's all kinds of things you need to know about the use of deadly force that have changed since you were out in the field."

Michaels looked at the shotgun. "Yes. I can see that. So, what do I owe you?"

Howard named a price.

"That seems awful low."

"Well, the gun I don't shoot, so it might as well have a good home. Box of shells came out of my gun safe at home, been around forever. The only out-of-pocket expense I had was the safe, so that'll cover it."

"Thanks again, John."

"Let me know when you want to go shoot. Might be I could give you a couple of pointers."

"I'll do that."

After Howard was gone, Michaels contemplated the

shotgun. He'd never kept a gun in his house—well, not this house. He had a pistol back in the days when he'd been in the field, but he'd never felt the need for a gun at home once he'd been kicked upstairs. He had the issue taser, and for a long time that had been enough—once. There was nothing like having a couple of killers drop by to make you feel like a gun in the bedside table or closet was maybe not such a bad idea after all. He might never have the need for it again, he hoped not, but he had come to appreciate the NRA slogan: It was better to have it and not need it than to need it and not have it.

Be interesting to hear what Toni would say. He hadn't consulted her about it.

9

On the **Bon Chance**

"Okay," the tech said, "here it is."

They were in Media, a ballroom-sized place divided into cubicles, thick with computers, printers, duplicators, and other electronic impedimenta.

Chance looked at the monitor, a 21-inch flatscreen connected to a top-of-the-line Macintosh computer. The Avid software and the computer's hard drive would allow up to a hundred hours of film storage, and with such a nonlinear editing system, you could do all kinds of things. Wipes, fades, dissolves, blue-screen, holoprojics, whatever. It was a powerful tool, used in a lot of movie and television productions, and with it you could take an ordinary piece of film or CGI and do amazing things.

To the world, CyberNation must be about amazing things.

Onscreen was the computer-generated image of a soaring marble and stone cathedral. Dust motes swam in beams of sunlight lancing through low-hanging clouds.

The point-of-view camera moved in on a simulated dolly toward the arched building.

Music began, a Bach fugue with thundering organ chords.

As the POV shot approached the massive doors to the building, they began to open and dissolve. Doves flew out and scattered. The music began to morph into a classic rock 'n' roll number with the words seeming to grow right out of the organ notes, something with a heavy, driving beat, all about American dreams and suicide machines. As the music changed, so did the image, from a towering pseudo-Gothic edifice to a futuristic nightclub. The camera continued to dolly in and through the doors, and inside the club dozens of beautiful people danced together, frantically gyrating to the rock beat. Sweat made their thin shirts and blouses stick to perfect bodies. The men obviously all lifted weights, the women didn't wear bras and didn't need them.

Overhead, lasers flickered through clouds of colored smoke, and the slogan CYBERNATION—WE CAN TAKE YOU ANYWHERE YOU WANT TO GO!" appeared superimposed over the dancers, with the sign-up URL under it.

The scene froze. "That's the intro. What do you think?" the tech asked.

"Not bad," Chance said. "But dial down the volume on the music a hair, and when we get the slogan super, I want a wah-wah sting that echoes the bass line. And see if we can vibrate the words a little. Who is doing the voice-over?"

"Foghorn Franklin."

"Good. He's perfect. What happens from here?"

"We're still working on the wire-frame dinosaur stuff, and the space aliens, but we've got the harem sequence and the shopping at Harrods almost done. The wire-frame'll be ready for texture in a couple of days."

Chance nodded and turned away from the Avid. She glanced at her watch. She hadn't heard from Roberto yet. She wondered how he was doing.

He was probably doing just fine. She worried too much about the details, she knew that. It was hard to trust people to do what you told them to do, and with good reason. Once upon a time, she had been a corporate manager, on the fast track to the vice presidency of a Fortune Five Hundred company. She'd been making good money, had been well-respected, and had been kicking ass and taking names, but she'd had to quit. People kept screwing up, doing things differently than she'd told them, and it drove her up the wall. The idea of being a decent manager was: You hired good workers and turned them loose, and they didn't call until the job was done, except if they had problems. The reality of it was: You inherited a lot of deadwood in whatever department you took over, and it was a while until you could figure out who worked and who shuffled papers and pretended to work. Yeah, once you got the lay of the land, you could fire the lazy ones, but then you had to spend time looking for somebody new, and that was always the devil-you-knew-versus-the-devil-you-didn't. You'd read this great resume, the guy would show up and give a good interview, and as soon as he got the job, he'd turn into a brain-dead lame donkey you couldn't move with a flaming two-by-four shoved up his butt. Half the time you couldn't lop off the deadwood in the first place because they'd sue for one kind of discrimination or another—gender, age, race, whatever. You could catch somebody stealing the petty cash, flashing old ladies in the subway, or snorting cocaine in the lunchroom and it wasn't enough to get rid of them if they had the right leverage.

And office politics? Stupid bosses who'd Peter Principled out? Backstabbing coworkers?

Don't even hike *those* trails . . .

Chance smiled at the memory. Being in charge of most places was no picnic in the park. The reason she had taken this job was that they let her start from scratch, hire anybody she wanted, and she could get rid of anybody who worked for her with two words: *You're gone!* There was no appeal. She didn't have to answer to anybody except the Board, and as long as she met the goals of the business plan—which she herself produced—nobody cared *how* she got it done. She couldn't imagine a better job.

Roberto was good, and she should trust him to do what was needed, but she was still too hands-on. She still worried every time her neck was essentially in somebody else's hands. She'd have to work on that. She needed to relax—'Berto was the best she'd ever found at his kind of work.

But if he didn't call in the next hour or two, she was going to be bent out of shape.

San Rafael, California

Killing the three was the easy part. After he had gotten everything from Dowling he wanted, and a whole lot he hadn't cared about, he very carefully choked the man out, using the special hold he'd learned from a Vale Tudo jujitsu fighter in Brazil. Enough so the guy was unconscious, but not so he'd die. Then he had retrieved the bodyguards one at a time, choked them out, and put everybody into the limo. He'd driven to the spot, only half a mile away, choked them all again to make certain they were out. Then he accelerated toward the guardrail overlooking an eight-hundred-foot drop-off, and locked the car's brakes in a hard skid that stopped right at the edge of the pavement.

He backed it up a few yards. Then he repositioned one of the unconscious guards in the driver's seat and strapped him in with the seat belt. He jammed the guy's shoe into the side of the accelerator, and the engine roared. He shut the door, reached in through the window, and shifted the automatic transmission lever into drive.

The car lurched forward and gathered speed. It hit the

rail with plenty of momentum, punched through, and rolled out over the long drop-off.

It made a lot of noise going down, tumbled and flipped several times. Santos was able to follow the car's fall most of the way, until the car's lights went out, probably because the battery had been knocked loose.

Adios, amigos.

It was not totally foolproof, but nobody would have any reason to look past the obvious: The driver for a corporate vice president, on the way home in the dark on a mountain road, had seen a deer or coyote or some other animal, slammed on his brakes, and too bad, had skidded right off the cliff. Yes, a trained accident investigator might notice that the safety railing was perhaps not damaged as much as a high-speed impact would warrant. But a California Highway Patrol officer would see skid marks that matched the limo's tires, indicating that he had tried to stop. The men would have died from injuries sustained in the wreck, and there would be no sign of drugs or other injuries that could not have come from the impact, Santos had made certain of that.

Accidents happened. A real CHP officer with any time on the job would likely have seen a dozen incidents just like this, and if that was what you were looking for, then that was what you would see. There would be no reason to think anything else.

Maybe the insurance company would send an expert out to check on things. Even so, such an investigation would take time, measurements had to be made, tests run, reports written, and even then, a conclusion would not be certain.

So, Mr. Acidente Experto, why is it you think this was not an accident?

Well, the guardrail did not show damage consistent with a high-speed impact.

Perhaps the metal in this rail came from a particularly strong batch?

Not according to my tests.

Yes, but—how do you know how fast the car was going when it struck the guardrail, eh?

The length of the skid marks is indicative of substantial velocity.

Ah, but putting on the brakes slowed the automobile down, no? Perhaps enough so that the impact was considerably lessened? Is this not possible?

Yes, it is possible . . .

As he hiked back toward where he had a hidden car waiting—one with license plates he had swapped with a car in the long-term parking lot of the *aeroporto* in San Francisco—Santos smiled to himself. If, a week or a month from now, the authorities did somehow become convinced that the limo's destruction had not been an accident, that would not matter. By then, the information he had been sent to collect would have been used. How? He didn't really know or care, that was not his problem. He had been sent to get it, he had gotten it, end of story. There was no way to tie him to the incident in any case. He had bought the car under a false name. Nobody knew him here, and nobody who might have seen him would know who he was or where he had gone. He was just another black man, and they all looked alike to whites, no?

He would call Jasmine when he got back to San Francisco, using a disposable mobile phone. A short message telling her answering service the job was complete. That would make her feel better. Missy was wound too tight. The only time she loosened up was in bed, and even then, she never let everything go; there was always a part of her still in control. He intended to get past that eventually. Bring her to pure animal pleasure, no mind left, just howling and quivering in ecstasy. It might take a while, but he didn't mind—getting there would be half the fun.

And once he had her there, she would be his slave. Then he would dump her and find another. The world was full of women.

10

Washington, D.C.

Toni was expecting the postman; the most recent order of faux ivory slabs for her scrimshaw should be here about now, so when the doorbell rang, that's who she thought it was. Not that she had gotten much scrimshaw done since the baby was born, bits and pieces while he was napping, mostly. Nobody had told her what a full-time job one small human child was.

She opened the door, but instead of the postman, Guru stood there.

The old lady smiled at Toni's startled expression. "Hello, best girl. Surprise."

"Guru! What are you doing here!"

"Waiting to be invited into your house."

Toni opened the screen door and held it wide. "Come in, come in!"

Guru—which in Bahasa Indonesian meant "teacher"—picked up her suitcase and moved past Toni into the house. She also carried a heavy, wooden cane.

The old woman, whose name was DeBeers, was coming up on her eighty-fifth birthday. She'd had a stroke back when Toni was five months pregnant, and was supposedly recovered completely. Toni had seen her when she'd taken the baby back to show off to her family six or eight months ago, and Guru hadn't been using a cane then.

But before she could ask, Guru read her mind: "The stick is for defense, not for walking. Do you think I could come all the way from the Bronx on a train unarmed? Did I not teach you better than that?"

Toni laughed. Of course not. *Pentjak silat* was a weapons-based art. You only used your hands if you didn't have anything else available. Guru used to say, "You are not a monkey, use a tool. You can fight with your hands. You can also butter your bread with your finger, but why would you if there is a knife handy?"

Toni waited until Guru had put her bag down and found a seat on the couch. "I'll go make the coffee," she said.

"That would be nice," the old woman said. "You have any of my nephew's Javanese beans I sent you left?"

"Sealed in a vacuum bag to keep them fresh," Toni said.

"You are a good girl. How is our baby boy?"

"He's terrific. Taking his nap right now, he'll probably be awake soon."

"This is also good."

Toni hurried off to grind the coffee beans and put them into the gold mesh filtered drip pot. She used bottled water—Guru was particular about her coffee—and once everything was going, she hurried back into the living room.

"I am happy you are here," Toni said. "You should have called. I would have come to the train station and collected you."

"And miss the look on your face when you saw me? No."

Toni smiled again. Guru had been family since Toni had begun learning the martial art of *silat* from her more than sixteen years ago. Toni had been thirteen when she'd seen the old lady, past retirement age even then, clean up her front stoop with four thugs brave enough to threaten an old pipe-smoking granny. Guru had come from Java with her husband as a young woman, raised a family, and been widowed before Toni had been born. Her husband had taught her the family martial art usually reserved for men, and she in turn had passed it along to Toni.

It would not be polite to ask the old woman why she had come nor how long she planned to stay, but as usual, Guru was ahead of her. She said, "I will take care of the baby while you work."

"Thank you, but, uh, I wasn't planning on going back to work," Toni said. "Not for a while, at least."

"Plans change, best girl. I think maybe you will go back very soon."

"I don't see how—"

The phone jangled. Toni was tempted to ignore it, let the computer take a message, but Guru waved at her. "You should answer that," she said. "I will go and check on the coffee." She smiled.

Toni shrugged. As she reached for the com, she saw the ID.

"Hey, Alex. What's up?"

"Trouble here in River City," he said. "Got a major blowout on the web. It's like somebody poked a stick in a nest of fire ants, they're running around, mad as hell, biting everybody close. You know, I wish your mother hadn't gone home, I could sure use your help on this."

Toni stared into the kitchen at Guru, who was pouring the coffee from the pot into a carafe, humming to herself.

It had to be a coincidence. Had to be.

But deep in her soul, Toni didn't believe it. What she believed was, Guru had *known*!

She couldn't have known that Alex would say that. And yet, there she was, making coffee, as if Toni had called and asked her to come up and watch the baby. She had come here, knowing Toni could use her help.

How was that possible?

"Toni?"

"Um. Yeah. Guru is here."

"Really? That's great. How is she?"

"Fine. She came to watch Little Alex so I could go back to work."

Alex didn't say anything for a few seconds. "Coincidence," he finally said.

"She said I'd be going back to work sooner than I expected. She got here ten minutes ago."

There was a long pause. "Coincidence," he said again. "I have to believe that. It's too spooky otherwise."

"Tell me about it."

"Coffee is ready," Guru said from the kitchen. "Hello to Mr. Alex."

"Guru says hello."

"I heard." Another pause. "Well, you might as well come on down here. I really do need all the help I can get."

Net Force HQ
Quantico, Virginia

Michaels cradled the receiver and shook his head. Someday, he was going to have to sit down with that old lady and ask her how this *tenaga dalam*, the "inside magic" she claimed to know, worked. There was probably some scientific explanation, but damned if he could figure out what it was.

Meanwhile, he had bigger problems. He voxaxed Jay Gridley.

"Talk to me, Jay."

"We got it tracked to Blue Whale," Jay said.

"Which is?"

"Major West Coast backbone server. Couple-three big nodes there."

"What happened?"

"Don't know yet, boss."

"Go find out."

"I'm gone."

Michaels stood and headed for the door. His phone was going to ring in a minute or two, and the director of the FBI would be on the other end of the connection, wanting to know what the hell was going on. Since he didn't have anything he could tell her, he wasn't looking forward to the conversation.

His secretary looked up at him as he passed her desk. "I'm going to the bathroom," he said. "When the director calls, tell her I'm indisposed."

Becky said, "Take your virgil with you. I don't want her yelling at me."

Virgil was short for Virtual Global Interface Link, a device slightly larger than a cigarette-pack that was a phone, modem, computer, weavewire fax, GPS, credit card, scanner, clock, radio, TV, and emergency beacon all in one. They weren't common devices, not in the version Michaels had, and it hadn't taken him long to figure out that the FBI had his virgil monitored and sat-tracked 24/7. They said this was for the safety of high-level personnel. If you had a powered FBI-issue virgil attached to your belt, you could run, but you couldn't hide, and unlike the civilian models with fudge-factors built in to keep terrorists from using them to guide ballistic missiles to targets, the military GPS was accurate to within a couple of feet. Michaels was fairly sure it would work even if it was turned off.

If you actually went to the rest room and took the virgil with you, they could tell which stall you were in.

"Battery is dead," he said.

"Uh-huh," Becky said. "Right. And there aren't a half-dozen new batteries in your top desk drawer where they always are?"

"I'll replace it when I get back."

"Chicken."

"That's me. Bye."

San Francisco, California

The night was alive with flashing lights, fading sirens, and the crackle of fire dining on everything it could chew and consume.

The building, a five-story job built after the big quake of 1906, was burning like, well, like a big house on fire. Black smoke poured from the upper two stories, flames shot out through imploded windows on the third floor. Pumper engines filled the street with red lights and throaty mechanical drones. A hook-and-ladder with a mounted inch-and-halfer giraffe line blew water into the upper story, while ground-based hydrant-fed three-inchers as stiff as wooden beams spewed water into the third and fourth floors. Cops kept the lookie-loos back, and firefighters ran back and forth, moving hoses, gearing up with air tanks and masks, doing what they were supposed to do.

Jay Gridley, dressed in a stiff and clumsy fireman's turnout suit—coat, bunker pants, gloves, boots, and helmet, light reflecting off the glo-flex strips on the clothing—stood with a group of other firefighters near one of the building's entrances.

A captain stood there in front of a chart on a stand. He listened to a handheld tactical radio, looked at the team, and said, "Okay, here's the situation. We got the building cleared of people so far as we know. Fire started on the third floor, which is two-thirds engulfed, and is spreading laterally and going up fast, but the first two floors are still cool. I want your line here." He pointed at the chart. "Baker and Charlie squads are entering the structure from the east and south, and setting up here, and here."

Gridley wasn't up to speed on real fire fighting tactics.

He'd started creating this scenario a few days back, but hadn't had time to do the research, so he doubted this was how it would work in RW. Would they go into a building on the ground floor if the floors above it were burning? Not something he'd want to do. His scenario was based on entertainment vids he'd seen, and everybody knew the movies never let truth get in the way of a story.

Fortunately, in VR, it didn't actually have to mirror reality. It didn't even have to look that good, unless you wanted to invite somebody else in to play. It was only the anal-retentive types like Jay who wanted the scenario to be as real as possible—most people didn't bother. For Jay, the test of his creation would be to bring in a squad of real firefighters and have them look around, nod, then say, "Yeah, this is how it really is." He figured if you could fool somebody who really knew what it was like, you had a decent scenario.

Most people could buy off-the-shelf software and be perfectly happy. Most people weren't Net Force's top VR honcho, Smokin' Jay Gridley. If he couldn't do it right, he didn't want to do it.

The captain finished his directions. The team started into the building, dragging a stiff and heavy pressurized hose. The power was out, so they switched on helmet and hand-carried lanterns. The sounds they made were loud in the darkness, and the roar of the fire a couple of stories up was muted but audible, the building vibrating as it was being eaten alive by the orange monster. A lot of firefighters anthropomorphized fire, Jay knew that much. They talked about it as if it were some kind of malevolent creature rather than what was essentially a real fast version of rust-oxidation and combustion . . .

Back at Net Force HQ, Jay and his team were working their computers, trying to find the source of the problem at Blue Whale—and they weren't alone—but in this scenario, he was about to take a turn up a dark hallway by himself to get closer to the source of the fire. Not something any sane fireman would do, and certainly not alone, he knew at least that much.

As the team moved to the location where it was supposed to deploy its hose, Jay slipped into the stairway and started climbing. The smell of burning material and the hint of smoke in the stairwell was a nice touch, he thought, congratulating himself.

As he climbed to the second floor landing, then past it, he suddenly thought about Saji. Despite her life-is-about-suffering Buddhist thing, she was very excited about their upcoming wedding. And while the idea of being without her and back like he'd been before they had met was as bleak a scenario as Jay could imagine, he had to confess to himself that he'd had some second thoughts. Getting married had never really been in Jay's life plan. Oh, sure, he had figured there'd be women in his life, maybe even children someday, but the reality of it was different than the vague imaginings he'd had. That he would marry a Buddhist he'd met on-line while recovering from an induced-stroke—a woman whose net persona had been that of an old Tibetan lama—had never figured into his fastasies. And now that the actual date had been set and the plans were being carefully laid, the idea that he was going to be *married* to somebody had begun to hit home.

One woman, for the rest of his life. Day in, day out, always around . . .

Yeah, the sex was great, and yeah, he loved her, couldn't really imagine being alone, no Saji around; still, there was this . . . finality about the idea of saying "I do" and signing a lifelong contract that had never really occurred to him until it was actually staring him in the face . . .

He got to the third floor. Took off his right glove, pressed it against the door. The door was cool to the touch. He took a couple of deep breaths of the stale-tasting compressed air from his bottle, then reached for the doorknob. Worry about getting married later. Right now, he had a job to do. Some guys were screwing with the web, and he was the guy who was going to track them down and stop them.

They obviously didn't know who they were messing with . . .

***On the* Bon Chance**

The fire scenario was okay, but overblown. Jay had always been too gaudy about such things, spending too much time on how good something looked when he should have been concentrating on how well it worked. Style and not substance.

Still, as Keller stood there in his fireman's gear, watching Jay work, he had to give him credit. He was sniffing in the right direction.

Keller waited until Jay went past, heading for the source of the "fire." Maybe he could figure something out, maybe not, but he wasn't going to get the chance. Keller followed Jay up the stairwell, being careful to stay out of sight, tracking him by the sound of his boots on the steps.

Once Jay was on the right floor, Keller moved in. It was dark, smoky, hot, all in all, a pretty good representation, as such things went. Jay was always big on details. But that was the curse of a small picture man, wasn't it? Couldn't see the forest for the trees in the way. No long-range vision.

From a cabinet near the door, Keller pulled a thermite bomb, shaped like a bowling ball. He triggered the timer for ten seconds, then rolled it across the floor toward the unseen Jay Gridley. Heard Jay stop and listen.

See you later, Jay. You lose this round.

The bomb went off in a flare that destroyed the scenario as Keller dropped out of VR and back into his cabin on the *Bon Chance*. He pulled off the sensory gear, laughing. "You never had an opponent like me, Jay. I know all your best moves. You don't have a prayer."

11

***On the* Bon Chance**

An old man, maybe seventy-five or so, sat in a recliner in a low-rent room, pointing a remote at a battered television set, pushing buttons, but getting only scrambled, frantic pixels whirling on his screen.

A deep, masculine voice said, "Tired of losing your net service? Unable to log onto the web because your server can't get its act together?"

The old man clicked the remote a couple more times, then shook his head and tossed the control onto a scratched table next to the worn and scuffed leather recliner.

A big, happy-looking German shepherd padded over to the old man. In his mouth, the dog held another remote, a silvery, glittering, truncated cone-shaped device. The old man looked at the dog, who dropped the device into his lap and gave him a dog smile.

"What's this, boy?" the old man said.

The dog gave one sharp bark.

The old man picked up the remote.

The opening notes for Strauss's "Thus Spake Zarathustra" began playing quietly in the background.

A deep voice said, "We at CyberNation understand your frustration. And we have a guarantee—if you are ever kept off the net for more than an hour on a CyberNation server, we'll not only give you your money back for that entire month, we'll give you your next month of service absolutely free."

The music grew louder. *Boom-boom-boom-boom-boom-boom . . .*

The old man looked at the dog and raised one eyebrow in question. The dog barked once, and it was obvious what he was saying. "Go for it!"

"At CyberNation, we are always here for you, twenty-four hours a day, three hundred and sixty-five days a year. You have our word on that, and we put our money where our mouth is."

The old man pointed the remote at his television set.

The music's volume increased so that it rumbled over the old man and dog as if a full symphony orchestra was in the next room.

The set morphed, changed into a giant window that expanded to cover the entire wall. People stepped out and into the shabby living room. There was an Indian holy man in a turban and long flowing white robe; a black woman in a grass skirt, bare from the waist up; a cowboy; an Arctic explorer; a big-game hunter. In addition, a rhino, an ostrich, and a small dinosaur stepped from the window into the suddenly expanded living room. All of them seemed to get along famously.

The music reached its peak, thundering Strauss, horns blasting their dramatic sting.

"Anywhere, anytime, any*body* you want to be—CyberNation can take you there. Come along. Join the millions of satisfied citizens of the net in mankind's greatest experiment. The future is waiting for you."

The old man and dog both smiled as the music faded.

"What do you think?" Chance said.

Roberto said, "An old man and a dog?"

"Not everybody goes for the sex ads," she said. "Dogs are always good. You know the old story about the book title?"

'Berto shook his head.

"Well, the theory is, people like dogs. They also like Abraham Lincoln and they like their doctors, for the most part. So a book title that would guarantee instant sales would be *Abraham Lincoln's Doctor's Dog*."

'Berto smiled.

"It's all about demographics. We catch a lot of the young male computer geeks with the sex come-ons. But we also have specific ads tailored for generation Xers, aging baby boomers turning into AARPers, young mothers, as many large groups as we can identify and niche-market to. Net, TV, radio, print ads, movie trailers, billboards, bus benches, sports sponsorships—everything from T-shirts to signs on racing cars—high school cable ed, you name it. Since the Blue Whale scramble, we've picked up eighty-eight thousand new subscribers on the U.S. West Coast alone."

"That's good, right?"

"Not as good as we'd hoped. The Net Force ops got in and patched things up faster than we expected. We should have gotten twice that many new linkers."

He shrugged again. "So?"

"Truth is, things aren't moving along as quickly as we want. We are falling short of our projections. It looks as if we are going to have to . . . step things up."

"More ads? More software scrambles?"

She looked at him. Butter wouldn't melt in his mouth. "Don't pull my chain, Roberto."

He chuckled. "You have a new piercing you haven't told me about, Missy?"

"Screw you."

"I'm ready when you are."

She smiled. Well. He had his charms, even when he played at being duller than he was . . .

Net Force HQ
Quantico, Virginia

Dressed in Net Force sweats and cross-trainers, John Howard stood under one of the chinning bars at the obstacle course, rotating his head slowly to stretch the muscles of his neck. Physical training was another thing he'd slacked off on during his short-lived retirement. Not that he'd stopped completely—he'd kept up morning calisthenics, and he still hit the weights down in the basement a couple times a week, plus he jogged most days for a few miles; still, he hadn't run the course in almost a month, and normally he'd do it at least twice a week.

Probably he'd lost a couple of steps, but not that much.

He jumped up, caught the steel bar, palms forward and slightly wider than his shoulders, and started doing chins. He knew after the first couple that his usual twelve or fifteen routine was out of the question. By the fifth one, he was straining, and it was all he could do to gut out ten.

He was glad Julio Fernandez was not here to see this. If he had been, Howard would have had to find three or four more reps somewhere, and like as not, he'd have pulled a muscle doing 'em.

He let himself hang for a few seconds after the tenth rep, to stretch out his lats, then dropped to the ground, disgusted with himself. Who was it—Gertrude Stein?—who'd said that after you hit forty it's all patch, patch, patch?

Didn't matter who said it, it was sure true. On the one hand, he still felt like a kid of nineteen. Yeah, his hairline showed a little more face than it used to and there were little tufts of gray at the temples. But there weren't too many wrinkles, and his general shape and weight wasn't that different from twenty, twenty-five years ago. If anything, he'd put on some muscle since his first hitch in the regular army. But the days of partying all night and then working a full day were gone. The occasional strain or bruise took longer to heal, and if he didn't stretch and warm up before he started working out hard, he got a lot more strains and bruises than he had as a kid. He thought he'd come to terms with getting older and slowing down, but he realized that didn't mean he could slack off. He wasn't going to get any younger or stronger, but if he didn't stay on top of things, he was going to get older and weaker a lot sooner. A layoff like this just pointed out what he knew was so—you might not be able to win in the end, but you were going to get there quicker if you didn't resist it every step of the way.

He took several deep breaths and looked at the obstacle course. He had his stopwatch, an old mechanical sweep-hand job he'd picked up from a Russian surplus place. Like that shotgun he'd given the commander, the Russians still did a lot of stuff the old-fashioned way. Not necessarily because of any desire for quality, but because they didn't have the technology to do it on the cheap. You could get a windup pocket- or stopwatch with an eighteen-jeweled movement for less than fifty bucks; a shotgun that was sturdy and well-made for maybe three, four hundred. Try that in the U.S. If you could even find such things, they'd cost an awful lot more.

He decided to skip the stopwatch and just run the course. He didn't really want to know how much he'd slowed down. He'd be happy just to get through without breaking something.

He set himself, and got ready to go. He was a religious man, he believed in God, and he'd been right with Jesus for a long time. He believed he would be admitted to the Kingdom of Heaven if he led a righteous life and he worked at it. But like the old joke his father used to tell, he wasn't ready to go *now*. He had a teenaged son and a loving wife, and he wanted to stick around long enough to smile at his grandchildren. Retiring had been part of that, but he realized as he gathered himself to hit the course that sitting back in a rocker on the porch and watching the world go by might not be the solution. You could get hit by a runaway bus sitting on the porch—that had happened to some guy in D.C. only a couple months back—instead of being shot by some psycho while you were leading a Net Force military team. God had His plan, and Howard's number was gonna be up on a certain day, on a certain hour, no matter where he was or what he was doing. He'd thought that he'd been tempting fate, but after that bus had left the road and squashed a guy younger than he was who'd been sitting in a porch swing, he'd realized that death could come from anywhere at any time.

Run, John, and worry about the meaning of life later—it won't get you through the obstacle course, all this thinking.

He grinned. That was true. There was a time to think and a time to move. Right now, moving was the order of the moment.

He took a final deep breath and began his sprint.

Michaels looked up from his desk to see Toni, dressed in business clothes, standing in front of him.

"Hey, babe."

"Commander," she said with a short nod.

"Uh . . ."

She smiled. "If I'm going to be working here, even temporarily, we need to keep it businesslike."

"What, I can't grope you in the hall?"

"Not unless you want a sexual harassment suit."

They both smiled.

"Okay," he said.

"So, what's the situation?"

"Better than we'd hoped. Jay and the gang managed to

find the problem with the server pretty quick. They had help from InfraGuard and the NIPC out of the CWG."

"And how are the National InfraGuard Protection Center and Crime Working Group?"

"Same as always. If they could make a wish, you and I and all of Net Force would disappear in a reeking puff of sulfur and red smoke."

Toni chuckled.

"Anyway, give them credit, they pitched in and helped Jay."

"How'd the terrorists get in?"

"Passwords. They had them up to the highest level."

"Social engineering," she said. "They bribed somebody."

He shook his head. "Maybe not. The VP in charge of Blue Whale's security was killed a few days ago, along with a couple of ex-FBI bodyguards. At the time, it looked like a simple traffic accident—car ran off a cliff, no signs of anything hinky. That seems awfully coincidental."

"Yes." She started to say something, then noticed the shotgun in its case, propped in the corner. "What's that?"

"A shotgun," he said. "John Howard got it for me."

"For what?"

He took a breath. "To keep at home."

He wasn't sure exactly what he expected, but with her being a new mother and all, he was halfway thinking she'd be against the idea. Instead, she said, "Good idea. We need a gun in the house."

His expression must have shown his surprise. She said, "What, you thought because I like knives I have something against guns?"

"Well . . ."

"*Silat* teaches you to use the proper tool for the job. There are times when a gun is necessary."

He nodded. "How is Guru?"

"She's fine. Looks great, no slurring of her speech, seems to move like usual."

"You aren't worried that the baby will be too much for her?"

Toni grinned. "He woke up from his nap squalling. Didn't want a bottle or his binky, wasn't wet, no poop, just yelling his head off. Guru took him from me and he shut up as if she'd turned off a switch. *Click*! just like that, and he was cooing and grinning. I couldn't believe it. I looked at him, said, 'Who are you? What have you done with my baby!' "

Michaels laughed. "Get her to teach you that trick. That's worth a fortune."

"You're telling me. Okay. So what do you want me to do?"

"Same thing you used to do. I've talked to the director, she doesn't have a problem with you being here instead of there. You'll be a consultant, so we can pay you. This most recent attack on the net/web is surely the responsibility of the same group who hit it before. And if they killed the VP to get the security codes, then they've raised the stakes. If they are willing to murder, this is going to get uglier before it gets prettier."

Toni nodded. "I hear you."

"So let's get to it. Your old office is yours again. It's good to have you back, Ms. Fiorella."

"It's good to be back, Commander Honey."

He laughed.

12

Quantico, Virginia

Any amusement the FBI recruits might have felt on seeing Net Force's Commander in a sarong over his sweatpants left at least several of those minds after Michaels slammed their owners onto the gym's mats hard enough so they bounced. He enjoyed this way more than he should. He'd seen the grins when he and Toni walked in, heard a few chuckles from the recruits on seeing his clothes.

They weren't laughing *now*, were they?

Toni had shown some simple self-defense moves, using Michaels as the dummy, and he'd dusted the mats pretty good himself. Then she called for volunteers and had him demonstrate the techniques so she could point out what he was doing and why.

He had earned the right to toss these guys, he figured, aside from the sarong-inspired amusement. He'd paid his share of dues. A couple months ago, when Toni had been working with him on his sparring, she'd put on a pair of boxing gloves and had danced in and out, throwing fast punches. He'd gone after her during one attack, trying to surprise her, and he'd forgotten to cover high-line while he was busy blocking a kick. For his inattention, he'd caught a right overhand smack in the left eye. Even with the glove, he'd worn a mouse and shiner for a week after she'd punched him. Of course, he had felt a certain amount of malevolent glee when he explained the shiner: *Hey, what happened to you, you run into a door?*

No, actually, my wife punched me in the face. She beats on me all the time.

People who didn't know about Toni and *silat* hadn't believed him. Of course, they'd thought he was joking.

"All right," the FBI combat teacher said. "Everybody see what just happened there?"

The recruits looked puzzled for the most part. Well, no, they *hadn't* seen it.

Duane Presser, the big Hawaiian said, "Don't let that funny-looking sideways stance rattle you—watch his feet, how he angles in and sectors off. You concentrate on his hands, you're gonna get tripped. You watchin' his feet, he's gonna whack you wid dat elbow. Watch alla him. And watch the distance—this stuff assumes a knife in hand, so you got dat extra half-step to worry about. You all see what I mean?"

"I see it, Chief," one of the recruits said, his voice full of confidence.

Michaels looked at the man. He was young, maybe twenty-five, tall, and fairly muscular in his sweats and T-shirt. He had a couple inches in height and maybe fifteen, twenty pounds in weight on Michaels. He also had a buzz cut, and what was left of his hair was so still so black it looked like a raven's wing. His skin tone and facial features indicated some Native American background in his ethnic tap. He'd been watching, not volunteering, and Michaels figured that meant he was smarter than some of the first gung ho chargers to step up. It was a good idea to see what an enemy knew before you risked an attack.

That could be a bad sign for Michaels.

"So, you think you can get past his defenses?" Duane asked.

"Yes, sir, Chief, I believe so."

Duane nodded. "Show us."

When the big recruit stepped up to the mat, Michaels saw Duane flash his big grin at Toni, where Raven couldn't see it. He wished he had Duane's confidence.

When Raven got closer, he said, sotto voce, "Nice skirt, sir."

Michaels smiled. SOP, trying to anger an opponent. He said, quietly, "Yeah. Don't look up it while you're down on the mat, son."

"Not gonna happen. Sir."

"Okay. Let's see. Show me what you got."

Raven slipped into a side fighting stance, left foot forward, circled his hands over his face and groin. From the smoothness of the movement, Michaels realized the kid had brought this with him when he joined the feds—it was too slick to come from the Hawaiian's six-week self-defense course.

Raven said, "What I got is a black belt in tae kwon do, sir." He sneered, bounced around a little, and edged toward Michaels. "But I won't hurt you too bad."

Oh, good. A martial arts jock who wanted to prove his stuff was superior. Michaels was, he had to admit, a little nervous. He'd been studying *silat* pretty extensively with Toni for more than a year, working out hard, practicing pretty much seven days a week, rain or shine, and he was far from a finished student. Still, he was improving. Toni didn't pull her punches, and she'd had a few people she knew dance with them at the gym a few times, to make sure Michaels had different-sized and skilled opponents, to help teach him distance and timing. He wasn't great, but he was not a total dweeb anymore. He hoped.

The kid had just made a mistake—he'd bragged about his black belt, which, like the skirt comment, had been to intimidate Michaels, to make him nervous, but he'd given too much away in doing that. If you thought you might be facing a tiger, that could be a problem. If you knew you were facing a lesser cat, that made things easier.

TKD was mostly a sport these days, though there were some old-style guys around who were excellent fighters, according to Toni. The sport guys liked to kick, they did that to score points, and they liked to kick high, to the head. Standing sideways like that, Raven was going to have to use his front foot if he wanted any speed. A spinning or round kick from the rear leg was going to take too long to get there.

All of this flitted through Michaels's brain fast, a second or two, then the attack came.

Raven danced in and threw a high roundhouse kick at Michaels's head.

He was limber, and he was very fast. Michaels ducked, and the kick sailed harmlessly over his head. As Raven came down, Michaels tapped him lightly on the ribs, no force, to see what the kid would do.

Raven sprang back, out of range. "That punch wouldn't have done anything," he said.

If he really knew how to fight, then that tap should have convinced him he'd made a mistake. If he was rattled, however, it didn't show.

Michaels glanced over at Toni. She shook her head. The kid didn't have a clue.

He came in again, twirling and throwing a quick combination of kicks—a front snap, roundhouse, and axe-kick, intending to bring his heel down on the top of Michaels's head or shoulder with the last technique. It was a good sequence, fast and well-executed.

He must have expected Michaels to back up and block, since that was probably what he was used to seeing, and if that happened, he would tag him.

Michaels didn't back up.

Instead, he dropped low as he stepped in and caught

Raven on the hamstring of his kicking leg with his right shoulder. No punches, no counterkick, no sweep, just a step and the shoulder—

The kid flew backward, lost his balance, and fell. He managed to turn the fall into a diving half-twist and roll, and came back up. "No problem!" he said, too loud and too fast.

Now he was rattled. A smarter, more experienced fighter would have backed up and thought about it, gotten cautious, but Raven hardly paused. He knew this stuff, he was gonna make it work!

The third time he came in, he threw a powerful right punch and right snap-kick at the same time, and if he was pulling either, Michaels couldn't tell. The kid wanted to whack Michaels, for embarrassing him, and he wanted it to hurt. He was extended, balanced on the ball of his left foot, his supporting left knee almost locked.

Michaels slid in, blocked the punch with a left heel-hand to the kid's face while scooping the kick aside with the back of his right hand. He pushed with his left hand and lifted hard with his right, palm toward the floor like he'd been taught, and Raven went back and down, stretched out horizontally. He slammed into the mat flat on his back, and the impact knocked the wind out of him. Before he could move, Michaels dropped next to him, swung his right fist up and over and down in a hammer blow that landed smack in the middle of Raven's chest. He pulled it some, but it still hit hard enough to make a nice *thwock!* on the sternum. Then he opened his fist, slid his hand up to the kid's throat, and pinched his windpipe. With any pressure, he could break Raven's voicebox, and the kid knew it.

Raven slapped the mat, to show he was done, but Michaels kept the pressure on the throat pinch. He said, "On the street, you can't tap out. If I squeeze, you're a dead man."

The look of panic on Raven's face was what Michaels

wanted. He relaxed his grip, rocked up onto his feet and stepped away, turned in a half-circle with a crossover *si-loh* back-step, and looked for more potential attackers.

There weren't any. He relaxed, moved back to where Raven still sprawled, and put out a hand to help him up. The kid waved him off.

Michaels wanted to make sure the lesson stuck, so he said, quietly, "Thanks for not hurting me too bad, son."

Raven shook his head. Youth would be served—but not today.

The Hawaiian grinned real big again and said, "Okay, so what'd he do wrong?"

A short redheaded woman with freckles said, "He got out of bed this morning?"

Everybody laughed—well, except for Raven there, just sitting up.

Raven came to his feet, gave Michaels a choppy nod, and said, "Okay, it works pretty well for a fairly big guy like the commander. But how about somebody like little Red Riding Hood there against somebody my size?" He pointed at the woman who'd spoken.

Michaels looked at Toni, and shook his head as she stepped onto the mat.

"Let me show you," she said.

Poor kid just had to learn things the hard way, didn't he?

On the Bon Chance

Santos thought about gold.

Ouro, the shining yellow metal that was the real measure of wealth. Missy was talking about fiber optic trunk lines crossing rivers underneath rail bridges, but Santos was wondering when he could get to a coin dealer to buy more Maple Leafs. He could do it on-line, of course, but he didn't trust computers. Too easy for them to crash, especially now. He grinned a little at that.

No, he would rather get to the Mainland and one of the dozen or so dealers he used, each who knew him under a different name, none of which were his own.

The spot price was down a little from last week, only ten or twelve dollars, and the coin prices were higher than spot prices for bullion, of course, to cover minting and such, but still, this would be a good time to buy.

Missy said, "—the main cables cross here, and here—" as she pointed at a map of the United States.

Canadian Maple Leafs were the standard for gold coins. They were pure—99.99 percent gold, unlike the American Gold Eagles, which were only 22-karat, alloyed with a few grams of silver and copper. Krugerrands were only 90 percent gold, even more alloy in those, though they were good for working the *berimbau* string. Chinese Pandas were so-so. The Australian Kangaroos and Koalas were better, nearly as good as the Canadian, but the Maple Leaf was the way to go, for gold. Everybody in the world knew this.

Platinum? That was different. The American platinum Eagles were okay, and this metal was harder and worth almost twice as much as gold at current market prices. He had a few of those, but the white metal seemed colder, more . . . sterile than gold. He had nearly two hundred one-ounce Maple Leafs now, and in a few months, he would have three times that many. A year from now, maybe a thousand altogether. Paper came and paper went, especially back home, but gold was forever. When he had a thousand coins, then he could go home. It would not be enough to make him a millionaire, but still, he would be a man of substance. Worth more on the black market there than here, too. He could teach his art and not worry about the rent. If he had students who were adept but poor, he could carry them, as his *Mestre* had carried him. Then he could get serious about his art, study all day, every day—

"Are you listening to me, Roberto?"

He smiled at her. "I am listening, though I do not see why I should bother. A trained monkey with a stick of dynamite could do this."

"And he'd be cheaper and would eat less than you," she said. "But we aren't going to blow up anything. We take out a section, no matter how big, they can fix it in a matter of hours. Even if we took the bridge down, a boat would lay a temporary cable in a day or less. No, we cut it in six places, each break many miles apart. They fix one, it still doesn't work. They find the second one and fix that, it *still* doesn't work. By the time they find the third break—which will be in a remote area and booby-trapped, tempers will be very short at the phone company. They'll have to hire more inspectors, more security. We wait a week, then do it again, in six different places. They'll be tearing their hair out."

"A good plan," he said, more to keep her happy than because he really cared. Cutting plastic cables was no work for a fighter. A man needed challenges, real challenges, from other men. Facing off, one-on-one, or one-against-many, that was worthwhile. But such work allowed him to amass wealth, and that was a goal to be attained for the long run.

He followed her with half his attention, nodding or murmuring now and then so she would see that he was listening, but considering with more of his thoughts the more important question of acquiring more gold . . .

San Francisco Bay
San Francisco, California

John Howard's assault team swam through the cold and murky waters, using rebreathers instead of scuba to better hide their exhaust bubbles. The wetsuits and gloves were the best quality, but the chill still seeped in around the seals. They used flippers and muscle power, no sleds or scooters, to make sure they didn't make any noise a sound sensor listening for motors might pick up.

The target was two hundred meters ahead, and they wouldn't be able to see it until they were almost there. Not that they would miss it—an oil tanker almost as long as three football fields and riding deep and heavy in the water wasn't something you were going to swim around or under with it laying broadside to you—it drew more than ten meters. At five-meters approach depth, what they would see would be a wall of steel plates above and below.

The tanker had been hijacked in Indonesian waters by Tamil terrorists and sailed to a spot just outside San Francisco Bay to draw attention to the terrorists' cause, whatever the dickens that was. If their demands were not met, they would, they threatened, blow the vessel to kingdom come, allowing hundreds of thousands of gallons of crude oil to escape along the California coast.

Such an event would be an ecological disaster, not to mention very bad for tourism from Big Sur to Santa Barbara, at the least.

This wasn't going to be allowed to happen. While authorities negotiated and delayed the terrorists, Howard and his team moved. The plan was simple: Get to the ship, scale the hull, prevent the terrorists from rupturing the bays holding the cargo, by whatever means possible. They would have to be quick, and they would have to be perfect—one psychotic with a fast hand would be disastrous.

They weren't expecting enemy frogmen, but they were prepared, just in case. Their dive suits were equipped with the latest high-tech toys. They had LOSIR coms, infrared sensors, and bubble comps that fed heads-up displays in their full-face masks. Aside from that, each member of the six-man team carried weapons that would work in water or in air. Primary defensive arms were the Russian 5.56mm APS underwater assault rifles. These were selective-fire, gas-operated weapons. The firing mechanisms for these were based on the Kalashnikov rotating bolt system, and except for the oversized magazines that held twenty-six rounds, they looked a lot like an AK assault rifle. The projectiles were drag-stabilized darts, the cartridges based on 5.56 × 45mm NATO rounds. The darts were twelve centimeters long. The effective soft target killing range in air was slightly over 100 meters. The underwater range at this depth was about thirty meters. In water this murky, if you were close enough to see an enemy diver, you would have more than enough punch to take him out—the fléchettes would blast through a face mask or wetsuit, no problem.

Each of Howard's divers also carried 7.62 × 36 H&K P11 dart pistols, five-barreled weapons with sealed chambers. The effective range of these was much less than the Russian assault rifles, about thirty meters in air, half that or less underwater. Furthermore, once you'd fired your five shots to reload the weapon you had to send it back to the armorer—it was a factory-only procedure. Howard figured if it came to that, things would be pretty bad—if two dozen–plus rounds from the Russian weapons weren't enough to do the job, another five from the handguns probably weren't gonna help too much. Still, it was better to have it and not need it . . .

Suddenly Howard got a shimmery red sig on his heads-up display. His team's transponder-coded heat-sigs were false-colored blue, so red meant company. A beat later, a second red image came into view. His display told him they were thirty meters out, right at the limit of their assault guns. The pair of reds moved slowly from east to west.

On patrol, he figured. *And they haven't seen us yet.*

Visibility was no more than seven or eight meters in the cold water, with nightfall coming on fast and about to drop that to almost zero. They wanted to be at the tanker hull soon, where they'd use the gecko-foot climbing pads.

As soon as it was dark, they'd ascend. Timing was critical; they couldn't afford to mess around out here.

Howard stopped swimming forward and used hand jives to signal his men, all of whom but the tail were in visual range. He could have used the line-of-sight infrared coms, but it was possible the enemy had LOSIR, too, and even though his transmissions would be coded, the unfriendlies might pick up a stray signal. They wouldn't know *what* it said, but that it was there at all would let the cat out of the bag.

Howard pointed into the murk, held up two fingers, then pointed at his eyes, ending with the jive for a question.

I see two enemy frogs ahead. Everybody see them?

He got affirmative hand signals from everybody.

He pointed at his two best men, in the direction of the enemy divers; he pointed at his watch, then made the classic fingertip drag sign across his throat.

His two men affirmed the order and quickly swam off into the gloom.

Howard turned to watch them go, following them visually for the few meters he could still see them, then with his sensors.

The two blue forms slowly closed on the two red ones. When they were within visual range of each other, the enemy divers apparently noticed his men. They took evasive action—

It seemed as if it took a long time, but in reality it was over in a couple of heartbeats. He didn't hear it, and he couldn't see it, except for the sensor images, but the two red forms stopped moving. The blue forms approached, merged with the red, and formed an odd-looking purple as his suit computer tried to figure out what color to paint. Then the two red forms began to sink, vanishing from the sensor's range in a few seconds.

Howard waved at the rest of his team. Time to move in . . .

Net Force HQ
Quantico, Virginia

The priority call bell chimed and automatically cut the VR scenario as it had been programmed to do. Since only two people had that priority code number—his wife and his boss—Howard was quick to answer. He did so without checking the caller ID.

"Yes?"

"John, it's me," his wife said. Her voice was tight, on the edge of panic.

"What's wrong?"

"It's Tyrone. He's been in a car wreck. He's at Mercy General. I'm on the way there now. The nurse who called said he's banged up and his leg was broken, but he's going to be okay."

Howard's sudden fear, launched like a missile by her first words, dropped fast. *Thank you, Jesus, for sparing my boy.*

"I'm on the way," he said. "I'll meet you there."

Howard touched a button on his virgil as he stood and pulled off the VR gear.

"Alex Michaels. What's up, General?"

"Sir, this is John Howard. My son has been in an automobile accident. He is injured but not critically so. I'm going to the hospital."

"Take a copter," Michaels said. "It'll be a lot faster this time of day."

"Sir, it's personal business—"

"Take the aircraft, John. Consider it an emergency readiness drill. We'll eat the cost if anybody kicks."

"Thank you, sir."

"Call me when you can."

"Yes, sir, I will."

Howard ran toward the helipad, calling ahead as he did so. It was good that nobody got in his way as he moved—he would have had trouble slowing down.

13

Net Force HQ
Quantico, Virginia

"How'd the demonstration go?" Jay asked. It was good to see the boss and Toni working together again.

The boss said, "I believe the FBI recruits learned a certain amount of respect for small women with extensive martial arts training."

"And men in skirts, too," Toni said.

Jay missed the byplay on that, but both Michaels and Toni thought it was funny.

"So, what do you have for us?" the boss said.

Jay looked up from his flatscreen. It was just the three of them. General Howard's son, Tyrone, had busted his leg pretty good in a car wreck, so Howard was out at the hospital. Tyrone had his leg in traction—a pin through his shin hooked to a sandbag over a pulley. He was gonna be there a few more days, at least. Jay had dropped by to see him. He was a good kid. Lieutenant Julio Fernandez was out testing some new piece of equipment.

Jay said, "Well, not that much. After that hit on Blue

Whale, everything died down again. But I started following a lead I got on CyberNation."

"CyberNation? Are they still around? 'Information should be free?' "

He looked at Toni. "Oh, yeah, they're bigger than ever. And they have a point, you know. That genie is out of the bottle, it ain't goin' back in."

"Uh-huh." She didn't sound convinced.

Jay shrugged. "And every time the net jigs instead of jags, they get more subscribers. Makes a good motive."

"Lot of people could have motive," Michaels said. "All kinds of things thrive in chaos. Have you got anything that makes them a better suspect than a thousand other companies whose stock went up when the net stuttered?"

"Nope, not that I can prove. I've got one interesting thing, might be a coincidence."

"Which is . . . ?"

"You know the vice president, the security guy for Blue Whale who got killed?"

"Yes. Something more on the cause?"

"No. Still an accident, far as the cops are concerned, though they are checking into it further. If somebody cooled the guy, he was good. But here's the thing: A couple days before he died, our VP went on a cross-country trip and did a little offshore gambling off the coast of Florida, on one of those international water floating casinos."

"Did he lose more than he could afford?" Toni asked. "Somebody trying to collect?"

"Not according to his coworkers. When he got back, he was up six grand, a happy man."

"What, then?"

"The gambling ship where the dead guy won his money? The thing is refitted, was formerly some kind of tanker, registered out of Liberia, and is now called *Bon Chance*. The ownership of this beast is real muzzy when you try to pin it down, runs through a fistful of dummy corporations. But at the top of this chain of hide-the-owner razzmatazz? A corporation called InfoMore that belongs lock, stock, and barrel to—tah dah!—our friends at CyberNation."

The boss raised an eyebrow at that.

Toni jumped in. "So you're saying that maybe somebody from CyberNation picked up on who the Blue Whale veep was, followed him home, and extracted security codes from him before they drove him off a cliff?"

Jay shrugged, though he was glad to see Toni hadn't lost too many steps and could see where he was going. "Naw, I'm not saying that, that's too big a stretch given what we got. Only that it seems like a coincidence that needs to be checked out, is all. If the guy was murdered, and if it was for what he knew, then you have to at least think maybe there is some connection. Last place I tried to run it down was booby-trapped: The information I went after self-destructed when I got to it. That makes me suspicious, too. You don't booby-trap info unless it's something you want kept private."

Michaels said, "You think you can find a connection?"

"Hey, that's why you pay me the big bucks. Well, okay, the medium bucks. Which I've been meaning to talk to you about. I'm getting married, don't you think I deserve a raise?"

Michaels chuckled. "You already make as much as I do, Jay. You want to embarrass me by making more?"

"I could force myself to live with it, boss."

"Not for a while, you won't."

Jay laughed.

"So you're going to follow up on this?" Toni said.

"Yep. I haven't found anything pointing anywhere else, so this is as good a direction as any. And you got to figure, if CyberNation is involved, they'll have pirate servers set up somewhere to make it harder to trace 'em. Mobile is better than stationary, and a ship on the high seas is worldwide mobile."

"Good," Michaels said. "Keep us apprised."
"Always."

Somewhere in Colorado

Things had just gotten more interesting than Santos had hoped for. Setting up the fiber-optic cable attack had been easy enough. Six cuts, ranged at odd intervals over a two-hundred-mile section, all made at about the same time—not that that mattered. Once cut in one place, the thick cable wasn't transmitting anything, so they could take hours to do the other five breaks. The idea, however, was to get in, do the job, and get out. If anybody spotted one of the cutters in one place, by the time they got police after him, the attack would be over, the phone company wouldn't be able to set up extra security in time to do them any good.

Santos had assigned himself the most remote of the attack sites, where the cable was strung out over a gorge, somewhere in cowboy country. He was fairly high up in the hills, five, maybe six thousand feet, he guessed, from how thin the air was in his lungs. Even so, the air did have a clean and fresh, pine-treelike scent, and it gusted and swirled in a fairly stiff turn-your-head-around breeze now and then. It was cold up here, dark and crusty old snow piled in shady patches everywhere. It was clear and sunny, though, and warmer near the larger rocks where it was protected from the wind. It had taken him three hours to hike in from where he'd parked his four-wheel SUV, and he'd worked up a sweat under his warm clothing, though he'd kept his gloves on. His hands never seemed to stay warm when the thermometer's reading dropped to near freezing. He liked climates where you could run around with no shirt on if you wanted, tropical heat, with snow seldom, if ever.

When he had gotten close to the spot where he intended

to burn through the protected cable, using a few coils of Thermex welding cord he carried in his pack, he ran into unexpected company.

He thought this strange, since the place was in the middle of nowhere, a long way on foot from the nearest road.

There were two of them, big men. They wore back-country cold weather clothes—dark wool trousers and hiking books, plaid wool shirts and heavy Gore-Tex parkas, and orange caps with state logos on them. The logos indicated that the pair were game wardens.

Bad luck. For them.

Santos was not carrying a gun, and thus shouldn't be thought a hunter, unless they thought he was chasing mountain goats and throwing rocks at them, but the two men decided to give him a hard time anyway. Santos figured out why in a few seconds when one of them said, "Well, well, whadda we got here—a hiker? Hey, Jerry, you ever hear of niggers hiking?"

"Can't say as I have, Rich. They only have two forward speeds—cock-stroll and feets-do-your-stuff! But they show up nice against the snow, hey?"

Both men laughed at the lame humor.

That made it easier, not that it was necessary to be easier. He would have had to take care of them anyway, since they'd seen him, but it made him feel better that they weren't nice men.

Santos waited for the two to get closer. Both men wore sidearms in holsters, visible under the unzipped jackets, the guns being Glocks, probably in 9mm or .40. The one named Jerry had a scoped bolt-action rifle slung over his shoulder on a hand-tooled leather strap. Looked like a Winchester Model 70, no way to tell the caliber. A good weapon, the Winchester.

"Colorado game wardens. Let's see some identification, boy," Rich said.

"Am I doing something illegal?" Santos said. "I thought this was public property. I'm not hunting or fishing."

"Ooh, listen to that accent, we got us a foreign nigger.

You from Mexico, boy?" That from Jerry. "Habla Spi-cko?"

"We want to take a look in that backpack of yours," Rich said. "See if you have a gun you might be using to illegally hunt with. Hand it over."

"Okay," Santos said. "You're the law."

Both men smiled, glancing at each other, secure in their ability to whipsaw this one black man into subservience out here in the cold mountains.

He swung the backpack into Jerry's face, hard, and before Rich could react, Santos did a cartwheel and kicked the surprised man flush on the mouth. Yes, it was a flashy move, one his *Mestre* would have slapped him for trying so quickly in even a street match, but these were not players, they were white racists. He wanted to bash them with *style*.

Rich went down, hard, and as Jerry managed to recover from being hit in the face with the backpack, Santos danced in and slapped the man, slinging his arm around using the twisting of his hips like popping a whip to deliver the power. The heel of his hand connected with Jerry's temple and sent a shock up Santos's arm. A good hit.

Jerry sprawled, and Santos would bet gold against sawdust the man was out of it.

Rich came up, clawing for his pistol, but Santos got there, grabbed his wrist and wrenched it, turned the gun so the muzzle faced Rich's belly, then grabbed Rich's fist with his own free hand hard enough to trigger the weapon.

The explosion was very loud in the quiet afternoon.

The empty shell ejected in a lazy, slow-motion arc, glittered in the sunshine, and fell, bounced from a flat rock, and tumbled from sight.

It shocked the hell out of Rich as the bullet hit him in the belly, you could see that.

The wounded man released his grip on the gun and fell to his knees, trying to stop the blood flow with his hands. That didn't work. Red seeped through his fingers, dripping to the ground. It smelled like warm copper.

Santos grabbed the pistol, pointed it at Rich's head.

"No, please, don't—!"

Santos grinned. *"Vaya con Dios,"* he said. "That's Spicko, right?"

"Don't—!"

He shot the man right between the eyes.

Jerry was still down, feet twitching. Must have knocked him cold.

Santos took two steps, aimed, and put a round into Jerry's head. The man spasmed, then went limp.

Two men, armed, and too easy. He sighed. In his country, the women fought better.

Santos tucked the gun into his belt. He would get rid of it later, where it wouldn't be found. His prints weren't on record in the United States, but he didn't want this coming back to bite him twenty years from now. The authorities had long memories when you killed any of their own. Fingerprints, DNA, whatever they could get, these things stayed in the system forever. He had heard about guys picked up thirty years after they did a murder when something that had been sitting in a refrigerator at some lab for all that time matched with new crime scene evidence. He didn't want that, always to be looking over his shoulder.

He went to the bodies and squatted. He already had his gloves on so there was little risk as he went through the dead men's pockets.

He found two wallets on each man, which puzzled him. A look at the contents brought a big smile to his face. Huh. What do you know about that?

He dropped the wallets, collected his backpack, and headed back toward his target. He'd be done in an hour, long gone by nightfall . . . This high up, cold as it was, if the animals didn't get them, they would keep a long time, turning to dessicated mummies. But the authorities would discover what the scavengers left when they came to find the broken cable, which would be sooner rather than later.

When he was far enough away, maybe he'd use a throwaway phone to call the authorities about these two. Just to make sure they didn't go undiscovered. That would be amusing, no?

Yes. Most amusing.

Toni came into Michaels's office looking at a computer printout. "Here's something that will probably make the director happy," she said.

"What?"

"You know those two federal fugitives, the militia guys? Ones suspected in the killings of a couple of game wardens in Colorado a few weeks back?"

"Bank robbers and armored car hijackers, right? Numbers five and six on the Ten Most Wanted? The ones the regular FBI has been combing the mountains looking for for the last three months?"

"That's them. Seems some anonymous call tipped off authorities about where to find the pair. And sure enough, they had the game wardens' ID and some of their clothing on them when they were located."

"Captured alive? I seem to recall they swore they'd never be taken that way."

"They were right. But they were both cold when the local sheriff's deputies got there. Shot to death."

"Who shot them?" he asked.

"Nobody knows. I'd venture to guess nobody really cares, either. Somebody who saved the state and the federal government the costs of a couple of trials."

"Life is strange sometimes, isn't it?"

"Isn't it just? The local cops also found a major transcontinental fiber-optic phone cable nearby had been cut."

"Maybe the phone company shot them. Hear anything from home?"

"Yes, I just talked to Guru. Little Alex is sleeping. Has been no problem at all."

"Ask her if she wants to move up here permanently, be a full-time nanny. Just for, oh, fifteen or so years?"

"You think you're joking," she said. "I'm considering it."

"Now you're joking."

"Nope. She's an old lady and I love her. I owe her a lot—what she taught me helped make me who I am. She's all alone in New York. Her own family doesn't pay much attention to her. And she's really good with the baby. Would it be so awful if she lived in the spare bedroom and helped take care of him?"

Michaels blinked. The idea was something of a shock. "Uh. Um."

"Think about it."

He nodded. "Okay. I will."

14

Mercy General Hospital
Washington, D.C.

Tyrone lay in a restless, Demerol-induced sleep. His breathing was mostly slow and heavy, but now and then he would moan softly and breathe faster, and try to turn on the bed. When he did that, Howard would reach out and put his hand on the boy's head, speaking soft reassurances until his son calmed down.

Nadine had gone to the cafeteria to get some sandwiches and coffee. Howard expected her back in a few minutes. She was a wreck, had seldom left this room since they'd gotten here. He had tried to send her home to rest, but she wasn't having any of that.

Leave her baby here, in a hospital, alone?

Well. He was fourteen, and hardly a baby, but she had spoken with such fierceness that he hadn't brought it up again.

And he understood her feelings. Even though he was pretty much out of the woods, one or the other of them was going to be right here until they let Tyrone go home.

Tyrone's left leg was supported in a sling. A titanium pin the size of a big nail had been driven through his leg just below the knee, skewering his shin bone. The pin was connected on both ends by a looped cord to a cable, which was in turn attached to a big sandbag, supported by a pulley on the steel frame over the bed. They needed to keep things a certain way until they could do the rest of the surgery with plates and screws, an open reduction, they called it, and even then, the boy was going to wear a fiberglass cast for a couple of months, from his hip to his ankle.

It hurt Howard to look at it. The doctor had assured him that there weren't any nerves in the bone, and that the pain where the traction device pierced the skin was minimal. Where Tyrone hurt the most was where his muscles had been torn and bruised in his upper leg when the thigh—the femur—had snapped. This had happened when a half-ton pickup truck, driven by a forty-three-year-old construction worker, had crossed the center line and plowed head-on into the car in which Tyrone had been a passenger in the rear seat. His seat belt had held, but the car had compacted and accordioned enough so that the seat in front of him had been thrust back into his leg, breaking it just above the knee.

Tyrone's friend, a fourteen-year-old girl named Jessie Corvos, who had been riding in that front seat was in Intensive Care with massive internal injuries, and her prognosis was poor. The car's driver, the girl's older brother, Rafael, had three broken ribs, a punctured lung, shattered right arm, broken ankle, and had undergone surgery to remove a ruptured spleen, but was expected to recover.

The man who'd been driving the truck had a tiny cut on his forehead that had taken three stitches to close; otherwise, not a mark on him. The man had been playing pool and downing pitchers of beer with friends at a bar. He had been arrested for driving under the influence and released on bail. His blood alcohol level was 0.21 percent, nearly three times the legal limit when they'd tested it.

Howard had met Jessie and Rafael's father, Raymond, in the ER. The older Corvos had been pale and shaking, probably in shock, but there had also been in him a tightly suppressed rage. Howard had caught only a glimpse of it. It was like seeing a nuclear fireball through a pinhole some distance away from the aperture: only a speck of intensely bright light was visible, but to move your eye closer would guarantee instant blindness. Raymond Corvos was an accountant, a slightly built, balding man, and mild-looking, save for that hint of white-hot anger.

If Jessie or Rafael Corvos died, then Howard would not want to be the driver who had killed them—he had the impression their father would come for the killer, and Howard would not wish to be standing in his way when he did.

As he watched his sleeping child, he could understand that. Vengeance belonged to the Lord, and Jesus had preached forgiveness for sins, no matter how heinous; but if Tyrone died as a result of some negligent idiot too plastered to be driving, he could easily see appointing himself judge, jury, and executioner, even at the risk of his own soul.

There were some things a man had to do, no matter what the cost.

Nadine came back into the room, carrying a plastic bag and a drink holder with four paper cups of coffee in it.

"He wake up?"

"No. He's still out. Resting better, I think."

She handed him a cup of coffee with a corrugated cardboard sleeve on it. He pulled the lid off and blew on the hot liquid.

"They had tuna on white, turkey on rye, and ham and cheese on whole wheat," she said. "I got two of each. You want one?"

"Maybe later," he said. "Coffee's fine for now.

She nodded, took a cup of coffee for herself, and pulled

her chair closer to his, next to the bed. She reached out with her free hand, and he took it in his.

He knew they would get used to this. You could get used to almost anything if you had the time. One of them would eventually go home, shower, get a nap, bring back clean clothes, while the other stayed. They'd swap off. But with any luck, they'd be going home soon. There were portable traction devices they could hook up to Tyrone's leg, once the doctors were sure he'd be okay. The surgery that would come later was relatively safe. There were some rare, but potentially dangerous complications following this kind of accident they'd told the Howards about: fat emboli, blood clots that might break loose and get into the circulatory system to cause problems. After a few days, the risk of these would be minimal.

Tyrone was going to be okay. But—what if Howard had been off on assignment somewhere in some hellhole, doing Net Force's business when this had happened? It was bad enough, but—what if it had been worse? If his son had been injured so badly that he didn't make it? Died while his father was a thousand miles away, unable to get back in time?

When he thought about it reasonably, he knew this was an irrational argument. Tyrone could have died in the accident and Howard could have been a block away and it wouldn't have made any difference. You couldn't live your life looking over your child's shoulder, worried every minute of every day about what might happen to him. The Almighty had His own plans. And if He wanted to call Tyrone—or Nadine—home? Well, that's what would happen, and there was nothing Howard could do about it.

Man proposes, God disposes.

But in his heart of hearts, he felt that if he was *there* when the call came, Howard might be able to talk God out of it. Offer a trade, himself for his child or wife, and maybe God would go for it. There wasn't any basis for believing that, God was not known for horse-trading souls, but on some level, he believed it might be different if he was there to make the offer. So going away and not being around to try that deal was heavy on his mind. Maybe he had made a mistake in going back to work for Net Force.

It was something he was going to have to think about some more.

Net Force HQ
Quantico, Virginia

Toni stuck her head into Alex's office.

"What's up?" he asked.

"The BCIII sting is about to go down."

"Really? That was fast."

She nodded. "Turned out the 'Chinese hackers' were in Richmond, they didn't have far to travel. Jay's run the feed from a case—and a sticky-cam into the conference room's big monitor, if you want to watch."

Alex glanced at his desk. "Might as well. I'm not getting much done here."

The two of them headed for the conference room. Toni hadn't been here when this sting had been set up, but she'd seen others like it when she'd been working here before. It was simple enough. Certain kinds of criminal hackers into extortion had been around for years. Generally they'd break into a company's system, steal files, crash the system, or set up a worm or virus for later, sometimes all three. Then they'd contact the company and offer their services as "computer security consultants." If the company wasn't interested, they would trash or steal valuable files, put client lists on the net, and other manner of devilry until the company came around. A lot of midsized corporations found it cheaper and easier just to pay the hackers to go away, as long as they weren't too greedy, and the RBs—that came from "rule benders," which is what they liked to call themselves instead of "law breakers"—would take their money and move on to another victim.

No harm, no foul, and the company eats the loss as part of doing business.

But a few years ago, the FBI, then Net Force, began using their skills to create fake companies whose profiles were attractive to the RBs. They'd set up shop, drop fake histories and credit ratings into places where they'd be found and believed, and wait. Too confident of their abilities in the electronic world, the extortioners would never stoop to actually *going* to a library—using shoeware-to-treeware, they called it—that would give the lie to the fake histories posted. Only squirrels played in trees.

You're not an ape—use a tool!

The RBs were always looking for fat and easy targets, and the Net Force decoys were set out like overweight turkeys too heavy to run.

The latest version of the sting was BC Internet Industries, Inc. Called BC Three Eyes, or just Three Eyes, the company had just enough passware and fire walls to make a bent hacker have to work a little, and all kinds of apparent goodies there for the taking once they were past security. Like a brown paper bag full of unmarked twenty-dollar bills just sitting there on the sidewalk with nobody around, it was just too good for the RBs to resist. Three Eyes had gulled a dozen thieves over the last year—under different names and slightly different configurations, of course.

"BC" stood for "Big Con," one of Jay's little jokes.

Typically, hackers would attack, then demand payment. Sometimes, a company would require more proof. Sometimes, they would even hire the thieves to set up security for them, with the idea that it takes one to catch one.

Some of the RBs actually considered breaking into a company's system and screwing it up to be the equivalent of a job interview.

Three Eyes had fine-tuned their process. Once they had

an RB coming after them, they first sent a small amount of money, with a promise of more—providing the thief would be willing to do a hands-on, face-time demo to their own security people of how they could get past the safeguards. The pitch had been developed and honed by a brilliant shrink who had worked for State before he'd moved to the FBI. The pitch was designed to be psychologically irresistible to a hacker mentality. Hackers thought they were smarter than normal people. They were convinced of their superiority. They thought they could think circles around any company security honcho or federal agent. They wanted to show people just how smart they were. They needed the applause, and the Three Eye pitch played right into their beliefs. It did everything but bend down to kiss their feet. They ate it up.

The RBs, once hooked, were landed almost every time.

The big HDTV screen was lit, and several people were standing or sitting at the table, watching. The case-cam was a briefcase that belonged to one of the agents. Typically there were a pair of these, one from the regular FBI, one from Net Force, playing the parts of the CEO and security VP for Three Eyes. They would ask for a sit-down with the thieves, and the RBs could choose the time, place, whatever. Some of the thieves had been pretty clever. They had made calls from mobile coms to the agents, changed destinations at the last instant, and one guy even had the meeting take place in a house that had been made into a kind of giant Farady Cage, complete with wide-spectrum jammers to make sure the company execs couldn't transmit their position for help.

These guys weren't that smart, though they were careful.

The case-cam on the table had a small scanning unit that panned slowly back and forth almost one-eighty. The cam panned to the left.

"Check it out. Metal detector built into the doorway," Toni pointed at the screen, "to make sure our guys aren't carrying guns or knives."

The camera panned back. There were two men seated at the table across from the two agents, and two more men standing behind them.

"Who are the goons?"

"Bodyguards, we figure."

"Big ones."

"Six four, six five. Two-seventy, two hundred eighty, easy. Not fun in close quarters."

PIPed in the left corner of the image was a smaller, wider-angle view that took in most of the room. That would be from the sticky-cam, about the size of a dime and almost clear and invisible, stuck on the wall near the door by one of the agents when they'd arrived. The wide-angle image gave a better view of the play, and Toni picked up a remote and switched the picture-in-a-picture around.

Toni looked at her watch. "Right about . . . now," she said.

One of the agents—the regular FBI guy—removed an envelope from his jacket pocket and passed it to the two men across from him. The thief took the envelope and checked it, smiled real big, and showed it to his partner. His partner took it, riffled what was inside with his thumb, and also smiled.

While the two extortionists were looking at the money, the agent on the left, who was in fact one Julio Fernandez of Net Force, removed something from his pocket, which he pointed at the man across from him.

It looked kind of like a pack of white playing cards with a small handle and a circular hole near the middle through which Fernandez had stuck his finger.

"Strange-looking weapon," Alex said.

"Starn pistola," Toni said. "9mm stripper clip, five shots, all plastic and ceramic construction, including the springs, fragmenting bullets made from some kind of zinc epoxy boron ceramic. Light, but very fast, even from a snubby. Eighteen hundred, nineteen hundred feet per second. Bullet comes apart on impact, creates a nasty temporary stretch cavity."

The bodyguard on the left made as if to draw a gun hidden under his jacket in a shoulder holster. Julio waved the gun at him and said something. Too bad there wasn't any sound.

The bodyguard must have decided that Julio's weapon wasn't that dangerous. He pulled his own handgun, a big, black semiauto pistol.

It wasn't even halfway from the holster when Julio shot him. The resolution of the camera, while pretty good, wasn't enough for Toni to see where the bullet or bullets hit, but the man dropped the gun and staggered back against the wall, then slid down into a sitting position.

The second bodyguard evidently decided that trying to outdraw a man pointing a gun at your face was maybe not such a good idea. He raised his hands, fingers open wide.

"My, my," Alex said. "What's the world coming to when hackers bring guns to the party."

"We live in dangerous times," Toni said.

15

***On the* Bon Chance**

In the conference room next to the computer center, Keller called his team together.

"Listen," he said. "I know you are all doing outstanding work. Our projects thus far have been on target and very effective. However, due to the actions of Net Force, as well as other minor security agencies, our successes have not been as great as we'd hoped they'd be."

Nobody was happy to hear that, but it wasn't telling them anything they didn't already know.

"There are real world contingencies; of course, those have always been in place, and those in charge of such matters will go forward as necessary. Some efforts have already been made in that direction."

This drew a disappointed murmur.

He could understand that. It had been his hope all along that the programmers and weavers could do the job without resorting to cruder methods. That would be the real victory, to use the very tools of that which they sought to bring about and nothing more. The reality of it was, however, that there were still limits on what could be done electronically. The future had arrived, but there were still people out there who not only refused to log into it, they seemed to be heading back to the past. There were groups who still used typewriters, for God's sake. Fountain pens were making a comeback. Handwritten letters weren't going to replace e-mail, of course, but there were people who still corresponded that way. There were even people in the United States who not only refused to have answering machines or services, they didn't have *telephones*!

You couldn't reach people like that, couldn't frighten them with worries of Internet problems. They didn't care.

Fortunately, these Luddites were in the minority; but the computer revolution was not yet complete. Some things still had to be done the old-fashioned way. That's why men like Santos were necessary. If you were doing surgery, you needed a laser scalpel, but now and again, despite medicine's advances, you had to have a bone saw. Or, perhaps more accurately, a leech . . .

He was wandering. He drew himself back to the meeting at hand. "We are going to have to push up our deadline on Attack Omega," he said.

That drew louder grumbles.

"I know, I know. You are already running as fast as you can. There is no help for it—the decision comes from on high. We will be coordinating with the other agents of change on this, and we can't slip the deadline even by an hour. Whatever we have when Omega launches is what we have. I'd like for it to be as much as possible. Okay, let's put on our question hats and get them all out in the open . . ."

Later, after they had filed out, Keller sat at the table, idly tapping his fingertips on the wood, thinking. His team would give him all they had. And he would roll up his sleeves and help them—Jay Gridley was the linchpin around which Net Force's security operations revolved. Throw enough sand at Jay, and he'd grind to a halt, and if Jay was stymied, much of Net Force's interference would also be slowed, maybe stopped.

Whatever Santos thought of him, all it would take would be for Keller to point a finger at Jay, and he'd be a dead man. That was the surest way of removing him from the picture. And probably it was safer for Cyber-Nation to do it that way.

But . . .

Where was the honor in that? The skill? The *knowing* that he could take Jay on and beat him, using the weapons they had developed with their brains. Any thug could crack somebody over the head with a club. Beating Jay Gridley *mano a mano*, VR against VR, computer to computer, *that* was something to make a man feel good.

Kill Jay? No. Not with a gun or knife. Beating him at his own game, that was how he would do it. Defeating him intellectually, shattering his confidence, taking away what he thought he was, that was worse than death for a man like Jay Gridley.

Nothing less would do.

He took a deep breath. Well. Might as well get started. He had a couple of things he could give Jay to chew on. He smiled. Yes, indeed.

Santos finished his exercises. Drenched in sweat, he headed for the shower.

The workout had been good, but he was getting stale. It had been too long since he had trained against an expert. The solo dances were okay for maintaining muscle tone, to stay flexible and to keep alive the basics, but you did not learn to fight men by practicing alone. Mirror warriors were no threat. To keep a skill sharp, you had to hone it against another player of equal or better skill. Timing, distance, position, those could only be learned against dangerous opposition. The flow had to be there.

Soon, he would have to find players of enough ability to challenge him. There were none on this ship, none within easy travel range. Maybe in Cuba—he had heard there were some old-line players still there, hiding in the cane fields, practicing by moonlight, since the art was still frowned on, even after the Old Man was gone—but finding them would be the trick. There were some in the U.S., of course, even in Florida, but to get a *real* challenge, he would need to go home, that's where the best players still were, and that was not in the cards in the near future—not until this job was finished.

He sighed. A man had to learn to put off his wants to deal with his needs.

He turned the cold water on full blast, shucked his pants, and stepped into the shower. The cold needles made him catch his breath, but it was a good feeling.

Then there was the problem of Missy Chance to consider. She was sleeping with Jackson Keller, at least, maybe others—who knew? One of the barmaids in the casino had told Santos this while she had been enjoying his body in her room, after he had returned from dispatching the vice president of the server company.

Santos soaped the long-handled and stiff-bristled brush and began to scrub his face and neck.

He saw no irony in finding out that his mistress was sleeping with another man from a woman he was screwing. Men were allowed to be with more than one woman, God had made men that way, but a woman who was unfaithful? That was wrong. He could not blame Keller for wanting Missy, though he, too, would have to pay. But if it was not rape, and he could not imagine that happening to her, then Missy must be made to . . . atone for her action.

He moved the rough brush down, scrubbed his shoulders, his armpits, his back.

Missy was expert in bed, but she was too sure that such ability made her superior to other women. It did not. In the dark, they were all the same, true?

She must be made to understand that some things could not be allowed by a man such as Santos. Not allowed.

Washington, D.C.

"A nightclub?"

"Not exactly," she said. "More like a . . . roadhouse," she said.

Michaels looked at Toni and raised one eyebrow.

They were in the living room. The baby was asleep, and so was Guru.

"We haven't been out since Alex was born," she said.

"Yes, we have," he said.

"Not by ourselves," she said.

"We didn't have a baby-sitter," he said. "And if we *had* had a baby-sitter, we wouldn't have trusted her."

"Well, we do now," she said, smiling. "Guru."

"She's a witch, you know. She's put a spell on our son. No baby should behave that well."

"Alex . . ."

"So, what is the attraction of this roadhouse exactly?"

"The food is supposed to be terrific, and they have a great live band."

"As opposed to a great *dead* band?"

"Has anybody ever told you how funny you are?"

"All the time."

"Yeah, well, they lied."

"Now who's being funny?"

"Anyway, the band is called Diana and the Song Dogs."

"What kind of music do they play?"

"Well, it's kind of, well, uh . . . country/rock/folk/blues fusion."

"Oh, please. Not another of those new-age bands playing touchy-feely elevator music—"

"No, no, nothing like that. It's just the kind of music you can listen to while having a beer. Foot-stompin', bug-squashin' music."

"Had a lot of that in the Bronx, did we?"

"We had radio. We had television. Why, we even had transportation that could take us to places outside our neighborhood."

"Ah. I see."

"No, you don't. But you will."

"Are you sure you wouldn't just rather stay home and enjoy the quiet? Just the two of us in the house? Alone?" He waggled his eyebrows. "Guru can take Alex to the park for a couple of hours—"

"We are going out. I am *not* going to become one of those women who, if she ever gets the chance to talk to anybody, prattles on about what color her little darling's last poop was when she changed his diaper."

"What color was it?"

"Go get dressed, Alex," she said. Her tone was ominous.

The roadhouse was called the Stone Creek Pub and Grill, and it was far enough out into the Virginia countryside that it took a while to get there. There were a lot of trees, so there was plenty of oxygen in the air when they found a parking spot in the crowded lot. And there were animals living in the area, too—less one skunk somebody had run over, adding a fragrant stink to the evening breeze.

"Jeez, what an odor," Toni said.

"You wanted to come here."

The place appeared to be a converted barn, lots of open woodwork and bare walls with old metal signs and horse harnesses and such hung on the walls. They managed to find a table, and it was noisy, filled with people, and busy. Still, Michaels was fine once he had gotten up and past the inertia. Toni was right; they needed to get out more. Having her back at work was good,, but hardly restful. Becoming parents had put a big crimp in their lives. Michaels really didn't mind, since he would usually just as soon stay home as go out after a hard day at the office. But it was all too easy to turn into a couch potato who stayed home all the time, warm and secure in the nest. The baby hadn't helped that. It was easier to be where they had everything they needed; if they went out, they had to pack diaper bags with bottles and clothes and rattles and stuff, and it was a hassle. He had gone through that with Susie when she'd been a baby, but he had forgotten, it had been so long.

The waitress came, took their orders for pints of beer. Toni got something called Ruby—beer "with a hint of raspberry," ick—and he got one called Hammerhead, which seemed appropriate. The waitress promised to be back for their sandwich orders in a few minutes.

The band consisted of a woman in jeans and a work shirt with a guitar slung around her neck, a guy with a fiddle, another on a double bass, and one more with a mandolin. They cranked up and started playing a lively tune that did have a folksy-bluesy sound to it. The harmony was pretty good, and the song was something about doing cartwheels on a gravel road or some such. The woman singer—Michaels assumed she was Diana and the men were the Song Dogs—had a pleasant voice and an animated face. When she sang lead, she belted it out pretty cleanly, and she sang a nice harmony for the bass player in a couple of places.

She had her web page address painted on the front of her guitar.

Well, you could hardly get away from that, even here in the country. Hank Williams would have been amused.

The beer came, and as she promised, the waitress dutifully took their sandwich orders. Michaels went for the barbecued chicken, Toni got the Reuben, and they decided to split a small order of fries.

The band began another song. The words were hard to hear, given the noise of the diners, but everybody seemed to be having a great time. And, Michaels had to admit, he was feeling pretty good himself. It *had* been a long time since he and Toni had been out together.

The band got through another tune and the food arrived. The basket of fries was huge, the sandwiches also generous, and the waitress brought catsup and vinegar and mustard and plopped them onto the table. Along with a ream of napkins.

"I'm glad we decided to get a small order of fries," Toni said.

He saw why they had gotten all the napkins as soon as the barbecue sauce squished out of the sandwich and ran down his chin.

For the band's next number, a harmonica player appeared from somewhere to sit in; the Song Dogs sang about traveling on the railroad and long stretches of empty prairie, and the blues harp wailed like a train whistle, long and mournful.

Michaels watched Toni, enjoying the look of pleasure on her face as she watched and listened to the band. This was what life was all about, wasn't it? Watching your woman have a good time, and being a part of that? Drinking beer, eating greasy fries, listening to a band—how much better did it need to be? He could do this. Definitely.

And maybe that's what part of your problem has been lately, Alex, hmm? Too much willingness to drop work and go home to play with the baby? To lie in bed with Toni when before you'd have been up and at work before anybody else got there?

Michaels felt a stab of guilt at that thought. It was true. Yes, he still did a good job. But for the last few months, his heart just hadn't been in it the same way. He wasn't a company man the way he had been before. He wanted to enjoy this wife, this baby, in ways he hadn't enjoyed his first wife and child. He had put them second, behind work, and as a result, he had lost them. He wasn't going to lose Toni and the baby.

Was that fair to Net Force? Didn't the agency deserve a boss dedicated to it first, before anything? When he thought about it, yeah, maybe. Then again—who could do a better job than he was doing? Even at three-quarter speed, he was still faster than anybody else around, wasn't he?

Uh-huh. Now there's a great rationalization.

Come on, he told himself. *Isn't it better for the com-*

pany if I'm relaxed, comfortable, at ease with myself? Doesn't a happy worker do a better job?

There's an even funnier one, Alex. Give us another.

He was beginning to get seriously pissed off at his inner voice when his virgil cheeped. He and Toni exchanged looks. This was not apt to be good news.

16

Casablanca, Morocco
June 1937

The wind off the desert was hot, dry, and carried in it a mix of powdery dust and fine sand that swirled through the alley as if alive, changing into an irritating, gritty mud as it got into Jay's eyes.

A good touch, that, he thought. Even if he did have to think so himself.

Here in Northern Africa as in Europe, everyone knew war was on the horizon, if not exactly where and when it would arrive, and things were about to change, as they would change everywhere.

Jay stepped into the nightclub and out of the wind, amid the babble of half a dozen languages. There were well-dressed foreigners in their silk and linen suits, mostly men, a few women. Natives, dressed in colorful robes and hats designed to keep the sun and sand out, sat at some of the small round tables, drinking something mysterious from brown bottles.

It was almost like film noir: dark and moody with stark contrasts everywhere.

The ceiling fans twirled slowly, barely stirring the warm air. The piano player worked on some heart-breaking torch number, and a native bartender cleaned drink glasses behind a long, curved mahogany bar that had been age-polished to a dull gleam. A mirror behind the bar reflected the racks of liquor bottles: scotch, bourbon, gin, vodka, absinthe . . .

Standing at the bar drinking scotch neat was Jacques, Jay's contact. Jacques wore a double-breasted ice-cream suit with a red handkerchief in the coat pocket, spats over his white leather shoes. He had slicked-back black hair and a pencil-thin mustache. He was a spy, of course, Algerian, and probably too long out in the cold. Or the heat, as it were.

"Bon jour," Jacques said as Jay approached the bar. "Emile, a drink for my friend!"

The bartender gave Jay a fish-eye look. "What may I serve you, friend?"

"Absinthe," Jay said. What the hell, it wasn't going to drive him mad here.

The bartender shook his head and went to fetch the bottle.

"Hot day, no?" Jacques said.

"Hot enough."

The bartender returned with a dark green glass bottle. He poured a small bit of the liqueur, which was also as green as an emerald, into a glass. Then he poured a shot glass of cold water over a perforated teaspoon full of sugar and allowed it to drip into the container. The absinthe's green turned a smoky, opaque white as the sugared water mixed with it. Without the sugar, it would have been too bitter to drink, and even so, it still bit the tongue pretty hard.

Jay knew from his research that the drink, which was partially made from wormwood, was illegal most places, and was traditionally used by artists and writers. Van

Gogh had used it, and the theory was that absinthe was what had driven him mad enough to lop off his own ear. It was supposed to eat holes in your brain with regular use. How charming.

Jay raised his glass to Jacques. "Good fortune," he said.

"Bon chance," Jacques replied. They clinked glasses, then drank.

"You have some information for me?" Jay said, after they put their glasses down.

"Oui, my friend. I believe I have *exactly* what you want. At a price, of course."

Jay raised an eyebrow. "Whatever it costs, I'll pay it. Tell me."

But before he could speak, there was an explosion. A gunshot, Jay realized, as he saw the blood blossom on Jacques's chest, over the heart.

What the hell—? This wasn't part of the scenario—!

Jay dropped to the floor in a deep squat and looked around in time to see a native dressed in one of those funny Shriner hats and a white-and-blue striped robe run out of the club.

Jay got up and sprinted for the exit, chasing the man. Who was this? How had he breached Jay's VR construct?

In the alley, Jay saw the assassin running away. Bull*shit*!

Jay took off. Whoever he was, he wasn't nearly fast enough to outrun Jay Gridley in his own damned scenario!

But even as Jay gained on the running man, he realized he wasn't going to catch him. The reason—reasons, actually, at least six of them—appeared right in front of him.

Half a dozen men, bare-chested, in basketball shorts and shoes, holding baseball bats, chains, knives, and what looked like a pitchfork, stepped out of the shadows between Jay and his quarry.

"Yo, yo," one of the basketball players said. "What's your hurry, baby?"

These guys were anachronisms—they didn't belong

here, weren't right for the time, even if they'd been Jay's constructs. And they weren't.

What the *hell*?!

As they moved toward him, Jay realized he didn't belong here, either. He didn't have time to come up with any kind of effective defense. The scenario was blown.

He bailed.

Net Force HQ
Quantico, Virginia

Jay pulled the sensory gear off and threw it at the computer console.

There hadn't been any real danger, of course, only to his construct. After the business with the mad Brit, he had made damned sure there was no way to turn his computer into what was effectively a capacitor that might be able to deliver an electric charge through the sensory connections. But it was galling anyhow, to be forced out of your own scenario!

How had this happened? Somebody would have to know where he was, be able to get past his wards, and be good enough to reprogram the input without Jay spotting him. For all practical purposes, it ought to be almost impossible—well, at least with a player of Jay's skill it ought to be. That it had happened was irritating—and scary.

It had to be one of the guys who had bollixed the net and web. They'd already shown how good they were, and now they were putting it right in his face.

Now it was getting personal.

He swore again. He needed to figure this out. And, as much as he hated the idea, he also needed to let the boss know. If nothing else, it meant they were getting closer. You didn't get that kind of response if you were wandering around in the woods lost somewhere. He must be trampling awful close to somebody's hidden marijuana patch.

Washington, D.C.

Toni listened to the music with one ear, and Alex's conversation with the other. It didn't take long for her to figure out it was Jay Gridley on the other end of Alex's virgil.

After a minute, Alex broke the connection.

"What's up?"

He shook his head. "Jay thinks he's getting closer to the bad guys who screwed the net."

"That's good."

"Maybe not. He says they must have set him up. Gave him a place that he thought he could get some information, then when he went in, they jumped him—electronically speaking."

"Yes?"

Alex explained it to her. Apparently Jay had been rousted from his own scenario. Which must have really bent him out of shape, Toni knew. She'd never met a computer geek who didn't think he was God's gift to electrons.

"But other than a bruised ego, no harm done, right?"

Alex nodded. "That's how I see it. But as he pointed out, whoever did it must know he's looking for them. And they knew where he might be apt to look. Which means he's maybe on the right path."

She nodded. "Maybe. Or maybe they just set a whole bunch of snares and one of them snagged Jay. He gets his foot out, goes charging down the trail, and maybe he's heading exactly opposite of where they are."

"Could be. I don't have Jay's expertise to say."

"But it sounds as if the bad guys do. Not good."

"No."

"Do we need to go home? Or to the office?"

"No, no reason for that. Jay was just giving me a heads-up. I asked him to keep me in the info stream."

"So, you wanna dance?" She nodded at the band.

A few couples were up, moving to the music.

He grinned. "Might as well. Can't get any work done here, can I?"

***On the* Bon Chance**

Keller leaned back in the form chair, stretched his neck and shoulders, removed the sensory head- and handsets. He smiled. "Well, Jay, old son, that must have been a shock, hey? About to download a juicy bit of information and *blap!* your source gets potted and the alley is full of NBA villains." He chuckled. "I hope you had autosave on. You'll want to go back and look at it again, I am sure."

He stood, bent at the waist, touched his toes, bounced a little. He straightened, sat back in the chair, took a couple of deep breaths, and let them out, then reached for the wireless headset. By now, Jay would have had time to think about what had happened, figured it out, and gotten pissed off enough to jump back into the net to hunt down whoever was responsible. Keller knew he would have done the same thing in Jay's shoes.

So. Now we give old Jay a new place to look. But carefully. He won't hit the next trap as easily. It needs to be . . . more subtle.

Keller slipped the gear on. Boy, this was gonna be fun.

Jasmine Chance was not a fanatic about it, but she did do enough exercise to stay in shape. It was harder to be a femme fatale if you were built like an overripe pear—a size six on top and size fourteen on the bottom. She used the stairclimber and the weight machines in the ship's gym for forty-five minutes a day. She wasn't going to be winning any Olympic events, but she was tight enough to make most twenty-five-year-old women jealous. Not bad for somebody past forty.

She leaned against one of the mirrored walls and took a big slug from her water bottle. She was hot, and sweaty enough so her headband wasn't stopping it all from running into her eyes. She wiped her face with a towel. Another fifteen minutes and she'd be done. Then she could shower and maybe have 'Berto help her stretch some other muscles. Yes. She'd give him a call, have him meet her in her cabin in half an hour or so. That would be pleasant.

But when she punched in his name on the ship's intercom, there was no answer.

She tried his phone. Got a leave-a-message recording.

Chance frowned. Maybe he was taking a nap, had the intercom and his phone turned off? Wasn't supposed to do that, but everybody did.

She called Security.

"Yes, ma'am?"

"Is Roberto Santos in his cabin?"

"No, ma'am."

She waited a couple of heartbeats. "All right. Do you know where he is?"

"Yes, ma'am."

She waited a few seconds, shook her head at the literal-mindedness of the security officer. "Would you mind telling me where? And if you say, 'No, ma'am,' I guarantee you'll be looking for a new job in about thirty seconds."

"Yes, ma'am. He took a chopper to the Mainland about an hour ago. He's probably in Florida by now."

Now she really frowned. What? She hadn't told him he could leave the ship! What the hell was he doing?

Why the hell was his com turned off?

"Anything else, ma'am?"

"Yes. Get me the pilot of the helicopter—call me when you have him."

She shut off the intercom. This was unacceptable. Unacceptable! Who did he think he was?

She threw the towel on the floor and headed for her cabin. She would find out exactly where Santos had gone, and he had better, by God, have a very good goddamned reason for going there!

Fort Lauderdale, Florida

Santos drove his rental car to the area called Sunrise, to the Saw Grass Mills Mall. It was a huge place, full of outlet stores, acres of parking, most of it occupied. There was a very ugly construction near an entrance, some kind of modern art perhaps, that looked like a giant unfinished house frame, colored the same shade as a pink flamingo.

These North Americans were nothing if not gaudy, especially in Florida.

He glanced at his watch. He was forty-five minutes early, and that was good. He wanted to be here in plenty of time to set things up.

He wore tan linen slacks, alligator leather shoes with rubber soles, and a pale blue sport shirt, and while it was winter, it was certainly warm enough so that he did not need a jacket. He did, however, wear a long and loose tan suede leather vest, under which he had concealed a .45 Colt Commander in a waistband holster over his right hip. The weapon was small enough to hide under a vest, but fairly potent. A hit from just one of the bullets would make any attacker pause and think seriously about stopping what he'd had in mind before he was shot. And while guns were not his joy, he knew well enough how to use one. And in this case, he would be a fool *not* to have a gun, for there was enough money involved to be tempting to many people.

He found a spot more or less in the shade of a building and pulled into the slot. When he came back, it would be by a long and roundabout method, to assure that he was not followed.

The meeting was going to be in the middle of the mall, people moving past left and right, in plain view, so the chances of either side trying to steal from the other were lessened. Not completely impossible, a robbery, but he thought it unlikely.

At stake was a fair amount of cash. Hardly a fortune, but enough to buy outright, say, a new and fairly well-made automobile. The cash he had in a cheap black nylon backpack on the seat next to him, in nonsequential twenty- and fifty-dollar bills. Amazing how much room it took.

What he was supposed to buy with those thousands of dollars was a hundred coins, Maple Leafs, almost pure gold. And the reason he was meeting the seller in a mall was because the price of those coins was three-quarters market value.

Which meant, of course, that the deal was in some way illegal. Probably the coins were stolen, but there were other reasons they could not be sold to a legitimate dealer: a divorce, perhaps—one spouse trying to avoid splitting the proceeds. Or maybe someone's grandfather passed away and they were avoiding the inheritance penalty. Or just somebody who did not wish to pay income tax on the proceeds.

Whatever. The reason did not matter to him, only the price. If the coins were good, where they came from was not important. They would join his others in the bank vault, and eventually wind up back home. There were no serial numbers on coins.

It was too good a deal to pass up, but because of that, Santos was cautious. Thus he had brought the gun. He would be alert before, during, and especially after the transaction. The gun was cocked and locked, and it would be the work of half, maybe three-quarters of a second to have the pistol out and firing.

If the deal was some kind of sting, the seller would find that he, too, had a stinger.

The place was huge. He saw signs for a Banana Republic, a Hard Rock Cafe, cinemas, Disney, Neiman Marcus, Calvin Klein, dozens and dozens of others. Such choices they had in the States.

The mall was too cool, and the air itself smelled stale. These *norte americanos* did not know how to live with warmth. They hid from it, kept it at bay with air conditioners that cranked up when the temperature wasn't even hot enough to melt an ice cube on the sidewalk.

He found the arranged spot in the mall, a place with skylights, benches, and potted tropical trees: thirty-foot-tall palms, small banana trees, like that. The floor looked to be wood, or some clever fake. He passed the place, strolled down the mall, looking for somebody who might be paying too much attention to that area.

A loop in both directions came up clear. There were a lot of people milling about, in and out of the stores, and it was noisy. Parents put children on little choochoo trains, couples strolled along hand in hand, old people exercised in pairs, moving quickly in their thick-soled walking shoes. He saw nobody who seemed to be watching the appointed rendezvous. He did see a couple of uniformed security guards on patrol, and that was good.

He found a small shop selling sporting gear from where he could watch the meeting place, and he stood there and pretended to look at fishing reels.

A few minutes later, his coin seller arrived.

The man was fifty, overweight, red-faced, wearing a Hawaiian shirt with blue blossoms against a black background, yellow Bermuda shorts, and leather sandals. He had a cell phone clipped to his belt. He carried a briefcase. A hundred ounces of gold—that was only 2.8 kilograms, 6.25 pounds, not very heavy. The man looked around nervously, wiped his face with a handkerchief, then sat on one of the benches. He put the briefcase on his lap, both hands gripping it tightly, and looked from side to side, searching for Santos.

Santos hoped the security guards didn't come back. The

man was entirely too nervous. He looked guilty just sitting there.

Appearances could be deceiving, of course, but this man in yellow shorts did not look dangerous. He looked terrified, and exhibited none of the coolness Santos would expect from a professional thief. Amateurs were bad—he'd rather deal with pros—but this Yellow Shorts here seemed to be no more than he appeared.

Santos scanned for backup. It took all of ten seconds before he spotted a woman about the man's age, fifty feet away, pretending to be window-shopping as she held a cell phone to one ear, but obviously watching Yellow Shorts. She wore a sundress and straw hat, and carried a big straw handbag.

A wife, maybe? But—no. On reflection, they had a kind of sameness about them.

A sister, he decided.

He would bet that Yellow Shorts had his cell phone turned on, so that the woman could listen to the conversation. Amateurs, to be sure.

Sundress could have a gun in that bag, just as Yellow Shorts could have one in the briefcase, but Santos did not think so. The coins, he decided, might be theirs, but they needed the money, and for some reason could not get it from a dealer. A dead relative, or one gone senile, possibly?

He did not intend to let his guard down, but he was less concerned than before.

He waited until a couple of minutes before they were to meet, then strolled out into the mallway and toward Yellow Shorts.

"Mr. Mayberry?"

Yellow Shorts looked at him as if Santos were a wild gorilla escaped from the zoo. He thought for a minute the man might jump up and run away.

"Yes. Mr. uh, uh, Ouro?"

"At your service."

"You're . . . black."

"I am? Oh, dear."

Mayberry gave him a tepid smile.

"Let me sit next to you," Santos said. "I will show you mine, and you show me yours."

He sat, opened the top of the backpack, pretended to be searching for something within, and held it so that the man could see the bills.

In response, Mayberry opened the lid of the briefcase and showed him the coins.

No gun.

The Maple Leafs were in pockets of clear plastic sheets, ten to a sheet in two rows of five, stacked ten deep. Santos could tell at a glance they were real. Faking such things was possible, but these were not fakes. To be sure, he said, "May I?"

Mayberry nodded. It seemed to Santos that the man's head would fall off, it bobbed so hard.

Santos removed one coin and felt it. It was real enough. He tucked it back into its pocket and closed the briefcase.

Pedestrians streamed by, unaware of the transaction taking place.

"It would probably not be a good idea to count here, but if you wish, you may take it into the bathroom over there and do so." He handed Mayberry the backpack.

"I, uh . . ."

"It would be no problem. You could leave the coins with me for security, and your sister can watch to make sure I don't run off."

Mayberry gasped.

Santos glanced over at Sundress in time to see her jump as if stung by a bee.

He smiled.

"How could you know that?" Mayberry said.

Santos shrugged, a lazy gesture.

"I—there's no need to count it. I'm sure it is all there."

Indeed, it was, but the man was a fool to trust him. In fact, Santos knew he could take the coins, and the backpack, and walk away, and Mr. Mayberry—or whatever his real name was—would do nothing to stop him. He could hardly call the police if there was some taint to the gold, and he could not physically stop him. But Santos was an honest man. He was saving twenty-five percent on the value of the Maple Leafs, a bargain. He was no thief.

"Very well, then. Our transaction is concluded, no? Enjoy the day."

With that Santos stood and walked away with the briefcase.

All his business should be so easy. But just to be safe, he would take his time getting back to his automobile, and he would make sure he wasn't followed. He had another backpack in the car's trunk, and he would transfer the coins to it—just in case. Perhaps Mr. Yellow Shorts was not a terrified amateur at all, but some kind of wonderful actor and criminal genius. Perhaps he might have put a tracking device into the briefcase to allow some . . . more violent confederates to follow along to relieve Santos of his gold elsewhere?

In which instance, the footpads would find themselves following a delivery truck, or wondering why their target had taken refuge in a garbage bin . . .

He smiled at the thought. If pressed, he would bet all the gold in the case against a dime that this imagining was not so. Still, it paid to be cautious when carrying a couple of kilos of gold around, no? Men had been killed for much, much less.

He went into a shop and found an exit in the back with a bar across the door that said an emergency buzzer would sound if the door was opened. He pushed the door open and stepped out into the warm sunshine. A short ways down was another entrance into the mall. He walked there and went back into the building.

He had heard that there were supposed to be a couple of good Brazilian restaurants in Fort Lauderdale. Perhaps he could get a real *caipirinha*, heavy on the lime and light on the vodka, maybe some *churrasco* steak or chicken and even some *torta de banana*? He had not had good banana pie since he had been in the U.S.

He would ask the car's computer where to find such a restaurant. With the money he had saved on the coins—at least ten thousand U.S., for sure—he certainly could afford to indulge himself in some real food for a change . . .

Ah. Life was good.

17

Net Force HQ
Quantico, Virginia

John Howard walked down the long hall to his office, oddly glad to be here.

Tyrone was out of danger, and home, and Howard felt as if he could go back to work without worry. Julio had had an adventure, breaking up an extortionist's operation, and Gridley and crew had been working hard on the latest net assaults.

Fortunately, he hadn't missed much.

He'd had a couple of long talks with his son. One of the perks of having a teenager confined to bed and depending on you for everything he couldn't reach was that he was forced to talk to you now and then, if for no other reason save to ask for his laptop computer, more DVDs for his video player, or another soft drink or glass of iced tea. The boy drank like he was trying to set a record for most liquid downed. Had three piss jars by his bed full most of the time.

Tyrone had asked about work, and Howard had given

him what was available for public consumption, plus a little more. After all, his son *was* a computer whiz who had once helped Jay Gridley track down one of their miscreants.

When they had gotten to Jay's theory about CyberNation maybe being somehow responsible, and the prevailing attitude as to where CyberNation could go and what it could do to itself when it got there, Howard had gotten an earful.

"You're wrong. These people are on the right track."

"A bunch of thieves? Putting copyrighted or trademarked stuff out without paying for it?"

"It's not *theft*, Dad. Knowledge should be *free*. If you're some poor backwoods family in Kuala Lumpur or somewhere and there's a way of growing rice that doubles your harvest, shouldn't they know about it?"

Howard had shrugged. "I can see that, but—"

"That's an easy one. Same thing for drugs. Suppose you run a Third World country, and half your population has a deadly disease, and the formula for a drug that will cure it is available, shouldn't you be able to get it, make the stuff, and cure your citizens? The big drug companies say no, you have to buy it from them."

"There's two sides to that argument, son. The big drug company maybe spent millions creating and developing that formula. Years of work and testing, getting government approval. So you're saying that they should just give it away for free?"

"No. I'm saying that they are making huge profits, so why shouldn't they be willing to cut some slack to sick people who will die because they can't afford it? Doesn't the end of saving lives justify the means here?"

Howard said, "But if you extend that logic, there might not be any profits. If they have to give away their stuff for free to everybody who can't afford it, they go bust, and then no new cures are developed. Nobody gets a haircut if the barbershop is out of business."

"You're twisting what I'm saying."

"No, I'm telling you that in our world, there ain't no

such thing as a free lunch. Somebody somewhere *always* pays for it, that's how it works. Yes, maybe some rich company could afford to make less profit to benefit others, but when you start drawing that line *for* them, you're forcing people into communism. That's a bad system."

Tyrone, sprawled on the bed and unable to escape, crossed his arms over his chest. "You don't understand."

"So educate me."

Tyrone scooted up a little. Like his mother, he had to use his hands to talk, so the tight body language went away. He said, "All right. Look at CyberNation. They are offering international citizenship. You join up, pay them, and you get connected to the world. You can get a college degree, find any information that's available, and they'll even offer you a kind of social security. What's wrong with that?"

"Nothing, except that it's a castle in the sky, son. You can't *live* on-line. No matter how many hours of the day you're plugged in, you still have to have a physical location somewhere. You can roam the planet in virtual reality, but your butt will be in a chair in Washington or Texas or Sierra Leone."

"So?"

"So, as a citizen of a geographic location—a country—you have to obey the rules and regulations of that place."

"But CyberNation is going to cover that—"

"They can't. They gonna pay your taxes for you? Keep up the roads and schools and national defense? Lookit, what if CyberNation decides to issue driver's licenses to its 'citizens.' That mean you don't have to get one from the state?"

"The U.S. recognizes licenses from other countries," Tyrone countered. "If you come here from France or somewhere, you can drive, as long as you have insurance and your license is valid at home. Jeez, Dad, every *state* gives out licenses, but you can drive in every other state with it. It's called reciprocity."

"But that's temporary, son. If you are passing through

Arizona and you're licensed in Mississippi, that's fine, but if you move to Arizona, you have thirty days to change your paperwork. That's how it works most places."

"Yes, but—"

"No 'but' about it. You live in a place, you have to toe whatever line that place calls for. But skip all the citizenship stuff for a minute. Let's get into the 'universal access to knowledge' business. Let me ask you something. You see anything wrong with recording a movie you like to watch off the cable without buying the commercial DVD of it?"

"No, I don't see anything wrong with that. *You* do it all the time."

"Right. But I'm paying for it. I pay the cable bill, and if I set up the HD to record a program I want to watch later, or because I won't be there when it comes on, there's nothing wrong with that. But if I take that pay-per-view program, run off a copy, and sell it to somebody else, is that right?"

"Why not? You buy a book, a knife, a frying pan, it's yours, you can do anything you want with it. You can sell it to somebody. That's legal."

"One that I paid for, yes. But let's say I run off fifty copies of a novel, or a DVD movie, and sell them at a discount, then what I'm doing is depriving the cable or satellite company of potential revenue. Fifty people who might have paid for it won't. Not to mention I'm getting a profit off of something I had no hand in creating."

"But what if you give them away? You aren't making any profit."

"Same difference. I'm not earning money, but I'm in essence stealing from the people who paid to produce it, because those fifty copies come out of the company's profit."

"But what if the people you sell them to wouldn't have bought it at full price?"

"You're saying it's okay to shoplift if you don't have the cash to buy something?"

"No, I'm not saying that. But listen. Here's an example: There's this piece of music I got from the web. It's a parody thing. Somebody took the words to a hot rock song, and put them to the music of a TV sitcom. It's really funny. But the rock stars didn't think so, so they sued them. You can't buy the song anywhere. So if I download it, who do I hurt? Nobody makes any money on it, it isn't available commercially."

Howard nodded. "I can see that. Parody is a valid argument and protected under our laws. But the rock stars could argue that the words are their property so it shouldn't be available without their approval. They own 'em, they can sell the song or let it sit on a shelf until it turns to dust."

"That's not right. What if somebody bought a famous work of art, a Picasso, or the Mona Lisa or something, then they took it out into the yard and slashed it up, set it on fire? Could they do that?"

"Legally, yes. It would be theirs, they could do that. Morally? I wouldn't want to be them on Judgment Day standing in front of God trying to explain why they'd destroyed one of the world's treasures."

"That's my *point*, Dad. Something can be legal but not moral. Didn't Jesus say if you had two shirts and your neighbor didn't have any, you should give him one?"

"Not exactly, but close enough. The thing is, while *we* follow Jesus's teachings, not everybody does. Laws have to be based on moral and ethical principles, but they have to cover *all* the people. And at the heart of western civilization is the concept of private property. And that includes intellectual property, too. You take a man's living when you steal his songs or books or secret formulas. Most laws are moral by society's standards."

"Like laws that allowed . . . slavery?"

Howard stared at him. "You gonna throw *that* up into *my* face? You're not any darker than I am, son."

"Sorry. But slavery *was* legal for a long time. That didn't make it right."

"No, it didn't. And those laws were changed."

"And it took them, what, two hundred and fifty years to get around to it? We've got laws now that will be changed, too. This is the information age, Dad. Old concepts will have to make way for the new ones. The cat is out of the bag, and it isn't gonna go back in."

Howard smiled at the memory of his conversation with his son. He was coming along pretty well, Tyrone was. He wasn't always right, but he did know how to think, and that was important. He had some good points—

Somebody said, "Penny for your thoughts, General, sir."

He looked up, saw Julio standing there.

"Maybe a nickel, you grinning like that."

"Just remembering a conversation with Tyrone."

"He's doing better, I take it?"

"Not a whole lot since you saw him yesterday, but overall, yes."

"Good. You here to work?"

"I am. Let's go into the office and you can catch me up."

"Well, I can try. I can't work miracles, sir. Hard to teach an old dog much of anything."

"If you learned how to change a diaper, Lieutenant, anything is possible."

They grinned.

Jay Gridley stared at his computer console. He should be working. He should be climbing all over the web like a million baby spiders, running down every lead, trying to find the bad guys who'd been screwing things up. But instead, here he was mired waist-deep in inertia, unable to get moving.

Thinking about getting married.

It still seemed like the thing to do, to get married. He loved Saji. He wanted to be with her.

Well, fool, you are *with her, aren't you?*

Maybe that was part of the problem. Nothing much was really going to change if they had a big wedding, signed documents, and made it legal. Oh, they'd get toasters and teapots, and they'd go on an RW honeymoon—Saji wanted to spend a week on the beach in Bali—and all that, but everything else would be the same, wouldn't it? The lovemaking, the time they spent laughing, none of that would be any better if they were married, would it?

Not that he could see.

Of course, you could twist that both ways. If it didn't make much difference, then why *not* get married? They'd belong to each other legally, in the eyes of man and God, and if they had property, or even children, there would be certain protections that came from that. On balance, there was maybe a bit of a plus on the marriage side.

So why did he feel as if he had just gone over the first drop on a SuperTall roller coaster at Six Flags, with his stomach trying to crawl into his throat?

What was there to be afraid of? Especially since it had been *his* idea in the first place? He could remember how scared he was that Saji was gonna say no when he asked, and how relieved he'd been when she hadn't.

What's the deal here, Gridley?

He shook his head. He needed to talk to somebody who was married. Maybe Fernandez, he hadn't been with Joanna that long, and he'd been a bachelor for a lot more years than Jay had. Maybe he could offer some insight.

Jay hoped so. It was bugging him that he couldn't concentrate on the job as much as he needed to, not to mention that it bugged him these guys were screwing with him personally.

***On the* Bon Chance**

Chance had in mind to ream 'Berto out, figuratively, anyhow. Yes, he was a perpetual motion machine in bed and that counted for a lot, and yes, he was as good a hammer for smashing enemies as she could want, but he had to understand that she was the boss.

When she found him, he was in the ship's gift shop, buying shaving lotion.

"Roberto," she said, a little louder and sharper than she had intended.

The shop's clerk, a young man in black-rimmed glasses, glanced up at them from where he was stacking candy on a shelf.

'Berto turned slowly and gave her a lazy and insolent raised eyebrow. "Ah. Hello, Missy."

The clerk turned back to his chore.

Roberto looked like a big tom cat, sure of himself way past confident.

Time to crack the whip a little. "You weren't supposed to leave the ship. Where did you go?"

"You know where I was, Missy. Did not the helicopter pilot you asked remember where he landed?"

She felt herself flushing under his gaze. This wouldn't do, not at all. She had to stay in control of the situation. "He remembered. What I want to know is why you left without telling anybody."

"I don't tell anybody when I'm going to pee, either. Nobody needs to hold my hand for that, nobody needed to know about my business in Fort Lauderdale. Because it was *my* personal business."

"You have responsibilities—" she began.

"And I do them," he said, interrupting her. "You have a problem with how I perform, either on the job or in bed?"

The clerk stopped stacking the candy and apparently realized he had urgent business on the far side of the gift shop. He went there in a hurry.

She lowered her voice. "No, I didn't say that."

"Or maybe I didn't worry about telling you because I thought you might not even notice I was gone, that you might be busy."

"What are you talking about?"

"I hear Jackson fills in for me when I'm not around. As much as he can, anyway."

She blinked, caught flatfooted by the statement. Okay, so he knew. But she wasn't going to give anything away. "I don't know what you are talking about." She had learned that in the corporate world a long time ago—when in doubt, deny everything. If somebody had a video of you doing something, if they had ten nuns and a priest as witnesses to . . . whatever, it didn't matter—you stuck to your story.

"I mean I don't think his equipment measures up," he said, deliberately skipping what she'd meant. "But you would be the one to know that—you the one doing the measuring."

"I don't think is the place to talk about this," she tried.

"You came to find me," he said. "This is where I am."

"Maybe we could go to my cabin," she said.

"No. I don't think so. I think maybe we don't be so . . . personal, if you know what I mean. We can talk business here, in the conference room, someplace, but not your cabin. I don't like the way it smells there now."

Was he *dumping* her?

No, she decided. He was miffed. His manhood was insulted. Okay. He could pout for a while if he wanted, but he wasn't ready to give her up yet. She couldn't believe that. She had too much power that way, it was her strength. Men never walked away from her until she was ready for them to go. Never.

"Fine," she said. "But next time you leave the ship without telling me why and when, you might as well stay gone. I won't have you compromising our mission. If you had gotten into trouble, been picked up by the police for something, where would that leave us? This is more important than just you, Roberto."

He smiled. "So you say." He went back to selecting his aftershave.

She felt a flash of anger so hot she wanted to kill him, right there where he stood.

He was going to pay for this. Dearly.

18

Washington, D.C.

Toni held the training *kerambits* she'd made, traced from her real ones onto a piece of stiff leather, then cut out and the edges rounded off to make them relatively safe. Relatively safe, because a hard hit with one could still leave scrapes and bruises. The points and inside edges of the leather blades were coated with lipstick, so that any place they touched left a red mark. Both she and Alex wore old white T-shirts and gray sweatpants that would show the marks if they were touched with the red.

Alex himself had a longer plastic knife, one that came from a G.I. Joe toy set, the rounded point and dull cutting edge also coated with waxy red.

Toni circled him in the empty garage—the Chevy convertible was finally repaired and sold, and he was without a project car at the moment. Gave them room to work out on rainy days such as this one.

"You have the longer weapon," she said. "And in a knife fight, size *does* matter. But I have two blades to your one, so you have to be extremely careful. Slashing is mostly defensive," she said. "Slashing can kill you, but it'll take longer. Your advantage is, you can stab for a faster killing stroke, but these knives are so short that I'll have to rip out a big blood vessel to do you any damage by slashing."

"That's comforting," he said.

He held his right hand, with the knife, in front of his face, kept his left hand under his right elbow. She could almost hear his thoughts: *high-line, low-line. High-line, low-line . . .*

"Knowing what you can do with a weapon, or what your opponent can do, is vitally important. Against an opponent with any skill, you will almost certainly get cut in a knife fight. The trick is to limit where, and how bad. You might have to take a nasty cut to end a fight in your favor. But better to be stitched up in the ER than on life support in the ICU."

He'd heard her say that often enough. He nodded.

When she came in, she did it fast, and his slash and poke was right on the edge of desperation. She got in, but she was aware of being touched on the arm and body by his blade. She jumped back as he flailed away at her again, missing.

"Okay, what do you see? Take a look in the mirror."

He moved a couple of steps so he was in front of the mirror they'd picked up at a garage sale. There was a red strip on the side of his neck, and three other less-defined ruby splotches on his chest, belly, and inside his left elbow.

"Well. Looks like I'm dead, Jim," he said.

"Yes, you are. Now, look at me."

He did so. Toni had a red long line on the outside of her right arm, and a small spot under her sternum.

"You see?" she said. "I'm your teacher. I have been training and practicing this art for more than a dozen times as long as you have. With real knives, I would have cut your carotid and probably the radial artery in your antecubital fossa—inside your elbow crook there—plus slashing you in the gut and chest. But even so, you would have opened my arm—which I could have survived—but also stabbed me in the heart."

She touched the spot on her chest.

"Without quick first-aid care, one or both of us would probably have died after that trade, but we'd both have bled. A weapon changes things."

"Yeah, so I see."

"Against a knife bare-handed, you are in deep trouble. Even with a knife of your own, you can get chopped down."

"And the moral of this story?"

She smiled. "If somebody comes at you with a knife, run. If you can run, don't attack unless there are several of them, in which case, you take one out, *then* run. If you stand your ground, you have to cover your centerline, that's your advantage."

"But maybe we both die? That's an advantage?"

"Everybody who carries a knife doesn't have great skill with it," she said. "You have to assume they do, of course, and move as if that were the case, but the truth is, most people who might attack you with a blade wouldn't have gotten any of those hits I did except the arm. They wouldn't have gotten me, either. And don't forget, I have *two* knives, short though they are."

"Bad for my wardrobe, though."

She smiled. "You can always buy a new sport coat, sport."

He smiled.

"Okay, let's try it again. This time, block with your free hand, dorsal side, and sector to the outside of my attacking hand when you do. Getting out of the way of an incoming knife is usually a good idea—if you miss the block, at least you don't get skewered. After that, we'll switch, you attack and I'll defend. That's when the *kerambits* work the best."

Later, when they were in the shower washing off lipstick marks, Toni said, "There's an exercise I want you to learn."

"I'm game," Alex said. "Come closer."

"Not that kind of exercise. A mental one."

"Oh."

"Don't sound so disappointed. It'll be a couple of hours yet before Guru and the baby get home. It won't take long."

"What kind of exercise?"

"Posthypnotic suggestion."

He scrubbed her back with the bath sponge. "Uh-huh. Sure."

"Look, I know you don't think a lot of the spiritual and magical sides of *silat*. You think it's all mumbo jumbo."

"I didn't say that."

"Give me the sponge, I'll do your back."

She soaped the sponge and began scrubbing between his shoulder blades. "You don't have to say it for me to know it. But hypnosis is a perfectly valid tool, and you can do it yourself. It's nothing more than autosuggestion with a focus. You visualize things, practice them in your head, and it improves your skill."

"You sound like Jay."

"No, listen. Take athletes. At the Olympic level, nearly all of them use visualization to help their performances. They practice their exercises—whatever they are, from swimming to downhill skiing—in their imagination."

"Careful, I'm ticklish there," he said.

"No, you aren't. Shut up. You ever practiced your *djurus* while sitting at your desk, just thinking about them instead of actually moving?"

"Sure."

"Same thing. Tests on athletes show that mentally practicing can lay down nerve memory channels just like doing it for real. Not as much, but some."

She squatted, and soaped up his butt and hamstrings. "So practicing mentally is useful," she continued.

"Okay. So?"

"What's your biggest problem with *silat* practice?"

"Aside from you?"

"I'm serious."

He looked over his shoulder. "C'mon. How serious you expect me to take this while you're rubbing my ass with a soapy sponge, Kemosabe?"

She smiled. "Think of me as your teacher and not your beautiful naked wife in the shower."

"That's hard."

"It better be. But try."

He nodded. "I'm too tense," he said. "I haven't learned how to relax when I move. I use too much muscle."

"Right. So what we do is, we take you to a state of relaxation and suggestibility, and teach you how to get there posthypnotically."

"You can do that?"

"To a degree, yes."

"Okay. Is that before or after we make love?"

"Before."

"Aw, come on."

"Maybe instead of, if you don't hurry up."

He hurried.

When they had finished showering and drying themselves, she had him lie on his back on the bed. She stretched out next to him, but not touching him. "Okay, close your eyes."

He did so.

"You comfortable?"

"Yep."

"All right. I want you to imagine you are in the hallway of an office building. It's an older place, but well-maintained. To your right is an elevator. Walk to the button that calls the elevator—it's an old-style mechanical one. You push it, and it lights up.

"The elevator arrives—you can see the number light up above the door. You're on the twentieth floor. You hear a soft chime. The door opens, the elevator is empty. You step inside."

Michaels wasn't having any trouble following along, but it felt kind of silly.

"The elevator is an old one, but in good condition. It's nice and warm in here, quiet, the light is soft. Push the button marked with the number one."

Michaels mentally pushed the button.

"Above the door are the numbers for the floors of the building. Twenty is lit in red, and the elevator starts to descend. As you watch, a few seconds later, twenty blinks off and nineteen lights up, and there's a soft chime as the elevator slowly passes the floor.

"Eighteen lights up, again, the soft chime.

"Now as the elevator slowly goes down, you begin to feel relaxed. The elevator settles very slowly, but you're in no hurry, you've got all day.

"As you pass seventeen, sixteen, fifteen, you become more and more relaxed. The numbers light, the chime sounds, and you are becoming even more placid, more comfortable. There is nothing but the numbers descending, the soft tones at each floor.

"You pass fourteen, twelve, eleven, ten, nine. Save for the chime, all is quiet. The motion of the elevator is smooth, soothing."

Her voice was a soft drone, lulling him.

"Eight, seven, six, five, four, three . . . two . . . one.

"The elevator stops. The door opens. You step out into the hall. To your right not far ahead is an open door. You walk into the room, there is nobody around, but there is a couch, long, cushy, very inviting. Lie down on the couch. You are so comfortable and relaxed you don't feel like moving a muscle, you are practically melting into the cushions."

Well, this wasn't so bad, Michaels thought.

"So there you are, warm, comfortable, relaxed, lying there on the couch. You aren't sleepy, just slack. No worries, no noise, nothing to bother you. Your breathing is slow and even. Life is good."

Yeah.

"You don't need to move, but if you did need to, you could do so quickly and easily, because you are so relaxed, no tension to slow you down. Concentrate on how relaxed you are, see how it feels, see how simple it is to just lie here and be this way."

Pretty good, actually.

"Here's a little trick. To get back to this place, this relaxed, comfortable, no tension feeling, all you have to do is say to yourself out loud, 'Relax, Alex.' That's all. If you say that, you'll feel just like you feel now, no matter what is going on around you. You'll breathe slow and easy, your muscles will hold you up, you'll be able to move as quickly as you need to, but there won't be any tightness in you. Just say, 'Relax, Alex,' and that's what will happen."

She waited a few seconds.

"Now, you stand up, and walk back to the elevator.

"Good. You push the call button. The doors open right away and you step inside. Push the button for the twentieth floor. The numbers start to light up, starting with one, then two . . . three . . . four. As the elevator rises, you still feel calm and relaxed, but more refreshed now, as if you have just had ten hours of sleep.

"You pass five . . . six . . . seven . . . but there's no hurry.

"The lights blink, the elevator chimes softly as you pass each floor.

"You watch the numbers flash by. When the elevator gets to the twentieth floor, it stops. You take a deep breath and let it out. As the door opens, you open your eyes—"

He blinked at her.

She smiled.

"That's it? I ride an elevator down, you tell me to relax, I ride it up?"

"Yep. How do you feel?"

"Well, I feel fine. Great." He raised a skeptical eyebrow at her. "That's what being hypnotized is? There's nothing to it."

"What, did you think you were going to turn into Frankenstein's monster? Cluck like a chicken? Not be able to remember anything?"

"Well, yeah, okay, kinda."

"It's not like that. It's a state of heightened concentration. If you do this little exercise a few more times, it will be reinforced. It's not magic—it just allows you to focus your thoughts better. You can get pretty much the same thing by meditation or prayer."

"And this will work?"

"Try it, next time you get tense."

"Okay. I will. But right now, I have something else in mind."

She laughed. "Why am I not surprised . . . ?"

Later, when Guru had gotten home with the baby and they were all getting ready to go out for dinner at the new Mexican place, Michaels thought about the workout and hypnosis thing. That short and long knife business could be taken as a metaphor for his life. Getting in close had consequences, it was more dangerous in some ways. He had a new family, and compared to his first one, it was . . . different.

Toni was much more a part of his reason to get up every day than Megan, his first wife, had been. Maybe it was Toni; maybe it was only because he was older and a little wiser and able to appreciate what he had now more than he had been able to appreciate it then. He didn't love his daughter Susie any less than he did Alex, but he certainly hadn't been there for her in the same way. Something he'd always regret.

Whatever. But lately, work just hadn't been calling to him the way family did. If he won the lottery tomorrow, would he still get up and go to work every day? Ten years ago, five years ago, even a year ago, he would have said yes, no question.

Now? Now, he wasn't sure about that at all. Maybe he would take a few months off.

Maybe he would take off permanently.

It could be that part of it was because he was at the top of the mountain at Net Force. Anything higher in government was going to be some kind of political appointment, and not likely to happen. He didn't slot neatly into either party. Most of the time, he voted Independent, sometimes one way, sometimes another, and there were times when he couldn't bring himself to vote for *anybody* running. He liked to think of himself as fiscally conservative but a personal liberal. Could support a right wing Democrat or left wing Republican, but wasn't really either. Pretty much smack in the middle of the silent majority's road. So unless he opted for the private sector, he'd peaked out in his biz.

Being commander of Net Force was as good as it was going to get.

Or maybe it was a midlife crisis. He had been face-to-face with death a few times in the last couple of years, and that made a man stop and think about the meaning of it all, something he had never done much before. Being introspective wasn't part of what he'd learned at home. When your number was up, it was up, game over, and if the old saw was true that nobody on his death bed ever said, "I wish I'd spent more time at the office," then what exactly *did* you look back and wish you'd done better when you knew you were about to shuffle off?

Michaels realized for him, it was gonna be family first, and then work. It didn't used to be that way, but that's how it was now. He hadn't noticed when that had happened, that shift, but it had.

He could understand a whole lot better now why John Howard had taken a leave and had thought seriously about retiring.

Just when he thought he had a handle on life, it went and changed on him.

Damn.

19

Western Pennsylvania
June 1770

Jay crept through the thick woods along a deer trail with as much stealth as he could manage. This mixed evergreen and hardwood forest was disputed territory, and dangerous. On the Indian side, technically at least, this area still belonged to the Iroquois-speaking Six Nations—the Mohawk, Oneida, Onondaga, Cayuga, Seneca, and Tuscarora—but there was a Chippewa camp not far away, parties of Delaware passing through now and then, even some Ottawa in the area, supposedly. A white man clad in buckskins prowling in any of their territories uninvited might be viewed with a certain amount of hostility; better that nobody saw him.

The deer trail wound serpentinely through the forest, wide enough for a man to traverse, but a bit low in spots, causing Jay to duck overhanging tree branches. The smell of fir was strong, and his own sweat added a sour note to it. He carried a long rifle, a flintlock as tall as he was, a powder horn, lead balls and patches, a single shot pistol of a matching caliber, a sheath knife, and a tomahawk, much as any frontiersman of the era might. No coonskin cap, though—the idea of a dead raccoon on his head seemed ghoulish, even in VR. Instead, he wore a plain leather cap. Maybe there wasn't any real difference between cowhide and small furry animal skin, but everybody drew the line somewhere.

The mosquitoes were bad, but as long as he kept moving they didn't settle too thickly on his exposed face and hands; they couldn't penetrate the thick buckskin shirt and pants, nor what he wore under them. A few big wood spiders had spun card-table-sized webs here and there, and he avoided those when he saw them.

A bird called out ahead of him, a cheerful whistle he didn't recognize. A man couldn't know everything.

He came to a small clearing in the forest, a place where a couple of huge old-growth conifers had fallen and flattened a dozen smaller trees. The big trunks had mostly rotted away under sun and wind and rain, turning to reddish brown, pulpy food for termites, and fertilizer for the new growth that wiggled and broke through their corpses. There were also sedge grasses here, many of which had been nibbled short by the deer. It was maybe thirty meters across, the clearing, and the sun shined down upon it through the rent in the forest's thick canopy.

He waited a few seconds, listening, looking, sniffing the air. Everything seemed okay.

He started across the clearing. Halfway to the other side, he heard something behind him. A startled animal, perhaps?

He looked over his shoulder in time to see a Native American warrior step out of the brush. The man had an iron-tipped lance, and from his dress Jay realized he was a Shawnee. He had forgotten about them—they were a Johnny-come-lately tribe in Pennsylvania, having arrived here only around the end of the 1600s.

Another warrior stepped into view, also armed with a long lance. A third slipped from the brush, and he had a rifle much like Jay's, though the stock of his was decorated with a pattern of brass nail heads. They weren't wearing feathers or war paint, but they weren't smiling at him, either.

Time to leave the party, Jay, he thought. He turned to sprint away, but three more Shawnees materialized ahead of him.

Hmm. Another trap. How interesting.

One of the Shawnee chanted something. Probably something like, "Say your prayers, round eyes, you're a dead man!" but Jay shook his head.

"Not this time, pal," he said.

He dropped his long rifle, tore open his buckskin shirt to reveal a Kevlar and spider silk vest, along with an Uzi slung from a strap under his armpit. He pulled the black subgun out and pointed it at the three Shawnee in front of him. "Rock 'n' roll!" he yelled. "Rock 'n' roll—!"

He pulled the Uzi's trigger. Thirty-odd rounds of jacketed 9mm bullets spewed. The air filled with smoke and noise. At this range, it was hard to miss. He waved the gun like a water hose—

The soft lead bullet from the Shawnee's rifle whacked him square in the middle of his back. He felt it flatten against the vest, sting, but do no damage—

By the time he spun to attend to the other three, the extra-long fifty-round magazine was running low, so he limited himself to five-round bursts: *Braaaap! Braaap! Braaap!*

He held the final burst down, and stitched the sixth very surprised Indian across the thighs. The last ambusher fell; unlike the other five, he was down, but not dead.

The woods got very quiet after the angry roar of the submachine gun.

God bless the Israelis and their dependable technology.

He held the muzzle of the subgun up in front of his face and blew away the thin tendril of smoke rising from the hot barrel.

"How'd you like *them* apples, pard?"

He moved toward the wounded Shawnee. He had a few questions to ask him, and if he hurried he might get an answer before his opponent realized what was going on . . .

***On the* Bon Chance**

"Son of a bitch," Jackson Keller said. He grinned. "So you haven't lost all your moves after all, Jay. Good for you."

He looked at the holoprojic recording floating above his console. The packet Jay had managed to snag wasn't going to take him anywhere useful, but it was surprising he had managed to avoid the scenario-destroying trap like that.

Well. Maybe it shouldn't have been so surprising. At his peak, back in their college days, Jay had been sharp, as sharp as anybody. They had run with CIT's and MIT's best. It wasn't unreasonable that some small part of his edge wasn't completely dull. That just made it more interesting, didn't it?

So he avoided a trap. No big deal. The next one would be better. He reached for his sensor set. *Let's play, Jay. Show me what you got . . .*

His com chirped. He was tempted to ignore it and jack back into VR, but he glanced at the ID sig. Better get that.

"Hey," he said.

Jasmine said, "Hey. Listen, there's something you ought to know, just FYI."

"Sure, shoot."

"It seems that Roberto has, ah . . . found out that you and I have been . . . intimate."

Keller both felt and heard himself take a deep breath. And his belly knotted as if somebody had stabbed him in it with a shard of dry ice. "Excuse me? How did that happen?"

"I don't know. I didn't say anything."

"Well, I sure as hell didn't."

"It's not anything to worry about."

Not anything to worry about? Santos killed *people with his bare hands!* Keller had heard the story of the two militia guys at the site of the telephone cable cut. About the ex-FBI bodyguards for the Blue Whale veep. They'd all been trained, they'd all had *guns* and that hadn't mattered! He'd killed five people, *bap*, just like that! And there had been others . . .

He knew it had been a mistake to sleep with her. Good as she was, it had been a mistake.

He tried to keep his voice calm. He should have expected this. It was a big boat, but not that big. They weren't invisible. "Oh. Really."

"He's part of the team. He doesn't want to screw that up, he's making way too much money—he knows I'd fire him if he hurt you."

Well, wasn't that *comforting! I'm* dead, *but he's* fired?

He didn't say anything.

"Anyway, that's it. I'll be sending him on a little chore later today. We can . . . talk about it more when he's gone."

He blinked at the frozen holoproj over his computer. Was she saying what he thought she was saying? That once Santos was off the ship, they'd get back into the sack together? Was she that stupid?

Was he?

Careful there, Jacko. Pissing off The Dragon Lady might be worse than pissing off the stone killer!

He mumbled something, and she discommed.

His heart was definitely beating faster, and his breathing was rapid and unsteady, too. All of a sudden, this little intellectual match with Jay Gridley didn't seem anywhere near as interesting and fun as it had only a few minutes ago.

A man who looked like he was chiseled out of granite, who killed people without batting an eye, a man with old ideas of machismo, had found out Keller was sleeping with his woman. How the hell was Keller supposed to just smile and shrug *that* off?

He forced himself to breathe slower. Maybe she was right. Maybe Santos was too smart to cause any problems. They were all getting rich off this project, and they stood to get a whole lot richer once their shares started really appreciating in value. He wouldn't want to screw that up over a woman. Santos was not that stupid.

But Keller wasn't sure about that. Not sure enough to bet his life on it.

Capitol Hill
Washington, D.C.

Michaels surreptitiously glanced at his watch. Next to him, Tommy Bender, the Net Force lawyer, caught the look and squelched a smile.

The senate subcommittee room was hot and stuffy. There were no windows. The senators were talking for the camera again. One of the senators got up and walked away, as a second returned to his seat on the dais. They came and went like a roomful of small children who had drunk too much lemonade. One would go, another would return. There was more motion from the subcommittee than a soccer team playing a match. Michaels couldn't leave to stretch or get a drink of water, though. He had to sit here at the table looking up at the sometimes-six, sometimes-eight, sometimes-five of them milling back and forth like somnolent sheep. Already it had been two hours, and there were no signs of an end in sight.

Senator Theresa Genaloni, from the great state of New Jersey, made her obscure point about the dangers of invading citizens' privacy, and finally shut up. This hearing didn't have anything to do with on-line privacy per se, but she was the junior senator from her state, her party was in the minority, and this pissant committee was hardly Ways and Means, so she had to make her points where and how she could. Otherwise, how would the folks back home know she was on the job? She certainly wasn't delivering jobs in their direction, nor much in the way of pork-barrel spending.

Stewart George Jackson, the once red-haired but now mostly bald and gray junior senator from the great state of Arkansas, took over the microphone. Jackson liked to be called "Stonewall," after the Southern Civil War hero. He was usually called "SJ" by his staff. While these were his initials, somebody had told Michaels that they also stood for "Strawberry Jell-O," due to his extremely flexible ethics. Jackson had all the backbone of a baby squid. He'd sometimes switch sides on an issue faster than a speeding bullet. General Jackson must be spinning in his grave like an atomic-powered gyroscope every time somebody called Jell-O "Stonewall."

"Perhaps Commander Michaels can explain to this committee why this latest round of attack on the Internet structure has continued despite Net Force's efforts to stop it?"

What Michaels wanted to say was "Because I am here listening to the senatorial windbags blow warm hurricanes instead of at the office helping them?" That would have been very satisfying. Stupid, but satisfying. He had this fantasy every time he testified, and he had never acted on it; still, he thought about it.

"Don't do it," Tommy said under his breath. It didn't take much of a mind reader to glean what Michaels was thinking.

No, he'd better not say anything nasty. Not only would that be career suicide, his agency would suffer, and he didn't want to cause that.

"Commander?"

"I'm sorry, Senator. I didn't realize you were asking me to speak."

That earned him a glare from Jell-O, and grins from three of the other senators.

"We are following up leads on the attacks," Michaels said. "Our operatives have narrowed down the suspects and are getting closer to a resolution." You could always say that and it would be true enough.

"Would you care to give us more specific information, Commander? Who, where, and when?"

"I am sure you realize that this is an ongoing investigation, Senator. I would not wish to compromise it by releasing details in public. If you would like a private briefing, I will have my staff follow up."

Of course, Jell-O didn't care about the investigation, and would no more want to spend his time going over the details of it than he would want to give up cigars and whiskey. This was a piddling committee, and one had to milk what one could from it. Scoring a few points for law and order was always good for the voters back home to see. He would have a staffer listen to the report and boil it down to half a page or so, highlighting key words to be spoken in his syrupy Foghorn Leghorn drawl next time Michaels had to show up and sit in the hot seat.

The senator droned on, and Michaels listened with half an ear. This was the part of the job he hated most, the sitting in front of a bunch of old farts and being treated like a grammar school boy by men and women who, for the most part, couldn't understand what it was he did. They were mostly lawyers, half of them were technophobes, if not Luddites, terrified of anything more complicated than a phone or television set, and their main strengths seemed to be the ability to get re-elected.

Face it, if they had anything on the ball, they wouldn't be stuck on this committee, now would they? The only one here who had more than two neurons to spark at each other inside his hollow head was Wayne DeWitt, the recently elected junior from West Virginia. He was young, sharp, and technically educated, with a degree in engineering. He was one of the few senators willing to stand up and say that the idea of CyberNation was stupid in the extreme. He was a fairly right-wing Republican, but even so, Michaels was willing to cut him a lot of slack—better a right-winger with a brain than anybody without one.

Not very charitable of him, those thoughts, but, hey, if it was true, it was true.

He glanced at his watch again. Another two hours of his life he'd never get back.

Damn.

On the **Bon Chance**

Santos had left his most recent coin buy in a safe-deposit box at a bank in Fort Lauderdale. They'd be secure enough there, but he would prefer to have them in his own bank. He had worked out an arrangement with an assistant ambassador in Washington who flew home to Brazil now and again, and who had access to diplomatic pouches. For a healthy fee, he would transport whatever Santos gave him back there, where Santos's cousin Estaban would collect it and take it to the branch of the *BancoVizinho* where Santos did his business. He had an arrangement with a bank officer there to make sure his coins were well-cared for.

Estaban was blood, and the bank official was also related, by marriage, to another cousin. Both were well-paid, and both knew what would happen to them if they got greedy and decided to pocket a few of the coins. Once, when they were much younger, Estaban had seen Santos take out a crooked policeman who tried to shake him down too hard. Crooked or not, killing a *puño*, a "fist," as they were sometimes called in the shanty towns, was the act of a man with *bolas grande*. Those who dealt with Santos at home knew his reputation. He was not a man to be fooled with—aside from his own skills, he had a couple of paid friends in high places, always necessary in

Brazil, and he was protected, at least to a degree.

Once his gold was home, it would be safe enough.

When Missy ordered him to take care of some business in Washington, D.C., this was perfect. He would stop at the bank in Florida and retrieve his Maple Leafs, speak with the diplomat once he got to the capital, and all would be well.

The business Missy wanted him to handle? Well, that was of small importance. One man who needed to have a bad accident. He didn't even have to die, merely be put out of commission for a month or two. Easy as falling out of a tree.

He made a point of swinging by the computer rooms just before lunchtime. He saw Keller with two of his people as they headed for the private cafeteria. Keller was laughing at something one of the others said.

Keller looked up, saw Santos.

Santos gave Keller a quick two-fingered salute, a how-you-doin'-amigo? gesture, nothing the least bit threatening in it. He smiled.

Keller went pale, as if somebody had just punched him in the belly.

Santos didn't stop. He turned away and ambled off down the corridor. All he'd wanted to do was make Jackson aware that he *knew*. That was enough, for now. Let him sweat a while, worry that maybe something hard was coming. Because it was coming, no question. There were some lines you did not cross, and Jackson had crossed one. He knew it. How much it would cost, when, where, he did not know. And that was part of the payment, too.

Santos hummed to himself as he headed for the helipad. Good day, so far. Real good.

20

Net Force HQ
Quantico, Virginia

Toni sat at Alex's desk, going over operations reports. She was glad to be back. She'd forgotten how interesting this work was in the time she'd been away. As Alex's assistant, she had been privy to the inner workings of the nation's computer business, all kinds of information the average citizen didn't even know existed had come across her desk. When she'd quit—over a mistaken supposition that Alex had been too idiotic to correct—she hadn't missed work, because almost immediately she'd had an offer from the director to start a job for the mainline FBI. The pregnancy, then the baby, had stopped that. It had been the better part of a year, and she'd lost a few steps. But it was like riding a bicycle—the basic balance was still there, and with a little practice, she'd be rolling smoothly again pretty fast.

She felt a quick stab of guilt. Did that make her a bad mother, that she wanted to work? Shouldn't she be at home, doing mommy things, putting all this away until

Little Alex was old enough to go off to school? It wasn't as if they needed the money. And she did miss the baby, that was true. But her husband needed her, too, and what was she to do? Guru had showed up, and that had seemed like some kind of sign.

Still, she worried.

Well, it was only temporary, after all. A few days, a week, until the crisis was over, that was all . . .

"Boss still testifying?" Jay said from the doorway.

"I think so," she said. "Anything new on your front?"

"Yes and no. I'm on the right track, I got ambushed in VR again. But this time, I surprised the sucker. Didn't get a solid lead, unfortunately."

"Win some, lose some."

"Oh, this one ain't won or lost yet. Too early. But I have some feelers out on the CyberNation gambling ship, down in the Caribbean, and I'm expecting those to come in later today."

"You think they are responsible?"

"Gut-check? Yes. Proof? None."

"Lay it out for me."

"Sure." He came in, flopped down on the couch. He started ticking points off on his fingers: "One, CyberNation has a lot to gain if people switch to them because of net woes. Two, CyberNation has the talent to pull this kind of thing off. I don't have a complete list of their programmers and weavers, but I've seen their public face, and it is very slick, uses all the latest language. Three, their advertisements increased just about the time all this started, a vigorous campaign to sign up new members, stressing the integrity of their systems. Four, there's that connection with the casino ship and the dead guy from Blue Whale. Five, I haven't found anybody better, and I've been looking real hard."

"Circumstantial and iffy," she said.

"Hey, I got another whole hand of fingers here. Six, CyberNation is pushing on other fronts. They have a powerful lobby working in D.C., and in various major countries around the world. Isn't that what the boss is over on the Hill about today? Problems with the net that CyberNation claims it can cure?"

She shrugged. "So what are seven, eight, nine, and ten?"

"I haven't filled those in yet," Jay said, grinning. "But I'm working on it."

"How are the wedding plans coming?"

His smile faded. "Okay, I guess."

"Getting cold feet?"

"What? No!"

"Easy. I was just joking."

He didn't speak for a moment. Then he said, "Did you? Get cold feet, I mean?"

"Not really. Of course, I was pregnant, and I didn't want to have the baby by myself."

"Hmm."

"Hey, look, it's only natural to worry about making major changes in your life. I wanted to get married, but I did think about it. Alex was married before—what if I didn't measure up to his first wife? And he's got a daughter from that marriage, a great kid, but I had to wonder, was he going to be thinking about her when he looked at our child? It's not like buying a new pair of shoes, is it?"

"No."

"You should talk to Julio Fernandez. He got married after a lot of years on his own, he had to make some adjustments."

"I was thinking that. I mean, I want to be with Saji, no question, it's just, I dunno, scary sometimes."

"Welcome to the human race, computer-boy."

"Thanks."

John Howard looked at the computer log and stack of hard copy on his desk and shook his head. Forms and clogged e-file boxes were the bane of military officers everywhere. Yes, they had to be attended to for the command to continue working, and mostly, he managed to pass a significant amount of paper shuffling and signing off to senior officers on his staff, but if you missed a few days, your piece of it always grew, it never shrank. He'd been at it for an hour and a half, and hadn't really made much of a dent.

How important was most of this junk? An invitation to speak at an upscale military school in Mississippi? He knew the school. Enrollment was ninety percent white males, with a few women and minority students sprinkled in to keep things legal. Yes, he was the commanding military officer of Net Force, but they didn't want him—he'd bet dollars to dimes they didn't know he was black. It might be amusing to show up just to see the expressions on their faces. Then again, that wasn't worth a trip to Mississippi, was it?

Another e-mail was a cc notification from the NF Quartermaster from a military supplier in Maine that there was a recall on part number MS-239-45/A, due to possible stress fractures in materials that might lead to failure in critical situations. The Quartermaster would have already addressed the situation, but it still sounded worth knowing about. A man needed to see where his troops might be at risk.

A check of the Net Force parts catalogue, which naturally changed the supplier's part number to their own designation, NF-P-154387, showed the part in question to be the "flexible containment system locking device for a Model B dorsal-unit personal supply and equipment carrier." After years of military jargon, that one was easy: They were talking about the plastic buckle on a backpack strap. The B-model had been in service for approximately three years, according to the computer file, and had been superseded by the C-model.

If the buckles on the old packs hadn't busted by now, then it probably wasn't going be a problem that would bring the Net Force strike teams to their knees.

And how many man-hours had been lost to this tidbit? Here was a directive from the U.S. National Guard regarding the directive from the General Accounting Office, regarding the directive from the Department of Defense's Revised and Updated Guidelines for Officers Regarding Sexual Harassment.

Oh, please. How relevant to anything was a directive about a directive about a directive about guidelines?

His intercom chirped. "Yes?"

"Sir," his secretary said. "Lieutenant Fernandez to see you."

Julio had just left a couple hours ago, but anything to get out of this drudgery. "Send him in."

Julio arrived.

"Yes?"

"Sir. I'd hate to tear you away from all this excitement, but we've got a new shipment of goodies and there are a couple of things you might enjoy seeing."

"I really need to get this done," he said. He waved at his desk.

"You're the general, General." He started to leave.

"Wait a second, I'll go with you. This can wait."

Julio grinned. "I thought it might."

As they walked out, Julio said, "I ran into Jay Gridley out in the hall a few minutes ago. He seems to be a little nervous about his upcoming nuptials."

"What did you tell him?"

"That being married is worse than death by Chinese water torture, of course. That if I had it to do all over again, I'd jump in front of a speeding train before I said 'I do.' "

"You're a braver man than I thought, Lieutenant. What if that somehow gets back to Joanna?"

"I'll deny having said it to my last breath."

"Which wouldn't be long in coming if she thought you said such a thing."

Julio chuckled. "I'm a career military man, sir. Not much she could do would scare me."

"She could make you watch little Hoo on your poker night."

"I was only joking. I told Gridley that. I also told him it was natural that he should feel nervous about taking the big step. That everybody does."

"I never did," Howard said. "Never crossed my mind."

"And you were what—twelve when you got married? Never had a room of your own, much less a life before you met Nadine. You didn't have anything to give up, except your virginity, now did you, sir?"

Howard laughed. "Unlike you, who lived alone so long that you had to relearn how to pick your socks up because you had never had to do that before? No, I knew Nadine was the best thing that was ever going to happen to me. Just like Joanna is the best thing that ever happened to you."

"Yes, sir. But don't let that get back to her, either. I'd never hear the end of it if she knew that was true."

"She knows, Lieutenant, she knows."

If he had had time, Santos would have taken the train up from Florida to the District of Columbia. The East Coast trains usually ran pretty well, they were clean, and it was relaxing to watch the country roll past your window at a speed where you could see much of it. The trip would have taken most of the day, and he could have gotten up, moved around, stretched out, eaten, drank, enjoyed the drone of wheels on steel.

But time was a luxury he seemed to have too little of, so he caught the jet shuttle, and what would have been a relaxing all-day ride became a two-hour hop. Not counting the forty-five minutes they circled the airport, waiting to land.

He rented a car at the airport. The car was a full-sized sedan, as big as they had, and he took out full insurance coverage on it. The name on the card he used matched the name of his fake driver's license, both of which had been issued to a man in Georgia a few weeks ago. The card and license had not been used before, and the man whose name was on them had not reported them missing, since he had been dead before they were issued. It was a wonderful way to move around semi-legitimately. Somebody in CyberNation's computer hutch had figured this out, applying for credit cards and duplicate licenses in the names of the recently departed who already had such things before the family thought to let anybody know. The geeks rented post office boxes, applied under several different names, and had the cards sent there. Once they had been used for a few days, the IDs could be tossed into the nearest trash bin. Very neat, no way to trace them.

He drove to a local hotel. He wore a suit and tie, carried a briefcase, and registered at the hotel, which catered to businessmen, looking as if he was one of them. Just another middle-class white-collar worker earning his living, no one to remember.

The briefcase contained not papers, however, but the gold coins he had gotten at such a bargain rate. While the guards at the metal detectors in the airport had been curious, they hadn't even bothered to open the case to look. And if they had, they could have done nothing, because there was no law against carrying such things onto a plane. It wasn't as if he was going to beat somebody to death with them, although technically that was possible. Slip fifteen or twenty of them into a sock, it would make a nice, hefty blackjack.

Once he was checked into the hotel, he took a stroll, ducked into a big drugstore, and bought a cheap disposable cell phone with thirty hours of credit on it. He used this to put in a call to his friend at the Brazilian Embassy. Morgan, who could always used a little extra money, was happy to hear from him, and they arranged to meet for supper at a restaurant not far from the hotel.

Between now and then, Santos had plenty of time to study the information he had about his target. This one would be simple, nothing complex about it at all. As soon as he had the gold transported, he would locate his quarry, and then it was merely a matter of waiting for the proper moment.

Hollywood, California

Two tall and well-muscled black men in different NBA uniforms played one-on-one basketball in a gym bathed in supernal beams of sunshine pouring in from big skylights in the gym's roof. There was just enough dust in the air so the beams stood out, hard-edged and brilliant.

The men were the hottest small forwards from both teams in last year's championship finals, all-stars, guys who routinely got triple-doubles when they played—ten or more shots, assists, and rebounds.

The one with the ball was dressed in black shorts, shoes, and tank top, the other player in white-on-white-on-white.

The offensive player jinked left, then right, dribbled behind his back, and stutter-stepped, trying to get into position to shoot at the goal.

The defensive player stayed with him, slapping at the ball. Two fine athletes at their peaks, beautiful to watch, even if you didn't follow the game.

Both men sweated, fat drops that rolled and flew with their sudden moves.

The offensive player faked right, then twirled around to his left and got past the player in white . . .

Time slowed to a crawl. The ball bounced slowly, took two seconds to come back from the floor to the shooter's hand. The sounds of heavy breathing grew louder, and when the ball hit the floor again, it sounded like a cannon—*boom*!—deep and vibrant. The ball bounced up. The shooter caught it, jumped for the dunk, moving in glacial slow-mo, as the player in white leaped to block . . .

The pair drifted through the air, seemingly as weightless as the dust motes in the gym's air, floating oh-so-slowly toward the basket . . .

Time speeded back up to normal.

The offensive player slammed the ball down, playing well above the rim, and the net *ka-thwipped!* in that way it does only when the dunk is perfect. The two players came down and smiled at each other.

White Suit said, "Good move, brother." He slapped the shooter on the shoulder, went to fetch the ball.

Black Suit said, "Yeah, I still got a few. Here's another one for you—who's doing your Internet service?"

White Suit shrugged. "Same provider I always use." He tossed the ball to the other man.

Black Suit shook his head. "Naw, you need to lose that, man. I'm tight with CyberNation, it's the only place to be."

"CyberNation? I heard of them."

"I'm telling you, it's the way to go. They got VR so good, it'd help even *you* with your defense."

"I got a cramp in my foot, is all. Try it again."

Black Suit laughed and walked away, dribbling. White Suit dropped into a defensive crouch as the other player turned and started back toward him.

The words CyberNation appeared under the screen, with the URL. The scene faded to black, leaving the words alone on the black background with the sound of the dribbled ball echoing in the gym. The sound and image held for five seconds, then faded out.

PART TWO

The Butterfly's Wings

21

***On the* Bon Chance**

Jasmine Chance liked to be in charge, a big part of the reason she had taken this job. Here she was, with a corporate budget as big as the treasury in some small countries, on a gambling ship she had named herself, and after a fashion, *for* herself. She could, literally, decide matters of life and death. If that wasn't control, what was? But at the moment, with Jackson practically wetting himself, she felt a definite loss of mastery here.

They sat on the bed in her room. She'd thought sex was going to be the main thing on his mind, but she quickly realized she was wrong.

"He's going to beat the crap out of me," Jackson said. "I know it."

"Don't be stupid."

"You didn't see him, how he looked at me. I'm telling you, this is not somebody to mess around with. He might as well have sent me an invitation: You are cordially invited to a major ass-kicking—yours."

"Jackson . . ."

"I'm not joking around here, Jasmine. This guy isn't civilized. Yeah, he wears a suit and smiles and can make small talk, but that's no thicker than a coat of paint. Underneath, he's a savage. He's a killer! He wouldn't think twice about sending me to the hospital, or the morgue."

"He's just trying to rattle you, hon, that's all. He knows how much we need you. He's playing with your head."

"And he plans to be playing soccer with my *balls*. I'm telling you, I know."

"You need to relax." She put her hand on his shoulder. The muscles there and in his neck were bunched like wet, knotted ropes.

"Easy for you to say. Listen, I want off the ship. Let me go to the train."

The train was one of the other two locations for CyberNation's mobile computer centers. Currently, it was on a siding in Germany, somewhere near the French border.

"Keller—"

"I can take my team there. It won't be any different. The hardware is the same, the software we built in the last day can be encoded and uploaded in a few hours. By the time it finishes downloading, we can be halfway there."

"What will you tell your team?"

"No need to tell them anything except they should pack their bags. They do what I say."

"That's not the plan," she said.

"Neither is getting my head stomped in by a jealous assassin!"

She thought about it. It was the fight-or-flight syndrome. Maybe in his place, she could understand it. Still, it wouldn't really solve anything. What was to stop Roberto from hopping on a plane and dropping round to see Jackson on the train? When he had time to settle down and think about it, he'd see that. There was no safety in distance, not if somebody like Roberto really wanted to do you harm. But no point in saying that now. He was rattled enough already.

Of course, out of sight might be out of mind. She was sure she could divert Roberto's attention. She could buy him a new toy, something to do with his fighting art. Sooner or later he would feel the call from her to find a place where they could get naked. Roberto was, after all, very primal in his urges. Maybe it would be for the best if Jackson wasn't around.

"All right," she said. "Gather your team and make the arrangements. Roberto won't be back before tomorrow at the earliest. You can be gone before he returns."

His sense of relief was obvious.

"As long as we are here, why don't you lie down and let me massage your back? You're as tight as a violin string."

He started to protest. "That's what got me in trouble in the first place."

"Relax," she said. " 'Berto is in Washington. You'll be gone when he gets back, and we aren't doing anything we haven't already done a dozen times. What difference could it make now? Why not relax and enjoy it?"

She didn't give him time to think about it. She slid her hand down his chest and into his lap. After that, he had other things on his mind.

Net Force HQ
Quantico, Virginia

Michaels was in the Net Force gym, dressed only in a pair of shorts and workout shoes, practicing his *djurus*. The short dances encompassed all the moves that *serak* teachers had developed for fighting, armed and unarmed. Somewhere in the *djurus* were all the tools you'd ever need, he'd been taught.

So far, he had learned more than he thought he'd use

if he got into fights every day. But better to have too much ammo than too little.

The creator of the esoteric fighting style had been a cripple called Sera, so named either because he was wise as an owl, or had a hoarse voice, depending on which definition of the Indonesian word *sera*, you liked. According to the various oral histories and subsequent letters and books, Sera had been born with a clubfoot and missing part of one arm. Such handicaps would not seem to lend themselves to the development of expert fighting abilities. Nonetheless, that had apparently been the case. Evidently the man had been an extremely nasty fighter, and not a man to be sneered at, however gimpy he might have been.

The origins of the art and its first practitioner were somewhat mysterious. Michaels had poked around, trying to research it, because he was curious, and had run into half a dozen dead ends.

He shifted from *djuru* seven, coming up from the full squat and upward thrust to an attacker's face that ended it, to eight, moving on the triangle, or *tiga*. Later, he would practice the footwork on the *sliwa*, or square pattern.

He had worked up a good sweat; it rolled down his chest and back. He'd always thought it interesting he could get so much work out of stepping around a triangle or square that was less than two feet long on each side.

Djuru eight was essentially a blending of three previous *djurus*—four, six, and three—and since it was the last one he had learned, once he finished it he repeated it and started going backwards toward the first one. That was how you did the exercises, up and back on one side, then up and back on the other, so that each *djuru* got at least four reps, two on the right, two on the left.

Pak, or *Bapak*—those meant *sir*, or *most honorable older sir*, more or less—Sera's date of birth was unknown. He'd been listed as having been born as early as 1795 A.D.; however, this seemed unlikely, given the known lineage of students, and Sera was probably born a quarter century later, in the 1820s or maybe even the 1830s. Current practitioners could not even agree on the man's real name. The ones Michaels came up with were Eyang Hisak and H. Muhroji.

Toni didn't know any more about Sera than Michaels did; she'd always accepted what her teacher told her and let it go. Not that it really mattered, but it was a shame they couldn't give the man his proper due.

The birthplace and tribe of Sera were also open to question. Some claimed he was of the mysterious Javanese people known as the Badui. Since not much was known about the Badui—the White, or Inner Badui remaining cloistered even in modern times and admitting few visitors to their primitive villages—this was difficult to determine. If Sera was of the Outer, or Blue Badui, that would seem more likely, but if he was, he certainly did not stay there, according to the stories.

Others said Sera was born in Tjirebon, on the north coast of Java, east of what was then Batavia, now Jakarta. There was no consensus on this point.

Family history from Guru DeBeers and from what he could find on the web indicated that Sera trained in Silat Banteng, which came from the area of Serang, in northwest Java. From his exposure to Tjimande, which it is said he studied, and with his training in Banteng, Sera developed his own system, tailored to his physical handicaps.

Although the exact dates weren't known, it was probably sometime before the turn of the 20th century that Sera met the man who was to become his senior student, a hardass of a fighter named Djoet, who was supposedly born around 1860, and died in the late 1930s. Djoet subsequently helped Sera formalize the system, adjusting it for people with sound limbs. Djoet was reportedly trained in Silat Kilat, Kun Tao, and probably Tjimande.

Michaels made it back to the first *djuru*. He stopped, grabbed a towel, and wiped the perspiration from his face and head. The problem with the short haircut he liked was that it didn't soak up as much moisture. He had thought about wearing a headband, but decided that looked a little too yuppie-ish for him.

He glanced at the clock over the gym's door. The day was winding down, and he had managed to lose a fair amount of the tension he had soaked up testifying before the senate committee. Not all of it, but some. Another twenty or thirty minutes of practicing his forms would help more, he decided. Picturing some of the more obnoxious senators on the receiving end of his punches and elbows probably was bad karma, but that helped, too. Imagining the "*Urk!*" a fat politician would blurt as Michaels buried his fist in the man's belly was certainly politically incorrect, but also very satisfying . . .

Net Force Supply Warehouse
Quantico, Virginia

"So is this a great toy, or what?" Julio said.

Howard looked at the device. "It looks like a miniature version of Robby the Robot somebody stepped on."

And indeed, it did. A scaled-down version of the movie robot, the device was squatty, maybe eighteen-inches tall, and had a clear bullet-resistant Lexan half-dome atop the cone-shaped body, complete with a pair of articulated arms and tanklike treads. It was very wide at the base and narrowing toward the top.

"We call her 'Claire,' " Julio said. "Your basic self-contained radio-controlled mobile reconnaissance and surveillance unit, the main feature of which is optical and auditory gear, including state-of-the-art CLAIR equipment—that standing for Circular-Looking-A-class Infra-Red sensors. Aside from the regular cams, she can see heat sigs in the dark, has a fuzzy-logic come-back circuit so she won't bump into things and can find her way home if the RC fails, and little waldo arms for picking up things to examine under her microscope, should the need arrive."

Howard shook his head. "Uh-huh. What did this beast set us back?"

"Ah, sir, there's the beauty of it. Nothing. Not a dime."

"How did you manage that? Tell me we aren't running a stolen robot here, Lieutenant. Something you won in a poker game with your RA buddies?"

"You wound me, sir, to suggest such a thing."

"And butter wouldn't melt in your mouth, either. Give."

"Claire here is a test model, from CamCanada, up in Toronto. They specialize in making devices to inspect the inside of big pipelines, checking weld integrity, hunting for cracks, like that, but they are looking to get into the police and military market. This is one of three prototypes they sent off for tests. The Mounties have one, one went to some sultan somewhere in the Middle East, and we have the third. We test it out under field conditions, write up a report, and for our trouble, we get one of the first models when they go into full production, absolutely free of charge. Well. Except for the maintenance contract, of course. But that's nothing."

"Interesting."

Julio picked up a remote and pushed a button. The little robot whirred.

"It does all the usual forward, back, left, and right stuff, and the POV cam shows an image right here on the handheld. Digital images and sound, and instant capture of info on its own wireless modem and DVD burner, which are around here somewhere. Those can be plugged into just about any computer for study and analysis."

He held the remote so Howard could see it. "Everything is shockproofed out the wazoo, structural components are machined from titanium or aircraft aluminum, and you can supposedly set off a stick of dynamite ten feet away without hurting it. Got a gyroscope for balance, low center of gravity, and she's very stable."

He brought the robot close enough to them so he could

kick it. His combat boot drove it back a few feet, but it whirred and stayed upright. He touched a control. "This shuts off the gyroscope. Watch."

He moved to the little device, which was slightly shorter than knee-high, and managed, with some effort, to shove it over onto its side with his foot.

The robot whined, and a rubber-tipped metal rod extruded from the robot's side and shoved it back upright.

"Automatic righting system," he said. "She can pick herself right up and keep on going. A byproduct of BattleBot technology, I'm told."

He picked up another remote and pushed a button. The windowless warehouse got very dark.

Howard saw the remote control's screen light up, and the false-color IR images of himself and Julio, looking like two washed-out ghosts, appeared on the screen.

"Lieutenant, I believe you just turned me into a Caucasian."

Julio chuckled. The false-color computer-augmented image tinted Howard's skin slightly darker, but no more than a redhead's tan might be.

"Only with the lights off, sir."

He switched the lights back on. "But wait, here's the really fun thing," he said. He touched another button, and the robot hissed like a giant lizard, leaped two feet into the air, flew about four feet forward, and came down. It clunked when it landed, but not hard enough to knock anything loose.

Howard raised an eyebrow.

"Compressed gas jets. The tank isn't that big, so it's only good for eight or ten hops before it runs out, but if Claire here comes to a ditch that would take too long to go around, she can make like a bunny and leap right over it."

Howard smiled. "Might make recon of a building full of armed terrorists easier, at that. What are they going to run when they go into production? Any idea?"

"Ballpark only. They're saying a hundred thousand, Canadian."

"Lord, Lieutenant. For that much, we can buy an armor-plated car."

"Yes, but it can't do this."

The little robot hissed and jumped again.

"And it's free."

"What's the service contract run?"

"Practically nothing. Three years, maybe thirty thou, U.S."

"For thirty thousand American or so, I can find a lot of enlisted men who would spit and jump up, even if they can't see in the dark."

Julio shook his head. "Have I ever mentioned that the general is somewhat old-fashioned?"

"Never know when my buggy whip is going to come in handy, Lieutenant. It does the job it was designed to do and never needs batteries."

"Come on, John, give it a try. You know you want to." He passed the controls to Howard.

Well, yes, he did. It was just like playing with Tyrone's new toy on Christmas morning when the boy was nine. As his mother was fond of saying, If you couldn't have fun, what was the point?

Howard pushed the button, and grinned as the robot jumped again.

22

Washington, D.C.

Santos waited until the senator came out of the supermarket on his way home before he made his move. One of the most powerful men in this country, one of only a hundred altogether, and he not only didn't have a bodyguard, he drove a small car and did his own grocery shopping. Amazing. In Rio, a man in this senator's position would be guarded, chauffeured everywhere in an armored limo, and would not have the slightest idea what a carton of milk or a loaf of bread cost, unless somebody happened to tell him. What was the point of having power if you did not exercise it?

Santos had already driven the route the man would take to get to his townhouse. He had a woman there—not his wife, who was back home in West Virginia with their two teenaged children until the school year was done. Santos had seen the mistress himself when he had driven by earlier. The information about the wife and children was public knowledge, available to anybody who cared to look for it. Another amazing thing. Back home, men of wealth and influence knew that knowledge was power, and they kept it to themselves. Why would you give a potential enemy anything he might use against you? Foolish.

The senator from West Virginia swung his car out onto the street and headed home, driving in the right lane. Santos followed him, two cars back on the four-lane road. Three blocks later, Santos swung into the left-hand lane and passed the senator. He sped up slightly, just a few miles an hour over the limit, not enough to trigger photo radar or the interest of a traffic cop. He gained a block on the senator's car, pulling into his home street forty-five seconds ahead of the honorable Wayne DeWitt. He gunned the car's engine, sped a hundred feet down the street, and hung a skidding one-eighty turn. He stopped the car, his steel-toed workboot resting on the brake, but still in gear. He lifted a motorcycle crash helmet from the seat next to him and slipped it on, pulled the straps tight. The helmet had a face-shield of heavy clear plastic. He flipped the visor down into place. He already wore the heavy leather and rubber grappling gloves used by NHB ring fighters for matches, with the wrist wraps cinched tight. You could use your hands, but there was a lot of padding on the outside. He put a boil-and-bite mouthpiece into his mouth and slipped it over his upper teeth. Guaranteed for the first seventy-five hundred dollars of dental work if you hurt your teeth while wearing it, nine dollars at K-mart. A great deal. He wore a boxer's cup in a jockstrap over his leather pants, and a weightlifter's thick and wide belt covering his waist and his lower back under his leather jacket. Without special springs and belts, he was as protected as he could be in this car.

When the senator's car rounded the corner, Santos mashed the accelerator pedal.

One thing you had to give big gas-guzzling American V-8s—they had power to spare. He left tire rubber smoking on the asphalt as he took off.

He was doing almost fifty when he switched lanes and slammed into the senator's compact car.

It was at a slight angle—he wanted to be able to drive his car away, if possible, and there was too much chance of rupturing the radiator in a head-on, even against a smaller car.

There was a hard *thump*! and crash, and a sense of time slowing down, almost of drifting through space. Even though he was braced and ready, the seat belt tight, he still went forward into the air bag as it deployed. The face shield and gloves saved him from a flattened nose and brush burns on his arms as he hit the bag, which immediately collapsed. Striking an air bag in an accident was not, as some people seemed to think, like being hit in the face with a soft feather pillow. It was more like being punched by a gloved boxer, hard.

The big car's windshield didn't shatter, that was good, but something shiny flew up from the impact and hit on the passenger side hard enough to crack the safety glass.

He saw the senator's car spinning, saw the man's head hit his side window, blasting the tempered glass into squarish little bits that burst outward in a glittering fan of shrapnel. The air bag in the senator's car had gone off, but the deliberately angled impact had caused the senator to hit the bag well to the side, so the safety device didn't do as much good as it would have—another reason to avoid the full frontal smash.

Once past, Santos stood on the brake, and his car, already slowed by the crash, skidded to a noisy stop. He looked back in time to see the senator's car pinwheel into a fiberglass light pole that snapped off at the base and came down on top of the auto just as the car plowed into a row of bushes, wiped them out, and smashed the right rear panel into a thick oak tree. The tree shook violently, but held.

Santos put the car into reverse and backed up. Seemed to be driving okay, nothing scraping against the wheel, that was good.

He came abreast of the senator's car. No way they were

going to repair that, the whole front end was shifted to one side, the frame bent and badly distorted. Steam came from the ruptured cooling system.

The senator's head lolled through his shattered side window. Blood welled from his head and dripped onto the ground, and from the angle of his neck, Santos thought it might be broken. Certainly it was wrenched enough to damage muscles. The front of the car was collapsed enough so that the man's legs were probably pinned, maybe they were broken, too.

Good enough. Maybe he would die, maybe not, but he wasn't going to be playing golf any time soon, if he survived. And he would not be a thorn in CyberNation's side for a while, either.

Santos put the car into forward gear, and drove away. People were coming out of their townhouses to see what had happened. He kept his head down, knowing he was disguised by the helmet and face shield.

Once he was around the corner, he pulled the helmet and gloves off and spat the mouthpiece into his hand. He unbuckled the lifting belt, pulling it from under his jacket. He used a small pocket knife to cut the elastic on the jock and cup. With one hand he stuffed all the protective gear into a big shopping bag from Trader Joe's.

Three miles away he came to a major bus stop. There was a movie theater across the street. He parked the car in a movie lot, damaged front end toward the building, got out, and dumped the bag in the nearest trash bin. Anybody who found the bag would probably not be the kind of person who'd run straight to the police, and even if they were, what was illegal about gloves, a helmet, and a lifting belt? By the time anybody found the hit-and-run vehicle, he would be long gone.

He walked to the bus stop. Smiled at an old black lady who saw him coming. She smiled back.

A good night's work, this. Made a man proud.

Mount Fuji, Japan
July 2012

Jay Gridley sat on a bench provided for pilgrims and watched the sunset. Fuji-yama was a walk-up, lots of people climbed it every day. It was a volcanic peak, a stratovolcano shaped like a squat cone, but more than twelve thousand feet high, in Fuji-Hakone-Izu National Park, near Honshu. The sacred mountain was the highest in Japan. It hadn't had a major eruption since the early 1700s, but it vented steam and smoke now and again. Gave folks a bit of a thrill, maybe, to know it could possibly wake up and blow the climbers into the next world, however unlikely that was.

Most of the pilgrims started their ascent at the Fifth Station, about seventy-five hundred feet up, from where it took six or eight hours to make it to the top. The official climbing season ran from July to the end of August. Climbers on the north side used the Yoshidaguchi trail, which ran from Fujiyoshida City to the summit. The Fuji Subaru Line toll road met the trail at the Fifth Station, halfway up the mountain.

It was crowded—Fuji-yama was always crowded, sometimes hundreds of people walking in a long serpentine line, only a few inches apart, laughing, talking, enjoying themselves. It wasn't Mount Everest. More than a hundred thousand people a year climbed the sacred mountain. Now and again, one would die making the ascent, usually from a heart attack, but sometimes from heat exhaustion or dehydration. It was cool, maybe ten degrees above freezing at the top today, but a steady climb produced a lot of heat, and the heavy jackets tended to come off pretty quick.

The old saying in Japan was you were a fool not to climb the mountain once, and a bigger fool if you climbed it twice.

Jay watched the pilgrims slog past, many with walking sticks—canes, staves—backpacks holding small children, even a seeing-eye dog leading a blind man. Old, young, fit, flabby, tourists, seekers, dressed in every color of the rainbow and a lot of hues not found anywhere in nature.

It was not a totally safe climb, however, even for those in good shape. Falling rocks injured or killed people, if rarely. Those who wandered off the trail had sometimes fallen. And now and again, a tourist would be hit by lightning, sometimes out of the blue. Jay carried a small transistor radio Velcroed to his backpack, tuned to a time sig from somewhere. Supposedly, if the radio started blasting out a lot of static, it was a good idea to hit the ground and lie flat.

Weather was not particularly stable from the base to the top, and what started out sunny could be foggy, rainy, or snowy in a matter of a few minutes. The place made its own weather.

The Climbing Safety Guidance Center was located at the Sixth Station, First Aid Station at the Seventh. Climbing during the off-season was not encouraged. Those who felt the need were required to clear their climbing gear with the Fujiyoshida Police Station. Failure to do so as a tourist would get you kicked out of the country if caught, heavily fined if you were a local.

It was a good idea to bring proper clothing, water, food, and toilet paper.

Assuming you made it to the top, you could visit the shrine, mail a postcard at the post office, and explore the volcanic crater. You could also buy souvenirs, very expensive, and the big show was to watch the sunrise above the sea of clouds that often shrouded the earth below.

Jay had made the climb five times. In VR, that is. He wanted to try it in RW some day. Since meeting Saji, he was no longer worried that the real thing might not live up to the artificial experience.

Saji. Ah, there was something to think about when he got to the top. As he had been thinking about her most of the way up so far.

An old man, white-haired, seventy, darkly tanned, came

and sat on the bench next to him. He looked as if he might be Thai. He wore gray wool slacks over waffle-soled hiking boots, a white shirt under a blue Gore-Tex windbreaker, white cotton gloves, and dark sunglasses. He smiled at Jay.

"Nice day for a climb, isn't it?"

Jay nodded. This wasn't a private scenario, but a public one run by Tokyo University. Some, maybe all, of the climbers could be personas of real people. Many of the visuals were lifted right from the net-cams that watched the mountain year-round. "Yes, it is," he said.

They sat there, not speaking for a few moments, then the old man got up. "Well, that's enough rest for the wicked. See you around, Jay."

Jay nodded and smiled, and it was a full two seconds before he realized that the man had called him by name.

"Hey! Hold it!"

But the old man developed a speed and broken-field running ability that would have shamed a star football quarterback on a ninety-yard touchdown run. And he laughed loud and almost maniacally as he did so.

Somebody is seriously playing with me, Jay thought.

And it seemed to Jay in that moment that it must be somebody who knew him.

But—who?

***On the* Bon Chance**

Jackson and his crew were well away from the ship when Roberto returned from his mission. Jackson had called, was already working using his flatscreen and modem from the helicopter, and obviously feeling much better.

Chance had read about the senator's accident on the NetNewsNow headline page within an hour of the event. DeWitt would live, but doctors were not sure that he would walk again.

Too bad. But you had to factor that in—you couldn't make an omelet without breaking a few eggs.

DeWitt was a fly removed from the ointment.

Now, as she waited for Roberto to arrive at her office—she didn't want to invite him to her cabin and have him refuse—she considered yet again how she was going to play this.

Roberto wasn't the brightest bulb on the string, but neither was he stupid. He was cunning, in a sly way, but his view of the world was limited, much more personal than global. She was smarter than he was, she knew it, and manipulation was one of her strengths. She could bend him in her direction. She had the skills.

He smiled when he sauntered into the small office she kept. "Missy. It is done."

"I heard. As ever, you are a man to be relied upon. Thank you."

He shrugged.

"Listen," she said. "I have sent Jackson away."

His eyebrows went up.

"It was a mistake. You know how I am. I am weak about sex, I crave it. I am sorry. But it was wrong, I admit that. So Jackson is gone; he'll be working on the train from now on—you never have to see him again if you don't want. I'll make it up to you."

"How?"

"Anything you want."

He smiled.

She could almost hear the wheels turning in his head. Of course Missy realized her mistake, how could she not? He was much man, while Jackson was a boy, one who diddled computers and did nothing for real. Only a fool would prefer him over Roberto, and Missy, slut that she was, was no fool. This was only right.

"I will think about it," he said.

She held her smile in check. She had him.

"Thank you, Roberto." *Don't lay it on too thick,* she told herself, *just enough so he sees you as contrite, and willing to kneel for his forgiveness. Let him think about what he is missing—what he could be missing in addition to that.*

He would come around.

She watched him stroll out, walking with that cocksure swagger that men of physical prowess displayed, like big cats who could spring at any second, relaxed, but ready, a coiled spring waiting for instant release.

And he really was much better in bed than Jackson.

23

In the Air over the North Atlantic

Keller felt better. He knew intellectually this wasn't altogether realistic, his relief—Santos was as portable as he was, and if he really wanted to come and get him, he could; still, having a thousand miles of space between himself and the killer was better than not. Besides, he didn't think Santos would do that, come after him. Jasmine should be able to protect him, and certainly she could distract the man if she put her mind to it. She was very talented when it came to distracting men, Keller knew for sure. He'd never been with anybody like her, not even close. She knew things he had never heard of, never imagined. The tricks she could do . . .

That was the problem. He should have never let himself get into that situation in the first place, but, ah, she was something. How could a normal man refuse? She could raise a cold sweat on a brass monkey, raise some other parts of his anatomy, too.

Still, as soon as he'd climbed onto the copter, Keller had felt as if a great weight had been lifted from him. He was able to get on-line and screw with Jay Gridley some more without looking over his shoulder. To have fun with it.

He leaned back in the first-class seat of the 747 heading for Germany and stared through the window. Dueling with a man like Gridley, that was a civilized way of doing things. You used your skill, your wit, your intelligence. Your opponent appreciated these things, respected them, even if he opposed you. There were rules, many of them unstated but understood nonetheless, and adhered to, proper ways to engage and contend. Civilized men knew these things—they knew how the game was played.

A man like Santos? He appreciated nothing but brute force. Violence. It didn't matter to him that you were smarter, that you had talent and skill. No, all that mattered to him was the fist in the face, the foot to the crotch. He was a savage, no matter how you cleaned him up and dressed him, a jungle creature with a sharp stick. If you explained this to him, he would laugh. If you protested his lowbrow, knuckle-dragging demeanor, he would kick sand in your face. He would rather hurt people than not.

Keller shook his head. How could you reason with a man like that? You couldn't. Jasmine wound him up like some demented killing toy and set him loose to do her dirty work. She used money, not to mention her sexual favors, like a carrot to entice a mule into her bidding. You didn't take a stick to a beast like Santos. He would turn around and rip your arm off if you tried it. The man was an animal, with the morals of a cat. Pure evil, not a whit of guilt, a sociopath.

Still and all, Santos was necessary. CyberNation had to go forward. Whatever means were necessary were justified. Just as abolitionists of a century and a half past had broken immoral laws to help the slaves, so would those engaged in the fight to bring CyberNation to life be revered as freedom fighters decades from now. Living on the cutting edge was risky, but it had to be done—for the greater good. If a few men had to suffer so that mankind as a whole would progress . . . was this not how it had been since before the beginning of history?

Yes. It was.

A man like Jay Gridley, even if he couldn't be persuaded to your side of the argument, could be outmaneuvered, could be defeated, using the tools that would eventually be society's redemption. Deep in his heart, whether he would admit it or not, Gridley knew that the old rules, the old ways, had to move aside. Progress marched on. It always had, and if you stood in its path, you got run over, that was the way of it. The question was not if, but when. The choice was between evolution and revolution. Even Gridley would admit to that. He was for evolution, a status quoist, but he had not always been so inclined. Neither, for that matter, had the country. Had not the United States of America been born of revolution, guns against outmoded laws? Could they not see that such cycles would come again? That the fast wheel was sometimes better than the slow one?

People who were comfortable had a selective kind of blindness. They saw what they wanted to see, and ignored the things they did not wish to notice. Like a horse with blinders on, they had no vision save straight ahead.

Now and again, somebody had to come by and pull the horse's blinders off, cut his traces, and slap him on the rump. Run free, my friend! The future awaits you out there!

The drone of the big jet engines lulled him. Here he was, on a craft bigger than the ships that had crossed the seas from Europe to open up the Americas, a flying vessel that was so big and so heavy that no one on Earth would have taken a bet that it could fly, even a hundred years ago. The jet could travel thousands of miles without refueling, cover a distance in a few hours that would have taken the wind-blown sailors months in their wooden ships with canvas sail. The electronics in this bird would boggle the minds of the creators of Univac. You didn't turn back from such wonders. The future ran only one way, and the next revolution was not going to be in machines, but in knowledge. The global community would be one, together, able to reach out and touch each other faster than thought itself.

Once that happened, men like Santos would be superfluous. They could be quietly eliminated. The strongest man could be brought low by a bullet to the head. The hand that pulled the trigger need not be any stronger than that of a child. As the mammoths had fallen before the technology of the spear and fire, so, too, would men like Santos, who flexed their muscles instead of their brains, eventually join the ranks of the extinct beasts who were strong, but stupid.

The mind was more powerful. Brain won over brawn.

At least in theory. Given his recent experience with Santos, Keller realized there was going to be a transition period before the thugs and mugs went the way of the dodo. And during that period, it would be smart to stay out of the way of the brutes as they flailed about in their death throes. Yes, indeed.

Washington, D.C.

In bed next to Saji, both of them reading, Jay sighed.

"What?"

"This biz with this guy," he said. "I feel like somehow I'm missing something I shouldn't."

She put her book down and looked at him. "Oh?"

"Yeah. There's something, some kind of, I don't know, familiar feel to the traps and touches. Like the Fuji thing. Why appear as an old Thai? Why come and sit next to me and then give it away like that?"

"He knows you're part Thai," she said. "He's playing with your head."

"Yeah, yeah, but something is weird about it. I feel as if I should know this guy."

She sat quietly for a moment. Then said, "What else is bothering you?"

"Me? Nothing. Work is all."

She said, "Are you sure?"

"Sure I'm sure." He looked at her. "What are you getting at?"

A short time passed before she spoke. Then she said, "Are you really ready to get married?"

He blinked. The question that had been on his mind for weeks sounded terrifying when it came from her. "How can you ask that? Of course I am!"

"Okay."

"What—are you having second thoughts?"

She sighed. "Yes."

"What? Really?" He sat up straighter. His gut churned with sudden cold, as if he'd swallowed a cup of liquid nitrogen. "Why?"

"You know the Four Noble Truths," she said.

He shrugged. "Yeah. There's suffering in the world. There's a reason for this suffering. There's an end to it. There's a way to learn how to end it, using the Eightfold path."

"Close enough. And the Eightfold path?"

"What is this, a bedtime quiz?"

She shrugged. "You asked."

"Okay, we're talking, ah—right understanding, right thinking, right speech, right action, right livelihood, right, uh, effort. Lemme see, ah, right mindfulness, and—don't tell me, I got it—right concentration."

"Yes. And the Middle Path is the way many of us seeking enlightenment choose. Staying away from the extremes."

"Okay. So? What's this got to do with you having second thoughts about us?"

"I fear that my desire for you is sometimes too strong," she said. "That having a desire this powerful, that being so attached to it, will ultimately be the cause of suffering.

Not *being* with you, but *wanting* to be with you too much."

"Listen, I've tried to plug into this, but I've never really understood it. What does that mean?"

She smiled at him. "Admission of ignorance is the first step on the road to wisdom."

"Yeah, right."

"It's not that we can't be together, married, and happy. Each moment should be what it is, and there is much joy to be found in each moment. But the idea is to not be attached to that, not to want the joy so much that you can't experience it. You can . . . get in your own way. You can spend all your time trying to live for the future, full of expectation, or living in the past, full of nostalgia. Either will cause suffering, because you can have neither. The past is gone, the future never arrives."

"So are you saying you don't want to get married?"

"No, idiot, you're not listening. I do. Maybe too much, that's all I'm saying. I don't want to make you responsible for my happiness, because if I do, sooner or later, I'll be disappointed and unhappy."

"That's real comforting, sweetie."

"It's the truth. Reaching outside yourself for happiness is the big cause for suffering. I want to stand next to you, but not depend on your shadow to protect me from the sun. Suppose I put all my life into you, into us. And it works great, you give me back all I give you and more."

"Sounds right to me. What's the problem?"

"You change your mind in ten years, decide you don't want to be here."

"I won't—"

"Okay, better example—you get hit by a bus in six months. You don't have the choice to stay or go, your number is up."

"Are you saying you don't want to miss me if I get hit by a bus?"

"No. I'm saying that I want to be happy on my own, so that what I bring to us is real and true. Marriage is a partnership. If I don't come to the table with my half, it's not fair to either of us."

He shook his head. He really didn't understand. She was worried that she might want him too much? How was that a bad thing? His fear was that he would lose something of himself by marrying her. That was different.

Wasn't it?

He felt her hand slide across his leg. "Whoa. What have we here?"

"The moment, Jay. No past, no future, just right now."

He grinned. Okay. He could deal with that. Oh, yeah. Definitely.

But it bothered him that she was worried about the marriage thing. Given how he had felt lately, that shouldn't bother him at all, but it did. Was that a double standard? Probably, but—ah!

She overrode his thoughts with her actions, and in the moment, he stopped worrying and was happy.

***On the* Bon Chance**

Santos was satisfied, at least for the moment. He had made Missy do some things she ordinarily did not do—and that was saying something. She would be sore in new places tomorrow. He was not done punishing her, and Jackson would not get off just because he had run away to Germany, but he could wait. All in good time.

Did he trust her? No, certainly not. She was a slut, and she was out for herself, that had not changed, no matter what she said. Her skill would only buy her so much, but for now, it was worth enjoying. When he went home, he would find younger women who did not know the arts of love, and teach them to please him in the ways Missy did. Only they would not have her devious mind and need to be in control. Smart women, ambitious women, they were dangerous, to be avoided. Young, beautiful, and stupid, that was what he preferred. And if they got smarter with age? There were always fresh ones waiting to take their place.

As he showered, lathering himself with her hard-milled soap, he hummed a little tune. The next part of the project was about to start. There was only so much they could do with their computers and advertising, and soon it would be up to him and men like him to make things really happen.

He stepped out of the shower and dried himself with one of the huge towels Missy kept. He should go and practice his moves, now that he was relaxed. The ship's gym had room once you moved all the equipment back out of the way. Making love, having a hot shower, those were things that made a man want to go to bed and take a nap, but discipline must be maintained. He worked out every day, no matter what, no matter where he was, he found a way to do something. The fighting edge was one that grew dull if not sharpened frequently. It would be easy to justify a day off now and then. But if you could do that, you could justify two days off. Then four. There was no end to that, and the next thing you knew, you were fat and lazy, meat for some lean and hungry player who did not fool himself into thinking he still had the moves when he had let them rust away.

He found his striped workout pants and rubber sandals, grabbed a clean towel, and headed for the door.

Lying naked on the bed, Missy saw him. "You're not going to work out?"

"I am."

"But you must be tired."

"Yes. That does not matter."

"Why don't you come back to bed? You can work out later."

"I could. I will. But I am also going to work out now."

She shook her head, and he left. She could not understand. She was a woman. Women did not know the ways of men, not in the important things. Oh, yes, they knew about what a man wanted in bed, but about honor and discipline and what made a man a man? No. They knew nothing of these things. How could they? No more than a man could know about bearing children. It was just not in them.

24

Net Force HQ
Quantico, Virginia

In the conference room bright and early, Michaels listened to his team give their reports. Toni was here, Jay, John Howard, and Julio Fernandez.

Toni said, "Police are certain that the car that rammed Senator DeWitt's vehicle did so deliberately. There were no skid marks before the impact, and the hit-and-run car, which has been identified from paint and chrome chips, has been located, only a few miles away. Area residents got a glimpse of the driver, but he was wearing a helmet and heavy gloves, so no one got a look at his features. He could be white, black, or even a woman."

Michaels said, "And Jay thinks this ties to CyberNation. Jay?"

Jay nodded. "Yep. Just one more log on the circumstantial fire, boss, but it's burning pretty good right now. I've been poking around and have found some interesting stuff out about their gambling ship. It never puts into port anywhere, at least it hasn't since it was refitted and went to sea more than a year ago."

"That's unlikely. How does it resupply and refuel?" Howard asked.

"Fuel, mail, food, everything comes in either by helicopter or by special cargo ships that show up once a month. Since the ship is in international waters, nobody can bother it. There are no plans for the rebuilding and refitting on file, nothing since the original vessel was chartered. Libyan registry means nobody pays any attention to it as long as they pay the fees. There are webcams online, but only of the main casino and the outside. We don't know what all is on the ship. I've culled reports from various web pages, posts by tourists, and if you put them altogether, you come up with a composite picture that is missing a lot."

"Such as?" Michaels said.

"Such as, half the ship. Here, take a look at the graphic." Jay touched a button on his flatscreen, and a line drawing wireframe holoproj lit the air above the projection port. "There are passenger cabins here and here, on these decks." Part of the 3-D schematic lit up in red. "The casino is here. This is the pool, here is a gym, over here a big dining hall, and an entertainment hall."

More of the image came to life in different colors.

"If this area is crew quarters, and you allow for these decks to be dedicated to engines, supplies, miscellaneous storage, fuel, all that"—more colors flashed on—"then you throw in a couple more big spots for the hell of it, you still have a fair amount of the ship that looks to be empty. And none of the reports can fill in those unused decks."

"Maybe they are building more casinos?" Fernandez ventured.

"Nope, no signs of construction, no construction stuff delivered on the supply vessels for at least the last six months—I was able to get those manifests."

"So, what exactly are you trying to say here, Jay?" Toni said.

He shook his head. "I dunno enough about ships to be sure, but it seems to me you wouldn't leave all that space empty."

"That's generally true," Howard said.

"So, if that's the case, what is on these decks? I'm betting it's something connected to CyberNation and not to gambling per se."

"Such as?" Michaels said.

Jay shrugged. "I don't know. Maybe computers. Some kind of production facility, for all those ads they run. They do those themselves, I found out, no outside agency involved."

"Which means what, even if that's so?" Toni said. "Nothing sinister about that. They had some extra room, they put it to good use."

Jay shook his head. "They don't need the room. CyberNation HQ is in Switzerland. They have a twenty-story office building in Geneva, and a big honkin' warehouse there, too. What's a ship half full of slot machines and card tables compared to that?"

"You have a theory, though, don't you?" Michaels said.

"Yes, sir, boss, I do. See, if they were up to something illegal, the Swiss police could go and knock on their door and check out that building in Geneva. But what if they had something going on down in the Caribbean? Who has the power to go and check it out?"

Howard nodded. "Legally, nobody."

"Exactly."

"So you're saying you think the net attacks originated on that ship?" Toni said.

"I can't say that for sure. But if they did, how would anybody be able to find out about it? Or do anything if they could find out? Why does CyberNation have a gambling ship anyhow?"

"Maybe we better find some answers," Michaels said.

"I'm working on it," Jay said.

• • •

After the meeting broke up, Jay found himself alone with Julio Fernandez.

Julio said, "Sounds as if you have your work cut out for you on this thing."

Jay smiled. "Maybe not. I might be able to crack their personnel database. If I can find out who is working for them, maybe I can locate those people by other e-trails. You know, get hits on where they used their credit cards, made long-distance phone calls, like that. If they've got some crack programmers working on that ship, that would point another finger in their direction."

"You think you can blow past firewalls for a place like CyberNation?"

"Well, yeah, if I had a lot of time and a couple superCrays to play with. But there's an easier way. Social engineering."

Fernandez smiled. "I remember you talked about that," he said. "But is that legal?"

"Not in the strictest sense," Jay said.

"In what sense *is* it legal?"

"Well, okay, not in any sense," Jay admitted. "But let's say, for instance, that I know somebody who knows somebody who knows somebody who has access to the files, and I can trade him something for the information. That doesn't cost us anything."

"Not to put too fine a point on it, but isn't that exactly the kind of thing we are here to stop? Doesn't sneaking into somebody's computer system and stealing information constitute a crime?"

"Technically, yes."

Fernandez gave him a wry grin. "Uh-huh."

"But look, we're not talking about some honest citizen whose house we're breaking into to steal his TV. I'm pretty sure these are the guys who cost nations around the world millions and millions of dollars. People died as a result of the net going down in places. These guys wear eye patches and carry cutlasses. They're crooks."

"Slippery slope there, Jay. Blows right past the Fourth Amendment. Fruit of the poisoned vine and all like that."

"Since when did you become a constitutional scholar, Lieutenant?"

"I'm sworn to uphold and protect it. You are, too, given Net Force's charter. Once you start breaking the rules to get to the really bad guys, how long before you bend 'em to get to the plain old bad guys? And then the ones who are maybe not so bad, but that you don't like?"

Jay sighed. "Yeah, well, you have a point. There is probably another way to get to the information without doing anything illegal. Be harder though. And what if while I'm doing that, they hit again, shut down a hospital and kill off a bunch of patients or something?"

"That would suck. But still."

"You obey all the traffic laws, Julio, all the time?"

"Nope. And if I get caught, I don't kick, either, I pay the fine. But running a red light in the middle of nowhere at midnight when nobody is around is not the same thing, is it?

"Suppose you get the stuff you need and we use the information to nail these guys. No harm, no foul, right? But then one of their lawyers finds out what we did? The bad guys, who are guilty, get off, and you wind up looking for work, or maybe spending quality time in a cell in some country club *federale*, doing the warden's taxes for five years. It's the Rule of Law, Jay. It's what separates the good guys from the bad guys. We toss that out, we're no different than they are."

"Yeah, yeah. You're right. It was just a thought."

"Can't hang you for thinking. Not yet, anyway."

Toni took a coffee break, but she sat at her desk, fiddling with the computer. It had been a while since she had done any serious scrimshaw work—if any of what she had done while she was housebound during her pregnancy could be called serious—and she decided to check in on Bob Hergert, whose on-line class had taught her what she knew about the art of scratching lines on ivory and then filling them with black paint.

Bob's method ran heavily to stippling, of putting a lot of tiny dots on the smooth surface, using very sharp needles, some of which he made himself, since ordinary needles were too dull for the microscrimshanding he liked to do. Bob could put a realistic portrait on a piece of ivory no bigger than a dime, so detailed that you could only see the thing properly under a big magnifying glass or even a stereomicroscope.

There were folks who didn't consider that art, but Toni wasn't among them.

Port Orford, Oregon

Bob had redone his on-line shop in the past year, adding new material. Virtually everything he had produced for the last fifteen years was available for view, since he kept records of it all.

Toni strolled down the wide aisles—floor space was cheap in VR—and looked at the various pieces set out for inspection. She had a more specific reason for dropping by than just checking. John Howard's wife, Nadine, had bought her husband a set of faux-ivory grips for his revolver for his upcoming birthday. The newer versions of that looked so much like elephant ivory it would fool almost everybody, but cost a lot less, and didn't require that Jumbo die for your sins. Nadine had asked Toni if she might be interested in doing some artwork on them. Toni had done a gun butt once, for one of Julio Fernandez's buddies. The friend, an ex-green hat, had a cowboy six-shooter, and Julio had asked her to do something on one panel. She had done a simple design, with a beret over a thin scroll, with the words, "De Oppresso Liber" on the scroll. "To Free the Oppressed." The design and motto were right out of the Special Forces T-shirt catalog, so it hadn't been that hard. She wasn't pleased with the way it had turned out, the lettering wasn't perfect, and the shading was not quite right, though the recipient had seemed happy enough with it. Nadine Howard had something a little more complex in mind, and if Toni was going to do it, she needed some help.

The store had been sorted according to her needs when she logged in, so it was easy to find the pistol grips. There were quite a few of them. There was a nice set given to a retiring sheriff by his friends, his badge and name on them. Some that had fancy lettering and geometric designs. Some with a portrait of a grandchild.

The ones that caught her attention were a set showing the front and back of a nude black woman, who was crouched down in an outdoor courtyard, over what looked like a tile floor, surrounded by Middle Easternlike structures. The detail work was intricate—the columns supporting the arched roof were carved, the balusters, rails, parapets of the building, all were exquisite. A domed roof showed in the distance in the back view. You could see the reflection of the woman's foot on the tile floor. And the nude herself was gorgeous. She had short hair, almost a crew cut, a nose that looked as if it had been broken, and with five-power magnification, you could see that her eyes were light-colored.

She looked familiar.

Bob drifted over. "Hey, Toni," he said. "How's it going?"

"Hey, Bob. I might have some gun grips to do, and I thought I'd come and get some inspiration. This is beautiful work."

"Thanks. That's Dirisha. Look close at the back of her hand, right there."

Toni did. There was what looked like a small square with a tube sticking out of one side, extending out like a finger. She dialed up the magnification to get a better look.

"That's a *spetsdöd*," he said. "A dart gun. She's a character from a science fiction novel; I did this for the writer."

"It's incredible work, Bob."

"Thanks."

"I should live long enough to get this good."

"All it takes is practice, kiddo. If I can do it, anybody can."

"Yeah, right."

"Well, okay, a little talent helps. But mostly it's hard work. Oops, gotta run, customer. See you around, Toni. Let me know if I can help you."

"Thanks, Bob."

She bent to marvel at the gun grips again. Bob did his work under a stereomicroscope, and Alex, bless him, had surprised her with one. Which, as it turned out, was instrumental in solving a case he'd been working on, so it had been a pretty good investment for that alone. But if Toni was going to do work like this, it would take a lot more than a good stereoscope. Whatever Bob had to say about it, it took a lot of talent and patience to produce a work of art so detailed that under twenty-power magnification, you could count every hair on the woman's eyebrows, and not a one was out of place.

Lord.

***On the* Bon Chance**

Jasmine Chance looked at the numbers. New memberships were up, way up, but not nearly at the levels that CyberNation wanted. It had been a good campaign, the combination pushes, but it had pretty much peaked.

She leaned back in the chair and sighed. Well, she'd expected it to come to this. None of the governments they had lobbied were ready to step on board: There hadn't been enough of a public clamor, and that was what it was going to take. Politicians did not venture far from their power bases, everybody knew that, and the way to get legislation passed was to get enough static from the voters so the elected officials knew which way to go. Politicians were, by their natures, followers, not leaders. They reflected public opinion more than they shaped it. That made for more longevity in their jobs, and getting reelected was more important than any single piece of law they might sponsor.

So, it was time to step up things enough so that an outraged public would demand that those people who did their elected bidding got off the stick and fixed things.

Chance and her teams had to give them something to fix. Something it would take them a lot of time and money and effort to make right. And that meant taking down more than computer networks with software. It meant taking down hardware, and whether it was cutting cables or blowing up buildings, whatever it took was whatever it took.

She looked at her watch. Keller's team would need to be told. She'd put in a call to him to let him know the schedule was being moved up again.

Roberto would be tickled. He could cut loose, pull out all the stops, and that's what had always attracted him about this project. That and the money, of course. He liked being with her, no question, but she wasn't foolish enough to believe she came first.

Well. Sometimes she came first . . .

She grinned, and reached for her com. Things were going to get active around here.

25

Joe's Diner
Kansas City, Kansas
June 1955

Joe's Diner was a classic—or it would be, if it survived to the 1980s. Shaped like a fat hot dog bun, the front was glass from waist-height up. Inside, a counter with boomerang patterns on the Formica ran the length of the place, and was utilized by sitting upon bolted-to-the floor chrome-plated stools with red Naugahyde covering the padded tops. Joe's served burgers, fries, and toasted cheese sandwiches for lunch. For dinner, the blue plate special was sliced roast beef and mashed potatoes, both covered with thick gravy, and your choice of a vegetable—as long as it was canned green peas or diced carrots. For breakfast, you could get ham and eggs, bacon and eggs, or sausage and eggs, and they all came with hash browns. If you were looking for health food, you'd starve to death in Joe's, and nobody would feel sorry for you.

Only some kind of commie queer ate nothing but vegetables, and good riddance if he croaked.

Since it was early, Jay was having breakfast, and the light version at that: eggs, sunnyside up, two of them. Four little sausages, Bisquick biscuits drenched in melted butter. Hash brown potatoes in a puddle of warm oil. The heart-attack special they'd have called it in the twenty-first century. Sixty years before, this was what people ate regularly and never thought twice about. And if they wanted cereal to go along with it, they had Frosted Sugar Whatevers with whole milk, and a couple heaping teaspoons of granulated sugar on top of *that*. And nobody here called it White Death.

Jay glanced at his watch and then at the door just as the newspaper guy from the *Kansas City Star* arrived. This was a jaunty-looking bearded fellow wearing a gray fedora, a rumpled white shirt and tie, with a black sport coat slung over his shoulder, Frank Sinatra–style, and carrying a manila folder. Here was Mahler, ace reporter for the *Star*, a metaphor for the information transfer Jay needed.

"Hey, Joe," Mahler said. "Coffee and the Number Three. My Oriental friend here is buying."

Joe, the swarthy, heavy-set counterman in a once-white apron that would need a gallon of bleach and three turns through a washer with new, blue Cheer just to get back to gray, nodded and turned to the kitchen pass-through. He yelled at the cook, "Four-mixed-shredded-fatback-short-dollars-and-burnt!"

Jay translated mentally: *Four scrambled eggs, hash brown potatoes, bacon, a small stack of small pancakes, and white toast, well-done.* Well, just "toast" was enough, since white bread was the only option in this place at this time.

Joe poured a cup of coffee into a heavy china mug and set it down on a saucer in front of Mahler. Some of the thin brew—it looked more like weak tea—slopped into the saucer. Mahler spooned four teaspoons of sugar into the cup, poured a little glass bottle of cream into it, stirred the concoction a couple of times, then sipped at it.

Starbucks would have a field day here.

Amazing they weren't all diabetics, too.

"So, here's your information," Mahler said. He slid the folder across the counter toward Jay.

"Thanks."

"No problem. Anything I can do to keep those Red bastards at bay, you just call."

Jay smiled. The fifties were full of people worrying that the communists would be storming ashore at Palisades Park or Long Beach at any moment. Senator McCarthy had played the country's fears like a rock drummer on crank hammers his skins, at least for a while. And even after HUAC—the House Committee on UnAmerican Activities—finally faded, the Red Scare lingered until the Soviet Union broke up, almost forty years later. For a time, anybody who considered himself a patriot would do anything for any government agency who hinted it would help stem the Red Tide threatening to engulf the world . . .

"Your government thanks you, Mr. Mahler."

Jay opened the folder. Julio Fernandez had been right. He had been able to get to the information legally. It was the long way around, but it was all public information, and if you knew what you were looking for, and you knew how to look for it, it was all there to be had. He scanned the list, nodded at the names, and smiled again. The boss was gonna love this.

Mahler's breakfast arrived, and it was positively psychedelic-looking. Bright yellow scrambled eggs, reddish-brown strips of crisp bacon, a stack of pancakes the diameter of a saucer, piled eight high, and a second plate with four pieces of toast cut in half diagonally, each buttered, with eight more pats of butter in a tiny bowl. Man. Jay had done the research. They really did eat like this. It was a wonder any of them had lived to be thirty.

Net Force HQ
Quantico, Virginia

Michaels was in his office trying to make sense of the new budget sheet his comptrollers had put together when Jay walked in. Nobody knocked around here. What did he have a secretary for? She never even tried to slow Jay down, far as he could tell.

"Check it out, boss." He waved his flatscreen.

"I'm listening."

Jay handed Michaels the flatscreen and flopped onto the couch. "They got a boatload of computer programmers on that ship. Bet your ass that's where the attacks on the web came from."

"And you know this how?"

"Well, I was gonna rascal the personnel files for CyberNation, but Julio talked me out of it. Being as how that would be illegal, immoral, and probably fattening and all. But he got me thinking, and I dug it out using public stuff, perfectly legal."

"Dug what out, exactly."

"Okay, look at the list. What I did was, I borrowed a couple hours on the BFS machine at NSA and ran a bunch of INEST records through them."

Michaels nodded. BFS was the Cray computer nicknamed the Big Fucking Sorter, at the National Security Agency's newly refurbished underground complex outside Fairfax. INEST was the InterNational Education Statistics Terminal mainframe, based in D.C.

"Okay."

"And what I did was, I ran the top two percent of grads from top computer schools in the U.S. and Europe for the last ten years. I found out who they were, then crossed them with public records—drivers' licenses, property taxes, income tax, like that."

"I'm still listening, but I'm getting older here. We getting to a point? I'll stipulate that you are a brilliant fellow."

Jay laughed. "Well, okay. So what it comes down to is a whole bunch of these guys and girls who were the wonder kids of their graduating classes at CIT, MIT, Zurich U, U of Q, and all, seemed to have taken up official residence in Geneva, Switzerland. Doesn't mean they all went to work for CyberNation, of course, but the brightest of that bunch have been spending time and money in Fort Lauderdale, Florida, for the last six months. They went to Switzerland, then to Florida."

"Which means?"

"Guess which gambling ship has half a dozen flights from its deck to Fort Lauderdale each and every day? And records I can access show these folks tend to show up in the same cycle each week. I make that their days off. They live and work on the ship, hop the copter, and fly to town for Saturday R&R."

Michaels nodded. Circumstantial, but a really big coincidence if that's what it was. Occam's razor would slice that one to confetti.

"I can nail it down some more, but I think we've got a nest of programmers and weavers on that ship, and they are taking some trouble to keep it quiet, if not absolutely secret. And of course, the big question is: How come? And I think we all know the answer to that. They've gone over to the dark side."

"Well. I guess we need to find out for sure, don't we?"

Jay shook his head. "Harder to do. We might catch one on the deck webcam or something, but the ship's records aren't going out to the public. I don't think we got enough to get a court order for a search. Not that we could get one anyway. They don't belong to us, and I doubt Libya cares."

Toni appeared at the doorway. "What's up?"

Michaels nodded at Jay, and gave her a quick rundown.

"Good work, Jay," she said. "So what now?"

"Maybe somebody ought to take a trip to the ship and look around," Michaels said.

"All one has to do to get on board is show up at the

heliport and flash a little credit to get a ride out to the floating casino," Jay said. "Most of the patrons come from the U.S. Mainland, a few from Cuba and the other islands."

"You going to ask the FBI to check it out?" Toni asked.

"They don't have any jurisdiction there," Michaels said. "And between you, me, and the hidden microphone in my lamp, I don't trust the CIA as far as I can fly by waving my arms."

"What are you saying here, Alex?"

"It's the dead of winter. A little trip to the Caribbean to gamble and take in the tropical sun would be a nice break, don't you think?"

"Me, me!" Jay said. "I'll do it!"

"Nope," Michaels said. He looked at Toni. "What do you think, Miz Michaels? You up for a little work out of town?"

The look on her face was priceless.

After Jay was gone, Toni said, "You're serious."

"Yes, ma'am. We need to send somebody there to get the lay of the place."

"And you don't want to do it."

"No, my wife would kill me if I went off like that, leaving her at home with a toddler."

"Seriously, Alex. Why me?"

"As I recall, the last time I tried to avoid sending you on an assignment because I was being overly protective, I got my *ass* handed to me. I learned my lesson."

"Really." Her voice was as dry as the Sahara.

"Well, okay, I don't think it is going to be particularly dangerous, if you must know. You aren't going to have to do anything risky, just walk around and get a feel for things, get the routine down. I don't want you skulking into parts of the ship that are off-limits to the public, no trying to swipe computer codes, like that. I'll have Jay come up with some holographs of the programmers he's found, you can study them, so if you happen to see one while you are there, fine, but the main thing is to gather information readily available."

"For . . . ?"

"For when and if we might need it. I don't know exactly where this is going to lead, but let's take a couple of hypotheticals and run with them. Suppose Jay is right. Say that CyberNation is responsible for the attacks on the net. And they are being mounted from this ship in the Caribbean. What can we do about it without proof? They are on the high seas, and our laws don't apply. Sure, we could send a Navy destroyer or missile cruiser down to do a search—assuming we could convince the admiral commanding, Secretary of the Navy, the Joint Chiefs, *and* the president to go for it, not that likely a proposition. If we're wrong, international outcry would blow whoever was responsible—that would be me—right out of a job. Even if we were right, every Third World country on the planet would scream to high heaven about American imperialism and gun-boat diplomacy. The drawback to being a superpower."

" 'O! it is excellent to have a giant's strength, but it is tyrannous to use it like a giant.' "

He looked at her, puzzled.

She grinned. "I've been waiting years for a chance to use that. *Measure for Measure,*" she said. "One of my political professors at NYU was a big fan of Shakespeare; he used to throw quotes at us like peanuts to overfed monkeys—we pretty much ignored them. The only other one I can ever remember came from *Titus Andronicus.* Not much chance to toss that one into a conversation."

"They made a movie of that one, didn't they? All about rape and murder and vengeance? Real upbeat, cheerful stuff."

"Oh, yeah. The line was Aaron's: 'If there be devils, would I were a devil, to live and burn in everlasting fire, so I might have your company in hell, but to torment you with my bitter tongue!' "

"Must have been an interesting character, your teacher."

"Oh, yeah. He went to work for State a few years after I graduated. One of the China hands now, I think."

"Well, I'm impressed with your knowledge of the Classics. You want to go on this trip or not? I'm pretty sure I wouldn't have any trouble finding volunteers if you don't."

"Yeah, I heard Jay."

"Well, I certainly wouldn't force you. It's up to you. But you can't say I didn't offer."

She nodded, and thought about it.

"If we can get enough stuff to be sure CyberNation is the guilty party," Alex said, "and that they are doing it from that ship, then we can maybe do something about it ourselves."

"How do you mean?"

"John Howard's boys and girls are bored, so he tells me."

"The director would kill you."

"Not if we were right. It's within our charter, sort of—at least we won't be sneaking into some foreign country. We have as much right to be out on the ocean as anybody, right?"

"That's real iffy, Alex."

"Not as bad as some we've done and gotten away with. Remember the trips to Grozny? And to Guinea-Bissau?"

"That's how you justify it? Making it the least of several evils?"

"Why not? I remember situational ethics from college, too."

She shook her head.

"Besides, it's all vaporware right now. We don't know for sure that Jay is right. Maybe after we gather a lot of little pieces, we can puzzle it together."

"And you'd really be okay with me going?"

"As your husband and the father of your child, not so much. As your commander, I am more sanguine about it. You are a trained operative, you can take care of yourself, and the level of danger is very low."

"And leave my husband with a toddler?"

"I have Guru to help. And you've been griping about being cooped up in the house or office, worried that you might turn into a woman who talks about baby poop at social gatherings. Go. Take a couple days, lose a few dollars of the government's money in the slot machines, get some midwinter sun—properly skinblocked, of course."

She smiled. "Okay. I'll do it. Thanks, Alex."

"We live to serve. Guess I better give John Howard a call."

"You're sending him, too?"

"No, but he might want to start thinking about ways to sneak onto a ship in the middle of the ocean."

On the Bon Chance

In the lowest hold behind locked and guarded doors were the EMP bombs. They wore wooden frames, made from two-by-four fir boards, and sat on big pallets, also made of wood. They smelled faintly of something spicy, and that and a seawater-and-oil odor drifted about in the damp hold. Santos knew vaguely how they worked, these devices, but they were not his thing.

He had made the mistake of asking. The explosives expert practically peed himself as he talked happily about overlapping radiation pattern lobes and capacitors, coaxial this and coaxial that, of hardened components and planes of radiation.

Santos listened with half an ear, nodded, and murmured from time to time, so that the bomb man believed, perhaps, that he had some idea of what the man was talking about.

"We're talking fifteen, twenty megajoules in ten-hundredths of a microsecond," the man said, his face ecstatic with pleasure at having an audience.

The man pointed at the nearest bomb, which looked to

Santos like nothing so much as a torpedo in an old submarine movie. A little smaller and thinner, maybe. More pointed.

"This particular model uses PBX-9501. The armature is surrounded by a coil of heavy-gauge aluminum wire, that's the FCG stator. The winding splits into halves, to increase induction. It's cased in a heavy block of tightly wound Kevlar and carbon fiber, so it doesn't blow apart before it generates the field—"

A bomb that didn't blow things up. How odd.

Well, yes, it did explode and destroy itself, but its primary purpose was to fry sensitive components with a powerful electromagnetic pulse generated by the explosion. Very complicated. It seemed easier to him just to drop a blockbuster on the target and take it all out, but apparently magnetic radiation could go through concrete better than explosives, and besides, they didn't want to lose the infrastructure altogether, they would need it themselves later.

Like a biological weapon that killed people, but left the buildings standing, an EMP bomb was designed to kill computers, but allow the people to remain. A bloodless weapon.

"Not as good as the Vircators," the bomb man continued, "which are electron beam/anode devices that will vibrate at microwave frequencies. They can get forty gigs out of this design in the lab, but they are heavy and much more complicated—"

It was all just so much useless technical babble to Santos, who cared only that these giant finned silver turds would blow up when and where they were supposed to blow up, and do the job they were intended to do.

These looked big and heavy, but the bomb man had assured him they could be easily transported by common aircraft. Even though they had come via supply ship, they could, in fact, be carried on one of the big passenger helicopters, no problem. Each one only weighed as much as, say, four or five big men, and on a craft that could carry thirty or forty people, half a dozen of these devices would ride quite nicely.

The bomb man started off on some new techno-rant, but Santos waved him quiet. "Yes, I understand," he said, lying through his smile. "I need merely be certain you understand where and when they must be delivered."

"Oh, yes, I know."

"Good. Attend to that. I will check back with you as we go."

Santos strode away, his footsteps upon the steel grating echoing slightly in the warm, dank hold. You'd think it would be cooler down here, right next to the water and all, but it was not.

Timing on all this would be critical. His part was easy enough to accomplish, but a failure on the parts of others could be fatal to the mission. They had only a week, and everything must be in place and synchronized exactly by then. It was not much time when you had to deploy men, transfer bombs, and make certain you know exactly where and how to strike each target. But, it was what it was, and he was happier to be going into the field than sitting around waiting.

Moving was better than waiting, almost always. Once you got moving, to hesitate at the wrong moment, to look away from the goal, that could get you killed. Yes, you had to plan in advance, know your tactics so that you did not make a stupid mistake, but once you started rolling, hesitation was a killer. The man who blinked first lost. And that would not be him.

26

Crawfish Point
Galveston, Texas
October 1957

It was raining hard. There was a tropical storm offshore, maybe a hurricane, still far enough away so it wasn't any real danger to the state yet, but close enough to bring lots of rain and choppy seas in the Gulf. Yet, there Gridley came, in an old-fashioned wooden shrimping boat, arrogant as always, secure in the knowledge that he was invincible.

Lack of confidence had never been one of Jay's problems.

Keller, wearing a black slicker and hiding in a mangrove tangle at the edge of the estuary, with a scoped 30–30 Winchester deer rifle, watched Gridley maneuver the boat through the shallow water as he headed for the Gulf, checking for roots or half-submerged logs he might hit with the boat's propeller. Or did they call them "screws" on boats this size?

Once again, the scenario was over the top, much more

than necessary to troll for the kind of information Jay wanted. The man never let one simple vision serve when he could do nine visions complicated. And even the public scenarios he chose were major sensory sims, like that stupid climb up Mount Fuji. Please.

Keller grinned at that memory. That had shaken old Jay up some, when he'd gone over in persona and sat down right next to him. Old Jay hadn't expected *that*.

When the boat got within range, Keller laid the rifle's forestock on a gnarl of root and aimed. The rain slashed down hard, the wind blew, and the scope was wet and blurry. The trawler was bouncing up and down on the rough water, and enough of it was sloshing up through the mangrove roots to keep Keller soaked, despite the raincoat. It wasn't an easy shot.

He managed to put the first round into the wheelhouse side window, shattering it, but missing Jay by a good foot. He worked the bolt and fired again, aiming at the hull just below the normal waterline when the boat came up on a wave. He ejected the empty shell and chambered a third round, which he fired at the life preserver hung next to the wheelhouse. Must have missed that completely, he didn't see it hit.

The boat chugged on, no sign of Jay, who must be ducked down inside the wheelhouse, wondering what the hell was going on.

Enough. He had other business to which he needed to attend. This was fun, pulling Gridley's chain, but Omega was coming, and they had less than a week to get ready. Not nearly enough time. He was going to have to let this go. Too bad.

In this scenario, which was Jay's, Keller had a small boat hidden behind the mangrove island in the swamp flats just short of the Gulf where some nameless river emptied into it. Probably it had a name, come to think of it, since Gridley did stuff like that.

Keller dropped the rifle, for which he had no further use, and worked his way to his boat. Might as well check things out as he left. Gridley wouldn't have come here if he hadn't been looking for something in particular, and maybe Keller could spot it.

He reached the boat, and started to untie the line that kept the craft from drifting away. When he did, a monstrous figure rose from the water like the creature from the Black Lagoon.

Keller froze.

The monster said, "Surprise!" and Keller realized it was a man in scuba gear and a wetsuit. Behind the face mask, he recognized Gridley's basic persona, which looked pretty much like the real man.

Gridley had a big knife in his hand. He smiled and moved awkwardly toward Keller, his flippers slapping the water noisily—

Keller bailed.

CyberNation Train
Baden-Baden, Germany

Keller came out of the scenario cursing. Dammit! He had underestimated Gridley again! He should have known better! He threw the wireless sensory gear down hard, and regretted that instantly. These headsets weren't cheap. If he broke it, the replacement would come out of his budget.

He picked up the set, touched the test button. The diodes lit up green, one after another.

Thank God for small miracles. He put the set down more carefully, hanging it on its rack.

Overconfidence had been the downfall of a whole lot of programmers, and he had seen it happen enough to know nobody was immune, even him. Gridley might have opted for the status quo, turned into a fedhead, fat and happy, but he still had some moves. Keller was better than they'd been in college, but it wasn't smart to think that the Old Thai had stayed where he'd been. He was, after all, the head of Net Force's computer operation. He might not be as good as Keller was, but he wasn't a total lube-foot, either.

It was too bad he didn't have time to call Jay out for a full wrangle. To make it a one-on-one, no-holds-barred. To show Jay who was better now.

Well. There was no help for it. And no real harm done. Keller's net persona was a mule, a Joe-average construct that didn't look like anybody in particular, certainly not his real self. Even if Gridley had seen him, he hadn't seen anybody he could put a face to.

And even if he had known who it was, well, so what? Knowing who and figuring out where he was, finding him and doing anything about it before Omega launched wasn't going to happen. And afterward? Jay wouldn't be able to do much to him then, either.

The train was moving. That very morning it had left the siding where it had been for days, and was now only a couple hundred kilometers northeast of Dijon, France. It would arrive at the border shortly, where it would turn around and head back toward Berlin. The powers that were in CyberNation did not want their three mobile centers anywhere near their headquarters in Geneva. The ship was in the Caribbean, the train went back and forth between Berlin and the French border, mostly, half-loaded with tourists who knew nothing of the high-tech gear on board the other half. The third station was on a barge ostensibly being rebuilt at a shipyard in Yokohama, Japan, though it could be hauled off at any time. If the German authorities being paid to ignore the train developed pangs of conscience, or if the Japanese harbor officials who were bribed not to worry themselves overmuch about the repairs on the barge suddenly went mad, the ship was the safety, the most secure backup. If something happened to the train or the barge, or both, the ship would be the base nobody could legally touch. But any one of them was enough by itself to get the job done. All three were similarly equipped, and what one did was quickly uploaded to the others, so that at any given moment the lead team was never more than a few hours ahead of the others. Major data transfers were done four times a day in all directions, so if the train or boat or barge was suddenly hit by a giant meteor, there wouldn't be more than six joint hours of work lost to the remaining two centers.

It was a good system. Not Keller's design, but good, nonetheless.

Well. As much as he'd like to square off with Gridley and kick his ass, he had to get on with it. Omega was coming, and his group wasn't going to be caught short. Maybe after it all came down he'd go find Jay and show him up, but that would just have to wait.

Washington, D.C.
The Zoo

Jay and Saji walked along, looking at the tiger cage. It was cold enough so the big cats were inside their heated enclosure. A lot of the less furry animals seemed to be. For a long time after he had been mauled in VR by such a creature, it had been all Jay could do to look at the tigers. Now, he made a point to stop by the zoo every so often to remind himself.

He was only paying half his attention to the walk though, and, of course, Saji noticed.

"Where are you?" she said. "Not here."

"Oh. Sorry. I was thinking about the fishing boat scenario. I think I know who the shooter was."

"Really? How so?"

"Well, when I ran the lists of the best computer programmers graduated in the last ten years, I came up with quite a few I knew. Me, for one. A lot of guys I went to school with at CIT, others I knew from the net and web, conferences, like that. Some of them I've kept in touch with, others kinda drifted away, so I tried to run down some of the guys I used to pal around with that I haven't seen in years."

They passed the brown bear compound. The bears weren't around. Hibernating maybe?

"Yes," she said. "And . . . ?"

"A couple have died. One in a car wreck, one from cancer. Most of the rest of them went into the field and have done pretty well. A few dot-biz millionaires, some commercial software producers. Some got out of the field, went to work in other areas. One woman I knew who was an ace programmer opened a chain of daycare centers for school kids. One guy writes comic books and TV shows. A few did well enough to quit work and live in Hawaii or somewhere. A couple dropped out completely to raise organic carrots or whatever on dinky farms in Footlick, Missouri, or like that."

"Yes. And . . . ?"

"Two are missing. No record of them. Didn't die, didn't get married or change their names, just dropped off the face of the Earth. One of them was a weirdo we all expected would go ballistic one day and assassinate somebody. The other was one of my best friends, a guy named Jackson Keller. We exchanged a couple of Christmas cards after school, and then lost track of each other."

"I see."

"The thing is, I can't imagine he would drop out of the biz. He was gung ho, like most of us. I figured they'd have to haul his body away from the console if he died. But there's no sign of him anywhere from about three years after we graduated. Poof."

The insect house was not far ahead. It was always warm in there, if kind of humid, but it was getting chilly, and Jay nodded at it. "Let's go look at the bugs."

Inside, small children darted from window to window, looking at giant cockroaches, horned beetles, and all kinds of scorpions from around the world. It felt like a jungle, warm and damp, though the lights were fairly dim.

"So you think maybe this weirdo is somehow part of things?"

He shook his head. "No. I think it's the other one—my old buddy Keller."

She looked at an albino beetle the size of a mouse as it lumbered over a floor of fine-grained sand. "What makes you think that?"

"A couple things. The weirdo—his name was Zimmerman—never had the chops to make me look bad in VR. Keller wasn't quite as good as I was, but he coulda gotten better. And I've been thinking about that climb up Fujiyama. When the old Thai guy came and sat next to me. That's what Keller used to call me, back in college. Jay, the Old Thai. He was a year or two younger than most of us, a child prodigy who finished high school at fifteen."

"You think the VR construct was a hint?"

"I think so, yeah. And you know what it really feels like? It feels personal. Like this guy knows me, wants to screw me up. And his stuff is like the stuff Keller used to do—he was always big on ambushes. He used to say if you are going to duel with somebody, shoot 'em in the back before they see you coming, it'll save you a lot of grief. Their fault if they weren't paying attention."

"Huh," she said.

" 'Huh?' That's the best you can do?"

"What do you want me to say? Yes, you must be right, you brilliant stud!"

He grinned. "That would be okay, I like the sound of that."

She grinned back at him. "I bet." She looked back at the beetle. "So, if this is true, how do you find out for sure? And then what?"

"Well, to start, I can dig deeper in public records, see if I can find Keller anywhere. Maybe I'm imagining it, maybe he's got a job in Silicon Valley somewhere running some company and I missed him."

"Maybe he changed his name," she said.

"Why would he do that?"

"For all your smarts, you sometimes miss the easy stuff, Jay. What if he got into debt? Maybe some kind of white-collar crime? Needed a fresh start. Or just went bonkers and decided to start calling himself 'Ra, God of the Sun.' "

Jay watched the bug in the glass case going about its business. It had found something in the sand and was digging it up. Jay halfway expected to see the insect unearth a tiny human skull. "I don't think so. If he had, there'd be some record of it under his old name. First things I checked were criminal records, B&D stats, and Deja, and he was active on the net until about five years ago. After that, he's just gone. You'd think somebody who was planning on leaving would say good-bye—he was on a lot of newsgroups and professional pub pages, then he stopped posting. I had a searchbot scan all his postings: There's no mention of being in trouble with the law, or in debt, or wanting to change his name. One minute he was there, the next, he was gone."

"Black helicopters got him?" she said.

Jay smiled. "Uh-huh. Don't forget, I know where those guys hang out."

The beetle came up with something that looked like a little ball made out of Tootsie Roll, and proceeded to roll it across the stand toward a far corner of the cage.

"All right, then," she said. "Hunt him down and find out what he's been up to."

Jay nodded. Yes.

27

Washington, D.C.

The ceremony was outside, a bright June afternoon. A sea of graduates in blue caps and gowns sat in folding chairs in front of a raised platform. On the stage, a speaker called out names, and students walked across the stand to collect their diplomas. Most of the students looked happy as they accepted their sheepskins and shook hands with the principal. A couple of the boys mugged and did silly waves. One boy flashed the crowd, showing off jockey undershorts. A typical high school graduation, "Pomp and Circumstance" playing in the background, the proud parents smiling, crying, fanning themselves with programs, watching their progeny morph from children to semi-adults.

Later, a tall blonde girl stood with her arms around two of her girlfriends while her parents, then the parents of her friends took pictures.

As the festivities wound down, students hugging each other, slapping each other on the back, punching shoulders, a father and son walked side by side toward the parking lot. The family resemblance was strong, the boy a younger copy of his father. The father stopped walking and said, "Here, son."

The boy took a small plastic card from his father, looked at it, then back at his dad.

"Your first year of membership in CyberNation," his father said. He was blinking back tears.

The son looked amazed. "But—but you think this is stupid!" He waved the card a little.

"Times change, son. People change, too—they have to, or they miss what's important in life."

The boy looked at the card.

"Your mother would have been so proud."

Behind them, a woman—the spirit of the boy's mother—shimmered and appeared ghostlike into view. The father and son looked at the spirit, who smiled at them.

With the spirit of the wife and mother watching, the boy and his father embraced.

"CyberNation," said the deep voice. "It's today, it's tomorrow. It's forever."

A small graphic appeared under the father and son, and in small print the words CYBERNATION appeared.

Michaels pointed the remote at the television in disgust and clicked the set off. "Have you seen this? A three-hanky commercial for an *Internet* service."

Toni came out of the bathroom with the electric toothbrush in her mouth. "What?"

Michaels waved at the television. "The CyberNation ad."

She held up a hand, a "wait a second" gesture, then went back into the bathroom. A moment later, she was back. "Let me go check on the baby," she said.

"Already did. He's sleeping like a rock."

She moved to the bed and sat. "You were saying something about the TV?"

"Yeah, the CyberNation tear-jerker commercial."

"Which one? The old lady abandoned in the nursing home by her children? Or the young guy talking to his wife's tombstone?"

"The high school graduation."

"Oh, that one."

"These guys put Coca-Cola, the phone and insurance companies into the minor leagues. Most manipulative thing I've ever seen."

"Wait until you see the thirteen-year-old girl orphan on the street and the cop who comes to help her," she said. "Equal parts of pathos and pedophilia."

He shook his head. "Don't they have any shame?"

"Not if they sell the product."

He shook his head again.

"So, have you thought any more about what we talked about? Guru?"

"You really want to do this?"

She nodded. "Yes. She's as much my grandma as anybody. Every day from the time I was thirteen until I went off to college, I spent two hours with her. Sometimes at her house, sometimes on the steps out front, sometimes in the park. Rain or shine, whatever else was going on, she was there for me. She gave me a skill that's the core of who I am. Whatever else happened to me, I was always sure I could take care of myself if somebody wanted to put his hands on me and I didn't want him to. It was the basis of making my way in the world. If all else failed, I could kick somebody's butt. I didn't have to be afraid."

He smiled at her.

"She's useful here. Little Alex loves her. I love her. And I owe her. For so much. She's eighty-five, she won't be around much longer."

He chuckled. "She'll probably outlive us all."

"Alex—"

"Okay. If you really want this, then, yeah, okay. Ask her."

"You sure?"

"What I'm sure of is that I want you to be happy. Whatever it is. If that means having a coffee-swilling deadly old nanny living in the guest bedroom, what the hell."

He didn't think he'd ever seen her smile any bigger. She hugged him, and once again he marveled at how good that made him feel, to make her smile.

What was it Jay's girl Saji had said recently? Making somebody smile lightens your karmic burden? Well, if that was the case, he intended to be karmically clear on Toni's grins alone, if he could.

CyberNation Train
Kassel, Germany

The train was stopped, some kind of mechanical problem, just outside Kassel, still three hundred or so kilometers southwest of Berlin. Some of the team had taken the opportunity to get off and stretch their legs, but Keller saw no reason to do so. He had never been a fan of outside. When you could go anywhere in time or space in VR, could control the weather, the smells, the action, why would you bother tromping around in the cold and dark next to a train track in the middle of nowhere? Where you had no control at all, save that of your own body's ability to come or go? That's what the Luddites didn't understand, that virtual reality was so much better than the real world because you could make it do exactly what you wanted it to do. No wild cards, no chance that you would be caught in an unexpected snowstorm, or bitten by a mosquito chock full of malaria. In VR, life was what you wanted it to be.

This was the real reason that CyberNation would succeed, more than anything. As VR became more and more like RW, the ability to have anything you wanted, to see, hear, taste, touch, smell, and feel it exactly as you wished it to be, that was heaven. Give the people what they want. Build a better mousetrap, and the world will beat a path to your door. That was always how it had been, and that was how it was going to continue to be.

There were some things you still had to do. Serious VR players, really serious ones, could hook up IVs and catheters so they could stay jacked in for days, not having to eat or pee. Keller had done that a few times, been in VR for forty, fifty hours, even sleeping on-line, being fed dreams by programs that knew how to input them. Usually, however, he had to interface with the real world often enough so he couldn't do that. Just like now, he had to go pee. It was a bother, but there was no help for it without a Foley running through your dick into your bladder.

He went to the toilet, which on this old-style car was a pretty big place—five stalls, five urinals, a tile floor, mirrors, sinks, the whole enchilada. Normally, they closed the toilets when the train was in the station, because when you flushed the toilet, a hole opened in the bottom and it fell right out onto the tracks. There were laws against that now in a lot of places, but people who ran private trains didn't pay attention to them. Who was going to follow a train across the country looking to see if it was dropping turds and piss onto the tracks out in the middle of nowhere?

He stood in front of the urinal for what seemed like a long time, emptying his bladder, zipped up, and started to wash his hands.

"Hello, Jackson" came a voice from behind him.

Keller froze, as if he had seen Medusa and turned to stone.

Smiling behind him, reflected in the mirror, was Roberto Santos.

Keller forgot how to breathe. He managed to manufacture a grin that felt like a rictus. "Roberto. Wh-what are you doing here? Something wr-wrong?"

Santos moved to the door. Locked it.

Keller's heart turned to a block of dry ice. His mouth went dry.

"Nothing wrong, Jackson. Just balancing things out."

"Wh-Wh-Whuh—?"

"You touched my woman. You knew she was mine, and you went with her. Missy is fine, she is hot. I know it was her idea, making the two-backed beast, I know how she is. Woman's got tricks that would make a plaster saint hard. I know turning her down is not easy. But she was mine. She still is, until I say otherwise."

"Listen, Santos, it was a mistake, a mistake, I'm sorry, I really am, I'm sorry, what can I do to make it up to you?"

Santos smiled. "Don't worry so much, Jackson. I'm not gonna kill you. It won't even show. But you got a debt; it has to be paid."

"Santos, don't! You don't want to do this! Jasmine will fire you!"

"No, she won't. Because you won't tell her."

"I will! I will!"

"No," he said, "you won't. And you know why? Because if she fires me, I will come back and kill you. But only after a long, long time of you wishing you were dead. You understand?"

Keller's fear gripped him so hard he started to shake.

Santos moved—so fast! and hit him, just under his sternum.

He . . . couldn't . . . get . . . any . . . air—!

Santos smiled. A man enjoying himself.

As Keller tried to get his wind back, Santos hit him again.

It hurt so bad—!

The rental car was cold when Santos started it, and it took the heater a while to warm things up. He hated the cold. Even in a jacket, with gloves and a hat, he felt the chill trying to get to him. Yes, they had winter at home, but it was the kind of winter where you could walk around in a T-shirt and shorts. In June, when it was the coldest, it dropped to maybe sixty, sixty-five most nights. Mean temperature year round was seventy-something. It got hot sometimes—now, in the summer, you could work up a sweat; it actually got cold sometimes, but rarely. Those were not the normal things. In Rio, the temperature was almost always perfect. It was God's country, and men who lived there were fortunate above other men.

Here and now, there was ice in the ponds and lakes, and patches of snow in the shadows, with more to come. How could people live in such places?

Well. They were Germans, weren't they? And all Germans were at least slightly mad.

The plane he was going to catch was at a private airport about thirty miles away. From there, he would fly to a big airport in Berlin, and from there, back to the U.S. He was supposedly making sure that preparations for the big attack were in order, and in a way, he was. He had already talked to people he needed to talk to, and he would see others. Missy wasn't expecting him back for a couple of days.

Putting fear into Keller was part of the preparations as far as he was concerned.

He smiled at the memory of Keller, lying curled like a newborn on the floor in the train's washroom, a pool of yellow vomit next to him. He hadn't really hurt the man, nothing permanent. Never hit him in the face. He would be sore tomorrow, belly, ribs, back, thighs, and he would bruise some, but nothing that would show when he was dressed. He was a flower-picker, Jackson was, his ping-pongs the size of BBs, more girl than man. It hadn't been particularly satisfying to beat him, like slapping a child. He had offered no resistance, but it had to be that way. There were things that a man had to do if he was going to remain a man and not turn into an old woman.

He hadn't decided yet how he was going to punish Missy, but he was smart enough to know he needed to wait until the attack was finished. There would be a bonus for successful completion, a big bonus, enough so he could walk away if he really wanted to do that. At the very least, he had to wait until that money was converted into gold and on its way home. It would not be quite as much as he wanted, but it would do. A man like him could always find more work if he had to find it.

The heater had finally begun to unfog the windows and offer enough warmth so he didn't have to tense against the cold. Better. Not good, but better.

Keller would say nothing to Missy. If he knew anything, Santos knew when a man would stand and fight, and Keller was not such a man. Missy was more dangerous. She could put a knife between your ribs if you pissed her off bad enough and closed your eyes at the wrong time. That was part of what he liked about her. She was soft where it counted, she could wring a man dry of his essential juices, but she was also hard in her mind. He would punish her, he had to, but it must be in such a way that she could not revenge herself upon him.

He might even have to kill her. A shame, but sometimes, that's what you had to do. People died every day. That was how life was: You came into the world, you lived your time, you left. All that mattered in between the coming and the going was how you spent your time. And for Santos, that and *O-Jôgo*—The Game.

All else was no more than a shrug.

28

Washington, D.C.

The lobbyist's name was Corinna Skye. She was a drop-dead gorgeous natural blonde who looked five years younger than her thirty-five years. She was tall, slim, busty, and was a six-handicap golfer. She wore a charcoal-gray power suit, the skirt cut just short enough to show she had great legs without being titillating, a white silk blouse, and a dark red scarf. Her shoes were dark gray handmade Italian leather, one-inch heels, five hundred dollars a pair. She was smart, funny, and while many in political circles considered all lobbyists high-priced whores, she had never slept with a senator or congressman, though many of them had tried to make that happen. She had graduated first in her class at Columbia in political science, and was considered the best lobbyist on Internet issues in the country.

Chance sat across the table from Skye in the booth at Umberto's. The salad had been perfect, and the handmade fresh pasta was outstanding—Chance had gotten the bay shrimp in heavy cream and would have to pay for it on the stairclimber later, but it had been worth it.

"With Wayne DeWitt's unfortunate accident—a terrible tragedy—things'll be easier on the senatorial side," Skye said. She didn't know that DeWitt's injuries had been on Chance's orders; she wasn't in that loop.

She continued: "We've gone to a full-press in the House. Congressman Kinsey Walker—he's a D from California—will offer his bill on Monday. We have the votes to get it out of committee, though we're still eight shy for passage in the House—but we'll get those."

"Assuming it passes in the House and Senate," Chance said, "what are the chances of a presidential veto?"

"Ordinarily, I'd say it would be nailed, at the very least pocketed. But the administration has a couple of pet projects on the table, the National Parks bill and the new medicare thing, and they'd sell their wives and mothers to a Turkish dope dealer to get either of those passed. We have some votes to trade. More than enough."

"Good."

The waiter came by. Would the ladies care for dessert and coffee?

Just coffee, they both said.

"You do realize that this bill is not what we'd hoped for," Skye said. "It's about half-strength."

Chance nodded. "Yes. But it's a start. Once this is established, then it's like new taxes, it won't go away, and we can strengthen it next session. The first part of making an omelet is to collect some eggs."

Both of them smiled, women of the world.

As they sipped their coffee, Chance reflected that in another life, she might have been friends with Skye. She preferred the company of men most of the time, men were so much easier to manipulate, but there were occasions when sitting somewhere and talking to a bright woman was more relaxing. True, there was always a certain amount of competition, even with women, but as long as there were no men around to control, girl talk could be a breath of fresh air. Testosterone did get overwhelming at times.

Take 'Berto, for instance. He was a man's man, willing to buy a drink and slap a back in fellowship, or, at the drop of a hat, kick in his drinking buddy's teeth. No complexity about him, no convoluted layers to his thoughts, he had simple wants and needs. For him, life was one giant game of king-of-the-hill. As one of her yoga teachers would have said, 'Berto lived in his lower *chakras*, the belly and the phallus, and had yet to realize his higher potentials. The yoga teacher would have earnestly believed that 'Berto had higher potentials. Chance knew better. 'Berto had three things driving him: fighting, sex, and good food, that was it—

"I've seen the latest TV spots," Skye said, interrupting her internal musings.

"What did you think?"

Skye chuckled. "The people who make Kleenex must love you. Even Kodak hasn't got anything so soppy."

"Subscriptions are up twelve percent since we started running the new series."

Skye wiped a bit of lipstick from her coffee cup with a napkin. "Doesn't surprise me. I'd expect them to be effective. Subtle doesn't work for television viewers. Lowest common denominator and all. Speaking of which, I know a woman who slept with one of those basketball players."

Chance raised an eyebrow.

"Hung to here," she said, slapping the inside of her left knee. "And she says they must make Viagra out of his blood."

They both laughed.

Chance nodded. Yes, a smart woman was a great break from mule-headed men. She glanced at her watch. "Well. I need to run along. It's been great visiting with you, Cory."

"As always. I'll call you with updates."

"I appreciate it."

Chance waved the waiter over and paid the bill, and Skye merely nodded her thanks. Another thing a man would quibble over. Skye cleared half a million a year, easy, and she wasn't going to make noise over a little hundred-dollar lunch tab, one way or the other.

As she left the restaurant, Chance looked around. Washington was a dreary city in the winter. It was beautiful in the spring, all the flowering fruit trees, but when the gray and cold settled in, all the marble and wide streets couldn't offset the gloom. She had a couple of other errands to run, including a visit to a key senator. While Cory Skye was scrupulous in her personal life, Chance would use any weapon she had to win a contest. If that meant screwing a middle-aged married senator stupid—which was no great chore, given the starting point of his IQ—she had no problem with that. Whatever worked.

Toni was excited. It had been some time since she had been in the field, back when she and Alex had had their troubles on that trip to England. She smiled at the memory, which was bittersweet. Such heartache they'd gone through, for what was basically a stupid mistake, on both their parts. More his than hers, but, she had to admit, she had jumped to a conclusion she shouldn't have.

She had packed for warm weather, one bag she could fit into the overhead bin on the jet. She was only going for a couple of days, and she had had enough bad experiences with checked baggage to last a lifetime. Once, on a flight to Hawaii, her suitcase had vacationed in Japan.

Documents had provided her with a new ID—driver's license, credit cards, even a library card, no passport needed—that showed she was Mary Johnson, a divorced secretary from Falls Church, Virginia. She was on holiday, going to play the slot machines and soak up the sunshine in the warm Caribbean. She had her flight booked, along with a single cabin on the *Bon Chance*. It was enough cover to check out the ship, she'd be in and out, and nobody would be the wiser.

"You still packing, girl?" Guru said. She came into the bedroom, Little Alex slung over her right hip.

"Guru, I don't know how you expect him to practice walking if you never put him down."

Guru smiled and bounced the baby on her hip a couple of times. He laughed.

"Don't you worry about him learning to walk. Pretty soon, I start teaching him *djurus*. Time you get back, he'll be a fighter."

"I'm only going to be gone three days."

"Plenty of time, eh, best boy?"

Little Alex laughed again.

"You sure this is all right?"

Guru shook her head. "Child, I raised a houseful of babies. This little one is an angel compared to a couple of my boys. We'll be fine. And we'll watch out for big Alex, too."

Toni nodded. Guru had recovered from her stroke all right, but she was in her eighties. Then again, her mind was still sharp, and the years of *silat* practice had given her a balance most people didn't have in their thirties. Little Alex couldn't be safer, and anybody who thought the old lady pushing the baby stroller was a victim would learn a hard lesson otherwise. It was just so strange to be catching a jet and flying off on her own. It felt . . . weird, somehow. That kind of thing belonged to her life before Alex and the baby.

"Go, I think I heard the cab honking," Guru said.

Toni took Alex and hugged him. "You be good for Guru," she said. She kissed him, and felt a pang of something like loss when she handed him back to the old woman, and hugged her in the transfer.

Once she was in the cab, Toni found she had to force herself to breathe slower. Her belly roiled with nervousness. An adventure. She was going on an adventure.

On the CyberNation Train
Outside Berlin, Germany

Keller ached all over. He had taken half a dozen ibuprofen tablets, and they had taken the edge off, but every move, every breath, hurt. He had never felt like this. Once, when he was fourteen, his mother had run a stop sign and their car had been broadsided by another driver. He had wrenched his shoulder and elbow, banged his head against the glass, and had a sore spot on his hip, and he'd thought that was bad, but that was nothing compared to this. Yet, when he looked into the mirror, there was almost no sign of the beating Santos had given him—he had some bruises on his chest, his belly, his legs and back, but they didn't look nearly as bad as they felt. They were just light brown splotches, a little purple in a couple of them. How could it hurt so bad and not look worse than it did?

Santos was a devil, a monster, a psychotic thug! He should get a gun and shoot him!

But even as he dressed, trying to avoid moving as much as he could—he had to sit down to put his trousers on—Keller knew he would not do that. Even with a gun, he was afraid of Santos. If he missed, if the man didn't die immediately, he would come for Keller, and that would be that. The man would kill him, slowly and painfully. And pain was not something that Keller wanted any more of, ever.

I-5, South of Sacramento, California
August

Jay wound the RT/10 Viper up into fifth gear and blew past the guy in the Shelby GT at ninety-five. In a few seconds, he was doing a hundred and fifteen, eating up the highway, speed still climbing. This stretch of road was straight as an arrow and in the middle of the desert, nothing to see, and even at this clip, he wasn't gonna get through it any time soon.

He shifted into sixth, and the little car had enough to surge when he did. Who's your daddy, baby? Huh?

The guy in the Mustang must have stepped on it, Jay could see him in the rearview, starting to gain. Jay laughed. The Shelby was fast, maybe even faster than he was on the top end, but he had a mile and some on the guy by now, and by the time the Mustang wound it up and pegged the speedometer, Jay would be at the exit to the olive place and the race would be over.

The olive place was where he was meeting his contact in this scenario, and he was being nothing if not careful this time. He came in with an anonymous persona, a female one at that, under a phony name and addy, and anybody looking for Jay Gridley wasn't gonna see that guy in this car. It would be almost impossible to figure out who he really was, and even if he went places where traps had been set for Jay—which he didn't plan on doing, thank you very much—he was going to make it look like he—or she, in this case—had wandered in there by accident.

There was the exit. The Shelby GT was coming up fast, but not fast enough. Jay put on his blinker and was off the interstate and down to sixty before the Mustang roared past. He heard the man in the car yell at him, and shook his head. Why, none of it—he'd never had that kind of relationship with his mother. The very idea!

The Viper burbled and rumbled, as if anxious to get back up to speed, but Jay nosed it into the olive place's parking lot, a big graveled area that had to run three acres, and parked.

The desert heat beat down on him in the little convertible, and he felt it much more without the wind, hot as that was.

He tossed his long blonde hair back over his shoulder, adjusted his boobs with the backs of his hands, and walked toward the building, the red miniskirt barely covering a very shapely female ass.

Inside, he slipped his shades off and into his purse. There were racks of olives in various jars, ranging from drinking-glass-sized ones to convoluted monsters five feet tall. Mostly they were big, fat green things, pits still in them, but here and there were some stuffed with pimento, and even some black ones that had been pitted.

There were also bottles and tins of olive oil, ranging from cold-pressed extra virgin or somesuch on down. How could oil be better than virgin?

An old lady with a big straw hat and a matching handbag cruised the aisle, her shopping cart half full of jars and cans. She smiled at Jay's young woman persona, and Jay saw the white rose pinned to her yellow sundress that told him this was who he had come to meet.

"Hot day out," Jay said.

"Yes, isn't it? Nice and cool in here, though."

"I wonder, have you seen any Tuscan bread?" This was the code phrase, in actuality, a key to a firewall's back door.

"Funny you should mention that, dearie," the old lady said. "I had picked up two loaves of that very thing, but I realize now I should put one back, one is more than enough for just me, since the mister passed on. Here, why don't you take it? Save an old lady a trip?"

"Why, thank you, ma'am. That's very nice of you."

"No trouble at all, dearie."

The old lady pushed her cart away. Something was stuck to one of the rear wheels, it bumped slightly every time it hit the floor. How annoying. Jay always got that cart when he went grocery shopping.

Jay went to pay for the loaf of bread.

Outside, he opened the packed, removed the bread, and broke it in half. Inside the bread was a mini DVD, the size of a half-dollar coin. Rainbow colors sparkled from its surface in the hot sun. Jay smiled. Easy as falling off a chair.

He hiked his blonde's short skirt up to climb back into the low-slung Viper, and accidentally flashed a man in a Cadillac who pulled into the lot as he hopped into the car. Oops.

But he had half of what he had come for. Another stop a bit farther south, and with any luck, he would have it all. Half the trick to finding information on the web and net was knowing how to look. It was all out there, but if you couldn't narrow your search properly, you'd never find it. After years of practice, Jay knew how to look: It had become almost instinctive, more an art than a science. Yeah, you could turn searchbots loose hither and yon and gather up tons of data, but sometimes you just knew where to go, without knowing how or why you knew. That was zen, Saji said. Knowing without knowing.

Whatever. As long as he could do it. And he could. A few more minutes and he would be ready to start kicking ass and taking names, and he would start with his old buddy Jackson Keller. Because if Keller was in some way responsible for the attacks on the net and web, and more important, if he was responsible for the attacks on Jay personally, then he was gonna be extremely sorry. You don't step on Superman's cape, and you don't mess with Smokin' Jay Gridley. No siree.

29

Washington, D.C.

The baby was asleep, as was Guru, and Michaels was propped up in bed, watching the news when the com chimed. He reached for it, thinking it was Toni.

"Hey, boss." The visual blossomed on the receiver, a tiny hologram of a face that definitely wasn't Toni's.

"Jay. What's up?"

"I've got good news, better news, and not so good news."

"Oh. Give me the good news first."

"I found Jackson Keller."

"I didn't know he was lost. Who is Jackson Keller?"

"Long story. Short version: I believe he is the guy running the web/net attacks."

"Good. Where can we collect him?"

"Well, see, that's the not-so-good stuff. I'm not exactly sure where he is. I know where he was, up until a few days ago, I think, but I'm pretty sure I know who he's working for."

"And that would be . . . ?"

"The better news—CyberNation."

"You're sure about this?"

"Yep. Want me to dazzle you with my brilliance?"

"Do I have a choice?"

Jay ignored that and said, "I scanned public tax records in the U.S. and found he had paid federal taxes last year on foreign income grosses of $250,000. I checked incorporation records, and found a Delaware company called Molotov Software Programs, Inc., the president being one Jackson Keller. Apparently the vice president is his mother, the secretary-treasurer his uncle. That's got tax-dodge or scam written all over it.

"From what I was able to determine, all of MSP's income for the last three years came from another corporation, Systems Upgrade, Inc., which turns out to be a shell owned by Future Tense Computer Engineering, which is, when you run it down, another shell, owned lock, stock, and barrel by—ta dah!—CyberNation.

"Corporate credit cards—Visa, MC, AmEx—have been issued for MSP, Inc., from the International Bank of Zurich, and Three-Cees and TRW both say that the credit is good, which means he pays his bills on time. Without a warrant, I can't get into real specific details on those transactions, but I've checked commercial usage location lists and gotten hits in southeast Florida for the last three months. Before that, he spent some time in Japan, and before that, in Germany. Apparently CyberNation owns some rolling stock and some other ships. The train carries tourists back and forth between Berlin and France, and there is some kind of repair work being done on the boat, or barge, or whatever, in Yokohama."

"He does some traveling," Michaels said.

"Yeah. But the south Florida thing is the deal—he goes to the same places the other programmers on the gambling boat go. Last hit was less than ten days ago, so my guess is he's on the boat. I dunno what his connection to the CyberNation stuff in Germany and Japan is, but I'm gonna find out."

"You think this is the leader of the assault team?"

"I'd bet money on it, boss. He's a programmer out of CIT, second in his class."

"Isn't that where you went to school?"

"Yeah."

Michaels heard something in Jay's voice. "What?"

"I know the guy. I used to know him, anyway."

"Second in his class, you said? He must be pretty sharp."

"Not as sharp as the guy who was first in the class."

"Ah."

"I'm gonna dig some more. When I think I got enough for a warrant, I'll shoot it past Hang 'Em High Harvey, and then we can pin this moth to the collecting board."

"Good work, Jay."

"Thanks, boss. Discom."

After he broke the connection, the com chimed again. This time, it was Toni. She looked tired, but she was smiling.

"Hey, babe," he said.

"Hi. I'm all settled in. I'm at the airport Hilton in Fort Lauderdale. I'll catch a shuttle copter to the ship in the morning."

"You're calling from the hotel?" It had been a while since she'd been in the field, but surely she hadn't forgotten something so basic?

"Not on the house phone, I'm using the coded cell."

He nodded. Net Force had field phones that looked ordinary, but sent and received shifting-code encrypted messages; even if somebody managed to trap the signal, they wouldn't be able to translate it into anything they could understand, unless they had a matching transceiver. Michaels's house com was so equipped, just as all the virgils were. SOP.

"How's the boy?"

"He's fine. Conked out about eight. Guru has him in bed with her. She's gonna spoil him."

"How are you doing?"

"Cold and pitiful in this big old bed all alone."

"Poor baby. I'll be all alone in this big old hotel bed, too."

"You better be." That got him a smile from her.

"I just got a call from Jay." He explained what Jay had just told him.

"Does he have a picture of this guy? Maybe I'll spot him on the ship."

"I'll have him upload one to your flatscreen if he has one," he said. "I'll have him bury it in a picture of your aunt Molly's seventieth birthday or something."

"Thanks."

There was a short pause, then she said, "Thank you for sending me to do this. I appreciate it."

"No problem. Just don't do anything other than what is in your mission plan."

"By the numbers, Commander Honey, don't worry."

But of course, he did. Despite what he had told her about how low risk it was, the husband and lover in him didn't like sending her anywhere. He worried about the plane's safety, the helicopter ride, and street traffic, not to mention being on a vessel that he now knew was enemy territory. He knew Toni would resent it mightily if he tried to keep her home and completely out of harm's way, but that's what he felt like doing.

They talked a few more minutes, said their good-nights, and discommed. It had been a long day and he was tired, but sleep was a long time in coming. This was the first time he and Toni had slept apart since they'd gotten married, and he didn't like it. Not even a little bit.

Woodville, Mississippi

This was not a town where you would expect to find a major Internet locus, Santos thought. Probably why it was here. Not far from the Louisiana border, in the southwest corner of Mississippi, Woodville was a sleepy place that time seemed to have touched only lightly in passing, at least in its last few decades.

Santos drove the old pickup truck along the Lower Woodville Road carefully. The day was gray, overcast, and cold. This was just a scouting trip to be certain of the information he had been provided. He was a black man in a small Southern town, and while racial profiling was not supposed to be allowed by police departments in this country anymore, he knew they still did it in such places. On the surface, the old tensions had been smoothed over. But a few inches down? Everybody here remembered who had been property and who had been slave masters, just as they did back home. People of color had carried the water and picked the crops. Nobody forgot that. A shiny new rental car would have made him suspect; a beat-up ten-year-old truck with local plates made him less likely to be noted. He wore a baseball cap and an old pea jacket over a workshirt and overalls, windows rolled up against the cold—just another lower-class Negro not worth paying any mind to, Thank you, Officer.

He would only get two passes by the location, one going out, another one half an hour later coming back. Any more than that might raise suspicion, and he did not want that.

The road ran next to a sluggish little river that he assumed was Ford's Creek—he'd been on Ford's Creek Road before, the place he was looking for was farther north, where Lower Woodville Road branched and another section of creek road picked up again, so that would make sense. He would make a pass, drive for fifteen minutes, then turn around and go back. From there, he'd keep right on going, local highway 24 east to Highway 61, then south on that all the way to New Orleans and a flight back to Florida. By mid-morning, he would be back on the ship.

But that was later. Now, he had to pay attention to what he had come for.

A few minutes later, he saw the driveway leading off to the west. There weren't any signs, but a hundred feet off the road was an eight-foot-high chain-link gate and a wooden kiosk behind it. He couldn't see the guard in the little building, but surely there must be one.

That would be the place. What else could they have worth guarding out here?

To be certain, he would have one of CyberNation's lease-time spysats do a pass overhead and confirm it. Or maybe they could just pull one of the CIA's public domain views—they had covered most of the world, and had pictures of anything not considered secret that could be had just by downloading them from the Internet. Whatever. That was not his job. He only needed to get the lay of the place, a feel for the location, for when he came back.

Some of the targets would be blown up electronically. Some would be taken out with more conventional explosives. And some would be captured and utilized for CyberNation's own ends, at least for a short while. This location needed to be functional for a critical few hours after the shit hit the fan, and he was going to see that it happened that way. After that, who cared?

At first, he hadn't really understood how this was supposed to be good for business. Missy had explained it simply. When a citizen's water or power shuts off, he doesn't care *why*. The reason why is not important, the only question that matters to him is, When will it be back on?

If somebody's Internet service dies and they need or want it badly enough and there is somebody standing right there with a shiny wire that will reconnect things just like that, a lot of customers will switch, no questions asked, except maybe how much, and how soon? And the answers will be, less than you were paying before, and immediately. These were the answers they wanted to hear.

With the surge of added customers clamoring to join up, CyberNation's political base would instantly grow stronger. Authorities would of course worry and wonder who was responsible, and they would certainly suspect CyberNation, who would benefit from such chaos. But they would have no proof, and the man in his little house in Nowhere, Indiana? That wasn't his problem—all *he* wanted to do was collect his e-mail or download his pornographic pictures.

It was simple human nature. In the right place, at the right time, a bottle of water would be worth a fortune. Timing was critical.

Santos could see it when she explained it that way. People here must be very stupid, but then again, people everywhere were mostly stupid. That was how it was.

That was not his problem, either.

Berlin, Germany

When the pain got to be too much—and it was actually worse the second day, more hurtful than it had been on the first!—Keller got off the train when it stopped and went to a doc-in-the-box, in Zehlendorf, not far from the *Universitat,* to get some medicine for it.

The doc-in-the-box was part of a chain that stretched across Europe, centered in the U.K. They didn't ask questions, and if you didn't want to show them an insurance card, they didn't care as long as your cash or credit was good.

The doctor, a gray-haired and gray-bearded old man name Konig, who looked to be in his late sixties and who resembled an old picture of Sigmund Freud, examined him, prodded and poked a little, and said, in fairly good English, "So, you fell down a flight of stairs, is that right?"

"Yah."

The old man smiled.

"What?"

"I've been a doctor forty-six years, my friend. In a land where narrow and steep old stairs are common. If you fell down a riser, it was after somebody beat you."

Keller, still bare-chested, blinked at the man, more surprised than annoyed at being called a liar. "You can tell that by looking? How?"

"Look here." He made a fist and touched it lightly to a brownish-yellow splotch on Keller's chest. "See? Stairs are flat and smooth. Even if you hit the edge of a step, it leaves a line—not a shape that matches perfectly a human fist like this does. Somebody punched and kicked you. Over a woman, was it?"

Keller started to deny it, then shrugged. Who cared if this old man knew? He would never see him again. "Yes."

"Beautiful?"

"Yes."

"Not your wife. Her husband?"

"Boyfriend. A big, stupid brute."

"Ach. That is the problem with the beautiful ones, *mein Freund.* I see nothing broken, so this brute must have held back a little. Here is a prescription—you can fill it at the *Apotheke* out front when you leave, if you wish. It is a generic version of Vicodin 5/500—acetaminophen and hydrocodone bitartrate. Take one or two every four hours if you need them for pain. Do not drink alcohol or take sleeping pills with these. Be careful if you drive, it can make you drowsy or slow your reactions. You should be feeling much better in a few days."

"Thank you."

The doctor waved him off. "The cost of love is dear sometimes, yah?"

Keller stared at him. Love? Lust, maybe. Never love. Not with a woman like Jasmine Chance . . .

He gave the prescription to a woman in the built-in drugstore on the way out, but when he went to pay for it and the office visit, he didn't have enough cash in *deutsche marks.* He shrugged and handed her his Visa card.

While she was scanning the card, he unscrewed the cap and dry-swallowed two of the pills.

By the time the cab got back to the train, he was feeling pretty good. Hardly hurt at all, unless he really thought about it, and why should he? The train would be turning around to head back toward the French border in a few hours. Best he get back to work, now that he could sit without it hurting so bad.

30

Fort Lauderdale, Florida

Toni leaned back in the seat and watched the dust boil up under them as the big transport helicopter lifted from the pad. You'd think there wouldn't be any dust, what with the choppers taking off and landing all day, not to mention the frequent rain here, but there it was.

The craft, a Sikorsky S-92, held eighteen passengers, and was full. Most of them actually were, she assumed, what she was supposed to be: tourists going to the gambling ship, which, as the flight attendant had announced, was ninety miles offshore where it was a pleasant seventy-eight degrees and sunny right now. A far cry this time of year from Ice Butt, Minnesota, where you could spit and have it freeze before it hit the ground. As long as there were winters like that, tropical resorts would have customers.

According to the posting in the hotel, they scheduled these flights on the half hour, starting at six A.M., with the last one returning from the ship to the Mainland at midnight, thirty-seven flights a day, split up among three aircraft. Which meant at capacity, they could move over six hundred and fifty people a day to and from the ship from this one heliport, and there were at least three other ports in operation just on the Florida coast, not counting those in Cuba or the other islands. At forty bucks a head for the trip, that was a hundred grand a day to pay for aviation fuel. Which also meant that if the things ran at full operation, and each of the passengers lost on average, say, only a hundred dollars each at the casinos, the gross would be over a quarter of a million dollars a day from the Mainland alone. Almost eight million a month. Assuming the Cubans had anything to lose, and anybody coming from elsewhere also did, that could work out to more than a hundred million a year, easy. Of course, they might not run to capacity day in and day out, and there would be operating costs, and even a few winners, too, but if even a quarter of that was profit, it would be a tidy sum. Better, Guru used to say, than a poke in the eye with a sharp stick . . .

The copter spiraled up and outward to its cruising altitude, only a few thousand feet, Toni would guess, and leaned into the rising sun. Fifteen or twenty minutes out, they passed a matching copter going the other way, a mile to port.

She looked over the passengers without staring at any one in particular. About what she'd expect. There were several couples, sporting fresh sunburns and wearing shorts and colorful Hawaiian shirts, likely going to see if they might be able to win back some of their children's college tuition.

There were a few women who appeared to be traveling alone, most of them also middle-aged, although there were a couple of younger ones in their mid-twenties who looked as if they might be former beauty queens. Hunting for rich husbands, maybe? Or perhaps high-priced hookers going to offer their services to winners looking for a way to spend their free money?

A couple of men looked like she'd always pictured high

rollers—dressing in western chic, with ostrich-skin cowboy boots and string ties, wearing Stetson hats.

There were some young guys, college-age, Toni guessed, laughing and talking among themselves, off on an adventure. Several of them had already cast appreciative glances at the ex-beauty queens.

There was a very fit-looking shaved-bald black man of thirty or so in a yellow silk T-shirt and khaki trousers, with dark sunglasses, who leaned back in his seat and appeared to be sleeping. He wore a gold Oyster Rolex on his left wrist, a gold nugget pinkie ring, and a matching bracelet of heavy gold links on his right wrist. From the way he sat and the look of his musculature under the thin silk, Toni's first impression was that he was a cop, or some kind of security officer, a bouncer, maybe. He might be asleep, but he looked as if he could go from zero to sixty in a heartbeat.

Behind him sat a couple who looked to be in their early seventies. Retirees from some colder climate moved to Florida, she figured.

Not that exciting a group, and nobody who looked like what she thought an international computer terrorist ought to look like.

Well, what did you expect? Geeky-looking guys with pocket protectors and horn-rimmed glasses, their fingers glued to Palm Pilots or flatscreens?

She grinned at herself. Figuring out who might be a heavyweight Bulgarian weight lifter was something you maybe could do by looking, but computer wizards came in all sizes and shapes. It was a fallacy to think they all looked like classic movie nerds. She of all people ought to know that—here she was pretending to be a tourist when she was, in fact, a spy.

Well. She'd be at the ship in a few minutes, she'd get checked in, find her cabin, then take her camera and wander around, snapping perfectly innocent pictures of whatever was open to public view. She had the picture Jay had sent late last night, she'd strained it from the covering JPEG of her mythical aunt. It was a college yearbook image of this guy Keller, and Jay had added ten years to it with a plastic surgery art program. The hair might have changed length or color, contacts could change eye color, too, but the shape of the ears and head would be the same. Even crooks having their faces remodeled seldom did their ears.

She had memorized the picture, then wiped it from the flatscreen's drive, overwriting the file so it couldn't be recovered. Like Alex said, she was just supposed to gather small bits of information they could use, but it would be embarrassing at the least if her flatscreen got lost and wound up being scanned by some curious tech-head who found something he shouldn't find.

So far, so good.

As the commuter helicopter approached the gambling ship, she saw that the actual landing site was a huge flat-topped barge anchored a few hundred yards away, with several long passenger boats shuttling people back and forth from it to the floating casino. She counted six helipads on the barge. There were three craft similar to the one she was in on the deck of the barge, with another one taking off, and a fifth one circling for a landing. That made sense—all those copters taking off and landing on the ship itself would be a windy, noisy commotion better left elsewhere. Smart.

***On the* Bon Chance**

Santos watched the dark-haired woman walk away from the shuttle boat toward the cabin check-in queue, and nodded to himself. She moved well, inside her balance, something most people did not do. Something in her stance, her carriage, it indicated some kind of physical training. A dancer, maybe, or a gymnast, she had the hip swing and that muscular roll to her walk. She wore a T-shirt and shorts, running shoes, no socks, and pulled a carry-on bag behind her, a big purse slung on a shoulder strap. Very sleek in the butt and legs. She was alone, wore no rings, a tourist from the States. Were he not so busy with all the things he needed to do right now, she would be a pleasure he would like to try. Missy would love that, wouldn't she? To see him with another woman? She was so sure of herself in that way, she would not believe a man could prefer somebody else to her, it was a major part of her power. And she had reason to believe in it, she was most adept in those ways.

Hmm. Maybe he was not as busy as he thought. When you could kill two birds with one stone, was that not a rock worth throwing? And how long did it take to slip out of your clothes and into a good-looking woman anyway? He could skip a workout in the gym, trade that for one in the bedroom, yes?

He grinned at the thought. Missy would steam like turtle soup . . .

"Hello, 'Berto."

Speak of the devil.

Without further planning, Santos allowed his gaze to linger on the woman from the helicopter as she walked toward the registration area. Missy could not help but notice he was looking at something other than her. He held his stare long enough for her to be sure of it, and for her to turn to see what held his attention. He caught the flash of anger as it lit her face. She turned back to look at him. It was there only for a moment before she hid it, the irritation, but it was there. Ah, good. Already he felt a warm satisfaction.

"Your trip was successful?"

"My trips are always successful."

"Made some new friends, did you?"

He shrugged, slow and lazy, gave her a small lopsided grin, but said nothing. Not yet, but if she wished to think so, why shouldn't she? It would serve his interests.

Her smile didn't change to look at, but it grew chilly; he could almost feel it. "We have a lot of things to discuss. Why don't you meet me in my office in an hour." With that, she turned and walked away, and he could see the anger in her steps.

Ah, better and better!

Now, of course, he more or less *had* to follow up on the attractive brunette with the dancer's stroll. He would talk to the clerk at the room check-in and ask about her. Find out who she was, which cabin she was in. It was a big ship, but not so large as all that. He could find a way to run into the woman on deck or in the casino, maybe even the gym, since it was obvious she worked out. He had access to the ship's security cams, and could find out where she was easily enough. A chance meeting, a little conversation, perhaps a drink, and they would go on from there.

A man had to do what he had to do, but, he had to admit, some jobs were more fun than others . . .

Zehlendorf Forest
Berlin, Germany
Summer 1959

Jay was in tracking mode, a skill Saji had taught him when he'd been recovering from his stroke. He walked carefully along the dirt road, cutting sign, looking for the smallest indication that his quarry had come this way.

The road was easy. It was dusty, and upon it, the passages of somebody in a vehicle or on foot were simple to spot, no problem. Somebody looking to hide his trail could brush the tracks away with little effort, but because the dust was so fine, it showed every tiny detail, and erasing something itself left a sign that was more interesting than the tracks. A man trying to avoid pursuit could change his mode of transportation, from a car to a bike to a pogo stick; he could change his shoes, and with a little bit of misdirection, lose a pursuer who was following combat boots when they turned into running shoes. But wiping away all tracks? That might seem smart on first thought, but really wasn't if you knew anything about how to follow a trail.

Sometimes, as Sherlock Holmes was wont to say, it was the absence of the dog barking in the night that was important.

The lack of impressions on a dirt road were more telling than any bootprint.

Carpet-walkers would sometimes glue carpet to the bottoms of their shoes, so as not to leave impressions, but that worked on sand or rocky soil, not on a red-dirt road with baby-powder-fine dust; instead, it would leave distinct patches of relatively smooth tracks. And somebody dragging a branch or burlap sack behind them would likewise wipe out the tracks, but leave drag lines that would last through a dry and moderately windy day, even though rain would eventually patter them down.

No, a smart runner would get off the road entirely, head for the rocks or streams where any tracks either wouldn't show, or would be swirled away in a few minutes or even seconds. And he would double-back, angle off in false starts, and head in the wrong direction long enough to gull a so-so tracker before he circled around for his true destination.

But if somebody was taking only the barest precautions, and they didn't really think they were going to be noticed or tailed, they weren't likely to be as cautious. You didn't go into full alert and stealth mode every time you went out to collect the mail from your box, or the paper from your front lawn—what was the point?

Keller wore carpet shoes, and for most people, most of the time, his basic moves would have done the job. Nobody driving along the road would notice any tracks. Anybody walking but not looking wouldn't notice the smooth patches. Even somebody looking for tracks of a particular kind of shoe would probably miss 'em. But Smokin' Jay Gridley wasn't just anybody, was he?

It was a nice day for a walk. Greenery everywhere, flowers in bloom, the smell of pollen and dust in the summery, early evening air . . .

Ahead, on the right, was a weathered wooden building. It had a caduceus painted on the side, the winged staff with two snakes twined around it, indicating a doctor's office, the paint weather-worn and faded from black to a light gray. Yes, this must be the place.

Jay walked to the front door. The office was closed for the day, and the door was locked, but the latch was an old-style spring lock, and it took all of ten seconds for Jay to open it with a skeleton key he pulled from his pocket.

It was dark and quiet inside. Jay looked around, didn't see any alarms. He flipped a light switch up. There was a four-drawer steel file cabinet full of patient files next to a big wooden desk. The drawers were locked, but he opened them with a couple of bent paper clips. So easy when you knew how.

He found the file quickly enough, too. Keller hadn't even bothered to use a phony name, and had paid for the office visit and medication with his corporate credit card—which is how Jay had tracked him here so quickly.

He read the report. "Fell down stairs" was what had been written on the new patient form. The physical examination showed multiple contusions and abrasions, no broken bones or torn ligaments. In one corner, in tiny, neat lettering was a note: "Altercation c̄ jealous boyfriend over woman," it said. The letter "c" had a line over it, and the words were underlined twice. Apparently the good doctor, one Willem Konig, M.D., had gotten a different cause for the injuries than had his receptionist.

So. Whaddya know. Keller had gotten his butt kicked for fooling around with somebody else's girlfriend. *That* was interesting. Keller had never been a ladies' man in school, but you never could tell. Jay himself hadn't been that much of a lover back then, either. Things changed.

He put the report back into the drawer, closed and relocked it, looked out the window to make sure nobody was around, then exited the building, locking it behind him. Technically, he was bending the law here. While he had a legal warrant to do an electronic search, that permission only extended to the U.S. borders. While Net Force did have reciprocity agreements with dozens of countries, including Germany, and the U.S. federal warrant would eventually have gotten a counterpart here, he didn't have time to wait. He wasn't planning to use this information in court, so it didn't have to have all the i's dotted and the t's crossed, as long as it helped him find his quarry.

Outside, behind the doctor's office, was a small hill. Jay climbed to the top and looked around. Krumme Lake was to the west, a short distance away, on the edge of the Berlin Forest. The Grunewald area was right over there. There were roads, a train track, and what was still West Berlin, deep in the eastern heart of a divided Germany, that wouldn't be reunited for decades. The Cold War was still cranking up in this era.

So, Keller was in Germany, or at least he had been yesterday, and a routine request from State to the German government for any use of Keller's U.S. passport had come back negative, so if he was gone, he must have done it illegally. Given his current status, Jay couldn't say Keller wouldn't do that, but since he didn't know anybody was looking for him, there wouldn't be any compelling reason for him to sneak out of the country.

Why Germany? Who was the jealous boyfriend who must live here who clobbered Keller? Where had he gone?

That was the problem with searching for information. Sometimes you came up with more questions than answers . . .

"Hold on a second," Jay said aloud. Wasn't there something else about Germany he had come across recently? Something about a barge . . . ? No, that was Japan. It was a train. CyberNation ran a tourist train or somesuch here. And there were the iron horse's tracks, right there. Maybe it was a sign.

And maybe not. But it gave him something he could check. Train schedules were public information. Find all those that had passed on this track down there for the last couple of days, run them down, find out where they went. Find out if the one owned by CyberNation was around. If it was, that would certainly be a big coincidence, wouldn't it? And a great place to go and look . . .

31

***On the* Bon Chance**

Toni played the tourist, mindful of what she had come to the ship to do. She carried a cheap electronic camera, and she took pictures of her room, the exterior decks, the swimming pool, and the helicopter barge. She bought a gambling credit card for two hundred dollars and played the slot machines. She lost eighty dollars over a period of four hours, then hit a three-cherry payout for a hundred dollars. She had lunch in one of the cafeterias, a club sandwich and iced tea, with a slice of very good banana cream pie for dessert, and that cost her half what it would in most D.C. restaurants.

In the early afternoon, she slathered herself with coconut-scented sunblock and lay in one of the deck chairs near the swimming pool. It was hot, but a nice breeze off the water kept things bearable.

A steward came by and asked her if she wanted a drink. She ordered a margarita, and when it came, it looked like a big green snow cone.

She went to her cabin, showered, put on shorts and a T-shirt, then took her camera to the ship's stern, where passengers tossed bits of food to a flock of hovering seagulls. She took pictures of the birds, and more views of the ship from that angle.

The periodic drone of passenger helicopters landing and taking off from the barge was noticeable, but not overly loud.

She could get used to this. Too bad Alex wasn't here to enjoy it with her.

Late in the afternoon, she went back to her cabin and changed into workout clothes, bike shorts and a halter-top, running shoes, white cotton socks. She didn't want to practice *silat* while she was here, even in her room, but she could at least ride the stationary bike and maybe do a few sets on the weight machines. She draped a towel around her shoulders, tucked her room keycard into her left sock top, and headed for the gym.

There were a dozen people in the gym, which was down a level from her cabin. The place had eight or ten weight station machines, pneumatic rather than stacks of iron, six bikes, three stairclimbers, two treadmills, and in one corner, a heavy punching bag hung on a thick nylon strap, the bag itself center-wrapped with layers of duct tape. Toni wished she could work the bag, but she didn't want to draw any attention to herself. Even in this day and age, a little woman beating the stuffing out of a punching bag drew raised eyebrows and male interest. Men who might not ever speak to you while you were on a bike or stairclimber would feel the need to say something if you were kicking a heavy bag. It was somehow a challenge to their masculinity.

Toni got a free bottle of spring water from a dispenser, found an empty spot in front of the mirrors, did a little stretching and a few warm-ups, then moved to one of the cardiobikes. The one she picked had one of those fan blade front wheels, so the harder you pedaled, the more air you had to move. This was good, because it helped keep you cooler. The electronics allowed a choice of difficulty. She started off slow, and built up resistance after a few minutes.

She was halfway through what she figured would be a forty-minute ride when the black man she'd seen on the copter ride came in. He wore an old pair of baggy shorts, no shirt, rubber sandals, a white cotton headband, and had a towel around his neck.

The shorts had the *Bon Chance* logo on them. He must work here, she realized. If he was a tourist, the shorts would be new, not old and worn as they were, right?

Toni sipped at her water. The man was well-built, all muscle, no fat on him. Not like a power lifter, but more like a boxer a few days from a championship match.

He moved to the hanging bag, kicked off his sandals, tossed the towel next to them, and went through a series of stretches.

He was very limber for somebody with that much muscle, she noticed. She was curious to see if he was going to work the bag, or that was just a place where he loosened up.

It didn't take long to satisfy her wonder.

The man stood in front of the bag, and started slapping it. Open-handed, first with the palms, then with the backs of his hands, he developed a rhythm—palm right, backhand right, palm left, backhand left, over and over, until the sound of the strikes sounded like somebody working a speed bag, *wapata, wapata, wapata, wapata.*

After a couple of minutes, with a sheen of sweat beaded on his head and body, he switched to elbows, and the rhythm was slower, but similar. Right horizontal elbow inward, then back, followed by the left, *bap-bap!*

Toni kept pumping, watching the man in the mirrors rather than looking right at him.

He switched from elbows to punches, using hammer fists in the same pattern. Then he went to his knees, and then to a series of instep-then-heel kicks. Right, left, right, left.

He was working really hard. Most people didn't realize how difficult it was to strike a heavy bag like that—it took a lot more energy than riding a bike or walking on a treadmill, a lot more. And not wearing bag gloves was hard on the hands, too.

The timer on Toni's bike cheeped. She looked down at it. The black man had been working the bag for twenty minutes, and while he was sweating profusely, he didn't look particularly tired.

The guy was in incredible shape. And though she couldn't tell from the strikes what his art was, he was obviously deep into some fighting discipline. He moved in balance the whole time, and his hits, while fast, were also powerful. Interesting.

She warmed down on the bike for another minute, gradually slowing her pedaling. She stepped off the bike, wiped her face with the towel, finished off her water, then started for the exit.

The black man stepped back, threw a hard sidekick at the bag, and lifted it a foot into the air, to drop back on its nylon strap hard enough to shake the mirrors. He reached for his towel, wiped his face and head, slipped his feet into his sandals, and walked away.

He was a few feet behind Toni when she stepped into the hall.

"You a dancer?" he said. He had an accent, sounded like Spanish or Portuguese, maybe.

Toni looked at the man. Was he hitting on her? In her guise of divorced secretary, she would probably be receptive to such things. He was a strong, good-looking man. Then again, she was supposedly from the South and might have a racial prejudice, so perhaps she ought to seem a little timid. If he worked here, maybe she could find out some things from him.

"No," she said. "Not really."

"You have the legs," he said. He nodded at her.

Toni gave him what she thought would pass for an embarrassed smile. "Well, I try to keep in shape. Are you a boxer?"

He shrugged. "Kind of."

He moved up next to her as they walked. "Your first visit to the ship?"

"Yes. You've been here before?"

"Oh, yeah. I work here."

"Really? What do you do?"

"I'm with Security," he said.

No surprise, but Toni raised her eyebrows. "How exciting."

He shrugged again. "Pretty dull, mostly. You maybe want to get a drink later?"

Toni pretended to be more nervous than she felt. "Uh, well, maybe."

He grinned, showing perfect white teeth. "I don't bite, Missy. My name is Roberto Santos." He put out his hand.

"I'm Mary Johnson." She took his hand. It was damp, but warm, and she could feel the power in his grip, even though he throttled it way back. "From Falls Church, Virginia."

"It is my pleasure to meet you," he said. He released her hand. "That drink?"

"Oh. Okay. I want to shower and change. Can I meet you somewhere?"

He smiled again. "How about the Lady Luck, that's the little bar next to the dining room outside the main casino. In an hour?"

"That would be fine," she said.

After he had gone on his way, Toni felt her heartbeat start to slow. It had been a long time since she had been in the field working a contact. That he was such a primal, physical man added something to her nervousness. This man was dangerous. No question of that.

On the CyberNation Train
Near Halbertstadt, Germany

When Jay sneaked onto the train, he kept it simple. This close to Keller, he wanted to be sure he wasn't distracted by historical details or esoteric odors in a complex scenario—Keller was, he had shown, too good to shrug off. So the train was just a train, the era was the present and real-time, and Jay's plan was to get in and out without raising a ruckus. He hadn't come to slap Keller's face with a glove and challenge him to a duel, only to find out whether he was here or not.

The duel would come later. On Jay's terms.

Not that even this much was easy. He made his way through the baggage car with his utmost stealth, stopping frequently to look and to listen. Cracking any of CyberNation's secure services would be extremely difficult, if not impossible. These were people who prided themselves on their ability to program and weave, and any chinks in their armor would be microscopically small. But the train ran on public tracks, and it had a connection to the railway system's computers, which were a lot easier to rascal. Jay wasn't hurting anything, he wasn't going to even peek at the rail system's files, he was just riding their coded sig into the CyberNation train. They had to allow it access, and while it wouldn't get him past their foot-thick firewalls, the information he wanted wasn't behind them anyhow.

Jay got through the baggage car. Just ahead was the conductor's office. Jay knocked, and when nobody answered he slipped the lock with a credit card and stepped inside. If the conductor had been in his office, Jay would have offered some excuse, gone away, and created a diversion that would have drawn the man out.

A file cabinet stood near the conductor's desk, but it was partially open, not even locked. Jeez, Louise! Not that the lock would have stopped him, but still, they didn't have to make it so easy. It was amazing to him how often people who should know better left their doors unlocked.

A few minutes shuffling through papers came up with what he wanted: a passenger list. He looked at several other manifests, on the off-chance somebody might someday notice he had poked around in here. No point in being obvious about what he was looking for.

Jay recognized several of the names on the passenger list from his own list of high-end computer program grads. And there, plain as day, was the name he had come to find.

Jackson Keller.

So, this was where he was, and this was where his primary team was, too.

Jay put the list back into the drawer, went to the door, peeked out. Nobody around.

He hurried back toward the baggage car. He had what he wanted. Time to leave.

"We've got a hacker incursion," Taggart said.

Keller stared at her. "Incursion? Not a failed attempt? Impossible!"

"Not in our systems. In the train's op comp. We got a bounce-back from Deutsche Bahn Access, said he wasn't who he said he was. I checked it: The hit came in off the sat pipeline from EuroAlliance One, not from any registered Deutsche Bahn connections."

"Let me see." He moved to the work station where Samantha Taggart, the security monitor for this shift, sat.

"Nothing to see," she said. "He's come and gone."

"What did he do?"

"Nothing to speak of. He accessed several housekeeping files. Didn't take anything, didn't leave a worm or virus behind. Probably some kid trying out a new cracker program."

"Which files? Never mind—" Keller tapped in a key sequence. The file list appeared in a real-time crawl on the holoproj. Mail manifest, cargo bills of lading. Passenger list. Station stops. Who would bother? There was nothing there to see.

"You back-walked him?"

"Far as I could. It was an anonymous sig from somewhere in the NoAtlantic Net; it frayed eight hundred ways from Sunday past that."

"That would be pretty sharp for a kid hacker."

"I used to do it when I was a kid. You used to do it. It's not that hard."

Keller chewed his lip. Nothing was taken. Nothing there to take, really. Who could possibly care where the train stopped, what it carried for cargo or mail, or who was on it—

He blinked. He opened the passenger file. There they were, his team, himself, the train crew. He felt a sudden cold rush in his lower belly.

Gridley!

He shook his head. "Can't be. He doesn't even know who we are."

"Excuse me?"

He looked at Taggart. "Nothing. Never mind. You're right, it was probably some kid screwing around. No harm, no foul."

But as he walked away, Keller's fluttering bowels didn't settle down. If it wasn't some kid trying to break into a system just for the hell of it, then who could it be? And the only answer was: somebody who wanted to know who was on the train. Maybe Gridley had figured it out. Maybe that old Thai persona Keller had used had been too good a clue. And if it was Gridley, and he knew Keller was on the train with his team, then they were in deep trouble. If the Americans thought this train had anything to do with the net and web disruptions, they would be all over the Germans to pull it to a stop and have a look-see. Somebody high up in the German government would surely owe a favor to somebody high up in the U.S. government, and even if not, there could easily be a quid pro quo offer in a big hurry: *Scratch our back, Hans, and we'll scratch yours, yah?*

And if Gridley knew about this platform, maybe he knew about the barge in Yokohama, too. It wouldn't be safe there, either.

He had to get off the train. Fast.

32

Net Force HQ
Quantico, Virginia

Michaels looked at Jay, then at John Howard, the other man in his office. "It's iffy," he said.

Jay nodded. "Yep. I don't have ironclad proof. But I'm positive of it. Keller is the guy leading the charge. He's got the chops, and CyberNation is the organization that stands to gain more than anybody. Last week, he and his team were on the boat, and now they are on a big ole electric train in Deutschland. If we can grab them, I bet we can squeeze a confession out of one of 'em. And sure stop anything they are planning."

"There's due process for you," Michaels said.

"Hey, the Germans got stung when the net went wonky, people all over the world lost money. If they don't have Miranda warnings, that's not our concern, is it?"

"I think you've been watching too many World War Two movies, Jay. They aren't all Nazis over there anymore. People have rights in Germany now."

Jay shrugged.

"What I want to know more about is this connection among the three locations," Howard said. "The train, the barge in Japan, the ship."

Jay said, "Triple redundancy. I think each of these has got identical computer systems set up. They share the information. If something happens to one, they still have two backups. That's how I'd do it. We got at least a backup off-site ourselves now, the new substation in D.C."

"So it wouldn't do us any good to take out the train by itself."

"Well, General, it would tell us for sure if these guys are the villains if we got a look at their hardware and software. Don't we have any spies who can do a walk-through in RT?"

"We've already got a spy on the boat," Michaels reminded him.

"Yeah, but she's not supposed to poke around in the private decks, just gather info that's public. Besides, we know that Keller is on the train now anyhow. I'm telling you, this is the real deal."

Michaels shook his head. "Even if I believed you—and it happens I do—we don't have enough to start arresting people, even via another government. And if we could shut down the train and the barge at the—where was it? the shipworks?—that would still leave the gambling ship down there in the Caribbean. If they are about to do something else nasty, wouldn't that be likely to precipitate it?"

Jay shrugged. "I dunno. Maybe. But they might not be ready to go for it yet. Our defenses have gotten better. It'll be harder next time. Plus if we get Keller and his big guns, that's gonna monkey wrench it. The second team won't be as good."

"If that's all they do," Howard said.

Michaels looked at him.

"Remember that cut transcontinental fiber-optic cable? Where they found the two dead militiamen? Have we considered that they might be linked?"

Michaels shook his head. "Why would you say that?"

"Well, sir, if it were me, I'd want a multipronged attack on something as big as the Internet. Sticking it with a knife in the hind leg will make it bleed, but that won't kill it, or even seriously slow it down. But if you shot it in the head, maybe set off a charge of dynamite under it at the same time?"

"The general has a point, boss. There is more than one way to shut off a node. Doesn't have to be with software, could be with hardware. My programmers can't fix that."

"Great. I need to hear this."

He leaned back in his chair and thought about it for a second. "All right. I'm going to present this to the director and get her thoughts about it. Meanwhile, General, you might want to fine-tune your ship-boarding scenarios. I'm expecting an update from Toni soon, so you can add that into your data files."

"Yes, sir." He grinned.

"You really like the idea of storming a ship at sea and taking it over, don't you?"

"Yes, sir. I know I shouldn't, it's dangerous, but it's what I'm trained to do. Every now and then, you like to see if your tools still work."

"Go sharpen them, John. I'm going over to see the director. Jay, you get back on-line and get me something, anything, I can use to convince the director we aren't grabbing at straws here."

"On my way, boss."

On the **Bon Chance**

The bar was relatively quiet, but the muted sound of bells going off in the casino filtered through the walls. People were smoking as well as drinking, there being no laws against it here. Even though there were apparently vacuum ashtrays on the tables and bar that sucked a lot of the smoke away, it still smelled like cigarettes, with a cigar or pipe thrown in to add their heavier scents. Cigarettes were nasty, but Toni had to confess that she kind of liked the smell of cigars and pipe tobacco.

Toni, dressed now in jeans, running shoes, and a dark blouse, arrived ten minutes early and looked around. She noted the exits, then found a small table next to the wall in the corner. She sat with her back against the wall. A row of curtained portholes ran along the wall at head level, but she arranged her chair so she wasn't sitting in front of one.

A young and pretty waitress in a short black skirt and white shirt was at the table fifteen seconds later.

Toni ordered, and it was only another minute or two before the waitress returned with a tall glass of tomato juice with a celery stick in it. Quick service.

Roberto Santos arrived exactly on the hour. He wore a dark suit, Armani if she was any judge, a black silk scoop-necked T-shirt, and alligator loafers. The shoes alone probably cost more than all the clothes she had packed. He also wore that gold watch, ring, and bracelet she had seen before. A walking Fort Knox.

He walked straight toward her table, as if he had known where she would be.

"Miss Johnson. Good to see you again."

"Mr. Santos."

"Roberto, please. Mr. Santos is my father."

They exchanged smiles.

The waitress was there before Santos settled fully in his chair, and she had a drink on her tray. It was mostly white, with streaks of brown in it. He smiled at the young woman and took the drink. "Thank you, Betty."

The waitress dimpled and almost curtsied, then moved away. Toni had the impression that if Santos said "Jump," Betty would be in the air in a heartbeat, and naked before she came back down.

Santos sipped at the drink. "Ah," he said. He looked at her and answered what he thought was her unasked question: "Coconut milk and Cuban rum," he said. "Very fattening. I have to work extra hard after I have one of these." He raised his glass to her and she held up her tomato juice. It looked like a Bloody Mary. Let him think so.

"To new friends," he said.

"Why not?" she said.

They clinked glasses.

She nursed her juice while he finished his rum and coconut milk and started a second one. He was very smooth, this Santos, not glib, but totally focused on her, appearing entranced by her every word or look, as if she were the most fascinating woman in the world. Which, in her fake identity, she certainly was not. It didn't take a genius to realize he was hoping to get laid.

Well, he was going to be disappointed, unless he could talk Betty the waitress into it, which didn't seem like much of a chore.

When she asked questions about his work, he managed to slip them, like a good boxer does punches, giving her almost no information. He walked around, he said. He watched for trouble. From time to time, he ran errands. Nothing special. Just a job.

Toni smiled and nodded and pretended to be impressed anyhow. He wasn't telling the truth. If something was going on upon this ship, Santos here was a part of it, she was sure of that. But—short of blowing in his ear and going off to his cabin with him—how was she going to find out what he knew?

"You have not had supper yet," he said. "We should go and eat."

Toni realized that extracting herself from this would be more difficult if they had dinner, and she was about to offer an excuse—a sudden unexpected visit from Mr. Red ought to do it—when Santos glanced away from her at somebody who had just entered the bar. He looked back quickly, and he wore a small smile when he did.

Toni looked at the entrance.

There was a strikingly beautiful woman standing there. She looked Asian, maybe Amerasian, Toni couldn't pin her nationality down exactly. She was tall, had black hair past her shoulders, so black it looked like shimmering ink. She wore a red blouse, tucked into a matching skirt that stopped four inches above her knees, hose, and heels. The clothes were snug enough to reveal a svelte hourglass figure, but not so tight as to look trashy. Toni was aware that the conversational background noise suddenly dropped in volume, and a quick glance around showed virtually everybody in the place was looking at the new arrival.

Except Santos. And given his obvious attraction to women, that seemed odd.

"Who is that?" she asked.

He looked at her. "Pardon?"

"In the red, over there."

He looked, pretending not to have seen the woman before. "Ah. That is Jasmine Chance." His accent thickened a bit, so that his next sentence came out, "She work on de boat, too." Not Hispanic, Toni decided. Brazilian, maybe.

The woman, meanwhile, was on the move, and it looked to Toni as if she was heading right toward their table, smiling like the Cheshire cat as she walked, heels clicking in the suddenly quiet bar. Here was a femme fatale.

Sure enough, she approached their table and stopped, still smiling. "Roberto."

"Hello, Missy," he said. He grinned back.

While it was all pleasant and smiley on the surface, Toni immediately felt that charged atmosphere that couples who'd been arguing sometimes had—just before they put on their public faces.

Bad blood here.

"Aren't you going to introduce me to your friend, Roberto?" Another smile, and if ever an expression was fake, this one was. It had crocodile all over it.

Santos held up a lazy hand. "This is Mary Johnson, she is an executive assistant from Falls Church, Virginia. Mary, this is Jasmine Chance. Head of Security. My boss."

"A secretary," Chance said, looking at Santos. Contempt practically dripped from her voice.

Toni felt a strong urge to stand up and slap the woman for that patronizing tone, but that wouldn't be in character, not at all.

"There was something you wanted?" he said.

Chance never moved her penetrating gaze from him. "An important security matter came up. Perhaps your friend could excuse us for a moment?"

Toni would have loved to stay and listen to this conversation, but it provided the easy exit she needed. She said, "Oh, of course. I was just about to leave anyway. I'm feeling a bit under the weather."

"I'm so sorry," Chance said, the words absolutely devoid of any sympathy at all.

"No need to leave," Santos said. "I'm sure this won't take long." He wasn't looking at Toni, either, but at Chance.

If looks could kill, anybody walking between these two would have been turned into crispy critters as if bathed by flamethrowers.

Toni stood. "Nice to meet you, Ms. Chance. Thank you for the drink, Roberto. Maybe I'll see you again."

She hurried away, just in time. She had to call Alex, and the window for the call was pretty narrow.

Back in her cabin, she went into the small bathroom and started the shower. That her room might be bugged was unlikely, but it paid to be careful. Once the water was running and making noise, she used her disguised scrambler phone to call Alex, vox only, no visual. There was a long-distance microwave repeater on the ship—they couldn't expect people to be without their phones even out here—but Toni's call went through a military comsat she knew would be footprinting the area for the next ten minutes.

"Hey, babe."

"Hey," she said.

"How's it going?"

"Fine. I haven't seen Jay's guy."

"That's okay, we think he's in Germany. Anything else?"

"I've managed to meet a couple of people who look interesting. You might have Jay run their names and see what he can come up with."

"Shoot."

She gave him Santos and Chance, described them. "Santos says he's with ship security, and that Chance is his boss. They have some kind of thing going between them, if that's any help."

"I'll pass it on to Jay. How are you doing?"

"I'm okay. I miss you and Little Alex."

"We miss you, too. He's fine, Guru is fine, I'm fine. Nothing to worry about here. Listen, I need you to plug whatever you've got, pix, thoughts, diagrams, into a file and upload it to one of the secure mailboxes. Mark it for John's attention."

"I won't be able to do it until the next comsat pass," she said. "Unless you want to risk using the ship's transmitter."

"No, it'll wait a couple hours."

"What's up?"

He explained Jay's theory about CyberNation's train and barge. He finished by saying, "I spoke to the director. Ordinarily, the government would be hesitant to move with so little hard evidence, but the powers-that-be uplevels are really nervous about this whole situation. There are going to be some strings pulled, some favors called in. The German train and the Japanese barge are going to get unexpected visitors. If what Jay thinks is right, that'll take two of the three computer loci out of action."

"Leaving the ship," she said.

"General Howard is working on that," he said.

"You're serious?"

"As a triple bypass. If this nest of electronic snakes is about to strike, we need to stop them before they do. Both Jay and John think they might escalate things from pure software attacks to physical attacks on servers and phone companies. That would really screw things up royally."

"Yes. So, I'm the fifth column agent?"

"No. You leave as scheduled. Finish up, catch the flight back to the Mainland, come home tomorrow."

"Alex—"

"Not open for discussion," he said. "If Net Force's military arm has to flex its muscle, that's who does the job, not the Assistant Deputy Commander."

She knew he was right. She was a mother, she had a toddler at home. She didn't have any business being on a military raid. Still, she felt the excitement at the idea.

"All right," she said.

The signal started to cut in and out, so they finished their conversation and discommed. Toni shut off the shower and went to collect her flatscreen. She would make notes, draw maps, and add in the pictures she had taken, and fold them into a compressed and encoded packet to send to John Howard via the scrambled cell phone the next time the comsat overflew her. One more day on the ship, and she would head home. It felt good to have gotten back into the field. And while she would have liked to stay on board if Net Force mounted an assault, she had other responsibilities now. It was the right thing to do. Although she hated thinking like a grownup. It made her feel . . . old . . .

33

In the Air over the Central Atlantic

Keller's jet was more than halfway to Miami when he got the frantic call from the train's SysOp.

German authorities had stopped them for a "health inspection," looking for, they said, a carrier of Lassa Valley Fever. Trash protocols had been instigated as soon as the police had arrived, the SysOp said. The onboard computers would be blank before anybody could download anything, all files burned and unrecoverable. There wouldn't be any sign of anything particularly illegal. Certainly it would seem suspicious, to have that kind of state-of-the-art computer setup on a train, and more suspicious that the machines were all empty, but there would be nothing the German authorities could charge anybody with that would stick. They could haul everybody in, but no evidence, no case, and all the players knew all they had to do was sit tight and CyberNation's lawyers would eventually spring them. Keller and his crew were safe, and they were what made the programs work.

It was scary, but not altogether unexpected when the

scrambled call came in from the Japanese SysOp a few minutes later. The barge's computers were history, too.

That left the ship, and if Gridley and his guys knew about the train and the barge, they had to know about the *Bon Chance*.

Fortunately, the ship was in international waters. If the U.S. could get a Coast Guard cutter or Navy ship to go there—not politically likely, according to Jasmine—the gambling boat's crew would see it coming fifteen miles away. Plenty of time to wipe those computers, too, though that would be a last resort. With Germany and Japan gone, all their work was on the ship. They would have to be damned certain it was endangered before they trashed it. Thousands and thousands of man-hours erased would hurt way too much.

He had better call Jasmine and let her know where he was and what was going on. Better she hear it from him first.

On the Bon Chance

In her office alone, Chance was absolutely pissed off. First there had been Roberto's little routine with that slut of a secretary—she could have strangled him when he looked at her all innocently and said they were just having a friendly drink. Now there were the goddamned hits on the train and barge, with a terrified Keller on his way back here practically peeing in his pants. She wasn't worried that the U.S. Navy was going to come calling as much as she was frustrated over the losses. How had they figured it out? Keller had told her it was impossible.

She was going to have to speak harshly with him about this.

And the schedule was going to have to be moved up, just in case. They only had one arrow left in their quiver now, and it had to be strung and loosed before their target had a chance to move out of the line of fire. She paged Roberto, a priority-one call. If he was interrupted trying to get into the secretary's pants, too bad. She sent half a dozen other pages, also P-1 calls. She didn't like the way this felt. Not at all. She did not want it to come unraveled now, not when they were so close to winning. Better to move and win a partial victory than to stand still and lose it all. The clock was ticking, and if time ran out before they launched, it would be all over.

Net Force HQ
Quantico, Virginia

Howard looked at Julio. "So, what do you think?"

Fernandez shook his head. "It's just simple enough it might work. Gridley can get the computer stuff done?"

"He says so."

"So if we get approval, we'd go when?"

"Tomorrow. After dark."

Julio shook his head. "Technology. Amazing stuff."

"Put together three squads, mixed male and female. I want thirty troopers, two pilots and copilots, the usual bells and whistles, given the limitations. Air transport, briefings, maps, assignments, I need everything ready to roll by 0600 tomorrow."

"Yes, sir. I'm on the way. Guess we'll see if the new top kick is as good as he thinks he is."

"He can't possibly think he's as good as you thought *you* were when you were a sergeant."

"Well, sir, that's because he couldn't possibly *be* that good."

Howard smiled.

After Julio had left, he looked at the computer images floating in the air above his conference table. The best plans were the simple ones, he knew, but maybe this one was too simple.

Only one way to find out.

***On the* Bon Chance**

Santos didn't like being hurried. Once he set his mind to a plan, he liked to have it flow naturally. Sometimes, you had to adjust to the unexpected, but this new bug up Missy's butt was too much, too quick. He'd tried to tell her, but she wasn't having any of it. Still pissed at him for the secretary.

Too bad, that. This speeded-up schedule was going to put a crimp in his seduction. The secretary was as good as on her back when Missy came in, all Ice Bitch, and started trying to pull his chain. She was gonna pay. It was just one more coin it was gonna cost her.

Meanwhile, he had to get his teams ready to move. Missy wanted it fast. Tomorrow, if possible, the day after at the latest. Too soon—but what could you do? He didn't want to miss the action.

Toni wandered around, taking more pictures, but feeling a sense of impending something. As the day wound down, nothing new happened she needed to think about. No sign of Santos, so maybe his boss had put the fear of God into him.

She briefly considered trying to get onto the private decks. Even went so far as to seem to get lost and wind up at one of the entrances to one such deck. But the electronic card reader would need a key, and as she started back the way she'd come, the door opened and revealed a couple of men standing on the other side, wearing photographer's sleeveless vests over their shirts, which in this kind of climate meant they were using the vests to cover pistols tucked into their belts—they certainly weren't cold.

One more small piece of circumstantial evidence, the armed guards. Of course, maybe they were there to guard a vault room, where the gambling winnings were kept?

Not likely. Most of what Toni had seen was cashless, all done on credit exchanges. You didn't need guards for that.

No, she would pack up and catch a late-afternoon helicopter out, head home. Earlier, she had heard somebody say it was supposed to rain tonight or tomorrow, a little tropical depression, not a hurricane or anything, but some wind and weather. She would just as soon be gone if that was going to happen—she didn't like to fly in the rain. She'd known some people who had been on a jet that tried to take off in a typhoon once. The jet had crashed and burned, and the folks she knew had been lucky to survive. Bad weather and flying didn't go together in Toni's book.

Le Boy, South Zone
Rio de Janeiro, Brazil

Jay looked around, and felt a little uncomfortable. The club was noisy, the music playing very loud, lights flashing, and people dancing. Most of the people dancing were men, there were only a handful of women, and some of them looked pretty mannish, too.

He turned back to his virtual beer. According to what he had learned, Le Boy was the biggest gay night club in the city. You kinda had to expect to see a lot of men, now, didn't you?

A tall, well-built bodybuilder in a pair of skin-tight leather pants and a tank top arrived at the bar to Jay's left and flashed him a big, toothy smile. "*Com lisença,*" he said, "*voce é ativo? O passivo?*"

Jay tapped the tiny translator hidden in his right ear, and the Portuguese the man had spoken was translated into English: "Excuse me, are you a top or a bottom?"

Even in VR, Jay flushed. "I'm waiting for a friend," he subvocalized. The translator turned the reply into Portuguese.

The buffed bodybuilder—they called them "barbies" here, Jay recalled from his research—kept smiling. "I could be your friend," the translator said in Jay's ear.

"Maybe," Jay said. "Do you know a man named Roberto Santos?"

His would-be friend's face went dark. "*Bicha*!" he said. Jay didn't need the translator for that one.

"He is a friend of yours?" the barbie said, his voice dangerous.

"No. An enemy."

The man nodded. "He is a bastard among bastards, a son of a whore, a fucker of his sister and grandmother!" He reached into his mouth and tugged. A partial dental plate came out—his top four front teeth were false. The barbie waved the plate at Jay. "He did this to me!" He put the plate back in.

Jay made sympathetic noises. "Tell me about him."

The barbie needed no more prompting. "He cruises the gay scene, though he is not gay. He sometimes goes into the—the dark rooms, and lets some poor boy give him oral sex. Then he beats him. He has hurt other of my friends. He always picks big men, strong men. He is a fighter, his fists are like iron. He enjoys hitting. He laughs while he does it."

"Why haven't the police arrested him? Has no one complained?"

The barbie nodded. "Oh, yes, many have complained. The police only laugh and shake their heads when they hear his name. He is protected. So protected that once he beat a man so bad the man died, and still the police did nothing. Santos is a devil."

Interesting. Jay had what he came here for. Time to move on.

School of Business
University of Hong Kong
Hong Kong, China

Professor Wang, a forty-five-ish woman with a pageboy haircut and a gray business suit so severe it made her look like a business nun, said, "Oh, yes, I remember her."

They were in a business library, the air conditioning blasting away. Jay nodded. "Anything you'd feel comfortable in saying about her?"

Wang smiled. "The words *comfortable* and *Jasmine Chance* don't belong in the same sentence. There's a story the students and staff used to pass around. Once, Jasmine was visiting the zoo, and there was a terrible earthquake. Some of the animals got loose. A pair of man-eating tigers escaped from their cage. Free and hungry, the tigers charged a group of school children. At the last second, Jasmine Chance stepped in between the hungry tigers and their prey. The tigers took one look at her, turned tail, and ran back to their cages in terror."

Jay chuckled politely.

"That's not the good part," Wang said. "The good part is, she charged the parents HK$400 each for saving their children."

"That sounds . . . harsh."

"Harsh? Let me tell you something I know is true. Jasmine wanted to be first in her class. But she was not doing well in one subject—and for her, not doing well was being second in her grades, only a high A instead of the highest one. So she seduced the teacher, a middle-aged man with a wife, four children, and three grandchildren. She got her first place. When the professor said he would leave his wife for her, she laughed at him. In great shame over what he had done and her refusal to accept him, he committed suicide. When somebody told Jasmine what had happened, she shrugged. 'Too bad,' she said. That woman is as moral as a shark. You don't ever want to get between her and what she wants."

Jay nodded. Even more interesting.

Net Force HQ
Quantico, Virginia

"So there you have it, boss. CyberNation has themselves a gay basher who apparently got away with at least one murder, and a woman who will do anything to accomplish her goals. I don't have a lot of other history on them, but Santos has been essentially a high-class knee-breaker for a couple of organizations, and Chance has risen up a couple of corporate ladders so fast she seemed to have wings. Add them into the mix, it just keeps getting thicker and thicker. Pretty soon, we have the whole cake."

"We're missing a couple of ingredients yet," Michaels said. "Your friend Keller wasn't on the train; neither were the others you listed who were supposed to be there."

Jay cursed.

"Yes, indeed. The German government is checking airports and other trains, but it appears he has flown the coop."

Jay cursed again.

"I believe you said that."

Jay shook his head. "Yeah. So, what now?"

"I am expecting a call from the director sometime in the next five minutes. If her clout is enough, we will be sending visitors to the *Bon Chance* in the very near future."

"I bet she named it after herself," Jay said.

"Excuse me?"

"The boat." He blew out a sigh. "Where is Toni?"

He looked at his watch. "She should be catching a helicopter from the ship about now. In fact, if you can access the passenger lists, I'd appreciate knowing which flight she is on."

"No problem. Mary Johnson."

Before Michaels could say anything else, the com chimed. His secretary said, "The director is on line one."

Michaels reached for the receiver, and shooed Jay out with a wave as he picked it up. Jay stood, but moved very slowly toward the door.

"Hello?"

"Commander. We have a 'go.' You better be right about this."

"Yes, ma'am," he said.

Jay raised an eyebrow from the doorway. Michaels nodded at him and raised one hand in a thumb's-up gesture.

"Yes!" Jay said in a stage whisper. He made a fist and pumped it.

Michaels wished he felt so positive.

34

***On the* Bon Chance**

Toni waited in line for the shuttle boat. The sky had gone gray, and while it wasn't raining yet, the wind had picked up and the southeasterly breeze felt damp. There was a full load of departing passengers waiting. Apparently more than a few people were worried about the weather, and didn't want to be on a ship ninety miles away from land if it got nasty.

The boat from the helicopter barge arrived and tied up at the base of the ramp, and after a few seconds, new arrivals climbed the stairs or wheelchair ramp onto the ship.

She hoped they had all come to gamble, because they surely weren't going to get much sun—

Hold on—

Coming up the ramp was a face she recognized. It took a second for her to realize why.

Keller. From the picture she'd seen. This was Jay's guy!

What was he doing here? He was supposed to be in

Germany, wasn't he? This must mean something.

As soon as he'd passed, Toni left the shuttle boat line, as if she had suddenly remembered that she had forgotten something. The gap she left filled instantly. She glanced at her watch. The comsat wasn't due for another forty-five minutes. Could she risk calling Alex on the ship's phones? She could keep it innocuous—*Hey, you know that picture you gave me? Well, I thought I had lost it, but I found it after all, right here on the ship.*

Anybody who didn't know who she was could hardly tell what she was talking about from that, could they?

Not likely. But if the ship's phones were tapped, and that would be easy enough to do since they were owned and maintained by CyberNation, they might wonder why a secretary from Falls Church was calling somebody at Net Force headquarters. Or maybe they might be even able to recognize Alex's name on the home phone or his virgil. And even if her scrambler kept them from hearing anything other than noise, maybe they would wonder what a secretary was *doing* with a scrambled phone.

Any of those would be bad.

No, she would wait until the next footprint so she could call on the secure line. There were still a dozen more copters leaving this evening, and she needed to get a better look at this guy, maybe even see where he went or who he might talk to—

As if some bored deity had been listening, Toni suddenly saw Jasmine Chance, now dressed in a black jumpsuit and sandals, step into view ahead. Toni turned away and put a hand up to block her face from view.

Keller went straight to her, and while she couldn't overhear his conversation, he was obviously pretty excited from the way he waved his hands around.

Well, well. What did this mean?

Alex would surely want to know about this. Yes, she could call him from the Mainland, or even from the shuttle copter, but there was no hurry, was there? Maybe she could find out something more before she had to leave.

In the Air near Fort Lauderdale, Florida

The old 727's rebuilt engines were reassuring in their smooth, dependable drone. They were only a few minutes out now, and Julio was going over the checklist a final time as they began their descent into Fort Lauderdale.

"Our boy Mr. Gridley here came through." Julio smiled at Jay, who sat across the aisle. "First squad and half of second squad will be on Bird A; third squad and the other half of second on Bird B."

Howard nodded. Next to him sat Commander Michaels. Michaels hadn't planned to come along at all, even to sit onshore, but he hadn't heard from Toni, who was supposed to have left the ship by now. According to Jay, Mary Johnson had not gotten on any of the shuttle copters for the Mainland yet. Maybe the weather had more people leaving than normal, delaying the flights, but Michaels was worried enough to go along. Howard didn't blame him. He knew how he'd feel if it was his wife there.

"Weather radar shows an ugly set of heavy showers moving from the southeast toward the target, the main body of which will have arrived by 2100—we're gonna get wet."

"I'll be sure to bring my umbrella," Howard said.

"Wind'll just turn it inside out, sir. Steady breeze will be almost thirty knots, gusting to forty."

"Go on."

"Troops all have Class III spider silk vests for armor—that's the best we can do, given the scenario—so nobody is real bulletproof. Augmented-LOSIR coms will be set on opchan Gamma, and we carry sidearms and subguns, plus the usual assortment of puke gas, flashbangs, and all like that, packed away in our luggage. Everybody knows what he or she is supposed to do."

Howard nodded.

The seat belt light and audible warning went on.

Julio said, "So, to condense things a little, we get there, take over before anybody knows what is going on, and capture the computers before they can trash 'em. Then our computer wizard here waltzes in and collects the evidence, the bad guys all go to prison, and everybody lives happily ever after."

It won't be that easy, Howard knew. *It never is.*

The jet started to descend; he could feel the pressure in his ears change.

"No word from Toni yet?" he said.

Michaels looked worried. "No. She should have called by now."

***On the* Bon Chance**

Toni had a problem. Her room was no longer available, she had checked out, and she didn't want to be wandering around the ship towing her suitcase. That made it kind of hard to skulk, when the wheels of your little carry-on were clacking over every imperfection in the floor. So when Keller went to a cabin, she ducked into a public toilet nearby, put her suitcase on the commode in an empty stall, locked the door, and climbed out over the top of the stall's door. It would have been smarter to have found a concierge and checked the bag, but she didn't want to get too far away from Keller, in case he came out.

He did come out, not ten minutes later, and she stayed far enough back so he didn't seem to notice her. This was working out all right.

He went straight to one of the guarded entrances to the private decks, and she couldn't follow him in there.

Okay. He was here, Alex needed that information, and that might be all she was gonna get. It was what it was.

When she went back to get her suitcase, it was gone. And her scrambled cell phone and flatscreen were in the suitcase.

This was not good. Not good at all.

Probably housekeeping had the bag. Somebody had reported the stall locked, a janitor had come by, found the bag. Nothing sinister about it. She had her wallet and ID, she could just go and find housekeeping and pick it up.

Maybe. Or maybe that wasn't such a good idea.

She sat in the stall and thought about the situation. If Alex and the Net Force teams were going to move on the ship, she didn't want to do anything that might possibly cause them problems. So making the phone call without her coded phone was out.

If they did show up here, chances were good they'd catch Keller—she could tell them he was here when she saw them. It wasn't as if she was the only civilian on the ship, now was it? There were probably a couple thousand tourists here—she wouldn't be in any more danger than any of them. Less, because she knew there might be a reason to keep her head down, and because she had some skill at staying out of harm's way.

If the suitcase was in the lost-and-found waiting to be claimed, no problem. But if they had opened it, seen who it belonged to, and wondered why it had been sitting in an empty, locked toilet stall, that might make them curious. It would surely make her curious if she were running security on a ship. Once they saw it wasn't a bomb, they might start to ask themselves other questions: Why on Earth would anybody leave their luggage there? What possible reason could there be?

The flatscreen was clean, no damaging files on it; she'd run the burn program. The cell phone was iffy. It looked fine, just another commercial model, tens of thousands of them around. There weren't any numbers programmed into it, and they'd have to be real inquisitive to take it apart and discover there was hardware and software built in that scrambled calls, coming or going.

But—just for the sake of argument—suppose they did that? Mary Johnson goes toddling in to collect her missing bag, and security—in the form of Jasmine Chance, who obviously bore Ms. Mary no love whatsoever for moving in on her Roberto real estate—decides to have a long chat with her? International waters, no constitutional rights, that would be, well . . . bad.

That word seemed to be cropping up a whole lot in the last few minutes.

Okay, she decided, that was what she would do. She would go to ground, find a hidey-hole, and stay there, see if Alex showed up. If so, good. If not, she'd worry about that when she got there.

Where to hide?

She had an idea. Probably the last place they'd look if they decided they needed to find her.

Chance called Santos into her office. He came in, a slow stroll, as if he had all the time in the world. He was like a big tomcat, coming and going as he pleased, not going to hurry for anything.

She wanted to slap him.

"Okay," she said, "whatever problems you and I are having, they have to go on hold now. We need to get this done, and we can sort the rest of it out later."

He shrugged. "Problems? What problems?"

Now she *really* wanted to slap him. Instead, she smiled. Fine. He'd pay for all this later. He truly would.

Santos looked at his watch. He had an hour and a half before he needed to leave. Plenty of time, since he was all packed, and since he could take the private launch to the copter platform without waiting for the regular boat. Maybe he should go and find that secretary? Fifteen minutes would be more than enough time to relax them both, no? Time enough for a shower afterward.

Why not?

He headed for the Security Cam Center. If she was still on board, she would have passed in front of a glass eye recently. The computer system that ran the surveillance gear couldn't search for a particular person, but it could, within limits, hunt for kinds of people. Women, brunettes, a certain size, smaller or larger. All you had to do was tell it what you wanted. Well. Generally. The computer probably wouldn't appreciate what he really wanted, and it couldn't see that as long as she had her clothes on anyway.

He smiled.

Fort Lauderdale, Florida

Michaels stood in line behind Lieutenant Fernandez, who was behind Jay. General Howard was already on board the Sikorsky. They all wore touristy civilian clothes, and carried assorted sizes and shapes of luggage. The bags were a little heavier than what most tourists would be bringing, but there weren't any metal detectors to pass through before boarding the choppers, so that didn't matter.

Everybody in the passenger line was from Net Force. At a different hotel helipad ten minutes away, another group of Net Force troopers stood in a similar line. Jay had booked them all into two flights, making sure nobody else would be on those particular craft but them. Well, except for the copter crews, and they weren't going to be a problem, the general had assured him. They didn't know the passengers were anything other than folks going to gamble. If something unforeseen happened, John had his own pilots who could take over.

It was simple enough. They would fly out to the helicopter barge, take the boat from there to the ship, and infiltrate the ship. It was not a direct assault, it was an undercover operation. By the time security on the ship realized it, it ought to be a done deal. Much less likely there'd be any shooting this way, and less chance of civilians getting wounded by accident. A pretty clever idea, actually.

Though Michaels had planned to stay in Quantico and wait until it was over, Toni's failure to report wouldn't let him do that. Right up until the last minute, he was hoping she'd call, but she didn't. And he wasn't going to let his people and all their hardware go without him, not as long as Toni was on that ship.

It wasn't politically or tactically smart, but hey, hell with it, he was the boss. At least for now.

The line moved along easily, with a military precision. Michaels had to grin at that. The copter's crew wouldn't have any idea their passengers were all part of the same group. Jay's work had made them appear to be from all over the country, singles, couples, a trio of college friends, no reason to think they were anything other than tourists.

As he climbed the short flight of steps into the craft, Michaels heard two troopers, a man and a woman, talking to each other.

"So, this your first trip to Florida?"

"No, actually, my family used to vacation here when I was a girl. Of course, that was up north, a little town called Destin, near Fort Walton Beach."

"Wow. I had an uncle who was stationed at the Naval Air Station at Pensacola. Small world."

Other troopers talked, establishing their cover. Michaels felt a nervous twinge in his belly, a quick flutter. He found a seat, tucked his bag between his feet, and buckled himself in. John had lent him his body armor vest. It was folded into the bag, along with a plastic handgun and a com headset. Since he had no active role in the mission, Michaels was supposed to find a secure spot and stay out of the way until the ship was secured, but if trouble popped up, he'd be able to communicate and he'd have a weapon and some protection.

He hoped Toni was all right. Yes, she could take care of herself better than most people, but even so, she wasn't a superwoman. Something could have gone wrong. Probably it was nothing—weather, crowded flights, her phone on the blink, that was all. But he couldn't help worrying. He loved her. And if she was all right, he didn't care how much she hated it, he was never going to send her into the field like this again.

35

On the **Bon Chance**

Keller had checked the operations center and everything was fine. Well, as fine as it would get. Chance's hurry-up was going to cause big problems. His team was good, the best, but they couldn't walk on water. They were at eighty-five, eighty-eight percent readiness, and if Omega launch was tomorrow, they wouldn't be able to improve on that. He had them all running full blast, and as soon as he had a chance to take a shower, get into some fresh clothes, and grab a quick bite, he would be right back there with them. He hated this. He wanted ten-for-ten for his part, but eight or nine was going to have to do it.

Maybe Santos the sociopath and his team of mouth-breathers could take up the slack. Not Keller's fault if they couldn't. He had been given a timeline, he had kept to it. If they wanted to hurry him along, fine, but in that case, they couldn't bitch about his work.

The door to his cabin stuck. He had to wipe the keycard three times to get it to open. Just one more little glitch in his life he didn't need. He flipped on the lights, went into the bedroom, and sat on the bed. Took off his shoes, his shirt, and undershirt. He was reaching for his belt buckle when a woman said, "I think that's enough for now."

He jerked around so hard he nearly fell down.

A short little brunette stood there in T-shirt, jeans, and running shoes.

"Who are you? What are you doing in my room?"

"Nobody you know, Mr. Keller. What happened to you? You get caught in a riot?"

She nodded at his bruises, which had developed several different shades of brown and purple.

"I'm going to call security," he said.

She shook her head. "No, I'm afraid you can't do that."

He blinked at her. She was, what? Five two, maybe a hundred and twenty, twenty-five pounds? He took a step toward the cabin's phone on the bedside table.

Somehow, she got between him and the phone and shoved him. He was off-balanced by the little push. He fell on the bed.

Screw this! He might get mauled by a man like Santos, but he was not going to be pushed around by some little *woman*! He jumped up, intending to slap her silly. He swung his hand at her face, hard—

She ducked the slap, and hit him with a brick in the ribs! Before he could recover, she did something to his feet, tripped him, and he fell back on the bed again.

He lost it. All the suppressed rage he'd felt at being used and abused by Chance, at being assaulted by that trained ape Santos, at being attacked by a woman in his own room, it all exploded. He screamed and leaped at her. He was going to choke the life from her—!

He came out of grayness, puzzled. He saw a woman sitting next to him, watching him. Who was this? Where was he? His thoughts were sluggish, as though wrapped in sheets of lead. He hurt, more than he had before. He needed a pain pill, that's what he needed. Had he been in an accident?

"Sorry," the woman said.

Part of it came back to him. He was in his cabin, on the ship. He'd come here, to . . . to do *some*thing, and this woman had been here. She had attacked him. Hit him with a club. Where was the club?

"Wh-who are you? What do you want?" God, he hurt.

"It's not important who I am," she said. "But we need to talk. I need you to tell me all about what you've been up to."

A surge of depression broke over him. This sucked! He had been beaten by Santos, threatened with death. And now, he had been beaten by a woman! A tiny little woman! It was embarrassing. He was ashamed. He felt himself starting to cry. What had he done to deserve any of this? It wasn't right!

"It's all right," she said, patting him on the shoulder. "I won't hurt you anymore."

That *really* made things worse.

In the Air East of Fort Lauderdale, Florida

The Sikorsky's intercom bonged: "Ladies and gentlemen, this is your captain. As you've noticed, we're getting a little weather here, and apparently the conditions are worse at our destination. While we could probably make it just fine, I'd rather not take the risk, so I'm afraid we're going to have to abort our flight and go back to Fort Lauderdale. Sorry for the inconvenience."

With those words, the big helicopter started a slow turn to port.

Howard sighed. Of course. It had been too easy. He looked across the aisle at Julio and nodded.

Julio unbuckled his seat belt, stood, then stepped into the aisle and headed forward.

One of the two flight attendants moved to intercept him. "Sir, please take your seat. The captain has the seat belt sign lit."

"I'm gonna puke," Julio said. He moved closer toward the flight control cabin, which wasn't far.

"I'll get you an airsickness bag, but you need to sit down—"

Julio said, "Sergeant Reaves?"

Reaves, a brawny man with a high-and-tight buzz cut, came up and grabbed the flight attendant, one arm pinning her arms to her body, the other hand covering her mouth. The woman tried to yell, but only a little sound got past the sergeant's powerful grip.

The second flight attendant, at the back, saw this and reached for an intercom mike, but a trooper caught her and sat her back in her seat.

Julio reached under his tails-out Hawaiian shirt and pulled his pistol, the old warhorse of a Beretta he carried, and hurried forward to have a little chat with the pilot and copilot.

A few seconds later, the helicopter turned back toward the southeast.

Howard looked at Michaels and gave the commander a little shrug. "Stuff happens," he said. "No problem."

Howard turned and motioned to his pilot to go forward. The man did. A minute later, Julio marched the copilot back and sat him in the vacated seat. His pistol was tucked back into its holster. He went back to his seat and buckled himself in.

"Everything okay, Lieutenant?"

"All systems green, sir. The captain has decided that cooperation is in his best interest, since our pilot is in the second chair with a gun and he's let the captain know he knows how to fly this thing. He wasn't ordered to turn back, it was his decision. ETA is thirty minutes. Might as well sit back and enjoy the ride."

A downdraft dropped the copter at that moment, a free fall that made them nearly weightless for a second or so. The fall stopped, and the craft shook as if it had bumped into something in the air. Howard looked at Julio.

"Think of it as a new and exciting ride at Disney World," Julio said. "The Upchucker."

On the Bon Chance

Santos looked at his watch and frowned. Forty-five minutes, and no sign of Mary Johnson. He had called and found that she had checked out, but the rain and wind were worse now, and they had shut down the commercial flights back to the Mainland, and according to their records, Ms. Johnson had not left yet. So she was here somewhere, and if she wasn't in her room, or in the casinos, restaurants, or bars, where was she?

Maybe she had found a lover? Was lying in bed letting the roll of the sea rock her and some lucky man into easy sex?

Well. It didn't really matter. Pretty soon, he would have to leave. Too bad.

His com rang. He pulled it from his belt and opened it. "Yes?"

Missy said, "Have you seen Jackson? He's supposed to be in Computer Operations and he's not."

"Haven't seen him," Santos said. And wasn't likely to, if Jackson saw him first. "You try his room?"

"He's not answering his phone, his pager, or knocks on the door."

"Maybe he's in a bathroom throwing up? Boat's moving some, and that Jackson, he's got kind of a weak stomach. So I heard."

"I doubt that."

"Or maybe he's getting himself a little pussy. I hear he likes that."

"Grow up, Roberto!" There was a short pause. "You'd better get going. The storm is getting worse, and you have to be on the Mainland."

"Don't worry about me, I'm not gonna disappear like Jackson."

He flipped the phone shut, tapped it against his other palm, then stuck it back on his belt. That was odd, that Keller wasn't around. He lived for his computers. Maybe before he took off, he should check Keller's cabin, make sure he hadn't had a heart attack or something.

Toni listened, astounded by the scope of the planned attack on the Internet. Keller, once he got started, was babbling like a man stoked on amphetamines, talking so fast he kept running out of air and had to suck more in big gasps.

Hacks. EMP devices. Men with guns and cable cutters. This was major. She was going to have to call Alex with this, it was too big to risk letting it get started. People were poised to do all this in a few hours, and authorities around the U.S., around the world, had to know.

Keller knew some of it, but not all. They needed to get the locations for attacks on the hardware, so they could stop them. Undoubtedly those were in the computers. Could Keller access those plans from here?

Yes, he could. He had his flatscreen. He could download those files. Would she like him to do it?

Toni smiled. This would justify her staying here! "Do it," she said.

It didn't take that long. When he was done, he burned the download into a mini-DVD and ejected it from the machine. "Here it is," he said.

Toni took it. She would call Alex, right now. If he wasn't on the way, this would be important enough to scramble a military copter and get help here. Toni said, "You did good, Jackson. Now just sit there for a minute while I make a call."

As she reached for the phone, somebody knocked on the cabin's door. No, not knocked, *pounded* on it, as if they were trying to punch a hole in it.

"Jackson! You in there, boy? Open up!"

Santos!

"No! No! Go away!" Keller yelled, before Toni could stop him.

Uh-oh. They were in trouble now—

Chance felt like a caged beast. She paced back and forth in her office. Where was Keller? Where was Santos? Why hadn't he left yet? Neither man was absolutely necessary at this point—the plan would go with or without them—but the lack of either would cripple things more than a little. Dammit! What was happening here?

In the Air

It was dark, the wind rocked the copter like a leaf blown by the winds of fate, and the rain was coming down pretty steady. Not a great night to be flying way the hell out over the ocean.

"There it is," Howard said.

Michaels looked through the window. A smear of bright light shined through the darkness. The helicopter barge. Past that, at least half a mile or so, he'd guess, was the gambling ship, also lit up like a Christmas tree.

Fernandez lurched back from the front of the copter, holding onto the seats as he came down the aisle, just barely able to stay on his feet. He got to them, sat, buckled up. "Landing is gonna be tricky," he said. "Our pilot wants to let the captain do it, it's his bird, he knows her better. The barge is rocking some, and their flight control doesn't really want to let us try it, but we have insisted—too dangerous to fly back, the captain said. They said we're gonna have to ride the storm out tied to the deck, 'cause they ain't running the transport boats, it's pretty choppy out there."

"It's a little far to be swimming in this weather, isn't it?" Michaels said.

Howard grinned. "Oh, I'm sure we can convince them to let us use the shuttle boat, if we ask real politely."

The copter dropped lower, spiraling in toward the landing barge. The deck didn't look very big from here. Kind of like a postage stamp.

Michaels leaned back from the rain-streaked window. The helicopter bounced and jerked to the left, then back to the right, and caught another wind shear that dropped them like a stone so suddenly that his stomach tried to climb up into his mouth. Behind him, he heard somebody vomiting. Into a puke bag, he hoped.

"Hang on, folks," the captain said. "We're going in."

36

***On the* Bon Chance**

Toni had, she figured, about two seconds before Santos came through the door, either by using a keycard or by kicking it down. He knew Keller was in here, no question.

But Keller was a quivering lump on the bed, curled now into a fetal position, hands over his face.

She had to get this information to Alex. And she didn't want to go one-on-one with Santos, not in a space as cramped as this cabin. Maybe she could take him. Maybe not. He was big, strong, fit, and trained, and she couldn't risk losing the data she had gotten from Keller. What to do?

The moment of panic flared, but then her brain started working. She realized that Santos *didn't know who she was, or what she was doing in Keller's cabin.* She could play that, but she'd have to do it fast.

She grabbed her shirt, pulled it off, then peeled off her sports bra. She held them in one hand, loosely covered her breasts, and hurried to the door.

• • •

Santos was having trouble getting the keycard override to work. He kept dragging it through the slot, but the little light stayed red. He was about to kick the door when it opened.

A half-naked woman stood there.

The secretary!? She was here with *Keller*!?

What god had he pissed off that this man, this *picaflor*, was sleeping with *two* of his women? That was it. He was gonna kill the guy.

"Roberto? What are you doing here?"

"I need to talk to Keller. He's supposed to be working. But I guess I can see why not. No wonder I couldn't find you."

"He's putting his clothes on," she said. "In there."

"Yeah, well, you wait right here. I got something for you." He cupped his groin, hefted it. "Bigger and harder than anything Keller has."

She smiled at him. Moved her hand with the shirt in it out of the way and took a deep breath.

Ah. Nice mambas.

Oh, yeah, this would have to be quick, but he could do that. Get Keller out of here, pronto, and get back to her. Leave Missy with a little something to think about—he'd make sure Keller told her about it.

He was already halfway ready as he moved past her through the short hall toward the bedroom.

Toni ran. She sprinted as if she were trying out for the Olympic hundred-meter dash team. She passed a couple in the hall, saw the man grin at her. Well, a half-naked woman running down the hall was probably not something they saw every day. She didn't have time to stop and dress. By the time Santos realized something was wrong, she wanted to be far away. She had to find another hiding place, fast.

The rain slashed down like a first-class hotel shower with good water pressure, and the blue-and-white-striped canvas roof on the shuttle boat didn't do much to keep the people under it dry.

Michaels was soaked by the time he got on the craft, as were the other "tourists." The rain came in almost horizontally when the wind gusted. The spider silk vest he wore under his shirt didn't help anything.

Next to him, Howard yelled, "I've left the pilots watching the crews of the two birds and two other troopers guarding the barge crew. They just developed serious radio and com trouble."

The way the boat was bobbing up and down, pitching and yawing, the helicopter crews were the least of Michaels's worries. There was enough light here to see the whitecaps and foam blown from the waves. He tasted salt then yelled, "Nice night for a boat ride!"

Whichever trooper was operating the engine cranked it up, and the shuttle, built to hold sixty people and only half full, moved away from its moorings against the barge. The motion got worse. Anybody who was prone to seasickness was going to be giving up everything they'd eaten for a month. Fortunately, that wasn't one of Michaels's afflictions.

The boat rocked and shook, pitched dangerously, but with its back finally turned to the wind, straightened out a little. It was still a long way to the ship.

As the boat slogged through the four-foot seas, Michaels's virgil buzzed against his hip. He'd left it on vibratory mode. Good, since he'd never have heard it in this wind and rain. He grabbed the unit. The caller number ID didn't mean anything, and the little screen was blank, no visual. He held it to his ear so he could hear better.

"Hello?"

"Alex, it's me."

Toni!

"Babe, what—?"

"Where are you?" she cut in.

"On a boat heading for the ship," he said. "We'll be there in five minutes."

"Thank God. Listen, I'm on a public phone. Jay was right, about everything. The balloon goes up tomorrow. I've got all the details. I'll call again later, but right now, I've got to go. I love you."

She discommed.

A malignant worm roiled in his gut.

"What?" Howard said.

"Toni. She's in some kind of trouble. Enough to risk calling on an open line. She says she's got the evidence we need."

"My God," Howard said.

"Hurry this thing up," Michaels said.

Howard made a hand signal. The boat's engine roared louder, but it didn't seem to move any faster.

Santos couldn't figure it out for a second when he saw Keller lying on the bed. What, had she screwed him stupid? He was just lying there, no shirt, in his pants, curled up in a ball. Was he afraid Santos was going to beat him again?

"Keller. Keller!"

The man whimpered. "Don't! I didn't mean to!"

Santos strode to the bed, reached down, and grabbed Keller by the hair, jerking him up. "What are you whining about?"

"I didn't mean to!" he said. "She beat me. She made me tell her!"

Santos turned to look behind him. "Tell her what?"

"About Omega!"

Santos let go of Keller's hair and slapped him with his free hand, but only once, then ran back to where he had left the woman.

She was gone, of course.

He looked out into the hall. No sign of her.

Santos pulled his com from his belt and thumbed the emergency button. "This is Santos," he said, when security answered. "There's a woman on board, short, black hair, maybe twenty-eight, thirty, calls herself 'Mary Johnson.' Dressed in jeans, running shoes, a black T-shirt. Find her. Find her now!"

The officer at the boat moorage was amazed. He looked at the boat with its drenched tourists. "You must be crazy to come across in weather like this! Somebody's head is gonna roll!" He looked at the boat's pilot. "And who the hell are you? Where is Marty? This is his shift."

The pilot grinned and shoved his Walther pistol into the officer's belly. "Marty got sick. If you behave yourself, you won't catch what he's got."

The officer froze; his face went white under his rain hat.

"Let's move it, people!" Fernandez said.

Michaels was first up the ladder.

Toni had solved the problem of where to hide by running past doors until she found one that was open. She slipped into a passenger cabin, saw a maid cleaning the room, and stepped into the bathroom before the woman got a good look at her.

In Spanish, Toni said, "Hey, you can leave that," she called out. "Come back later please, okay?"

The maid said, "*Esta bien, Señora*," and left.

Once the maid was gone, Toni checked out the cabin. No computer, so she couldn't try to upload the disc into a Net Force receptacle, or even some friend's mailbox. Damn!

She couldn't stay here long, she knew. Santos would have put out an alarm by now. If somebody asked the maid if she'd seen a *norte americana*, maybe Toni's speaking Spanish would throw them off. Maybe not. But the ship was rigged with surveillance cams all over, and she didn't want to let one of those see her. Alex had said he'd be here in a few minutes. If they were about to start some kind of operation, all she had to do was stay hidden until it was done.

That was all.

• • •

Michaels looked at his watch. In ten minutes, everybody on the assault team was supposed to be in position. In fourteen minutes, everybody would put on their specially augmented LOSIR headsets, and sixty seconds later, they would pull guns, fire off explosive charges that would blow open secured doors, and, in theory, take over the ship before anybody could wipe the computers. He had already slipped his headset from the bag John Howard had given him, and had it tucked away in his shirt pocket, ready to go.

But—where was Toni?

Michaels went belowdecks, and wandered the halls, looking. There were some security types with headcoms of their own moving around purposefully, and he was sure they were looking for Toni. Or maybe they were looking for tourists carrying bags. He slipped the bag with the gun in it behind a potted plant as two of the men approached him.

Unfortunately, one of them spotted the bag. "This yours?"

Michaels looked at them. "What? Never saw it before."

One of the guards picked up the bag.

Alex didn't want them opening it. Quickly, he said. "Hey, you looking for a little brunette?"

The man about to open the bag stopped so suddenly he almost fell. "You've seen her?"

"Yeah, she came out up on the deck. Back by the swimming pool."

"Thank you, sir." The man took off, talking into his com.

That would help, Michaels thought. As long as Toni wasn't hiding out at the swimming pool. But this was bad. He looked at his watch. Twelve minutes.

Santos didn't know what was going on, but he knew the little secretary was not what she pretended to be. He should have known. Those legs didn't belong to somebody who sat on her butt all day. This woman had moves. He was getting stupid to trust what he saw.

He had to find her. She was a spy, and if Keller had rolled over and given up the operation, it could mean big trouble. And as much as he hated to do it, he had to tell Missy.

When he found her in her office and did, she was not pleased.

"What?! Are you sure?"

"I left Keller lying on his bed curled up like a baby, sobbing," he said. "He gave it up."

"We've got to find her before she can get any of this off the ship!"

"My men are all looking. Somebody saw her by the swimming pool."

Missy shook her head. "Why would she go there? She can't get off the ship there. She can't hide there. Shut off all the outgoing communication."

"Already done."

"The swimming pool, no, that doesn't make sense."

"Maybe she isn't alone," he said. "Maybe she's meeting somebody."

"Find her, Roberto!"

Howard looked at his watch, then at Jay Gridley. "Stay behind me," he said.

"Don't worry about that."

Howard adjusted the spider silk vest under his still-wet Hawaiian shirt. It was too tight. But that's what he got for letting Michaels have his and using one of the spares. He loosened the side tabs a little. Better.

On the minute, Howard and Jay both pulled their augmented-LOSIR com headsets from their packs, designed especially to work indoors and around corners, and slipped them on. "Don't forget your nose plugs," he said.

Jay nodded, touched his nostrils. Already in.

"This is Howard. We are still on."

Howard stepped to the card reader, put a strip of plastic

explosive onto it, and waved Jay back. He looked at his watch, counted down the seconds.

"—four . . . three . . . two . . . one . . . now!"

The card reader flashed like a strobe and exploded.

After a beat, the door slid open and two armed guards jumped out, waving pistols.

Howard sprayed them with emetic foam, a burst that looked as if a can of shaving cream had exploded. Thick white billows of the stuff enveloped the pair. They both screamed, and both started retching. *Great night for reverse peristalsis,* he thought.

It would have been safer to have shot them, but they didn't want to kill anybody if they didn't have to.

Even as the guards fell, he was moving. "Go, go!"

Jay was right behind him.

37

Michaels heard Howard over the headset, then felt the small explosions through his shoes, and knew the teams had begun their assault on the computer decks. It would take only a few seconds, and with luck, they'd be able to shut down the computers before they destroyed their information.

He looked up and saw a ship security man with a drawn pistol running in his direction, and he flattened himself against the wall, playing the frightened tourist. The man didn't seem interested in him, but kept running.

As he passed, Michaels stuck his foot out. The guy tripped, sailed a good eight or ten feet, and came down on his face, screaming as he fell.

Michaels ran up behind the downed man and as he tried to stand, he kicked him in the head. The guy collapsed.

Score one for the good guys.

Santos was about to open the door of the room where the Cuban maid had seen a woman come in when his com buzzed stridently, the emergency pulse, long and loud rings.

"What?"

"Sir, we have some kind of trouble belowdecks! There's a—aaahhh!"

"What?! What?!"

Santos heard the sound of somebody vomiting noisily.

He snapped the com shut. The woman? Or her friends? Whatever, it was serious. He headed toward the stairs. He'd better see what was going on.

He rounded a corner in the corridor, and saw two men in Hawaiian shirts heading away from him. They were dressed as tourists, but they wore com headsets and carried submachine guns. He could see what looked like body armor under their wet shirts.

Not his people.

He pulled back out of sight. Grabbed his com, triggered the emergency caller.

This time, there was no answer. A minute ago, it was working fine.

Either his people were too busy to answer, which was not likely, or the ship's communication system had been shut down. Neither was good for him.

He knew what had happened. The spy had arranged to get her people on board. Maybe they had been here for hours, days. The place was done. If he hung around, he was going to be done, too.

It was time to leave this party.

If he could get to the launch, he could escape. The cigarette boat had a couple hundred miles of range, easy. In the storm, nobody would see him, and even if they had a ship with radar, they'd never catch him in it. It would beat him half to death in this kind of weather, but the cigarette could outrun anything afloat in these waters. Florida had a long and unprotected east coast. He would find a secluded spot. Once he was ashore, he would be safe.

Yes. He needed to go. Now.

But as he cut up and through the gym, he came across

another tourist with a headset. Fortunately, this one wasn't holding a gun.

"You're Santos," the man said.

"That's right. And who are you?"

"I'm a federal agent. You're under arrest. Sit down and put your hands on top of your head."

Santos laughed.

Chance realized when the com system shut down that something grave had happened. She saw a stranger run past, men with guns, and she knew instantly that the ship was under assault.

Her people weren't prepared for that, not a full-out military attack. They could dump the computer drives, but the security had not been designed to hold out against SEAL or Special Forces teams once they actually got onto the ship—that had never been in the cards.

Now, it would come down to lawyers and money. CyberNation would take care of her. She had seen to that. But her insurance to that end might be a liability if it fell into the wrong hands. Best she attend to that, right now—

38

Michaels stared at the man. The ship's gym was a fair-sized room with wall-to-wall mirrors and a thick carpet, exercise machines around the perimeter and mostly open in the center. Santos circled around a treadmill and leaped into a dive at the floor, hit on his hands, and did a front handspring directly toward him.

Michaels had never seen anything like this—!

Despite his training to go in when attacked, however, Michaels sectored off to his right, and the heel missed his nose by an inch. A good move, it turned out: If he'd gone in, he would have eaten it.

What the hell was this? Some kind of demented gymnastics?

The black man landed on his feet, then twirled around into a crouch facing Michaels. He danced from side to side, raising and lowering himself from almost upright into a full squat and back as if he were some kind of a crazed jack-in-the-box.

Reflections of Santos matched him in the floor-to-ceiling mirrors.

This was surreal, like something out of a Bruce Lee movie.

Santos had beaten a man to death, according to Jay, so let's not forget, he is dangerous.

Michaels kept himself angled at forty-five degrees, left foot forward, one hand covering high-line the other low-line, not moving.

"What kind of crooked stance is that?" Santos asked, grinning. "Not karate, not jujitsu. Not, for sure, *Capoeira.*"

Capoeira? That rang a bell. It was the South American fighting style the African slaves either created or brought with them from the Old Continent to the New World. Acrobatic stuff, but that was pretty much all he knew about it. He had heard Toni talk about it. That would fit. Santos was from Brazil.

"Welcome to *O-Jôgo, homem branco!*" The man leaped up and did a back flip, landed easily, one foot hitting before the other, one-two! He laughed.

Michaels felt another moment of panic. *Get a grip here!*

Santos shuffled to Michaels's right, almost as if dancing to some unheard tune.

Michaels didn't move. Let him dance. He wasn't doing any damage out there.

Santos jinked in, just at the edge of kicking range, then jumped back, trying to draw the attack.

Michaels held his ground.

The black man smiled. "You know something, don't you, Mr. White Man Federal Agent? But what is it, White? How well does it work?"

"Come and find out."

"Oh, yes, I will."

Santos shuffled the other way, stepped in, and feinted a high kick. He was too far away to connect, and outside Michaels's range. Michaels stayed where he was.

"You waiting for me to make a mistake?"

"Whenever you're ready."

Santos laughed. Then he twirled and whirled and

dropped, spun into a kind of crabbed cartwheel, and somehow ate up the space between them. His kick was low, and while Michaels dropped his stance, turned, and managed to get a sweeping block down, the kick was too powerful to do more than slightly deflect it. It glanced off his thigh instead of hitting it square on, but it still hurt even in passing.

Michaels should have blocked it, but it wasn't major. The goal here was not so much to win as it was to not-lose. The winner was the guy who got to go home, under his own steam, and well enough to be able to hug his family.

Santos shifted back and forth from foot to foot, waving his arms in a pattern that was probably supposed to be hypnotic. "Not bad for an old man," he said. "What you call this, *Branco?*"

Branco. Must mean "white." "Does it matter?"

"Just curious. Always lookin' to educate myself more."

"I'll tell you all about it after we're done. Maybe you can find a teacher in prison."

Santos laughed, a deep belly rumble. "That's funny. You expectin' to be around after we're done, me in jail? No way. Tell me now."

"I don't think so," Michaels said. He pivoted to follow Santos as he circled, switching his hands from high to low, still in the open-gate stance.

"Good economy," Santos said, nodding. "No wasted motions. Maybe I let you live so you can tell me about this. Chinese, maybe? Burmese? Why don't I know it?"

"You need to get out more. Lots of things you don't know. We have the ship."

"Maybe. But you don't have Santos."

Michaels took a deep breath. He let half of it out. "Relax, Alex," he said quietly to himself.

The days he'd practiced the mental exercise Toni had showed him paid off. He dropped lower, with just enough tension to stay upright. His breathing deepened, and he felt much looser. Considering his current situation, this was more than passing extraordinary.

Santos raised an eyebrow. "What did you just *do* there, Mr. Federal Agent?"

Michaels smiled. "Bring your pretty little dance closer and see." It was, Toni had always taught him, good *silat* to bait an opponent. Maybe it would make him angry enough to lose control, do something stupid. Probably not this guy, who looked as if he'd been carved out of stone and was just as impervious to trash-talk as he would be a hammer, but it didn't hurt to try.

"I will, don't you worry. But we have time, yes? No reason to rush. We might make the game last a while."

Santos feinted a kick and punch, then spun and dropped, put his hands down on the floor, and shot out a mule kick with his left foot, low, aimed for Michaels's knee—

Michaels sectored to the inside, blocked the kick, and threw a snap kick of his own at Santos's groin—

Santos twirled away, and Michaels's heel hit him on the thigh. The glancing blow didn't seem to hurt him, but at least it connected.

Santos whirled back around and did some kind of acrobatic twist, ending in a back fist at Michaels's head—

Michaels stepped in, his right fist covering his face, and did a block hit—

Santos leaned away, slipping the punch, but not quite enough—Michaels got one knuckle solidly into the other man's forehead.

Santos backed off, shook his head. "Good one," he said.

He came back immediately, dropped into a one-legged squat, and swept with his other leg extended—

Michaels didn't expect the sweep from that angle—it caught his left ankle. He started to lose his balance, pushed off with his right foot, and managed to hop over the still-sweeping leg and come down without falling. He stepped forward and into a closed gate, right foot ready to kick or *beset* if Santos stepped in.

Santos did another twisting aerial move away. He came down lightly ten feet from Michaels. "I like this stuff you do. It's tight, no wasted moves. Come on, tell me what it is so I can learn it. It will make my game better. Tell me, in case you aren't able to afterward."

"Don't worry about that," Michaels said. But *he* was worried about it. He wished he had a knife. Might as well wish for a gun. A hand grenade or a tank would be useful, too.

Santos laughed. "You worried, *Branco*?"

"Nah, I just don't want to be late for dinner. You're the one who should be worried. See, I know what your dance is—it's *Capoeira.* You don't know what I'm gonna do."

"Let's see!"

Santos flew at him—

The wound was minor, the handgun bullet had punched a hole through Howard's side exactly where the vest tab left a tiny gap between the front and side panels. The slug had caught mostly skin and fat, maybe three inches above his belt. Another inch to the inside, and the body armor would have stopped it. An inch farther out and it would have missed entirely. Bad luck. A freak shot. What you got for not using your own gear.

It hadn't done any crucial damage, though, and while his shirt was ruined and the nick oozed some, he wasn't going to bleed out from it. He would worry about it later.

The man who'd shot him had taken Howard's return fire square in the middle of his chest. He hadn't been wearing a vest, and the Medusa's two .357 semijacketed hollowpoints had punched holes right through his sternum, no more than a couple inches apart.

Julio would like that. A nice group. And so much for not killing anybody. Well. The guy should have thought about that before he shot Howard.

"General?" Gridley said, "You okay?"

"I've hurt myself worse shaving. I'll put a Band-Aid on it when I get a minute."

The voice on the LOSIR was Julio's: "We have the ship secured, General."

Howard laughed. He had never felt more alive. Risk was a part of life, he knew that now. And this was what he did, who he was. He was a man of war. A soldier. Death came to all, eventually, but he couldn't stop living in the meanwhile. "Good work, Lieutenant. Where are you?"

"With the computers. Deck D, amidships."

"We'll see you in a few minutes. Discom."

Gridley shook his head. "I'm gonna stop going out with you. Last time, I nearly got killed by some psycho drug fiend in California. This field work gets old fast."

"You get a fix on the commander?"

Gridley looked at his virgil. "Yeah, his virgil is about a hundred and fifty feet that way." He pointed. "But I can't get an altitude on him—he could be on the top deck or down below."

"Let's go find him. Our squads will mop up the rest of these bozos. Stay behind me."

"You don't have to tell me that twice. Saji would never forgive me if I messed up the wedding by getting myself killed."

Howard did a tactical reload, using a Bianchi speed strip to replace the two fired shells in the revolver. He snapped the cylinder shut, and headed past the row of slot machines and toward the blackjack tables. There was a corridor past those that led through a kitchen to a cafeteria. Michaels would have to be past that, according to Gridley's GPS sig. He brought up the briefing map in his mind's eye: past that, on this level, was a stairway leading up and down. Up was the main deck. Down was a gymnasium. There was an access to the locked-off computer deck that way, too.

Worry about it when you get there, John. Because if you aren't more careful, you might not get *there . . .*

• • •

"Just ahead," Jay said.

Howard nodded. He looked at Jay. "I'll go through first. Try not to shoot me in the back."

Jay laughed.

Santos came in, fists and knees driving, but Michaels knew how to deal with that—he launched himself to meet the attack—

Santos disappeared. He dropped into a weird, crablike pose, feet extended out in front, hands in back, face up but almost lying on the ground. Stupid position, his crotch was wide open. Michaels stepped in to kick Santos's balls for a field goal—

It was a trap!

Santos snapped one foot up and caught Michaels in the thigh, just missing his groin. The force was enough to spin Michaels around, and he nearly lost his balance. He stumbled, managed to get his feet back under him—

Santos came up, twirled in, and it was all Michaels could do to cover as a quick series of punches bounced off his arms, shoulders, and one against the side of his head that cracked him into a blinding flash of red—

The man had fists like rocks—!

Michaels felt for Santos, not using his eyes but his body. He threw his knee and right elbow, caught a hip with the knee, the side of the man's neck with the elbow. Not pretty, but enough to back him off—

Santos shook his head, whirled around, stepped out of range. He nodded. "I thought I had you then, good recovery. Now we havin' fun."

Michaels knew this was psychological warfare. He'd connected with two solid shots, and Santos didn't seem overly bothered by either. The neck hit had to hurt, but he was not going to let Michaels know that.

"Your head okay, *Branco*?"

Michaels was still rattled from the head punch, but he

couldn't let that show, either. "Why wouldn't it be? Did you hit me? Is that the best you got?"

Santos managed a smile as he circled, spiraling slightly inward. "Best I got? I'm not even warmed up yet. Let me show you. I am younger, stronger, faster, and more skilled. You have enough of your game to see this, no?"

Damned straight about that. He was better than Michaels, and he knew it. He wasn't going full out, he was playing, as if this was a friendly sparring match. Michaels felt it. He was in trouble here.

Well. Wasn't that what silat was supposed to train you for? To stay with somebody who was stronger, faster, and as well-trained?

Yeah. But this guy was some kind of world-class fighter. He probably trained for hours every day. He had the edge. He knew it, and Michaels knew it, too. *Silat* would let you keep up with most people, but it didn't make you invincible, certainly not at *his* level of ability.

But there was one thing he had going for him, and maybe he could stall the guy long enough for that to happen.

Michaels circled to his left, staying low. He said, "You want to hear a story?"

Santos flashed a smile. "Is it a funny story?"

"I think so."

"Go ahead. I need a good laugh. Been a bad day."

They circled, each to his left.

"Once upon a time, there was a gathering of animals in the woods. They talked about the rain, the sunshine, the state of the world. At one point, the talk turned to which creature was the most deadly in the forest, and Tiger proclaimed that he was the most dangerous animal.

" 'Really,' Dog said. 'Why is that?'

"Tiger laughed. 'Just look at me! Compared to you, I am bigger, stronger, and faster! My teeth are longer, my claws are sharper! I could break your neck with a single swipe of one paw! Is this not true?'

" 'It is true,' Dog admitted.

" 'Then you agree that I am the deadliest animal in the forest.'

" 'Maybe not,' Dog said.

"This angered Tiger greatly, and he roared his displeasure."

Santos grinned, gave a little foot feint, but did not follow up. Michaels shifted his hands, but did not take the bait.

"Just making sure that you're awake, White."

"I'm awake."

"Go on with your story. *Tigre* is angry."

"Yes. And he looks at Dog and says, 'So, you say I am not the deadliest animal? Who is, then? You?'

" 'Not me,' Dog said.

" 'Tell me! Tell me now, or I will kill you!' And he reared up and prepared to leap on Dog. But before he could attack, there came an explosion, and Tiger suddenly fell over dead.

"There behind the animals stood Man, smoke curling from the muzzle of a rifle.

"And Dog smiled his dog-smile and said, 'I am not the deadliest animal in the forest. But I have a friend . . .' "

Santos smiled. "That's not such a funny story, *Branco*."

"Oh, I don't know" came a voice from behind him. "I thought it was pretty good."

Santos stepped back and half-spun.

A black man, another tourist-not-a-tourist, stood there, aiming a handgun at him. He held the gun in both hands, and it was pointed right at Santos's heart. A second man stood behind him. He had a gun, too.

Too far away to get to them before they could shoot. Hmm.

"Commander," the newly arrived black man said.

"General. I am extremely glad to see you."

Santos glared at *branco*. "You cheated."

He smiled. "Yes. Cheating is good *silat*," he said. "That's the art I practice, by the way. *Pukulan Pentjak Silat Serak.* From Indonesia."

"Ah." Santos knew of the Indonesian forms. He had never faced anyone who played them before, but he had seen pictures, films. "Where is your skirt?"

"It's a *sarong*, not a *skirt*—!"

Santos leaped, turned the jump into a dive and roll, and as he came up, made that into another dive—

The gun went off, but a hair slow. The bullet burned across his back, the lightest of touches. A graze, that was all, nothing, no damage—

There was a large sealed window looking into the hallway just ahead of him. He was a step and a dive away from it . . .

The gun boomed again, loud in the enclosed space, and the bullet hit the glass in front of him, punched through, and spiderwebbed the glass with fractures. Good!

He launched himself at the cracked plate headfirst, hands and forearms up to cover his face. Hit!

He flew through the window in a spray of glass shards, tucked, rolled, hit the carpeted floor, came up, too much momentum, slammed into the corridor's far wall. That shook many of the glass fragments on him loose. He grunted as he flattened against the wall, pushed off and L-stepped away, shoving hard with his left foot, moving to his right, as the third bullet punched through the wall where he had been a quarter-second ago. But now he was moving down the hall, ducking low, and gaining speed with each step. In two heartbeats, he was out of the line-of-fire, the angle on the window no good to the shooter anymore. He pumped for all he was worth, feet digging into the rug, leaning into it, almost a fall. He reached a juncture, cut to his right, skidded across that corridor and into the wall, hit on his left shoulder, bounced off, and kept sprinting.

He laughed, loudly. He had a small wound on his back, and there was blood coming from little cuts on his arms, the back of one hand, but he was gone. They would never catch him from behind. He would find a way off this ship. CyberNation might be mortally wounded, but that did not matter. He would get away. He would go home. He would count his gold and have the last laugh.

But first, there was one small piece of business he needed to finish. Then he could leave.

Chance had the pistol and the disk with the blackmail insurance on it. Nothing else was important enough to worry about, not now. She didn't know how many of the invaders were on the ship, or if her people had had time to wipe the computers, but she would have time enough to destroy the disk, and that was all that she could do now. If they caught her, CyberNation's lawyers would get her out of jail, and once that happened, she would disappear. She had half a dozen false identities ready for use, money stashed under those names. This was a big loss, but she would survive. She could start over, under another name. Work her way back up. It might even be fun, that kind of challenge.

She couldn't risk hiding the disk. They might take this ship down to the waterline for all she knew, and if they found it, CyberNation would suffer a major, maybe even a killing blow. The files were damning—names, dates, places, a criminal prosecutor's dream. She had done it to protect herself in case CyberNation decided she was no longer worth having around, but now she needed their help, and anything that hurt them might hurt her.

It wasn't enough just to break the disk. Supposedly there were recovery devices now that could get information from fragmented DVDs. It could be glued back together, and while some of it would be lost, much could be salvaged. She couldn't afford the risk.

No, she had to make sure there was nothing left to recover.

There was a cigarette lighter on her desk, a fancy thing of carved jade and semiprecious stones, a gift from a former lover. She would burn the disk. The pistol would make sure nobody would get to her before the disk was destroyed, if need be. A few shots fired into the floor or ceiling would make anybody heading her way cautious. She'd only need a minute or two. After that, she would surrender. Sooner or later, she would make bail.

She hurried down the corridor toward her office.

39

Toni came out of the room; she looked carefully up and down the corridors. There were people milling about, a score of tourists who were puzzled and upset, but none of them were Santos or any of his guards that she could tell.

"What's going on?" somebody said.

"Pirates!" a fat man answered. "We've been taken over by hijackers!"

Toni smiled.

"What's funny, lady?" a bald man with a bad complexion said. "You think being hijacked by pirates is funny?"

"It's not pirates," she said. "It's just my husband, come to rescue me."

The man stared at her as if she had turned into a giant snake. She smiled again and started toward the stairs.

Boy, this was gonna be a great story to tell Little Alex someday. Maybe when he was forty or fifty . . .

40

"I never saw *any*body move like that!" Jay said.

"Did you hit him?" the boss asked.

John Howard shook his head. "Not so you'd notice. I didn't think a man could be that fast, rolling and all. He a gymnast?"

"*Capoeira*," the boss said. "South American fighting art."

"We'll get him," Howard said. "We have the ship. The more important thing is, our people control the computer room, and they've pulled the plug. Jay here can have a field day." He pulled a pistol from his belt and threw it to Michaels. "But just in case we run into your friend along the way, here. If you see him, shoot him."

Michaels nodded. "Oh, yeah."

As they were heading toward the stairs, Toni appeared. Michaels nearly knocked her down he grabbed her so hard. They hugged, spun in a circle. Jay could feel the relief coming off both of them like heat off a fireplace. And he had to admit, he felt a lot better himself. He had been worried a little.

Toni held up a mini-DVD. "The plans for the attack on

the net," she said. "They ramped things up. You need to get these locations to the appropriate authorities," she said.

Howard took the disc. "Yes, ma'am. Although they won't be doing anything from here. We control this vessel."

"You collected Santos and Jasmine Chance?"

"Not yet. But we will."

"He's a dangerous man," she said.

"Tell me about it," the boss said.

Santos saw that the door to Missy's office was closed, and when he got to it, he found it locked. She wasn't in her room, and he didn't think she would be trying to hide on the ship, she was too smart not to know they'd find her. No, she'd be here, and likely working on some scheme to save her beautiful ass. That was the thing about Missy, she always had a backup plan.

He touched the door, nodded once, and stepped back. He hit it with his shoulder and slammed it open, recovered his balance, and moved through the atrium to the inner office.

"Roberto! What are you doing?"

She had a cigarette lighter in one hand, a small pistol in the other. Something was burning in the ashtray on her desk.

"Come to pay my respects, Missy. Leaving you a little gift before I retire."

"What are you talking about? We don't have time for this!"

"Your left leg, I think," he said. "Just above the knee. I think that would balance us. I wasn't so rough on Jackson, but it wasn't really his fault, was it? When your woman screws another man, if it isn't rape, then *she* is the one who is responsible. All she has to do is say 'No.' You will have plenty of time to think on it when you are propped up in the cast waiting to heal."

She raised the gun. "You've lost your mind. I'm not

going to just stand here and let you break my leg!"

He grinned. "Easier on you if you do. You think that little gun is enough? You sinned, you know it. It's only justice."

"*You* talk about justice?! You were humping every waitress and change girl on the ship! You think I didn't know? Get out!"

"Men are men," he said. "It's not the same. You can't understand that." He took a step forward.

She dropped the cigarette lighter and grabbed the pistol with her other hand. Aimed right at his chest.

"If you shoot, I will break your neck instead. A leg is not so bad."

He took another step.

She shot him. The noise didn't seem all that loud, and the impact of the bullet, high and to his right, didn't hurt. It was like being hit with a finger-poke, nothing, really. He leaped—

Chance pulled the trigger, again and again, until the pistol clicked empty. She saw the holes appear in Santos's body, his chest, belly, one in his outstretched hand, but he kept coming!

She tried to leap out of the way, but he snagged her with one big arm, caught her around the waist—

She hammered at his head with the butt of the pistol, saw the skin tear on his scalp, watched the bright red blood gush, but he wouldn't let go . . .

He dragged her down, knocked the chair behind her away, slammed her back against the floor

"Roberto! Don't—!"

She kept hammering at his head. Saw him grinning through the blood streaming down his face. He slid his hand up her body, caught her by the throat. He squeezed, his big fingers biting into the vessels of her neck. Her sight went gray.

"Please! Don't!"

"Good-bye, Missy," he said. He leaned down and

kissed her. His blood dripped into her face. She tried to blink it away. Then it all faded. His smile was the last thing she saw.

Santos held his grip on her neck for a long time after her eyes rolled back in their sockets, until they settled back and the pupils dilated and stayed that way. When he finally let go, he was sure she was gone.

Too bad for her.

He tried to push himself up and away from her, but found that his strength had gone, too. He had never felt so weak. He inched forward a hair, but that was it. He could no longer support himself on his wounded hand. He collapsed across her body, his face next to hers. *Who would get all his gold?* he wondered.

That was his last thought.

In the bowels of the ship, the CyberNation programmers and security people had panicked. They hadn't done as good a job as they had on the train and barge. The men spraying puke foam and blasting flashbangs had moved too fast. There would be evidence here.

"Jay?"

"Already on it," Jay said. He moved to an undamaged console and sat. Toni stood behind him, watching. "I've got a freezer here. Let me get it slotted. That should kill their autowipe . . ."

From behind them, Julio Fernandez said, "General?" He came in, leading a couple of troopers.

"Been taking a nap, Lieutenant?"

"Something I think you and the commander want to take a look at. Hey, Toni, nice to see you're okay."

"Nice to be okay, Julio."

Howard nodded. "Keep an eye on things here," he told his troops. "Lead on, Lieutenant."

Michaels and Toni followed Howard and Fernandez up a short flight of stairs and down a corridor. In an office on the floor were two dead people: Jasmine Chance and Roberto Santos.

Michaels shook his head. "Lord. What happened?"

Julio said, "From the marks on her neck and the little hemorrhages in her eyes, I'd say she was strangled. He's got six bullet holes in him and cuts all over his head from where somebody hit him with that little .380 PPK over there. There's blood all over her hand and a pattern in it that matches the butt of the pistol. Way I see it is, he came at her, she blasted him, he lived long enough to choke her out. *Ai-uchi*, the Japanese call it—mutual slaying."

"My God," Howard said. "Mean people."

"Not anymore," Michaels said.

EPILOGUE

The wedding had been beautiful. Now, at the reception, Saji had gone to change into her traveling clothes. Jay had already shed his tux and dressed in his usual laid-back style. Toni stood next to Alex, who looked very James Bondish in his black tuxedo. John Howard and his wife, Nadine, were nearby, as were Julio Fernandez and his wife, Joanna. Julio held his squirming son, who apparently wanted to get down and destroy the place in a terrible-two frenzy. Something Toni could look forward to with Little Alex . . .

Saji's mother hugged her sister, crying. Jay's parents wiped away tears and beamed at their son from across the room.

Jay came over to shake Alex's hand. He said, "Thanks for everything, boss."

"You feeling better about this now?" Toni said, waving at the interior of the church's reception area.

"Oh, yeah. Just cold feet was all. I love her. I can't see that stopping. My parents are already talking about grandchildren. Can you imagine me being a father?"

"I think you'd do well at it," Toni said. "But there's no hurry."

"Off to Bali, right?" Alex said.

"Yep. Sun, sand, drinks with fruits and flowers in them, the whole enchilada. We're gonna make a pass by Thailand on the trip back, see some of my distant relatives, too."

"That's great, Jay."

"If you're sure you can get by without me, that is."

"We'll manage. With the train, barge, and boat out of commission, I don't think those folks will be causing us any more trouble for at least a little while," Alex said.

"But they were only wounded, not killed. They can blame somebody, offer him up as a scapegoat, keep going," Jay said.

Alex shrugged. "You take what you can."

"You sorry you didn't get a chance to go head-to-head with Keller?" Toni asked.

He shrugged. "Yes and no. It would have been great for the old ego to kick his ass up and down the block. But he lost, any way you want to cut it. He's in jail, an emotional wreck. Not much point in pouring water on a drowning man, is there? Besides, what could I do that would make him feel worse than getting the bejeezus beat out of him by a *girl*?"

She smiled. She looked up and saw Guru, dressed in a formal sarong and sandals, carrying the baby, who was in a cute little baseball uniform, complete with a darling little Baltimore Orioles cap. Guru came over and stood next to Jay as Saji reappeared, dressed in her traveling suit. She smiled at Jay.

"I think that's my cue," Jay said.

They left, amidst a hail of tossed birdseed—better than rice, because it wouldn't hurt the birds to eat any that didn't get swept up. As the limo drove away, Toni turned to Alex. "So romantic, a trip to Bali, don't you think?"

"Hey, we had Hawaii. Just as nice, and they speak the same language. You complaining?"

"Not me," she said. She took his arm. "Now we're at the good part."

"Oh?"

"Yep. And they lived happily ever after."

He laughed and she joined him in it.